MW00641604

LUSITANIA GOLD

Fred Rayworth

NewLink Publishing
Henderson, Nevada
2017

Lusitania Gold
Fred Rayworth
Copyright © 2017
All rights reserved

Line/Content Editors: Mary Einfeldt
Cover: Richard R. Draude
Interior Design: Jo A. Wilkins

ISBN: 978-1-941271-34-6/Paperback
ISBN: 978-1-941271-33-9/E-Pub

1. Fiction/Science Fiction/Adventure
2. Fiction/Science Fiction/Alternative History
3. Fiction/Suspense

www.newlinkpublishing.com
Henderson, Nevada
Published and printed in the United States of America

1 2 3 4 5 6 7 8 9 10

Dedication and Thanks

I can hardly believe it. Twenty-one years, 689 rejections and it finally paid off! When I gave up trying to be a musician back in 1995 but still needed a creative outlet, I found my muse with a computer keyboard. The story of how I came to that place is much too long, but once I tried my hand at that first (never to be published) novel and actually finished it, I knew writing was no flight of fancy, nor was it a hobby, but a passion.

The path from A to B was in no way easy, yet it was also so much fun that I persevered regardless of the roadblocks placed before me. If one has the passion and drive, those barriers become nothing more than learning experiences. I've had a lot thrown at me, yet not for a moment have I considered giving up.

I've been very lucky in that when I first started out, I found two authors who were kind enough to respond to me when I sought advice. Both gave great feedback and one became not only a close friend but my mentor.

Elizabeth Forrest, AKA Emily Drake, real name Rhondi A. Vilott Salsitz was a huge help with my first icky bug novel. I give thanks and a huge shout out for her early encouragement and advice.

I can't say enough about my friend and mentor, Carol Davis Luce. When I first ran across her novel *Night Passage* in our local bookstore back in the mid 90's, I loved it so much I felt compelled to contact the author through her web site and e-mail. To my great surprise, she wrote back and from there, our friendship blossomed.

Carol is the one who went above and beyond, gave me sage advice on what I was doing right and wrong, picked me up when I was frustrated and kicked me in the butt when I was feeling down. She also provided invaluable beta reads for many of my manuscripts including this one. If not for her, I wouldn't be where I am today as a writer. I'll always treasure her friendship. I have the honor of being named a character in one of her novels. Rock on Carol!

This book would never be in the shape it is now without the help of the Henderson Writers' Group (HWG). I preach constantly to writers about finding the right fit in a writer's group, and I hit gold with the HWG. I brought the rough draft of Lusitania Gold to the group many years ago and read every chapter, from start to finish over the span of almost two years. I received outstanding feedback from the likes of Donald Riggio, Lauren Tallman, Roger Phillips (RIP), Trudy McMurren (RIP), Audrey Balzart, Roger Storkamp, Douglas Davy, Sydnee Elliott, Vital Germaine, Nancy Sansone(RIP), Brian Yates, Darrah Whittaker, Morgan St. James, Jay Yarbrough (RIP), Gregory Kompes and too many more names to list. I know I'm forgetting people and I apologize if I left you out.

A special thanks to Clive Cussler and James Rollins. They both provided inspiration and support in their own ways, whether they knew it or not.

As for beta readers, before this novel ever reached the publisher, it went through several beta reads going way back to 1995 and beyond, when I wrote the first draft in Oklahoma and kept tweaking it as I changed jobs and we moved to various places. A special thanks to Diane Greenwood from Indiana for one of those early reads. Once in Las Vegas, I had outstanding help from the likes of Darlien Breeze (who also gave great feedback at the writer's group meetings), Bonnie Hall and Pamela Liddington Saxton. Of course, I can't go without mentioning again Carol Davis Luce, who gave me invaluable expertise and feedback (along with multiple beta reads) after the manuscript had gone through multiple-multiple drafts. Most recently, I also had my high school classmate and dear friend Judy Fryer read it and I really appreciate her most recent take on the story. Judy, you rock! Once again I apologize if I left anyone out.

Now, as with most writers who get published, it's not only the ability to put ideas to paper, it's having someone believe in you and carry through with it. I found my champion in another one of those readers at the writer's group, the former president of the HWG, Jo Wilkins. I've known her since I first joined the group in 2003. Jo has suffered through not only this one, but many of my other draft novels, so she knows my work. It's her undying faith in my little story that's the reason you are holding this book today. I have to give a huge shout out to Jo for believing in me and Detach and I can't thank her enough. Jo, you also rock!

I also must thank Richard Draude for the outstanding artwork and my outstanding editor, Mary Einfeldt.

I would also like to thank my wife Kim who's put up with my long hours tucked away in the computer room, away at writer's group meetings and wondering why I've never given up. She's put up with a lot!

Finally, this book, as with my last one, is dedicated to Tear Bucket, BBBSBFBR, Baby, I-Baby and Double Baby. You all know who you are.

PREFACE

There comes with any fictional endeavor, a lot of imagination and depending on the genre, a varying amount of research. To get to the heart of this story, I have to give you a bit of history about how *Lusitania Gold* came to fruition.

BEGINNINGS

When I first started writing in 1995, I had plenty of inspiration, but not enough hours in the day to get it all down on paper. The first thing I had to do was see if I could shift from being a failed musician to another artistic outlet. It had to be something where I had a potential muse, but at that time, I didn't know if I had the wherewithal to pull it off. That muse was for writing. The only way to find out was to give it a shot and in the very primitive days of word processors, I started The Cave, a science fiction adventure story. Before I knew it, I finished it.

The shock of pulling off a full novel gave me the inspiration to continue and I went to my first icky bug novel, The Greenhouse. For those of you that are familiar with me either personally or through my web site, icky bug is my term for B-movie horror. When I finished The Greenhouse, a good double the word count of The Cave, I knew I had not only the muse, but the chops to continue on with this passion of writing. This wasn't a hobby, even this far back. I have to write. I don't just want to. It's something I'd do whether I was published or not. As of this story, Lusitania Gold, it's taken 21 years and 689 rejections to get this far, with one fantasy novel under my belt and multiple short stories along the way. I was also able to parlay my expertise into a profession as a technical writer, once I retired from the Air Force.

With my urge for science fiction and icky-bug satisfied for

the moment, what I really wanted to do was action/adventure, or more politically correct in today's world of publishing, "adventure thrillers." With a huge bit of inspiration from Clive Cussler and a few others, I started Lusitania Gold.

Not only did I have the title, but I knew the beginning and the end before I typed one letter! That's right. I knew exactly what I was going to write before I started.

BACKGROUND

I've always had a fascination with shipwrecks, since my grandpa sat me on his knee (yeah, grandpas really did that) and showed me pictures and read to me from an Encyclopedia Britannia. This was in Lakewood California, well before it became known as Calee'fornia, sometime around 1955. We happened to have the L volume out and came to the end of the book. My eyes locked on the infamous image, a painting to be exact, of the Lusitania sinking. It was the first image I'd ever seen of an ocean liner and it was a doozy! Those four huge funnels still spewing coal smoke, the hull sticking out of the water at about a 45-degree angle, the hooked rudder and those gleaming propellers drew me in like a siren song. I never forgot that image and on that day, became fascinated with shipwrecks.

Over the years, I read up on the most popular wrecks enthusiasts are aware of such as the Titanic, the Morro Castle, the Empress of Ireland and the Sultana along with a few others that at the time, received little attention, mainly because of lack of body count. I became a Titanic buff, largely due to the movies and that one popular book at the time, long before James Cameron did his thing.

When it came time to write Lusitania Gold, I not only wanted to draw attention to the ship again, but I was inspired by two books by Clive Cussler, namely Raise the Titanic and Sahara. Both stories gave me inspiration for what was to become the story you have here today. Second, about two years before I started writing, in 1993, Bob Ballard dove on the real Lusitania and filmed it. From that video and subsequent book, I obtained a wealth of info to help with the story.

The seeds of this novel came together in the latter half of 1995 and in somewhere around December of that year, I finished the first draft.

DRAFT AFTER DRAFT

Over the two decades since I wrote it, the manuscript went through numerous major edits. Not one iota of the main plot has changed. However, that's not to say that a good bit of bloat hasn't been removed! The most significant changes came when I moved to Las Vegas and found the Henderson Writer's Group. I can't stress enough the importance of how valuable a good writer's group can be. Because of them, I trimmed and cleaned up my draft from 130,000 words to 97,000. It had nothing to do with the plot, just bloat. Something every writer needs to go through. There was no Kill Your Darlings either, because I never sacrificed any of the characters I felt were essential to the story.

Also, with the advent of a more reliable and expanded internet since I originally wrote it, I was able to research more details and update numerous facts and fictions to make them more believable.

REALITY VERSUS FICTION

Though there's some real details mixed into this story, in no way is it a non-fiction piece nor is it meant to be a college textbook! This is a purely fantastical, made-up, "wishful thinking" story. My hope is that you, the reader, will suspend your disbelief long enough to enjoy it. I did my best to add as many real details as possible, but in no way should you to take what I present in Lusitania Gold as real facts. If you want to know the reality of the story about this fascinating and often overlooked tragedy, there are numerous highly regarded works on the subject. I used some of them for my research.

LUSITANIA

GOLD

ONE

Emil Straub strolled along the promenade deck of the luxury liner *Lusitania*, filling his lungs with the cool sea-air that danced about his lapels and tousled his wavy hair. The way the huge ocean liner cut the waves amazed him, despite the ship's tendency to sway and lurch when the bow bit into a large swell. He noted the gentle motion of the deck below him, grateful he did not have to count seasickness as one of the many discomforts to endure on this stressful journey.

On a similar stroll a few days prior, he learned from a pair of engineers, who had taken the time to chat with him, that the straight-up bow did not allow for deflecting large waves in an efficient manner. The ship stood tall above the waterline, uncommon for an ocean liner. These features tended to make her sway in the water more than other ships of her class. One of the men said her designers considered this design flaw minor, because the ship could cross the Atlantic in record time with a large group of passengers. The sheer size and power of the vessel impressed Emil, despite the flaws.

The engines rumbled under his feet, and though the four huge funnels towered far above him, an occasional current of air allowed a wisp of coal smoke to drift down to the deck. The tangy smell left a metallic taste in his mouth, an unpleasant distraction from the briny salt air. He glanced at the third funnel towering above him, and decided it was time to move upwind. From the starboard side, the English coast displayed a mass of low, dark hills looming on the Eastern horizon. Earlier, he caught a glimpse of Ireland from the port side, but he preferred to stare out into the open Irish channel.

During the voyage, he had made regular trips to the ship's magazine and bribed several crewmen to let him into the compartment where he could eye his carefully marked boxes of ammunition. There were several cases of real bullets mixed in with his special ones. Only he and his contact in England knew which was which. Emil could not stand waiting any longer. He walked next to the second funnel toward the passage down to the magazine for another inspection. A wave of impending doom stopped him in his tracks.

Kapitanleutnant Walther Schwieger glanced up from his studies, the profile book given to all German U-boats lay neatly open on his small desk. He had been stalking the large ship for some time, and had identified the vessel as either the *Lusitania* or the *Mauritania*, both classified as armed merchant cruisers. Three torpedoes remained in his arsenal. He decided to save two for the trip home in case of another encounter. His government passed out the warnings that all British ships were fair game, and this would be a spectacular kill.

He gave a long, low whistle, taking in the sheer size of his target. He doubted his inferior torpedoes would do more than slow the liner down. Without warning, it turned right in front of him, making an irresistible target. He ordered the best and only G-type torpedo loaded into a forward tube.

"Fire!"

He traced the weapon with his eye, sweat trickled down his brow, his hands gripped the periscope handles in a viselike embrace. The bubble trail of the torpedo etched a straight path through the water to the massive ship.

Schweiger led a cheer with his crew when his torpedo exploded against the hull of the great ship. A few seconds later, a geyser shot up behind the first funnel, spewing smoke and debris in every direction. This second detonation shook his small submarine.

"So, the Americans are smuggling arms to those British bastards!" Schweiger took in the nods and cheers from his crew.

During their hasty exit, he remained transfixed, watching through the periscope as the great ship listed heavily. Hundreds of people scrambled for lifeboats that would not lower because of the severe angle of the hull. The last he saw of the liner was the stern rising out of the water, her hooked rudder and bronze screws gleaming in the sunlight. Though this should be a great victory, somehow, the sheer chaos and loss of life bothered him. He kept that thought to himself.

"This will be an historic day."

TWO

A blast of diesel, mixed in a cloud of fried onions and rotting garbage hit Joseph "Detach" Datchuk in the face on the way to his hotel through a tenement district in New York City. "Now you did it. The only way to see the real New York, far from the tourist spots, right?" He took a quick look around to make sure nobody heard him. The subway would have been a quicker and safer way to go, but he could not see things from deep underground. Now he was not so sure. Secured in a pouch under his shirt, he carried an old pirate log he had acquired in a shady exchange at an Irish pub a few blocks away. He eased a hand over it and glanced once again at his surroundings.

He passed a window and glanced at his reflection in a mirrored display. *I guess I blend in well enough for around here.*

The dense fog rolling in reminded him of London, though with a different variety of grime coating the decidedly New York architecture. He zigzagged between parked cars, overflowing trashcans, and the occasional homeless refugee in a refrigerator box. He turned down a deserted street with most of the street lights out. An impulse nudged him to turn around and find another route. A hoarse scream shattered the calm of the evening.

Ahead, a large masked man struggled with an elderly woman. He knocked her to the sidewalk.

Detach clenched his teeth. A primal fury bubbled to the surface, an overwhelming urge to go berserk on the scumbag.

"Oh, no you don't!" The old woman reached up and sprayed

5

something in the man's face.

"Aieee!" His hands went to his eyes. He howled.

"Back off!" She screamed again, louder this time.

Bam! Bam! Bam! Windows shut to block out the noise that echoed down the empty street, adding to Detach's fury. A broken two-by-four leaned against a metal fence nearby. He grabbed it.

While the mugger wiped at his eyes, Detach skittered around the fender of a beat-up car with the board raised above his head. With a shock, he realized that the assailant stood at least six-four, and had the build of a professional wrestler.

"I'll get you for that!" The man lurched forward, blindly grabbing at the frail woman on the sidewalk.

"Not in this lifetime." Detach swung his improvised weapon hard against the side of the guy's head. With a loud thump, the assailant dropped to the ground.

The woman, with a fearful but defiant look on her face, raised the can of mace and aimed it his way.

"Hey, I'm a good guy." Detach placed the board on the hood of a nearby car and held out his hands. Once she lowered the mace, he held out a hand.

"Are you okay?"

"Yeah, I think so." She straightened her dress and checked her bag.

"We'd better skeedaddle before Goliath here wakes up."

"Thank you, Son. I'm afraid I might be dead right now, or worse, if you hadn't come along."

"Dead or worse?" He looked down at the man and gritted his teeth.

The woman held up her hands. "Please let it be. We need to go."

Detach nodded and glanced around. Not a soul in sight. "You're right." The last thing he wanted to do was talk to the police, especially carrying a stolen book. His hand went to the pouch still tucked inside his shirt.

"Just let me get this." He picked up the board to remove the weapon from the scene. Before the old woman could tell him no, he struck the man in the right knee with all his might. The kneecap shattered with a satisfying crunch. If the scumbag managed to avoid the police, at least he would not be chasing little old ladies anymore.

Her small, crinkled eyes widened, a momentary imitation of youth in her shocked expression.

"Sorry." He shrugged and gave her a guilty grin.

"Would you mind escorting me home?"

"No problem at all." Detach followed the woman down the street and noticed how she watched every shadow and kept hold of the mace can. On the next block, he threw the board into a dumpster.

The elderly woman led him to the nicest in a line of run-down tenements. The brick walls were recently cleaned and a fresh coat of paint brightened up the wood framing, not peeling like other houses in the neighborhood. He glanced up and noted red and purple petunias in the front windows of the second floor. It was a good guess the woman lived there, the flowers a dead giveaway for a grandma. It reminded him of his own grandmother, who once lived in an old apartment building in San Francisco.

The night cooled and the fog thickened, dropping visibility to a dozen yards. Horns honked in the distance. The random screech of tires echoed here and there along with the sound of arguing in Spanish.

"Come inside," she said. "You look like you could use a nip."

He nodded. *I've come this far, might as well see her safe inside.*

By the time they made it up the front stairs, his new companion was wheezing with exertion. They entered a small foyer and passed the buzzers and mailboxes to a locked door. With a key fished from her purse, she sought the keyhole with trembling fingers and missed several times before shoving it home.

Like the outside of the building, the door looked newly painted. He caught a hint of fresh fumes in the air mixed with cooking and the odors of a very old structure. They followed a narrow hallway to a set of stairs.

With wobbly legs, she climbed, huffing and puffing. Her palsied right hand gripped the rail while she clutched her purse with the left. Detach fought an urge to carry her up. When they reached the second floor, she turned back and headed to the front of the building confirming his guess about the flowers in the windows. He watched the same ritual with the keys except with three separate locks. He was about to ask if she needed help when a key slid home in the first lock. She went through a similar struggle with the other two, pushed the door open and motioned him inside.

Detach sucked in his breath and stifled a curse, noticing the antiques filling the room. His smuggling background automatically put him in appraisal mode. He recognized Victorian, French, and Early American furniture. At a glance, he estimated the room contained at least thirty thousand dollars worth of items.

"Take a load off." She gestured toward the living room. "Brandy? Port?" The old woman's demeanor changed to one of confidence.

"Brandy will do fine," Detach replied, though he did not normally drink hard liquor.

She let out a loud cackle, disappearing through a door, which he assumed was the kitchen.

Afraid to sit on anything, knowing its value, he settled into a fancy Victorian love seat with extra thick padding. Comfortable for the first time since leaving his hotel, he scanned the room. The only things not antique were a few matchbooks. A non-smoker, Detach tried to ignore the stench of tobacco and had no trouble spying the source. He even recognized the seven ashtrays around the room as New Haven Railroad glass from the late thirties. Each of those beautiful works of art were full of butts.

Only one portrait hung on the wall. A colorized black and white photo of a barely-recognizable young woman smiled down at him. In her time, the old lady was a looker.

"Gladys Henson, one hot tamale." She reentered the room with two glasses in one hand and a bottle of brandy in the other. She cackled again, a funny laugh that turned into a coughing fit. She set the glasses on a French coffee table, filling them from the bottle. She peered at him with bright blue eyes.

He nodded and put a hand to his chest. "Detach...I mean

8

Joseph Datchuk."

"Detach? Datchuk? That's Polish isn't it?"

"German, I think."

"Ah...Germans." She sighed. "I used to have a real honey of German descent, rolled in the hay like a rabid dog too!" She exploded in a fit of cackling and coughing.

The heat crawled up Detach's face. *What kind of character is this woman?*

"Aah, years ago I could've given you a run for the money." She gave him a sly wink.

Detach squirmed in his seat.

"Lighten up, Honey. I just enjoy life more than most people my age."

"Uh, huh." He sipped the brandy.

"How old do you think I am?"

"Wayell..." He sensed her appraising him, taking his measure. "Oh, easy. 29."

"Hey smoothie, I'm over three times that."

"90?"

"Try a little more than that." She gave him a coy smile.

This lively woman did not look a day over eighty, despite the palsy in her hands.

"Wow is right. I'm 95." She gazed longingly out the window. "Try finding someone my age that can still have a good time." Gladys reached for her Virginia Slims and lit one up. She alternately puffed and sipped, remained quiet.

A clock ticked somewhere in the room, undoubtedly an antique. To Detach, the silence felt comfortable, but he did not like the cigarette smoke.

After enough puffs to leave a thick cloud in the air, she said, "You know, Honey, there aren't many people willing to stick their necks out for someone, especially in this town, despite all those hoo-ha feel good stories you see in the news, at least around this neighborhood." Her eyes watered. "There was the World Trade Center thing but that was a fluke, in my opinion, all for the cameras. I really don't know how to thank you. You allowed this old lady to maybe make it to a hundred."

9

He still had the sense she was measuring him, but why and for what? "I'd do it again in a heartbeat. Can't stand the odds being so out of proportion."

"You just about killed that animal." She cocked her head and listened. "Nope, no sirens yet. Probably still lying there in a heap, if he's not dead. No one in this neighborhood will give a crap until they trip over him."

"I didn't kill him," Detach said. "Tell you what though. I don't think he'll be able to chase a snail without a walker from now on."

Gladys cackled again. She peered into his face and he raised his brandy glass in an attempt to hide. After an eternity, she turned her eyes away and gazed pensively toward the flowers lining the front of the closest window.

"How long have you lived here?"

"Over ninety years."

"I take it you were born here?"

"Close by. Whole family used to live here. I somehow ended up with the place when the rest of them either croaked or left for greener pastures."

Detach almost choked at her choice of words. He had not heard anyone say "croaked" for ages. "Any family left?"

"Oh sure. I have three kids, seven grandchildren, and seventeen great grandchildren. They're spread all over the country."

He took another cursory glance about the room, in case there were other photos of family or loved ones he might have missed, but was met only with the solitary self-portrait. The busy walls displayed artwork and shelves enough knickknacks to keep him full of temptation. *Is that a friggin' Picasso?* "Why are you here by yourself?"

"Independence...nostalgia...besides, I own it outright. I'm not that lonely. I have family visiting all the time."

"I just didn't picture..."

"Say, honey, what do you do? You're obviously not from around here."

"Well, I'm a diver, marine salvage expert, and a few other

10

things." *No need to elaborate.*

"Hmmm." She furrowed her brow. "Like exploring old shipwrecks?"

"Sure. That's my favorite pastime when I'm not involved in a research project or salvage operation. Most of the salvage work I do is newer shipwrecks or spilled cargo. Not all that interesting, or with any historical value."

Gladys puffed on her cigarette, her eyes studying him. After a moment of silence, she smiled. "Honey, I just thought of a way to pay you back for your brave act tonight."

"Gladys, you really don't have to. The brandy's enough." Detach squirmed again in his seat.

"Look, it's now or never. I'm too old to keep the secret forever. I probably wouldn't be that good of a tumble in the sack for you either." She winked at him and broke out in a fit of laughter and coughing.

Detach struggled to think of a comeback.

"All these years and I never met a real honest-to-goodness diver." She had her eyes aimed at the rug as she shook her head and chucked.

"That's what I am, Mr. Sea Hunt." *Actually, I haven't done a conventional dive in over a year.*

"More brandy?"

Before he had a chance to respond, Gladys filled his glass again.

"Listen." She scanned the room as if someone else might be listening and whispered, "What I'm about to tell you has been a secret for over eighty..." She backed away and frowned. "Or is it ninety years? A hundred...before I was born."

Detach did not know if this lady was crazy or actually knew something, but a tingling in his gut and on the back of his neck told him he had better listen.

"Have you heard of the *Lusitania*?"

"The what?" The blood rushed to his head, a twinge rippled from the pit of his stomach. "Of...of...course. I've been fascinated with that wreck since I was a kid. The first picture of a ship I ever saw was the *Lusitania* sinking. My grandpa showed me an illustration in an encyclopedia when I was three years old. It started my fascination with shipwrecks, especially ocean liners. Were you a passenger, or should I say, survivor? Oh wait a minute, you are a little too young." He winced.

"Goodness no. But you remember that German boyfriend I spoke of?"

"Uh yeah," Detach choked back a snicker and fought to keep his expression serious.

"Like mother, like daughter. My mom had a German boyfriend, before I came along. She was a naughty girl too." Gladys gave him a sly wink. "She knew he was a smuggler. Even though Emil was an American, of German descent, she figured he spied for them. Remember, this was before we went to war with Germany. In fact, there were a lot of German sympathizers here at that time."

"I remember reading about that somewhere."

"Absolutely. She said Emil acted weird the last few days before he left on a trip for Europe. You can always tell when someone's getting ready to say goodbye." Gladys sucked on her cigarette. "That last night, he came for a visit, drunk on his butt. Couldn't get it up, but she didn't care. Momma was madly in love with him."

Detach forced back a laugh. *Where's this leading?*

"He booked passage on the *Lusitania*." She made a slicing motion across her neck. "The first thought she had was the warning the Germans put in the paper that said sailing to England was risky. She'd heard about the ships sunk by U-boats off the English coast. Momma warned Emil not to go, but he ignored her. She thought maybe since he was fiddling with the Germans, he knew something she didn't. He told her the German torpedoes were lousy and a ship as big as the *Lusitania* would hardly notice if one hit it. He promised to marry her when he returned and said he'd have enough money so they could live the easy life."

"Someone blew smoke up his butt about those torpedoes." Detach smirked. "They may have been lousy, but they did the trick on some pretty big ships, even before the *Lusitania*."

"Yup." Gladys nodded.

"So that's it. He got lucky, picked the wrong trip to go to England and went down with the ship?"

"I haven't even told you the good part yet, Honey." She reached over and patted his knee.

The tingling on the back of his neck increased. *What am I getting myself into?*

THREE

Faint noises from the street crept into the silence of Gladys' living room. A pall of cigarette smoke hung in the air like the smog over a steel mill. The only thing keeping Detach from coughing his guts out was the excellent brandy that kept his throat lubricated.

"Momma never told anyone else, especially my dad. He was a good sort, but the jealous type." Gladys blinked and continued. "I never even told my late husband or my family 'cause I didn't want to spoil a good thing with impossible dreams." She hesitated, casting a pensive glance out the window. "We all did pretty well for ourselves. No regrets."

Detach gazed around the room for a second time. He wondered again about the lack of photos. Her silvery hair had escaped in wisps from a tight bun at the nape of her neck, reminding him of his own grandma, "Granny Twinkle toes," except she smoked L&M cigarettes. Gladys took a few drags from her cigarette and he noticed that the palsy in her hands stopped whenever she inhaled.

"Aaaah!" She eyed him and said, "Sorry, have to stoke the habit." With one more puff, she continued. "Emil was secretive about his goings on. Being naive and love-smitten, Momma never asked. She was dying of curiosity, but in those days you just did not question a man on such matters.

"That last night, they had an argument about leaving on the *Lusitania*. She had this feeling. I guess the combination of their fighting, making up, and his drunkenness led him to spill the beans." Gladys laughed, hacked out a cough, and took a drag off the cigarette. "He was smuggling gold to Germany via England."

15

"Oh?" Detach leaned forward.

"Exactly. How were they going to pull that one off?" She smiled, clearly enjoying the suspense.

"Via England?"

"Here's the way he explained it to her." She paused as if searching for the memory. "Security was pretty lax around that time in England, despite the war. The real kicker was that they were going to smuggle it directly to Germany from the English coast! Think about it. What a slap in the face that would be to the Blokes if the German underground smuggled a fortune of gold right under their noses. They were even going to have a press release when it arrived in Berlin."

"But why burn a bridge that they might be able to use again?"

"All these years and we've never figured that one out. I thought it was pretty dumb to cut off a possible pipeline just to embarrass the British. Momma couldn't come up with a better explanation, either."

"How were they going to hide gold on the ship?" His heart raced and a familiar tingle rippled up from the base of his spine.

"The genius of this plan was the way they were transporting the gold. The Germans knew that the American government supported England under the table, even how much. They did it mostly with small arms and non-weapon type supplies, but there were probably artillery shells and other stuff too. The key to Emil's operation was the small arms." She tapped a finger on the side of her forehead and gave him a devious smile.

Aha! He remembered reading excerpts of the ship's cargo manifest that included gun cotton and sundry small arms supplies. There were also over four million rounds of .303 cartridges. He kept that thought in the back of his mind.

"As you may have guessed, they molded the gold into the shape of bullets and coated them with lead. Unless someone scratched one and exposed the gold underneath, the weight would be close enough that no one would notice. Besides, who would bother to mess with a dozen crates of bullets, useless without the cartridges, powder, and gun cotton?"

Detach arched his brows and felt a rush of excitement.

16

"Here we are with a lot of gold in crates of what everyone thinks are lead slugs. Emil said the network already had their man in Liverpool who'd divert the slugs and replace them with real ones he had stashed in a warehouse. No one would ever know the difference until it made the papers."

"If they had this elaborate network set up, how come we've never heard about it? I've never even heard a rumor."

"Good point. I wondered about that myself. Over the years, I did a little research and based on what Emil told Momma, most of the network didn't know what they were smuggling. The ones that knew must've all died during the war. Apparently, no one even suspected what happened. You're the first person to hear this story besides me."

"What about Emil? Did your mom ever find out what happened to him?"

"Unfortunately, he went down with the ship. He booked passage under a bogus name listed among the dead. And don't ask, I forgot that one a long time ago. Doesn't matter anyway. His body was never recovered." Gladys gazed out the window again and took another drag of her cigarette. "When Momma heard the ship went down, she mourned for months. Those fools grossly underestimated the power of the German torpedoes."

"From what I heard, the torpedo didn't cause enough damage to sink her. It was a secondary explosion that blew out a large portion of her hull below the waterline. One theory is that an empty coal bunker exploded and caused her to sink." He tugged his goatee and gazed at the wall "You know, this mission must've been too secret for their own good, especially since they basically shot themselves in the foot by sinking the ship."

"Honey, that's exactly what convinced Momma that most of the network didn't know what was going on. I've always assumed the conspirators in Berlin weren't talking either. Otherwise, they would've tipped off the U-boat commander."

"Actually, depending on how last-minute the scheme was, the U-boats weren't in regular contact with their command for weeks at a time. Besides, how would they get a message and an explanation out without alerting someone?"

17

"My research showed that the German navy didn't have much faith in the speed of their U-boats, or the quality of their torpedoes. They didn't expect Captain Turner to plop right down in their lap." She took another puff of the cigarette.

Detach tugged on his goatee again. "Some people think he screwed up, but I think old Bowler Bill, as he was called, got screwed by the British admiralty. He was framed and made a scapegoat."

"So, here's your mission, if you decide to accept it." Gladys did a very poor Mission: Impossible voice imitation. "Find the ship's magazine, and recover the slugs. I bet they sparkle when scratched." She winked.

"If I decide to pursue this further, what do you want out of it?"

"Nothing, dear."

Detach stared at her, surprised.

"Really. My family's doing just fine, and I'm too old to use it. I don't need the hassles that come with so much wealth. I don't think my family can handle it either."

"You're handing this to me on a silver platter, forgive the cliché."

"Hah. You still have to go down and get it. Plus, I don't have to remind you, there are some 'legal' implications."

"I'll bring you back a souvenir if I go through with it."

"Don't take any artifacts, just the gold. Remember, it's also a graveyard and a memorial to all those that were lost."

"Yeah, I respect that." *We can be delicate when we need to be.*

"Say, there is something…oh, but that would be like finding a needle in a haystack, and I don't care if it's a cliché. I'm too old to worry about it."

"What?"

"Well, you see, Momma gave Emil this locket with her picture in it. It was gold and looked like a small pocket watch. She said he kept it around his neck all the time. It would be nice to get that back. I don't have too many of my mom's things anymore. I realize that finding his skeleton in all that junk on the bottom would be near impossible. I watched the special Bob Ballard did

18

when he dove on the ship. I know it's in bad shape." Her eyes took on a faraway glaze. "Knowing the crazy fool, the way my mom used to talk about him, he'd have tried to move the gold out as the ship sank, or something equally stupid."

"Let me guess." Detach arched a brow and stared at her. "You must've watched the movie Titanic. Are you serious?"

"Okay, I did, about thirty times. But in this case, the locket is real. It would be a real hoot to get it back, though it's a shame I couldn't tell anyone where it really came from."

He studied the blushing old woman's face, not sure if she was serious or pulling his leg. When she didn't crack a smile and a tear formed at the corner of her eye, doubt crept into his subconscious. "I can't guarantee anything because the ship is in pretty bad shape. I might not even be able to get to the magazine. There's also a chance the gold is already gone, and someone else may be a millionaire."

"Let's hope not." Gladys smiled and offered him more brandy while she lit another cigarette.

Detach wanted to pinch himself and wondered if he had dreamt the whole thing. The only part that bothered him was her reference to the *Titanic* movie. Did that make her a crackpot, and this gold thing was nothing more than a wild story she made up? His gut told him she was not crazy.

He picked up his pace during the walk back to the hotel and used a different route in case the assailant was still where he had left him, or worse, the police had showed up. Despite the exertion, the fog crept into his bones and he picked up a chill. *The Lusitania, the Holy Grail of shipwrecks!* The vessel rested at three hundred and ten feet, the limit of conventional diving technology. A strong current constantly swept the ship with murky water and made exploration difficult. It reminded him of the *Empress of Ireland*, a wreck off Newfoundland. Sunk in one hundred and thirty feet of water, nasty currents, frigid temperatures, and thick sediment made the dive hazardous. He had cut his chops on that wreck.

His boss, Jams, head of Mason Industries, mentioned many times that he would love to send an expedition to the *Lusitania*,

19

but something else always came up. Detach had not done a conventional dive for over a year because he had been working on new technology that would make diving to great depths easier and safer. "Now I can try out that new gear in a real-world setting." He pumped his fist in the air. "Woohoo!"

FOUR

A screeching violin echoed through the house. Grace peeked around the corner into the hallway. A tall, slim African-American woman in a nurse's uniform crept to the half open door of Mother's room, stuck her head in for a furtive glance, and popped back out with a wince

Even this far back, Grace detected the odor of cleaning fluids, sweat, and insanity leaking out the door. The nurse cringed again when the old woman inside, Mother, hummed a melody as distorted and out of tune as the violin. Every time Grace went into that room, she witnessed her cadaverous face as it scanned the walls, taking in the aged photos. Mother always sang to the photos with a wicked grin on her face, as if taking pleasure in torturing the man in the images. At the dawn of the recording age, the old hag's mother, Grace's Grandmother, made the so-called music herself, recording it on wax. The noise was later transferred to wire recorder and eventually cassette, just like the copy she had.

The nurse backed away from the door, presumably so Mother would not see her. The hired help knew the consequences of disturbing her employer during one of those episodes. When she headed in her direction, Grace shrunk back through the shadows into the foyer and a door on the opposite side.

Grace waited for the nurse's footsteps to approach beyond the foyer door. She opened it and plunged through, startling the uniformed help. "Is she lucid?"

Glancing furtively down the hall, the nurse nodded and made a quick exit toward the kitchen.

When she was out of earshot, Grace muttered, "I know you hate it here, you useless bitch, but we couldn't get anyone else to do it. I'm sure those extra digits on your paycheck are the only thing keeping you here."

"Fates help me." She approached Mother's room and took a deep breath. "Time to get this over with." She stepped inside.

The room contained a large hospital bed over which hung an aura of impending death. Black and white photos crowded every wall, all of the same person. The man in the photos wore a maniacal gleam in his eyes, matching the eyes of the figure in the bed. "Daddy," Grace's great-grandfather grinned down at her.

"Mother, have you had your medicine today?" She gazed at the woman with a mix of hatred and love.

"Huh? Wha?" The old hag's startled expression turned into an insane grin. "How's Daddy?" She pronounced it "Day-dee."

Grace eyed the photos of her great-grandfather then turned back to her mother. The haggard-looking crone reminded her of a shriveled piece of leather. "I paid him a visit three days ago."

"Did you play my mamma's music, like I told you?"

"I always play that music like you tell me to," she said with an exaggerated sigh.

She hated, yet loved to visit "Daddy." He lay in a shrine she built for him because she did not like the way Mother had worshipped him in the past. She was her own woman, and had to worship him in her own way. Mother, at 101 years, was in no shape to go there and see what she had done, anyway. To make her trip more meaningful, Grace danced for him as the music played. She never revealed that detail, afraid her improvisation would upset Mother. The vile old crone had no idea.

"Aieeeyahahaha!!" Mother screeched in a maniacal wail, roughly in rhythm with the violin music.

Grace cringed. Listening to her mother sing with those broken-down vocal cords was too much. "I'll get the nurse to tend to you." She backed out the doorway, with no intention of meeting up with the useless nurse.

The rust-colored walls of the dark and humid room hinted at

a deeper rot within the structure. A round window looked out into blackness. She approached her granddad, the dim glow of a lantern casting deep shadows across his supine form. Handcuffed to the bed, he provided no threat to her.

Grace did a little ballet dance, hummed a tuneless melody, and waved a cassette tape in the air like a kid flying an airplane. After circling the bed three times, she reached for a cassette player on the left side nightstand. The lid popped open with a snick, she set the tape into the carriage, and snapped it closed, performing each step with exaggerated ceremony. She turned it over, opened the battery compartment, and popped out the old C-cell batteries. They clattered to the floor along with a large pile of others. From her shirt pocket she produced fresh batteries and installed them. Setting the player on the nightstand, she hit the play button and the screechy melody her grandmother had recorded ninety years ago disturbed the silence.

An exact rendition of her mother's singing came out of her mouth. She continued her ballerina dance around the bed, this time in the opposite direction. Her singing reached a crescendo and after a dozen orbits, she stopped, grabbing the water pitcher from the right-hand nightstand. At the bottom of the liquid lay a thick layer of sediment. Pitcher in hand, she sloshed it around to suspend the solids in the mix and poured some into a glass. She fed the solution into her granddad's mouth. The wild gleam in her eyes would give the Devil the creeps.

FIVE

Maria Delgado, the head secretary of Mason Industries in Galveston, Texas grinned at Detach from across a chessboard. Though he hated the game, he liked Maria enough to play whenever she asked. Besides, it gave him something to do while he waited for the boss. It was a small sacrifice for his habit of always arriving early to everything.

The phone rang, and Maria momentarily turned her back to the board. Detach moved one of her pieces, sat back, and tried to look innocent.

Maria turned around and looked at the board. "Did you move yet?"

"Wanted you to see it." He grabbed a knight and moved it to take one of her bishops, putting her in check.

"Hmm. Looks like you have the upper hand." She rubbed her chin.

"About time, huh?" Detach had never won a game with her.

"Let's see if I can get out of this one." With a studious expression, Maria scanned the board.

"Take your time."

"Okay, here we go." She moved a knight and took his queen, leaving the king exposed. "Checkmate."

"What?" Detach studied the board and saw the predicament. "I don't believe it."

"Tee hee hee." Maria said, "Next time you move one of my pieces when my back is turned, look at the patterns closer."

The door opened and the biggest cowboy hat he had ever seen floated into the room, accompanied by the sound of heavy metal music. Detach stood.

Eyeing the chessboard, Jams grinned and said, "Trying to give the boah' some culture?"

Maria smirked, looked pointedly at Detach and turned to her computer.

"I still have some other business, so just take a seat and I'll be with you in a moment." Samuel "Jams" Mason motioned Detach to follow.

Detach entered the luxurious office and plopped onto a couch below a photo of the *Titanic*. The locket Gladys told him about sprang to mind, but he dismissed it. The head accountant stood next to Jam's desk, his face red. He could never remember the guy's name.

"Ah' don't give a hoot about the bottom line. Give 'em what they want." Jams played with a pencil, balancing the eraser end on his finger.

"But sir, it'll mean a ten percent drop in profit for the next three months."

Jams let the pencil fall on the desk and flipped on his boom box, his usual way of ending a conversation.

"My God, you're over sixty. How can you stand that horrible noise?"

Jams gave a casual shrug. "It's a death metal band from England called Bolt Thrower."

"Do you understand any of the words? All I hear is growling."

"Not a clue. Don't care what the words are anyway. I just like the articulated vocal noises and the beat." He dropped the pencil and tapped out a double kick drum blast beat with his fingers on the top of his desk.

"Jesus!" The accountant backed out the door.

Detach snickered when Jams hit the stop button. The extreme music came several generations after the boss's peers, and he loved that Jams played that eccentricity to the hilt. The man got off on the heavy distorted guitars, the jackhammer drumbeat, and the unintelligible growling vocals, though he could never explain to Detach why. The music drove Mrs. Mason crazy and out of respect, the old man never played it in her presence. He gave few others that consideration.

Jams pulled off his hat and tossed it onto a ship's wheel mounted on the floor behind his desk. He scratched his gray crew cut and gazed at Detach over the top of the polished mahogany desk.

He used to have carrot-red hair, but Detach saw no trace of it now. However, the freckles remained. Short, at five feet two, he looked up to most people. He kept his chair hiked up so he could sit comfortably at his desk.

Jams pulled out a side drawer and lifted his legs onto it, sat back and closed his eyes.

Becky Mason, Jam's daughter, had once commented to Detach that she thought her dad bore a striking resemblance to a leaner and meaner Boss Hogg, from the television show *Dukes of Hazard*. Except for the red hair, freckles and a sort of Howdy Doody look Detach would never acknowledge in either of their presence.

His eyes wandered from his boss to that oversized cowboy hat. He got a kick out of the contrast between the Texas good ole' boy image and the obnoxious heavy metal music, always a pushbutton away. With the hat, the music, and his booming voice, he rubbed his competitors wrong at meetings, conventions, or anywhere he bumped into them.

"Too silent in here." Jams hit the play button again.

Detach preferred music of the 60's and 70's, but had been around Jams long enough to acquire a vast knowledge of death metal and other forms of extreme metal. He recognized Bolt Thrower's album, *The IVth Crusade*.

Jams hummed along with the roar and picked up a paper from a pile on his desk. "These are the results of the latest test on our new diving suit. Quite impressive. I'm proud of you guys."

A lump swelled in Detach's throat. He, along with head engineer Ruby Fenner and her team, had worked hard testing and modifying the suit. They spent many a day and sleepless night refreshing the coffee pots, neglecting yards and houseplants, and making excuses to friends and family to get that marvel of technology working.

"That's why I sent you off to New York. You needed a break.

27

Sharon and Becky told me you guys were working yourselves to death and I'm not insensitive to that. As it is, I had to drag you all away from the project. From the results I've seen on the screen, you have no reason to worry about an imaginary deadline. This suit will revolutionize deep diving."

At the mention of Jams' wife Sharon and daughter Becky, heat crawled up his face. Both beautiful women, Detach had very strong feelings, especially for Becky.

Jams swiveled his computer monitor to reveal a mechanical drawing of the suit.

The image triggered a myriad of thoughts in his subconscious. Two computers, a myriad of sensors, a re-breather, and a special mixture of chemically enhanced gasses put the suit in a category unlike any other. This setup allowed Detach to stay down for twelve hours with no decompression. The big drawbacks were thirst, hunger and limited waste elimination.

"I think it'd make a great space suit for long voyages, but NASA's deemed it too expensive." Jams spat. "Government!"

Detach sensed a rant coming on.

"I know that 'too expensive' was an excuse to keep NASA out of a political mess with other companies that have lobbyists. I was going to foot most of the bill anyway, but that didn't seem to count. The up-side of that deal means we're free from all the government red tape. We're free to do what we want. I always told you there was a good reason I don't believe in lobbyists."

"What did you really expect by going to them in the first place?"

"It sure wasn't to make a profit." Jams rolled his eyes.

Though Jams had earned his initial fortune smuggling, he was a patriot and had railed for years about how much he could contribute to the space program if they could get the suit to work.

A caption and arrow pointed to the power pack mounted just above the small of the back. Detach got a tingle in the pit of his stomach when he thought of the real secret of the suit. Ruby had developed cold fusion and engineered a working design they used in a variety of top-secret projects. So far, they were the only company on the planet to have a working version. Most everyone else had dismissed the principal as impossible, and thought they had proven so. *Some proof.*

He eyed another caption outlined in red. The suit had one critical component subject to failure. If the depth/position sensor acted up, it would cause erratic results in the control of movement. Otherwise, the system worked well beyond expectations.

Jams leaned back in his chair and stretched. "I always thought the suit looked more useful for space than the water."

"If NASA won't listen, screw 'em," Detach said. "We can use it."

The image changed to a 3-D version of the suit that rotated on the screen. The white composite skin could withstand extreme pressure, and an ingenious flexible joint design allowed free movement without rupturing. All around the suit, grilles indicated the locations of small high-pressure pumps. These extremely powerful jets allowed a diver to move freely in a ten knot current as if the water were dead still. A diver could work virtually unrestricted in many different environments with high currents and Detach had firsthand experience figuring that out. He almost drowned a few times, and once came close to a heat stroke because of the bugs in the design. However now, outside of that annoying sensor, the suit performed flawlessly.

The image changed to another view, this time of the helmet. With a clear bubble and unobtrusive connectors for the visual display, a diver had the choice of a whole screen of info and video or simple idiot lights, available at the touch of a button. A special coating on the inside of the helmet projected the images in the front at proper eye focus. Ruby explained that it was an illusion that fooled the eye into focusing at a greater distance to allow proper vision outside the suit.

"Like swimming naked."

"Huh?" Jams started and gave Detach an arched brow. "Is it that good?"

"I'm not exaggerating...much." Detach sat back in his chair and let his eyes wander. "I almost forgot." He pulled the pirate logbook out of its carrying pouch and tossed it on the desk. The book slid over the slick surface to stop in front of Jams. "I hope it's worth the money."

"Meh." Jams shrugged and picked up the book. "It ought to be an interesting search, historical value and all. Pirate treasure, my favorite."

"Say, who's that on the boom box now?" Detach did not recognize the screaming and growling.

"This Swedish guy. Calls his band Bathory, after the bloodthirsty Countess Bathory. He had a loose sort of band, but in the studio it was mostly just him. Unfortunately, he died a few years ago."

"Give me Blue Cheer, or even Iron Maiden, but that..."

"Wimp." Jams opened his center desk drawer, fished out another CD, and Detach winced, sure the choice would be obnoxious. The top of the mahogany desk glowed from a high polish and at Jams' right hand, the ring from a coffee cup stood out against the smooth surface like a mountain range. *I wonder what happened to the cup?*

Jams popped the CD into the player and a roar of sound filled the room despite the low volume.

Unable to resist asking, the music sounded vaguely familiar, but he could not quite place it. "Who is it now?"

Jams eyed him with a grin. "GWAR, *This Toilet Earth.*"

Detach recalled a videotape of one of their shows and had to admit, they did not just stand up on the stage and play. Their shows were outrageous and graphic with everyone in monster costumes as they killed a huge rubber dinosaur with fake blood spraying everywhere. Their original lead singer had also passed away not too long ago.

"How was the rest of the trip? Fill me in on what you told me over the phone."

"I ran across a very interesting story," Detach said with a sly smile. He related the story Gladys told him, leaving out her rescue and the *Titanic* reference.

"Boah', ah've' always wanted an excuse to explore the wreck." Jams exaggerated his Texas drawl. Then he changed to his "professional" voice, an unconscious habit when he formulated plans. "This is a golden opportunity to find out what really

30

happened. Also a great test for the suit."

"Yes it is," Detach agreed. It did not surprise him the way Jams perked up, his eyes got bright, his back erect, that gleam shone in his eyes when he told him the details of the *Lusitania* story.

SIX

The drilling rig swayed back and forth under Perry McManus' feet as it rode the deep swells of the North Sea. An icy wind slammed rain into the window in front of his face. "The swells are too high to start drilling, Laddie. That crew down there needs to focus on trying to keep this rig from sinking."

"Aye, Captain."

Perry gave the young assistant a sidelong glance. The kid liked to use nautical terms even though none on the rig were sailors. He let it pass.

The assistant handed him a fresh cup of coffee.

"You know, we're already behind schedule." Perry watched the dark brew as it sloshed around in his cup. "I'm under pressure to get this hole producing to make up for the rig that sunk thirty miles out that way."

"Yeah, I heard about that." The assistant shivered, clung to the window ledge and looked to the east.

"The company had a knee jerk reaction to get a replacement on the water and they shoved me into this job. Too many top executives had to pinch pennies on their Beluga Caviar and champagne because they lost that other rig."

"You *do* have a reputation for getting the job done."

Surprised, Perry grunted and turned his eyes to the crew down on the deck. Through the rain-splattered window, he watched them struggle with a piece of machinery. He thought back on how he ended up in this situation and without realizing it, he spoke aloud. "I can be a wee bit stubborn. It's tough to do a balancing act between speed and safety. This job's no exception."

33

"So I've heard."

"I bet you have." Perry did not need to hear more. They had reached the spot two days before, and he put the crew on double shifts to prepare the platform to get the drill into the seabed. In their rush, the tow vessel missed the mark by twenty miles and he let the home office know about it, but they ignored his complaints and nobody bothered to follow up. Compounding the problem, a huge storm headed their way. Now, in the midst of that storm, there would be a significant delay.

"You know what?" Perry looked at the young man. "I don't like this rig."

"Why's that?" The assistant reached up to the back of his head, wiped down a cowlick, making him look even younger.

"Time for your first lesson in oil rigs, Laddy. Instead of the quad leg design, which is normal for this region, we have a tripod. Each leg consists of computer-controlled cement pylons. Once in place, the computer lowers the pylons to the seabed, their weight sinking each at least thirty feet into the soft bottom. When the pylons are in place, we raise the platform eighty feet over the water. For the North Sea, the quad leg design provides more stability because of the rough seas." Perry shook his head in disgust. "In a rush to get back in business, the company grabbed this rig from an operation in the Arabian Sea."

"Are we safe?"

Perry took in the wide eyes staring at him. He saw no reason to candy-coat anything. "This platform consists of living quarters and an office module at one end, pipe racks in the middle, and the drilling rig at the other. The living quarters are supposed to be a breakaway module, but after years in the field, I can tell you they don't always work as advertised."

The kid nodded, his Adam's apple bobbed.

"Harrumph. Get used to it." Perry took another sip of the coffee. "We're expendable, despite what company propaganda may tell you."

"How deep is it here?"

"The water in this particular location is ninety feet and we took advantage of relatively calm seas to anchor the platform and raise it up. We did it in less than twenty-four hours. Problem is, the depth was supposed to be one hundred twenty feet. I told the home office we were twenty miles off, but with their lack of concern, I blew it off. This whole region is full of oil anyway. I'm sure we're going to hit a good spot."

The kid turned a worried glance down at the deck.

Perry did not usually let things get to him, but he was off kilter. This job did not feel right. Their tow ship had departed early to beat the storm and left them to fend for themselves. He wondered, despite the small footprint and tripod design, if the rig would last until the job was finished. He did not feel confident, but if he could just get things started, he could leave it to someone else.

Cold spray beat against the window. He cursed his luck before turning and facing the control console, his assistant close at his heels.

"I hope this blow doesn't capsize the rig." The kid gripped the windowsill, his legs planted firmly.

Perry examined an arched mercury level. Despite the legs being sunk into the seabed, the platform swayed from the tremendous pressure of the sea. He noted the list weaving from minus three to plus three degrees from zero bubble. "She's designed to operate anywhere from minus to plus eleven degrees, and as you can see, we're still within limits."

The intense swaying of the deck could have knocked an inexperienced crewman off his feet, but it calmed Perry that the kid already had his sea legs. It would do no good to have a puking whiner hanging over the rails. He studied the young barely-bearded face, "It's a bloody mess out there, laddy. Yer' gonna' get yer' wee bit a roughin' it."

"Aye captain."

For the next two days the platform swayed, the cold did not let up, and Perry watched the tilt bubble inching toward the eleven-degree mark several times. He had accepted this god-awful job and would not back out just because of a little storm, the wrong style platform, or the fact that they were on the wrong site.

35

On the third day, the storm broke. The weather returned to the bitter stillness that was the norm for the North Sea. Morning loomed gray, and it would likely stay that way until dark. Perry entered the sleeping quarters at five-sharp and yelled, "All right ye' laddies'. Let's get the bloody drill in the water."

With his assistant at his side, Perry led operations. He felt obligated to keep the kid up to speed on what was going on. Someday, the laddy might be in his position.

"First, they'll lower the drill shaft until it meets the seabed almost two hundred feet below the deck. The first few feet are always easy until we hit bedrock."

When the large shaft bit into bedrock, he stopped the drilling. "Next we install the rupture cap."

He liked that the kid paid attention as he explained. He spent the next few hours supervising installation of the rupture cap and his assistant asked a lot of questions. "Now it's time for intermediate drilling."

True to his reputation, Perry would not let the crew break, despite grumbling about the cold and long hours. He could not ignore the crew tiring from the extreme conditions, but he had a deadline. "Sorry if I don't seem sympathetic to the laddies. I worked under worse conditions before most of them were born."

Perry did not like that they had no backup, no satellite, and no surveys. This operation was on the cheap, and the company was taking a big risk without all the high technology that was available nowadays. They were basically working under conditions the same as three decades ago.

"Now we're going to sink the intermediate shaft through the surface pipe." Perry pointed down to the rig.

Soon, the drill hit bedrock and it ground its way through solid rock toward the goal far below. Perry noticed the shaft vibrated more than usual and then it started a wobble as it turned, picking up sympathetic vibrations.

"Is that normal?" The kid backed away from the rail.

"No, it's not." He did not want to stop drilling yet, and pushed a nagging memory to the back of his mind.

More than once, the joints almost vibrated loose as the shaft sank into the rock. Reaching a particularly tough spot, Perry signaled the rig operator to increase drill pressure. "Sometimes we hit a rough spot. Normal for this kind of thing."

"Yes, Sir."

The operator knocked the downward pressure up a notch. With a loud clang, the shaft shot down and disappeared, coming off the coupler.

"What the bloody hell?" Perry looked down to the water far below. A realization dawned on him like a slap in the face, that nagging memory at the back of his mind he should not have ignored. He had seen that happen before, once when they accidentally drilled in to a large underground —

"What's happening?"

He gazed at the panicked face of his young assistant as a rumbling deep in the earth shook the whole platform. It swayed in a circular pattern. Perry could only mutter, "God help us all." He held tight to the nearest rail. With a loud sucking sound, the platform vanished into the swirling sea. All hands met the cold water .

In less than thirty seconds, the only thing visible at the rig site was a whirlpool that disturbed the surface of the slate-gray water. When it subsided, the water revealed no sign of the oil platform or any of its occupants.

A geological station in Northern Scotland registered a 3.4 magnitude earthquake centered about one hundred miles north. The scientists were surprised because no known fault existed at the location of the epicenter.

The huge vortex stabilized as the cavern below filled with water. Hours later, three massive creatures popped out of the hole, seeing this world for the first time in countless millennia. The ice that had kept them preserved melted and brought them back to life as if only a day passed. Swimming south, instinct led them to warmer waters, much like a migration they had followed in the distant past. Large bulging eyes glared out at the world above a set of sharp jagged teeth. They were free, hungry, and pissed off.

Gorging themselves on easy prey, the creatures continued south. Waking up in a foreign environment gave them a nasty disposition, and they attacked even when they were not hungry. The propeller of a large freighter had the misfortune of being in the path of their mindless aggression. The thirty-foot length of the creature was ripped to shreds beneath the huge single propeller of an older cargo ship. The ship too suffered debilitating damage, and had to call for rescue.

Though they were born in a prehistoric environment, the creatures were smart enough to learn from the mistake of their ill-fated companion. They avoided the "fish with the spinning teeth." The second creature met a different kind of hazard when it bit into a white plastic drum of cyanide waste, carelessly left floating in the open sea. The bright white plastic drifted like a tantalizing beacon, and the lucky one decided it looked like lunch. In minutes, the unfortunate beast's air bladder emptied and the heavier-than-water carcass sank to the seabed.

The remaining creature moved on, distressed with this strange new environment. Its usual food source was nowhere to be found and the water was cold, though there were plenty of other creatures to sample. The prehistoric animal found a current that urged it toward warmer water. Eventually it met up with a huge mass, a creature that resembled a larger version of the one that killed its first companion. Dead and bent, the carcass lay on its side. A gaping hole in the body of the big fish's belly provided shelter. It sensed plenty of food nearby and this dead creature's shell provided a place to hide and spring on unwary prey. The creature decided to take up residence.

SEVEN

Paddy Flaherty sat with his lifelong pal Sean O'Hanlon at a table in the shadows at the back of their favorite pub, the Boar and Whistle, while he sipped on a Guinness. A smoky haze filled the room, dimming the gleaming bottles lined up behind the bar across the room. Forty brands of brew, some local, some part of the bar's collection sat on shelves amid knickknacks of the local football heroes.

"Bloody fish weren't there again." Paddy spat the words out in a curse.

"Stop draggin' yer tail in the water, ya' might haul in sometin'."

"Bloody boyfriend of a sheep. I see ya did as well."

"Lost me bloody net. Yanked the spar right off the back, too."

"Got too close to the bloody boot', didja?"

"Hardly, ya swill drinkin' bloke."

"So, was it the boot' 'er not?" Sean had lost a valuable net for the third time in a week and Paddy saw the veins throbbing in his forehead.

"Snrgh." His friend snorted. "Bloody no, wasn't the boot'. I was more thanna' kilometer off her bow."

"I know, a bloody Russian submarine took your bloody net." Paddy guffawed. Out of the corner of his eye, he noted patrons glancing at the commotion but they turned away so not to catch his attention.

Over the past two months, the local catch yield had dropped off and Sean was not the only one that had lost or dragged in a severely mangled net. Paddy was surprised his buddy got within a kilometer of the *Lusitania*, or as Sean called it, the "boot'." It sat on the bottom ten miles off the coast, almost a hundred meters down. It caught many a fishing net until the locals wised up. Paddy had lost a net or two there. Though he knew this new net problem was different, he could not resist ribbing his friend. Despite not being the smartest person in town, Paddy was sure Sean had been far enough away from the sunken luxury liner, especially with the price of nets.

"Many more fishing days like these'll mean poverty, mate."

"Arrgmph." Sean glared at him, bleary eyed. "Already there."

Paddy shook his head. *Ain't that the truth.*

There were no massive kills or other evidence that the fish died en-masse. Those with enough fuel ventured to more plentiful waters either direction along the coast but he and Sean could not afford the extra diesel. The lack of fish seemed to be restricted to the immediate area around Kinsale, and the signs were bad enough that Paddy heard it attracted the attention of the University in Dublin and the University of Pittsburgh in the colonies.

The only real money they made was working for the old woman . Last year, right after a major diving expedition left the area he found a note with a phone number in his mailbox. No envelope and no postage. With nothing better to do, he called. He should have thrown the note away, but something in the eerie tenor of the woman's voice compelled him to say yes. Through his IRA contacts, he had been able to obtain enough explosives to improvise a few depth charges. He was as surprised as Sean when a few of them actually exploded as they dropped them on the *Lusitania*. That clandestine night operation gave them enough money to pay off their boats. She never told him why he had to blow up a wreck that had already been used for target practice by either the Irish or British navy. He did not care. "Wish she'd call again."

EIGHT

The boss already had the expedition in the planning stages by the time Detach returned to Galveston from New York, and he was not surprised, since he gave him a heads-up on the phone before he flew out. They shared a mutual interest in the old liner. "What d'you think?

"Tell you what. You've got the mission, whatever you need." Jams looked up at the ceiling, then at Detach, square in the eye.

Detach almost laughed. They were going to try and steal a treasure right under the noses of the private owner of the wreck as well as the Irish government. "What if I don't find any gold?"

"That's only our secret excuse to explore the wreck." Jams winked and pointed to the pirate log. "No different than this pirate map. It's probably a wild goose chase too, but I don't mind paying to check it out."

Detach figured that once the *Lusitania* mission ended, he would be heading a pirate treasure hunt. Jams always asked Detach to take care of those *special* missions that were not on the books. He considered Jams his second Dad, his friend, and his partner, besides being the *Boss*.

"All I'm interested in is the riddle of the ship. I know what Dr. Ballard and his team found, and they're probably right about the coal bunker exploding. But it'd be nice to check out that other theory about the ship carrying more munitions than what they told the public, which some guys in England said they've proven."

Detach recalled Dr. Robert Ballard, the man who found the *Titanic*. In the years since, he had also explored the *Lusitania* and

41

derived the theory that an exploding coalbunker sank the ship and not the German torpedo. There were other theories being bandied about, but he had not heard about other divers finding munitions until recently. That would add another element of danger to this project.

"We've got superior technology capable of digging deeper into the wreck. We can do it safer on top of that. Maybe we can prove Ballard right once and for all. Maybe we'll find something entirely different. Who knows?" Jams looked off in the distance. "In any case, we have an excuse now to check the wreck properly. The suit as well."

"What about the wreck owner and the Irish government?"

"Being cleared now. We're going to film it. I sold the idea because of our advanced technology. We're going to be very open with them." He gave an exaggerated wink.

"Heh heh heh. Just like every other time." Detach grinned back.

"The videographers I hired will hook into your helmet video as well as take shipboard shots. All I want to know is the truth. Radically disturbing the wreck and taking souvenirs is the biggest problem and I assured them we'll take nothing and disturb nothing. That seems to be the biggest dispute of all. However, since nobody else knows about the gold..."

It would not be the first time they took what they wanted right under the noses of watchdogs hanging over their every move. "That's the tricky part," Detach said.

"All I ask is that you distribute the wealth fairly, okay?"

"Please!" Detach planned to limit his take to a modest percentage and give a larger split to his friends. After countless off-the-books ventures for Jams, he had more money than he could spend in four lifetimes. He could have retired at twenty-nine, but loved his work so much he stashed his money for a time when he would not be able to handle these missions anymore. "When do we start?"

"Tomorrow, nine in the morning, the boardroom. I'll gather some personnel to start planning. Oh, and I invited some Russians along for the ride."

"The who?"

Before Jams could answer, the phone rang. He grinned at the number on the display. "It's Maggie."

Detach had heard that name many times. Jams had an obsession with "Mad Jake" Malone, a turn-of-the-century industrialist, and criminal. His latest thing was buying Malone's real estate property which included obscure plots of land all over the south. Maggie, Mad Jake's great-great-granddaughter, was his pipeline.

"You might as well hear this, too." He punched speakerphone. "Talk to me." He sat back with his hands behind his head and winked at Detach.

"Hello, Jams. Did you get all the paperwork on that piece of property?"

"Maggie! I want to thank you for selling me that land."

Maggie chuckled. "My great great-granddad would have a heart attack if he were alive to see what's happened to his empire."

"You're a good woman, Maggie. Besides, you could use the money for that child care center you sponsor."

"You know me well, Jams. Getting rid of another piece of that worthless swampland is going to be for something good."

Detach arched a brow when Jams looked his way.

"I'd like to introduce you to my second son, Detach." Jams held out a hand. "Detach, introduce yourself."

"Uh, hi. Maggie?"

"Hey, I finally get to hear your voice. I've heard a lot about you."

"So you're Mad Jake Malone's granddaughter?"

"That's great great-granddaughter."

"Nice to meet you."

Jams cut in. "We had a little excitement here today."

"Oh?" she asked.

"We're going to dive on the *Lusitania*. Film it and everything. I even invited some Russians to participate."

"The *Lusitania*? Russians? That's nice." Her voice flat. "Don't you have all that advanced salvaging gear you use on oil rigs and stuff?"

"Not really interested, huh?" Jams rolled his eyes.

"I'm just happy for you."

"You're right. We have some new toys that may help confirm why the ship sank so fast."

"My grandma has mentioned that ship a few times, but it's not really my thing. However, I'm excited *for* you. I hope you find what you're looking for."

"I'll keep you posted as things develop. Since you've been so nice to me, you'll get a heads up before the reporters can get it on the air, how's that?"

"Hah! You don't have to. Still, I appreciate the effort...you know, it would be cool to get the inside scoop." Maggie's voice sounded like it was coming from inside a tunnel.

"No problem at all." Jams nodded.

"You're crazy for buying a bunch of worthless swamp, but I thank you for taking it off my hands."

When they hung up, Detach cleared his throat.

"She's my connection to old Mad Jake. Her family still owns most of his estate, which as I've told you before, is mostly swampland in the Deep South. I'm just nibbling at the edges."

Detach remembered sitting in the Mason's backyard and listening as Jams related the same old stories over and over again about the mad industrialist from the turn of the 20th century. He never understood the fascination, but he did not care as long as Jams was happy. The man could certainly afford to buy that wild land. One time, Jams told him he was going to donate it all to conservation groups to preserve the environment. It would not be useful for anything else.

Grace walked through the door after returning from her latest trip to see Daddy, when she overheard her daughter on the phone. The mention of the *Lusitania* drew her attention. By the end of the conversation, she heard enough to send a chill down her spine. She backed away and ran up the stairs to her mother's room.

"Daddy's in trouble." Grace told her what she'd heard.

"What makes you think they'll discover anything?" Mother asked with temporary lucidity in her voice.

"They have diving stuff nobody's ever tried before." After she found out Maggie was selling Daddy's land to the owner of Mason Industries, she investigated them and learned that they were top of the line when it came to underwater salvage. "They've also invited some Russians to help."

"Oh, my!" The old woman gasped. "Russians? If they find..."

"What do we do, Mommy?" A glassy-eyed stare crept into the old woman's face and Grace was afraid of losing her again. "Mom?"

"We must stop them in Ireland."

The hint of lucidity returned to Mother's voice and Grace relaxed. Mommy always had the answers when her mind was clear.

An hour later, Grace left the mansion. The tires on her Mercedes squealed, racing out the long driveway. If those Mason people dug too deep, they might find out the truth. Time to go to plan B.

NINE

The conference room always reminded Detach of the bridge of an ocean liner. An antique ship's wheel stood at one end, mounted to the floor, matching the one behind Jams' desk. Portholes lined three walls. The long table in the center of the room seated twenty people. Each station had a computer keyboard and flat screen monitor, mouse, and space for writing. The equipment lowered into the table and a lid flipped down to make the table flat when not in use. Teakwood paneling covered the walls, the wood salvaged from the deck of an actual ocean liner. His eyes wandered to the ceiling that housed video, projection, audio equipment, and a drop-down plasma screen, ready for virtually any visual media.

Jams sat at the head of the table, the ship's wheel to his back. His cowboy hat hung on one of the spokes. Detach always got a chuckle out of that eccentricity. The old man even had a ship's wheel at his house where the hat would sit when he was home. Every time they salvaged a ship, Jams collected the ship's wheel for himself, but only if it was the traditional spoked wheel. Somewhere he had a warehouse full of them.

The boom box sat next to his computer. He reached, as if to turn it on. All eyes went to the boss and talking stopped. Some winced while others smiled. If Jams wanted to get people's attention, a few seconds of death metal usually did the trick.

"Just seeing if you're paying attention." Jams chuckled and took his hand away from the obnoxious noise machine. He typed in a few commands on his computer keyboard.

The plasma screen came to life displaying an image of the

47

Lusitania at sea.

"Thanks to Detach, we've finally come up with a good enough excuse to explore the wreck proper. My interest is in finding out what really happened, and to test our new gear. He'll tell you the rest."

Detach trusted everyone in the room with his life. Over the years, he and Jams had carefully assembled this team of experts, people who proved their loyalty and trustworthiness, even over their expertise.

"While I was in New York, I ran across this little old lady. Her mother's boyfriend was a passenger on the ship and he liked to *move* merchandise."

Several people rolled their eyes.

"Well, this merchandise was a shipment of gold going to Germany." He repeated what Gladys had told him.

Barry Kruger, a thin man with sharp blue eyes and blonde Aryan features spoke up. "They were going to smuggle this gold right under the noses of the British? As ammunition?"

"Yup. Not only would they get the gold, they'd also embarrass the Brits just to rub it in."

"So what we have here is flawed genius." Barry smiled, revealing perfect teeth. "A good plan, but a Murphy's Law outcome."

"Pretty much." Detach could not count how many times "Mr. Murphy" spoiled his plans. "From what Gladys implied, there were quite a few crates of bullets, and by my guestimate, the treasure could be several tons. Since no one but us knows about it, they won't miss the ammunition if we happen to run across it."

"Uh huh." Barry shook his head. "We only have to do it under the noses of the Irish Government, the guy that owns the salvage rights, and the cameras we're going to use to document the exploration."

"Details," Detach said with a shrug.

Everyone in the room joined in a chorus of chuckling.

"Here's the deal. We carry on the exploration as advertised. I'll take care of the extraneous activities. You'll all get a percentage of what I find. No guarantees of course, but whatever we find, we find."

"Okay, now that we have that settled, let's get down to the details." Jams nodded to Barry. "Give us the tour."

Barry typed on his computer and brought a new image on the screen.

Detach scanned the detailed painting of the ship lying in a heap on the bottom of the ocean. He recognized it from the book Dr. Ballard wrote on his exploration a few years earlier.

"Basically, we're dealing with a scrap metal yard vaguely in the shape of a ship," Barry said with a sour tone. "She's in terrible shape. Besides the natural deterioration from the environment, the Royal Navy used her for submarine mine practice in the fifties. Conspiracy nuts say it was an effort to cover up evidence. Whatever the truth, they did a good job of it. As you'll notice, there's a massive tangle of fishing nets caught all over the superstructure, something we'll have to deal with, besides everything else." Barry took a swig of bottled water and continued.

"We'll be dealing with nasty currents, cold and murky water, and one other thing that Ballard ran across." Barry paused for emphasis. "Unexploded ordnance in the form of hedgehog mines."

Detach groaned along with several others.

"Can the diving suit take it if one explodes?" Jams asked.

A woman with a neat bob of shark-gray hair spoke up. "The suit's incredible, but one of those babies can blow a hole in the hull of a large vessel. I wouldn't want to be down there if it went off nearby."

Detach gazed affectionately at the head engineer. Ruby Fenner sounded like a whisky-soaked bar floozy. A going joke said she swallowed broken glass and gargled with battery acid to mellow it out.

"How do we handle this one?" Barry flipped his hands up and scanned the faces.

"Suggestions?" Jams said.

"Elroy Jones." Detach waited for the protests.

"Uhhhhh." Jams put a hand on his forehead. "Not him."

"Hey, we did the Gulf together. That man can disarm anything, plus he has plenty of experience deep diving."

"Is he even among the living?" Barry said.

Detach had brought Elroy Jones in on several of their ventures. Elroy's two weaknesses were alcohol and gambling. At one time or another, many of the people in this room either bailed him out of jail for drunken disorderly conduct, or whisked him away from someone he owed money.

The last job he did for the group went well enough, but soon afterward, Detach heard Elroy went into deep debt with a casino in Las Vegas, his hometown. He could not understand that since Elroy was the best blackjack card counter he had ever seen. "Look, he does have his faults, but he's the best explosives expert, bar none."

"Hmmm…" Jams tapped his finger on the table. "Tell you what. If you can find him alive somewhere—"

The door opened. All heads turned to a stocky, well-proportioned brunette who walked into the room.

"Sorry I'm late, people," Becky Mason said.

So glad she's back from Spain. In her mid-thirties, she was just two years younger than him. Everyone respected and admired her, not because of her dad, but because she continually proved her worth as a diver, archaeologist, and marine biologist. She could also pack a mean punch when provoked, a quality that made her more attractive to Detach.

"Well?" Jams asked.

"Have a seat," Detach offered.

"No thanks. I've been sitting for more than half a day already." She leaned over one of the consoles and typed, replacing the *Lusitania* painting with a map of Spain, and a newspaper headline from *El Pais* off to the side.

"That job was a load of trouble. Normally, the Spaniards are pretty lax about permits and such, but in this case, they gave us a lot of grief. Once that was settled, they had a Basque bombing. We had equipment troubles, boat troubles, diver troubles, and the icing on the cake was a rumor that we released a demon from its ancient prison." She stopped to catch her breath. "The

Catholic Diocese got involved and demanded we have a priest on call in case there was any truth to the rumor. Sort of 'preventive demonology.'"

"Did you accomplish anything?" Ruby said.

"It's not Atlantis." Becky dug in her pocket, pulled out a laser and aimed it at a spot of text in the article. Even though it was in Spanish, the meaning was plain. No Atlantis. "However, I was able to slip this out." She held up an object.

Detach joined everyone in a gasp. Becky held a gold necklace with an engraved oval frame. In the center, a huge blue stone the size of a walnut gleamed. He had never seen a sapphire that large.

"This alone would pay for the expedition, if we wanted to sell it." Becky looked at her dad. "I get the feeling it's not going anywhere."

"Are you ready to join in our latest venture?" Jams said.

"Sure." She nodded. "Let it rip."

"Let's see...oh yeah, explosives...where were we?" Jams looked around the room.

"Elroy?" Detach waited for a tirade, this time from Becky.

"Oh, yeah, him." Jams winced and rubbed his forehead. "Here's the deal. Find the man, check him out and get him here, if he's able. We don't need to drag his problems along. If he works out, I assume you'll be cutting him in on a share."

"Absolutely," Detach said, noting the sour expression on Becky's face. "As it is, he'll probably be taking one heck of a risk for us."

"We know it's going to be rough down there. Suggestions? Ways to boost the odds?" Jams waved a hand.

"It's about time we put some more of those miniature cold fusion generators to use, besides the ones in the suits," Ruby said.

"How so?" Jams' eyebrows shot up.

She typed on her keyboard with long, nimble fingers, dexterous despite their aged appearance, and the plasma display went dark.

With a burst of brightness, which made Detach blink, a ring of lights illuminated the Ballard book drawing of the wreck as it sat

51

on the ocean bottom. *I wonder how many hours she worked to create that simulation.*

"What I propose is this. We need a massive amount of light to see down there because the water's murky and dark at that depth. To get enough light conventionally would require a huge generator on the surface, which would take up a lot of space on the mother ship."

The mouse pointer went to the base of one of the stadium-like light fixtures.

"We rig independent light poles with their own power pack, anchor them to the seabed well enough to withstand the current, and control them remotely from topside."

"How bright are we talking about?" Detach already had an idea.

"Let's just say you'd probably be able to see them from the space station," Ruby said with a twinkle in her eye. "Of course, they're useless once you're inside the ship, but the lights on the suits will take care of that."

"Won't the water be a bright blur, even with the lights?" Barry waved his laser at the image. "All that sediment down there will diffuse the clarity."

"Aah...a little magic." Ruby held up her right index finger. "Each light will have a special filter that utilizes the most efficient light frequency to cut through all that crap."

"But wait a minute." Becky had been pacing behind Detach and asked, "Why are we bothering lighting up the whole area? All we need are the lights in our suits."

"Okay, Barry." Ruby turned to him. "Your thoughts?"

"It's like this." Barry settled his laser on the ship. "We're going to be filming for that video team. It's a big deal to appease the owner of the wreck and the Irish government. We'll be doing some major movement around there in our independent diving suits. Those lights will show not only the nets and crap caught on the hull, but will also show any munitions down there. Besides, it's a chance to try our technology in a real-world setting. Nobody has ever done that before."

Ruby walked to the end of the table. "All this may be for

nothing if the water is still too murky, the filters don't work, or a host of other issues. One of the stipulations is that we film as much of the debris field and the wreck as we can. To make everyone happy, I dreamed this idea up. It may come in handy again one day if it actually works."

"Mr. Diplomat, what about the Irish government? Is everything cool with the ship's owner?" Jams turned to George George.

Detach eyed George. The man's wire-rimmed glasses shifted while he pondered the question. A former career diplomat, he performed as their expert on international affairs. Small, with black hair combed in a pompadour, he looked like he should be in a Las Vegas lounge act. His name provoked a double take from most people. When asked his name he would say "George George." The usual response was "George George what?" That never seemed to be a problem overseas where double names were more common.

"Since this is going to be a public event, there'll be monitoring from both parties. To what extent, I'm not sure. We should be able to circumvent whatever they throw at us as soon as I gather the extent of their involvement." George let out a long sigh. "Maybe, if we get lucky, we can keep it to a minimum."

"Are we going to use *Lothar*?" Jams toyed with his pen, twirling it between his fingers like a baton.

Detach nodded. "Definitely my choice." The *Lothar* was their finest research vessel, commissioned ten years earlier when Jams acquired it from the Chilean government. Detach named it after Lothar and the Hand People, a sixties band his uncle turned him on to during a visit when he was still in high school. One of the ship's many features was the internal moon pool they used for work in bad weather, or when they wanted to be discreet.

"What about the interns?" Barry asked.

"Sure," Jams said.

As young divers training for careers in the organization, they would be useful for grunt work, though only one had experience with the new suit. Detach thought of the young and cocky men, too big for their britches. The deep dive qualified kid was the cockiest of them all. He figured James Broce would get his chance at the suit, though he wanted to slap the crap out of him for general principles. With the right direction, the kid would make one great diver.

"You know where Elroy is, Honey?" Ruby said.

"I have an idea." Detach gave Becky a wink. She returned it with an icy stare.

"Speaking of which," Jams interrupted, "it's time we get started on this thing. Let's meet at say, ten in the morning, day after tomorrow and see where we're at."

"I have one more question." Detach held up a finger. "If we're going to use the cold fusion packs for lighting, how are we going to hide that from our audience?"

"I already figured that one out dear." Ruby leaned over her keyboard. "Check this out."

She typed some commands and the overhead screen displayed the *Lothar's* main deck.

Mounted conspicuously in the middle, Detach noticed a large metal box with heavy cables protruding out one end.

"See that thing? It's the generator. We'll be using it to power everything on the surface. What we'll do is expand the casing, make it look bigger than it is. As far as the lights downstairs, we're going to rig dead cables to them to make it appear the generator is doing the work."

"That seems like a lot of trouble," Detach said.

"True, but who's going to be able to dive down and look closely outside of you and your team? Besides," she continued, "as you're all aware, the world isn't yet ready for cold fusion, so it's imperative that we keep the technology secret. If they get a gander at how bright those lights are, there's no way they'd believe batteries could do the job, hence the generator and cables. Besides, the cables also double as the lift capability to get the lights back up to the surface."

Barry waved his laser at the ceiling. "I've already seen those lights in action, and Ruby's right. There's no way anyone's going to believe a mere battery pack can keep them going for more than a few minutes."

"I can't argue with that reasoning." To Detach, the phony cables and generator would at least look plausible and should fend off too many questions.

"How are we going to explain the suits?" Becky said.

"Simple. We're not." Ruby waved a hand at Becky. "By all appearances, you'll be limiting your dives to a conventional time period and if anyone asks about the stabilizing system, we'll be vague. Trade secrets, proprietary technology and all that stuff."

"Every TV network in the nation might see them because of the videographers," George said.

"No one ever said we couldn't be discreet when we needed to be," Jams added with a grin.

The meeting adjourned, and Becky met Detach in the hallway. "I missed you."

"Elroy, are you kidding me?" She glared up at him, blinked, as if thinking twice about her tirade. "You did? I thought you were vacationing in New York."

"I don't know if I'd call it that."

"Well the answer is still no. I won't date you. But if you want to go get some lunch in the cafeteria, I'm in…and we have to talk about Elroy."

"Let's go." *Oh crap, I'm in trouble now.* They walked down the hall to the elevator, her hand momentarily touching his. Despite knowing what he was in for, he felt a warm rush of excitement

TEN

Detach put one foot in front of the other, each movement an effort in the oppressive heat as he trudged from the chow hall toward the barracks. The ground erupted nearby, shrapnel screaming by his right ear. He dove into a ditch to his left and landed on a uniform already planted there. Another detonation compressed the air around him. He rolled off the other man.

"Hey man, give a guy a break!"

"Sorry!"

Two more explosions ripped the air above them.

After screaming a tirade into the dirt that only he could hear, he turned to the coffee-brown stranger in his face, and abated his voice. "Just roll over a bit!"

He twisted around to obtain a more comfortable position, and prayed the explosions were nothing more than a random attack. In this place, there was no telling. Resistance had been almost non-existent, but that did not mean something would not flare up, as it was now.

After the commotion died down, he took stock of his ditch mate. He was face to face with a young black man, about his age, a wild and ornery look in his eye.

"I ain't been here an hour and get bombed!"

"Welcome to the Gulf. You can call me Detach." He held out his hand.

"Elroy."

Elroy had a firm handshake. "Welcome to our happy home."

He snapped back to the present as the seatbelt light came on. He wondered if he would find his old friend, and if so, what kind of shape he would be in.

57

They became instant friends, serving together as Navy divers in the Gulf. Elroy was the only outsider that knew Detach's fear of fresh water. During his time in the military, he never once had to dive in a lake. He kept that issue hidden from his superiors. He had confessed his limnophobia to Elroy in a drunken spree when they did an R&R in Germany.

"At first I thought you were joking. I can see in your eyes, you mean it." Elroy never joked about it or tried to use it as a way to poke fun at him. That kindness put Elroy at the top of his close friend list, which was very short at that moment.

When they got out of the military, Detach had called on Elroy's munitions expertise many times. Sober, Elroy presented the image of a consummate professional, and he completed each job without incident. However, when the job ended, the money he made usually went to the blackjack tables and his favorite hooch.

Detach deplaned at McCarran Airport in Las Vegas and a rental car waited for him at the gate. Becky's tirade still rang in his ears. In some ways, she loved Elroy like a brother, but she had also been on the receiving end of his issues and did not want him jeopardizing their trip. It took three beers to get her calm enough to go along with it. He knew once he got back with their friend, Becky would give no sign of her reluctance. *At least I hope not.*

He figured it was up to him to bring Elroy back, if he was still among the living, and he had a good idea he could find him at his favorite table in the *Circus Circus* casino.

Scanning the interior, he looked for a familiar face and saw a small crowd gathered around a table. A boisterous black man sat at the center of the crowd. Detach could already tell by his loud, slurred speech that Elroy felt no pain. He stayed behind his friend and studied the crowd. He spotted the pit boss, a burly man that looked like security, and another one in a more expensive suit, probably a manager. A substantial pile of black hundred dollar chips sat next to Elroy. The suits and pit boss gazed intently at his friend. On the ceiling, the camera globes glared like insect eyes, surely zeroed in on the big winner. A bad feeling settled in the pit of his stomach.

Detach knew Elroy's eccentricities. When he was very drunk, he would count cards. He never knew how his friend could keep track of the cards while stewed out of his mind, but somehow Elroy did better at it drunk than sober. The three men were about to pounce and he had one chance to head them off before his friend ended up in an embarrassing situation.

Detach bent down and whispered in Elroy's ear. "They know. Quit while you're ahead, or it'll be like New Orleans." He patted his friend on the shoulder.

Turning his head, Elroy's expression changed from recognition to a frown and he muttered, "Nawlins."

He had reminded Elroy of an awful experience in that city. It almost cost them their lives, not from organized crime elements, but the local police force. He noted the recognition in his friend's eyes.

"I'm done," Elroy gathered up his chips before the dealer played out another hand. An audible groan came from the crowd, and sighs of relief from the three suits. While Elroy gathered his chips, Detach went over to the pit boss and apologized for his friend.

"I'd like to offer him a free room," the guy said.

That would be a great way to get your money back, wouldn't it? "Sorry, but he'll have to pass on that. He needs to be someplace else."

He dragged his friend by the arm to the cashier to turn in his chips. Afterward, he whisked him to the parking garage and his rental car, not a word passing between them. He did not bother to ask where Elroy lived because he had been to his house many times. His friend lived with his aunt in North Las Vegas. Leaving Circus Circus, he headed north on Las Vegas Boulevard.

"Had em' beat, had em' cold."

"Sure you did, except you forgot that they had you cold the moment you started counting and winning."

"Gagmmph," Elroy snarled and passed out.

Elroy reeked of alcohol and Detach hoped he could get him to his aunt's house before they had a mess to clean up.

Fifteen minutes later, he pulled up to a house in a neighbor-

59

hood of dirt yards, peeling paint, dead weeds and gang graffiti covering boarded windows. Yet, amongst the bad were the neat houses with trim desert landscape, painted walls and well-kept abodes. Detach pulled up to one of the nicer homes with the curtains drawn. *What happened to Elroy's aunt? She never has the curtains closed.* He parked the car, went around and opened the passenger door. Elroy woke with a start and fell out of the car. He struggled to his hands and knees.

"Gaggmph, muthammph!"

Detach helped him to his feet and guided him to the house. Elroy fished for his keys and Detach had to take them from him to open the door. Once inside, he noticed a clean house that matched the outside. He led his friend to the bedroom and let him fall on the bed, unconscious. In the living room, he spotted a TV and an old-time VCR. "A VCR? You got to be kidding!"

At eight in the evening, Elroy stumbled into the living room. Detach looked up from his third movie. "It's alive."

"Mmmfmgrmph." Elroy disappeared into the kitchen.

Detach knew to let well enough alone until his friend woke up. In the Gulf, Elroy almost killed a young recruit who annoyed him when he woke him up from one of his binges. It had been a nightmare smuggling booze into the strict Islamic surroundings. As a result, people tended to overdo it. Even Detach drank more than he would anywhere else again. The place was that bad.

A few minutes later, he smelled coffee and food cooking. Tuneless humming replaced the unintelligible mumbling.

Elroy never seemed to suffer from a hangover once he woke all the way. Soon, he came into the living room and plopped into an easy chair. Coffee sloshed in a cup in one hand while he held a plate of reheated spaghetti in the other. "What did I do this time?"

"Circus Circus, blackjack, counting cards….need I say more?"

"Mmmm"

"The pit boss offered you a room."

"Lucky they haven't banned me for life, yet." His friend took a mouthful of spaghetti.

"I'm surprised they even allow you through the door."

"I haven't quite gone over the line yet. Now I have to lay low for a while." He stared at Detach as if seeing him for the first time. "Say pal, what're you doing here?"

"Where's your Aunt Meg?"

Elroy's face darkened. "Lost her last year, left me her place."

"I'm sorry." Detach liked Meg, a large roly-poly woman with a big heart.

"We were lucky she went the way she did. She died of a massive stroke in her sleep. Never knew what hit her."

Detach noted dampness in the corner of his bloodshot eyes.

"What's up? I know you well enough to know you aren't here on a social call."

Detach tried to look hurt but Elroy gave him a suspicious look. He told the story, leaving in all the details.

Elroy did not interrupt and maintained a serious face. When Detach finished, he stared him in the eye. "Look at us. We're both looking back on thirty. We're getting a little old for this, aren't we? Isn't that a touch of gray in your wig?"

"Not a chance." Detach grinned. "We're still kids."

"Don't feel like one right now. So, you have this suit. How maneuverable is it? I'll need to be dexterous, especially with that old ordnance a hair trigger away from roasting my cookies."

"With a little practice, you can pick up something as small as a postage stamp without wrinkling it."

"I'll have to see that to believe it."

"Look at this." Detach pulled out his wallet and took out a piece of plastic the size of a credit card with scratches on the face of it. "That's my payroll signature done in a ten knot current two hundred feet down, while being harassed by the local fauna."

"Huh." Elroy shrugged and said, "I'm impressed."

"You game?"

"How's that old fart with the noise machine?"

"He's doin' well. His latest kick's been Scandinavian Death Metal."

"That's the weirdest thing. A senior citizen playing heavy rock."

"Drives his business partners crazy, keeps 'em on edge."

"How's Becky? You get married yet?"

"Are you kidding? We haven't even had an official date. She keeps turning me down."

"Mmmph." Elroy took a slurp of his coffee. "Don't give up. She has the hots for you, trust me." A bloodshot eye winked.

"Well? What do you say? You game?"

"I've been doing a bit of writing." Elroy leafed a thick stack of papers on the table that Detach had not paid attention to.

"We should only be a couple of weeks. Can it wait?"

"Just one condition."

"Uh oh." Elroy's eyes gleamed in a way that made Detach uncomfortable. "What?"

"Jussaminute." Elroy stood on wobbly legs and went into his bedroom. He came back and handed Detach an eye patch. "Do the pirate."

"Ohhh." Detach groaned. "Do I have to?"

"Part of the deal."

Detach stood and put the patch over his right eye. On a stand next to the TV, he found a red dust rag. He tied it on his head with the excess hanging down the back along with his ponytail.

"Aaaar, matey, aaar," he growled in his best pirate voice.

Elroy burst out laughing and fell on the couch.

Detach had started his pirate routine in high school to get a laugh. Now he had done it so many times he hated it. If it would get Elroy to help on his project, he could tolerate it one more time. While his friend convulsed on the couch, Detach took off the patch and dust rag. "Think I'll keep the patch. Might need it one day since I threw the other one away."

ELEVEN

The room held an air of anticipation for the upcoming expedition. Afternoon sun streaked through the west windows, muted by a heavy tint on the glass. The air smelled of coffee and a mix of perfumes. Detach locked hands behind his head and leaned back to watch his friends and co-workers while Jams conducted the meeting.

"Where do we stand?" When nobody responded, Jams moved his hand to the boom box.

Barry Kruger stood.

Jams grinned and pulled his hand away from the CD player.

Barry leaned down, tapped a few keys on his computer and walked to the plasma monitor. An image of the wrecked liner displayed, the same painting they had used two days before.

"I've been going over this thing and we got a real mess to deal with. The ship's lying on the starboard side, the side we're trying to get to, and it's twisted with the bow sort of straight up. The whole superstructure's collapsed and any dive will be like trying to get to the bottom of a scrap heap."

Detach noted the expression on Elroy's face as his friend realized what they were about to do.

"What're all those dents and holes?" Elroy squinted at the huge screen.

Detach replied, "That's where you come in, my friend."

"Mmmm."

"Our primary entrance will be this huge hole in the side amidships." Barry used his laser pointer to highlight places on the image.

"Uh..." Jams frowned. "Isn't that a long way from where we want to go?"

"For some of it, yes, but we might have a relatively clear area to tunnel toward the bow if we stay as far below decks as possible."

"I see another large hole forward, closer to the area we're interested in."

"True enough, Detach, but ask yourself this. How did that hole get there? Does it look like a salvage cut or did something else blow it open? See what I'm saying?" Barry said.

"It might take some time to ensure it's a safe way in." Elroy's eyes moved back and forth across the screen.

"Exactly." Barry whipped the pointer from the screen to the ceiling and back. "I wasn't going to say anything, but something about this image bothers me."

"How so?" Jams waved his right hand toward the screen.

"I don't quite know. You see, the artist based this painting on photos of the original ship, underwater photos, and radar images. He used all that to make what I have to admit is a masterpiece. It gives us an idea of what the ship actually looks like down there."

"But?" Detach leaned forward and tapped the table with a finger. "We need to know before we get into it."

"I don't know exactly, but something doesn't seem quite right." Barry shrugged. "I wonder how much was actually seen, then guessed at. I wonder how they filled in the blanks."

"Are you telling me something's missing?" Jams splayed the fingers on his right hand toward the image.

"Not exactly. But..."

"Okay." Jams clamped his hand. "If you ever figure out what that is, let me know."

"Well, boys and girls," Mildred Pierce, their head researcher and librarian, said. She pointed at the screen with her finger. "I know one thing that's definitely wrong."

Barry slid his laser pointer to her, and she aimed it at the image. "That second smaller hole forward? It's not there."

"What do you mean?" Barry said.

"You see, when the artist first painted the ship, he added

64

the hole that previous divers thought they spotted. Ballard and his crew found out it wasn't there. Without proper lighting, the previous divers were probably looking at the big tear in the side, the one that actually exists." She pointed to another spot. "He added it just for historical value. The painting that made it into the book is the correct version."

"What about *Lothar*?" Detach changed the subject.

"She's, er', being re-fitted especially for the trip." Jams grinned.

Detach forgot that they were replacing the engines with cold fusion generators.

"What's *Lothar*?" Elroy asked.

"Remember that research vessel I told you about the last time you worked for us?"

"That decommissioned cruiser from, where was it, Argentina?"

"Chile. They weren't the original owners, but once they had it, they couldn't afford the upkeep. Besides, some well-placed people in the government owed him." Detach nodded to the boss.

"Big favors...yup." Jams did a drum tap on the table with his fingers. "Big favors."

"It'll be our home away from home?"

"That's about it. Wait until you see her. She'll surprise you."

"Oh?" Elroy arched a brow at Detach. "Can I assume it bears no resemblance to a broken down old warship?"

"Not quite." Becky put a hand on his shoulder. "Actually, it looks more like a broken down cargo vessel, at least on the outside."

The room erupted with laughter.

"Not to change the subject again, but..." Detach turned to Ruby. "What about the sensor problem?"

"Still a regular pain in the butt, asking all these questions," Ruby said with an exaggerated sigh. "Had to bring that up! The boys tried several modifications while you were enjoying yourself in Vegas, but it's still not right yet."

"Aw, geez." Detach threw up his hands. "We've mastered difficult technological problems, yet we still can't get a lousy sensor to work right?"

"It's like the Challenger failed because of a lousy o-ring." Barry sat down in his chair and leaned back.

"Can I assume then that Murphy's Law is alive and well?" Detach rubbed his forehead.

"Got it." Paddy mumbled into the phone before he hung up.

"Another job?" Sean asked.

"Aye. Say, that old man with ties to the IRA, is e' still around?"

Sean's eyes lit up. "We gonner' blow sumptin' up again?"

TWELVE

Detach crept through the basement library door to spy on Mildred Pierce. She looked like a typical spinster librarian with petite, curly gray hair, her eyes shooting a stern look over half-lens glasses at her computer screen. Never married but not gay like some people thought, she had once told him that she simply never found the right man and at age sixty-seven, she did not care anymore. *Wonder if I'll end up the same way, the way things are going with Becky?*

Detach admired Mildred for being so unique. Besides her talent as a researcher, she was an expert marksman, one of the best in Mason Industries. She also maintained a black belt in Tae Kwon Do. In the decades he had known her, she had a chance to show off her martial arts talents on several would be muggers and rapists. Two of them almost died in the process.

Her muttering voice echoed off the walls, and row upon row of books. Mildred's domain, fondly called the "morgue," resided in the basement of the main building. Her collection rivaled a small public library. Lined with shelves upon shelves of books, microfiches, computer terminals, and other research media, it even put many large city libraries to shame. Nobody dared take her up on her long-standing bet that she could name the title of every book in the room. Detach knew better.

Her desk sat in the corner farthest from the elevator and stairwell. He had plenty of cover to spy on her, with the desk buried among piles of magazines and papers. Nautical maps and photos of some of the expeditions she had researched for the company, successes and failures covered the walls in her personal corner. He had worked on them all.

The polished teak desk hiding beneath stacks of paperwork, had been salvaged by Detach from a well-preserved cruise ship wreck he had found years earlier. He fashioned the desk into a work of art for her in the carpenter shop on his own time. A reward for her superior work on an expedition to South America. The center was clear of the big piles of paper that surrounded her and he had a clear view while she worked. He wished he had a rubber band or even a spit wad. Next to her desk, a sink jutted from the wall. On a shelf beside it sat her "precious," a battered but still functional plastic coffee machine. She abused it when in her "do it or die" mode. Detach had spent many of those sessions with her, the longest lasting fifteen hours.

She tapped the monitor screen and mumbled, "So, we have ghosts."

"Ghosts?"

"Aaagh!" She jumped. "You scared the daylights out of me. Don't do that!"

"You were absorbed in your work. I'm not surprised you didn't see me." Detach gave her a guilty grin.

"You know me pretty well, don't you?"

"What we got, so far?"

"Pull up a chair."

He admired her ability to smell trouble and liked to get personally involved in the research. Finding out details prevented nasty surprises, and he could justify the long hours he spent with her. Mildred always told him she enjoyed his company and the second set of eyes. Together they uncovered details that kept trouble to a minimum, most of the time.

"We have several ghost stories that popped up for about five years after the sinking, but faded out as time passed." She pulled one up.

"*The Banshee of the Lighthouse* tells the tale of a nasty spirit that chased people along the shore at night, especially near the Old Head of Kinsale lighthouse. Think there was a basis for them?" Detach continued to squint at the screen.

"You mean outside of the normal superstitions?"

"Uh huh."

"Funny you should ask. I was just about to look for unusual activities along the coast during the era. Let's see what pops out."

"When it comes to seafarers and ghost stories in coastal towns, I've always had a great deal of suspicion. As a common tactic, maritime smugglers created ghost stories to cover up their activities. Playing on superstition, these guys often exploited the ghost angle until either they completed their operation or someone caught them. Often as not, they avoided discovery and their ghosts became the stuff of local legends. Just like *Scooby Doo*."

"Oh, boy." Mildred snickered. "On a more serious note, I set to work pulling up the local commerce reports. In many cases, and especially in certain foreign countries, historical data on the Internet is vague at best. In this case, I pulled up a substantial amount of stuff."

"I guess we should be lucky this isn't in Gaelic."

"Tell me about it. From what I've found so far, there wasn't much going on along that part of the coast. The war effort put the kibosh on most enterprises except for ammunition factories and war supplies."

"Hmmm." Detach scratched his head. "What about company holdings in the area?"

"Nothing much except fishing ventures. Now there was a... processing plant? Yeah, a processing plant." Mildred ran her finger over the screen.

"Hmmm. Nothing particularly unusual," Detach had a nagging feeling they had missed something.

"Since the ghost stories were active for about five years, let's look for businesses that lasted only during that time."

"Yeah, see if anything looks out of place."

Mildred clicked through several web sites, until one displayed that dealt with specific company histories. It included a database search engine, and she added the parameters for the counties around Kinsale. She chose the dates 1915 to 1920, and the companies that started and folded during that time span. She clicked on the search button and the screen changed colors and displayed three companies.

"Hmm." She wrote down the names on a paper pad next to her keyboard.

Detach loved to watch Mildred work. She reminded him of his aunt, Joyce, a kindly relative who tried, unsuccessfully to teach him how to play chess. He wished now he had taken her instructions to heart. Maybe Maria would not kick his butt every time they played.

Mildred reached for her coffee cup and took a sip. Her eyes got big as she spat the liquid out on the floor, narrowly missing her computer keyboard and splashing all over Detach. "Aagh! Cold."

"Aha ha ha ha!" Detach slapped his knee and rolled his chair out of the way, clearing a path for Mildred to reach her precious.

"I ought to pour a hot cup in your lap for laughing, smartass."

"Sorry!" Detach shut up. It was a good thing the floor was tile, he had witnessed her spit out cold coffee many times when she concentrated too much on her work.

"Okay, okay." Back at her computer with a hot cup of coffee, she said, "We have three possibilities. One is Flannery & Sons in Cobh. They made Army cots."

"Naah, don't see a connection."

"I don't think so either. The second one is...to heck with that, look here." She pointed to the third name on the screen and the detailed history below it.

"Uh huh..." Detach peered at the screen but from the distance, could not resolve the small font. "What do we have here?"

"West Wind Trading Company, LTD, out of Glasgow."

"So? Scotch and Irish don't mix?"

Mildred reached around and slapped him on the knee. "Shut up and listen. West Wind started a cannery and a small fleet in Kinsale. They built into an old warehouse and had only three ships. Problem is that only one boat was a fishing vessel and the other two were a cargo ship and utility vessel respectively."

"Utility vessel?"

"That's what it says, whatever that is." Mildred squinted at the screen, reading the details below the name. "According to this, they came into Kinsale in June 1915 and stayed four months. Never brought in a fish, but a host of foreign employees. Locals said a lot of them spoke French, but they were mostly dark skinned, and didn't bring families. They hired locals to modify the warehouse. After working for a month, progress on the warehouse stalled and the locals lost their jobs. The company struggled from then on, and in two more months, folded without doing any business. Packed up everything overnight and loaded it onto the two larger ships. They abandoned the fishing boat at the dock."

"If that doesn't stink, crap must be sirloin steak."

"That has to be the worst cliché I've ever heard." Mildred scowled at him.

"So, what's with this West Winds business?"

"Let's find out." Mildred closed the web site and went to another one.

Detach leaned back in his chair and waited.

"There are three West Winds Trading Companies, and none were from Glasgow. Keeping in mind the potential for historical errors, let's forget Glasgow and see what's what." Mildred worked her mouse furiously, pulling up data on all three companies. "Here we go," she muttered. "Candidate number one was a company dealing with Chinese imports in the 1870's on the West Coast, mainly San Francisco. Folded in 1899. Second one started in the 1940s and is still active today, novelties. Third was...hey, this is odd..."

"Odd?" Detach sat up in his chair. "Odd's what we're looking for."

"According to this, it's obvious West Winds was a front for something else."

"Mmm."

"Do you think they could've salvaged the ship and knew about the gold?"

"Considering the technology of the time, I don't see how, especially if they folded so soon after setting up. Maybe it has nothing to do with the *Lusitania*. Maybe it's something else."

"Hmmm. The trail's murky at best, but let's see..." Mildred

71

tapped away now using the keyboard along with the mouse. "Jake Malone."

"Mad Jake Malone? Jam's favorite character?" A tingle rippled through his spine.

"It seems so. The old rascal's popped up again."

"Mad Jake Malone was a turn-of-the-century industrialist. He had a hand in every major smuggling operation in North America and many in Europe. Mad Jake earned his name for several reasons, one of them, his ruthlessness. Rumor had it he once killed a man for passing him on the road. Then again, with Jam's obsession, you already know that, don't you?" Detach had heard the stories often enough. He assumed she did also.

"Oh I've heard plenty, too. This stinks to high heaven." Mildred sat back in her chair and closed her eyes.

"The old goat pushed the envelope of technology in the name of a dollar. When it came to maximizing profits, he bent or broke every rule of science to reach his goal. Some of his crazy ideas earned him a lot of money and inadvertently advanced technology." Detach could not help but admire the old rascal.

"He met his downfall when several of his employees killed him. He'd pushed them too far. The exact circumstances of his death remain a mystery except it happened in late 1915 somewhere in the South. Jams is the man to talk to about Jake. Early on, he started acquiring bits and pieces of Mad Jake's former empire. Most of the property amounts to swamp land and miscellaneous dilapidated buildings throughout that region."

"That's what he's been doing all this time. I knew he had a thing for Mad Jake, but I never paid much attention to it. When I got back from New York, he talked with Jake's great great granddaughter and bought another piece of swamp somewhere." He never realized how extensive Jam's passion was. "I guess everyone needs a hobby."

"Yup. And he hasn't done anything with it either, at least not yet." Mildred shook her head. "Jams can be so weird sometimes."

Detach did not like the link to Mad Jake. It was hard to believe the rascal knew about the treasure and had a way to salvage it from three hundred feet down without raising suspicions, especially considering the technology of 1915. "He was probably smuggling arms to the Germans or something."

"I wouldn't put it past the old scum bag, especially after what you just told me."

"Okay, that's it for now. I have another engagement." Detach stood to leave. "Still, I have a feeling we may run across this West Winds business again before this is all said and done."

THIRTEEN

A pall of cigarette smoke lingered in a haze, highlighted by the dim light in the bar. A mix of noises, from darts hitting a target, to glasses clinking, to mumbled conversation filled the room.

"Ish' a bloody shame," Sean slurred, so drunk he could barely speak.

"Stop yer' bloody whinin' mate," Paddy said with a snarl.

They sat at their table in the bar in an ugly mood, the fishing day like the last few, lousy. The only thing that went right was the fun he and Sean had dropping those barrels of explosives on the *Lusitania* the night before, and knowing the sweet payment heading their way. Not normally the trusting type, he had made an exception by doing the work in advance. Their employer always came through. However, a touch of fear also tempered his patience, though he would not admit it to Sean. The voice on the phone scared the wits out of him.

With the wind blowing seaward from shore, nobody heard the muffled thumps, at least from what Paddy had heard through the rumor mill. He did not want to explain what they were doing, not that anyone dared speak to him in the first place. Not all of their bombs exploded, but he saw no need to reveal that to their employer. After almost a hundred years on the bottom, he figured a few explosions would finish off what remained of the boat. He had no idea why the old bitch wanted the ship blown up, but he was happy to oblige. As a bonus, it might eliminate the hazard to their nets.

"Listen, you dirt bag!" Grace screamed into the phone. "I don't

75

care how much it cramps your piddly drug operation. I want you to keep people out of that property at all costs."

A sigh of compliance came from the other end of the line. Confident she had made her point, Grace slammed the phone down in the cradle. After a more pleasant conversation with this man yesterday, she heard some unfortunate fool had wandered into the protected area. A major screw-up like this, she had to set her guard straight.

Even though her stupid daughter just sold the property, she discovered that the crazy Texan, Jams, had no plans to do anything with the land. As long as he kept that up, she would continue protecting the area as she had for the past decade. If he decided to nose around, she would have to take more drastic measures.

She went to the window and gazed out on a rich green lawn spotted with blooming magnolia, cypress, and catalpa trees. Spanish moss hung from the cypress trees that grew on the side of a stream winding through the lawn and ending in a lily-covered pond in the distance. She loved the beauty and tranquility of this old-fashioned plantation. None of this would be possible without Daddy. The serenity of the view inspired a song.

"La la la la la…." She sang a tuneless melody.

FOURTEEN

A cool sea breeze drifted across the patio and caressed Detach's face. He eased back in a lawn chair and gazed to the open ocean. After a leisurely dinner with the Mason family, everyone gathered as dusk approached. For the first half hour, no sound distracted him from his thoughts except the occasional pop of an opening beer can as Elroy, the featured dinner guest, sipped Lone Star Draft. Becky sat next to Detach, just out of reach. Jams and his wife, Sharon, shared a porch swing, arms locked. Buster and Doodles, their two Basset Hounds lay in their usual positions, asleep wherever they happened to fall. The sky darkened and Jupiter popped out in the evening sky just above the horizon, a bright jewel over the dark ocean.

"You ready to give it a go?" Jams asked, breaking the long silence.

"Please!" Elroy waved his beer bottle in the air. A bit sloshed out on the ground.

"I second that," Detach said.

Jams chuckled. "I can assume that's a yes?"

Becky stood and went to the railing. "We still have some details to work out, but we should be on the way by this weekend."

"Hey." Sharon turned to Detach. "What did you and Mildred dig up?"

"Oh, boy." He had been waiting to drop this bombshell all day. "Mad Jake Malone."

"Pffft!" Jams sat forward, releasing his grip on Sharon's hand. "You've got to be kidding."

"He had a small venture in Kinsale right after the sinking, but

77

it folded within three months."

"How'd you come up with that?" Becky said over her shoulder.

"Mildred looked for unusual activities in the area to see if anyone might've beaten us to the treasure. We also searched for any local superstitions or other problems we might run into. Right after the sinking, ghost stories popped up."

"Ghosts? Crap!"

"Ghosts?" Elroy gave Jams a puzzled frown. "What's ghosts have to do with anything?"

"Ah, an old trick." Jams winked. "Often, smugglers start ghost stories to cover their activities, usually to keep the superstitious locals at bay. Seamen are prone to superstition."

"Do you think someone got to the treasure?" Elroy took a long gulp of beer.

"I doubt it." Jams eased back and put his arm around Sharon. "At the time this all happened, around 1915, the technology would've been too primitive for that kind of operation."

"What kind of ghost stories, Detach?" Sharon said.

"Weird ones, and not the boo kind." He yawned and rubbed his eyes. "More than one person saw the *Lusitania* rise out of the water and sail away in the night. On top of that, someone saw it sink again weeks or months after it originally went down."

"No way!" Becky half turned, her arm against the rail and snickered. "How could they see even a hundred yards off shore at night? That place is in fog most of the time."

"It's just like the haunted 'Chinese' graveyard back home with nothing but Hispanic people buried there." Detach recalled a local ghost story from where he grew up in California.

"Sounds like bull to me." Elroy swished his bottle around.

"Of course, but then again, something or someone inspired the stories. Since Mad Jake had an operation there, it makes me suspicious. Yet it may not have anything to do with the *Lusitania*." Detach did not believe that, but had to put it out there.

"For me it's the exploration. I'd hate to find out that someone beat us to the treasure, but there may not be anything to find, or it may be inaccessible," Jams said.

Sharon sighed and settled back in her seat. "Wouldn't be the first time you guys have come up empty."

"Okay, guys." Becky stood straight. "That's not the only odd thing."

She had Detach's full attention, and judging from the silence, everyone else's as well.

"You remember what Barry said at the meeting about how the ship doesn't look right?"

"Bah," Jams scoffed. "He's just paranoid. Doesn't like it when all the pieces don't fit the way he imagined them."

"Maybe Dad, but I have a feeling there's more than meets the eye." Becky rapped the rail with her fist.

"As long as the treasure's there, I don't care," Detach added. "And even if it isn't…"

"What the hey?" Jams shrugged and took a pull from his beer. "Be extra careful."

Once more silence. Detach stretched back and watched more stars pop out of the night sky.

An hour later, Detach stood at the rail, facing the sea with Becky. Everyone else had left or gone to bed. Waves crashed onto the sand. Watercraft zigzagged across the harbor, their lights accompanied by indistinct shadows. An occasional meteorite fell, adding to the beauty of the night.

"You know, I *do* like you."

"Then why won't you go out with me?"

"Humph." Becky gazed out at the ocean. "We've been diving partners for a long time."

Detach had a feeling what was coming next. He had heard it before. There was always that little bit of hope she would surprise him and say something different. "Best diving partner I've ever had."

"That's right. We trust each other, and work well because we're detached. Can you just imagine how the dynamic would change if we were lovers? You'd be that macho-protect-the-helpless-lady guy, instead of the solid partner you are now."

Same old speech. No point arguing with her. He had already tried that.

"I don't want to be treated that way. I love what I do and don't need the grief. Besides, even if we did get together, the question is, would we resent the restrictions?"

"You know, we aren't getting any younger."

"Yeah, I know. I'm...just not ready yet."

"I understand." *No I don't.* He knew she was right, but hated to admit it, even to himself. They faced the ocean, standing apart, hands firmly gripped on the railing. *What can I say to that?*

Detach had almost reached his house when his cell rang. Barry Kruger's number glowed blue in the darkness. "What's this all about?"

He hit the ANSWER button. "You're up late."

"Couldn't sleep. Something about the wreck is still bugging me." Barry sounded restless.

"Jeez, Barry, it's 1 a.m., you've been burning the candle down. It must be driving you crazy."

"Would you mind coming over for a little while? Maybe you can give me a second set of eyes."

"Hmmm." The request surprised Detach, but he never hesitated to help a friend. "Be there in fifteen minutes."

He drove down the darkened streets, his mind racing with every possible problem with the wreck, but nothing made sense.

Barry stood in his driveway, wearing a bathrobe.

"I take it you made an attempt at bed, but..."

"Something like that. Come on."

Detach admired the intricate landscaping of the Kruger house, though the lush lawn was dark now, the trees and bushes dark sentinels. The aroma of flowers he did not recognize filled the air. Recent hurricanes and floods had hit this neighborhood hard, but Barry had sunk thousands into repairs and he had effectively erased any signs of damage. That could not be said for many of the neighboring houses, even after all this time.

On the way into the house, Barry said, "I'm normally a heavy sleeper, but this nagging feeling at the back of my mind keeps waking me up. The past few days, I've been having problems with the ship, the structure of it, or something. Tonight, I couldn't sleep at all."

Detach knew his friend could pick out discrepancies that anyone else would miss. He once told Barry he should have been a detective, but knew the engineer did not have the disposition or people skills for that line of work.

"Here we go." A large-scale model of the *Lusitania* perched on a table in the middle of the den. Barry walked around it in a wide, slow circle. "I made this five years ago when Jams was thinking about an expedition. Pulled it out of storage. It's an exact replica from the *Cunard Lines* blueprints. Every detail's exact and to scale, including the last modifications made on her before she sank. It's painted wartime colors to subdue her appearance, including blackened portholes and the name letters on the bow and stern that used to be white. The bridge is even repositioned to account for a shift that occurred when the ship hit a wave too hard a few years before the sinking."

"Wow! That is an awesome job, Barry. You're a genuine artist."

Barry reached into his desk. With a remote, he turned on a sixty-five inch LCD TV and powered up his computer. He pulled up the detailed painting from the Ballard expedition. "It'll be hard to place everything exactly where it should be considering the deteriorated condition of the ship. What's been drawing my attention is the exact positions of several vents, the funnel bases, and portholes that don't match up to the model. By visualizing the stresses she went through in her dying moments, I calculated the distortions that would cause these discrepancies. They still don't add up."

"Hey, there." Barry's wife, Diane, wandered into the room. "You're going to drop over with a heart attack it you don't get some sleep, Honey."

Detach acknowledged her with a nod.

"Hi, Detach."

"I actually enjoy the challenge." Barry scratched his head. "I just wish I could pin down the problem here."

"Tell me again."

81

"It's like this." He turned to face Detach. "We, or rather you, are about to dive on this mess, and you'll need the best information to make the job safer. I've been finding anomalies."

"Like your monster movies," Detach said. Barry loved to find mistakes in movies, especially his favorite genre, monster movies. He called them anomalies instead of mistakes after he heard the term on an episode of *Star Trek*. It did not take much to get him going, and Detach had witnessed his rants plenty of times. A telephone pole in a fantasy setting, a hand flashing on the screen behind a monster, or a store that did not exist until the 70's popping up in a movie set in the 50's.

"What's wrong?" Diane put a hand on his shoulder.

"More like, what's right...no...wrong, it is. Wrong." Barry picked up a pencil and pointed as he spoke. "See these portholes? Notice the pattern and the spacing?"

"Sure."

Detach squinted to see them.

"Now look at the painting. Notice they're not only spaced different, but two of them are a different size?"

"Sure. But isn't that the artist's interpretation?"

"At first I thought so, but look here." He reached over to the computer and pulled up an actual photograph of the same area. "That's one area he obviously didn't interpret." The pattern in the photograph matched the painting.

"Could it be a modification you weren't aware of?" Detach said.

"Good thought, but besides the fact that it was never registered in any maintenance or design logs, why in the world would they change the porthole pattern? That would take major hull structural changes. It doesn't make sense."

"Uh huh." Diane shrugged.

"Now look here." He pointed to the base of funnels two and three. "See the positions? They're spaced different from the painting."

"I suppose there are photographs to verify that one too."

"Sure are. The collision with the bottom compressed it, but the decking is not buckled visibly or torn, as one would expect to account for that difference in spacing. Of course, you have to consider that most of the decks are collapsed on top of the twisted hull, but I took that into account also."

"Hey, what are these holes?" She pointed at the full painting now back on the screen.

"Those are the ventilators, see?" He drew a finger across the curved ducts on the model that pointed forward along both sides of the funnel deck.

"Okay, so they fell off. Hey…"

Detach saw it too. He stayed quiet to see if she noticed the same thing he did.

"They're not in the same places as the painting." Her head swiveled back and forth between the model and the TV screen.

"Aha!" Barry brought his hands together in a single loud clap. "Exactly what I found."

Detach noticed a significant difference in the spacing between the ventilators, the edge of the deck and the funnels. He saw no way that difference could be accounted for with the twisted hull.

"That's quite odd," Diane said. "What does it all mean?"

"It means your old man has too much time on his hands." Detach wrapped an arm around Diane's shoulders. He was not sure he should be worried. With so much else going on, this mystery would have to wait for another time.

"For crying out loud, why are you losing sleep over it?" She smiled up at Detach, shook her head and met her husband's blue eyes.

"I know it's ridiculous to get upset over what's probably nothing. All right, I give up. I guess there are plenty of bigger problems to get worked up over."

"Come on, silly, before we wake up the kids."

"I need to get some shuteye too." Detach yawned. "I'm actually glad you showed me this. It's something to ponder when we get down there."

When Barry turned everything off, Detach caught a glimpse of the ship as he went to the door. The light from a full moon leaked through the window and gave the model an eerie glow.

FIFTEEN

Jeremiah Laborteaux spit from where his two front teeth used to be, lost years ago in a barroom brawl. Brown spittle plopped into the brackish swamp water next to the *No Trespassing* sign his boat skirted on the property. Millions of mosquitoes and other bugs buzzed around his head and lit on every available surface. The damp reeked of mystery and death.

"Nobody tells me where I can fish and run my business." He tolerated the outsider with a deed encroaching on his territory. In this case, that crazy old hag had hired him to keep people out of the area. He did not believe that included himself. The woman paid well and was not a Northerner, so that gave her two plusses.

Jeremiah scanned the rotting terrain. *My kingdom.* He relished his leadership position in the local drug operation. The thrill of an occasional murder added a bonus. Along with his two childhood friends, Charles and Pierre, he smuggled cocaine and other drugs through the Louisiana swamps to fools that paid for it up north.

"You, mister Gator. You behave yourself now. One day I bring you another meal. You just be patient." He saluted a green snout poking above the muck. His thoughts lingered on the countless people long since consumed and decomposing in the swamp, all to maintain control in the area over the last decade. The thought of killing another one sent a tingle from his bladder to his stomach. The price for keeping their operation quiet resulted in a never-ending supply of unfortunate victims. The bonus he got for killing people to keep them out of the old hag's property made the extra murders that much sweeter.

The swamps had a way of making evidence disappear forever.

85

They had only screwed up once when someone found a few of the bodies. Dumb luck led the police to blame a known serial killer instead. Jeremiah set up a party when he heard they caught the guy and put him on death row.

He aimed his craft for Shamblewood Mound, the highest point in the area, and right in the middle of the old bitch's property. Local legends said the mountain simply appeared one day out of the flat swamp. Nobody noticed it until around the turn of the twentieth century. Desolate despite the proximity to Morgan City, it did not surprise him that no one had ever noticed it before. Even after the last series of devastating hurricanes and floods, the area around the mound remained impenetrable except for a run-down dock on one end.

"Brrr." His teeth chattered and a chill ran up his spine when his skiff approached the rotten old sign that marked the border of her property. He had been guarding the area for years. In the past, he could have ignored her warnings to stay out, but something in that voice creeped him out. After years of listening to her threats, curiosity got the better of him and he decided enough was enough. *The old hag'll never know, anyway.* He glanced around, more out of habit than from any real threat, turned the skiff past the *No Trespassing* sign and pushed forward into a dark channel beyond.

The heat of the day gave way to murky darkness as he navigated through the dense foliage. Jeremiah suppressed a shudder of nervous anticipation. He peered at a compass mounted on a shelf next to the rudder and maintained the general direction. An occasional alligator or snake revealed itself. Millions of vicious bugs created a song of danger. The oppressive, humid atmosphere stunk of rot. Though he grew up in the swamp, this section always made him uneasy.

After progressing through a twisting maze of channels, he spied a bright area ahead. He steered the skiff into the open and a clear pool the size of a small lake. A rotting dock on the other side marked an opening beyond that led into the dense foliage. Rising out of the dense growth, the mound loomed like an evil guardian. The dock indicated previous activity. He automatically thought of an illegal operation. *So, you old hag. You's up to something?*

Judging by the condition of the dock, he guessed that whatever the activity, it had stopped long ago. Why would the old woman still want him to guard it? With that question on his mind, Jeremiah pushed the boat to the dock, stood, and wrapped a line around a half-decomposed pole. The smell of creosote came from the timbers, strong enough to be detected above the reek of the marsh. No trash on the ground indicated anglers or anyone else had been there in decades. The only safe way to get to the opening in the brush was to walk along one of the support beams. He did not trust the wood decking and eyed numerous large holes dotting the surface. The wood's treatment passed its prime long ago.

A path of rusty nail heads led him safely to solid ground and an overgrown path. He noticed that boulders not native to the area covered the ground. Jeremiah reached for the gun he usually wore at his hip and found nothing, he glanced back to spot it on the seat in the skiff. Rather than go back for it, he patted the scabbard at his side and felt his trusty machete. He pressed forward, following a vague path over boulders, sand, small rocks and between dense foliage. The path moved straight toward the mound. Thick trees covered the pathway, blocking out direct sun. He hesitated, looking back again to where his gun sat in the skiff, he grunted and took out the machete. The path continued for a hundred yards more and ended at a door. The mound was not visible because trees and brush blocked the view. He assumed it was somewhere ahead.

A rotten wood door hung on a rickety frame with a hasp and padlock that was little more than a lump of orange. He pushed at the door with his boot and it crumbled around his feet in a cascade of bugs and damp wood chips. One look at the dark opening ahead confirmed that he would need a flashlight to see what lurked inside. He went back to his skiff to retrieve it and fifteen minutes later, flashlight in one hand and his gun in the other, he returned to explore what mysteries lay beyond the darkness.

He turned on the flashlight, a six-cell halogen unit, and

stepped into the gloom. Scattered debris covered the floor. Some of it used to be furniture, but now it lay in heaps of rubble in the shape of chairs, a table, a cabinet. The walls appeared to be cement and he guessed the room's dimensions at thirty feet deep, twenty feet wide, and ten feet high. There were no other doors or obvious openings. From the ceiling hung cables and the remnants of two of the oldest light fixtures he'd ever seen. One bulb remained intact, while a jagged piece of glass with a filament dangling down hung from the other.

"Electricity this far out?" There must have been a generator nearby.

Jeremiah went back outside and searched each direction from the doorway but discovered the vegetation so densely packed, he could not get around it. The marsh water came within three feet of the door on one side, tightly packed with cypress and other bushes. That ruled out exploring with the skiff. The generator would not be so easy to find, if it still existed at all.

With a devious smile, he sat on a fallen log. Abandoned and remote, he could set up operations and have a place to store large amounts of product. As a bonus, their secret pond, the new place they brought murder victims after those other three were discovered in their old dumping ground, lay less than a mile away, just outside the old hag's property line. His employer had inadvertently provided him with their new base of operations.

SIXTEEN

Detach stood next to Becky on the bow of the *Lothar*, their hands gripping the railing to keep balance. Moderate rough seas knocked the ship about, spraying them with a fine salty mist. On board, the main team included Ruby, Barry, Elroy, and the intern divers. The rest of their support team had already arrived in Kinsale on their other ship, the *Cooper*. The ever-present aura of Murphy's Law weighed on Detach's mind, aggravated by nervous twinges in the pit of his stomach.

"You've got to keep me away from the pubs."

"Aagh!" Detach almost lost his grip on the railing. Out of the corner of his eye, he saw a figure move into view. "Give us some kind of warning."

Elroy responded with a smirk. "Beautiful sea, isn't it?"

"What do you mean, keep you away from the pubs?" Detach knew exactly why, but wanted Elroy to openly admit it.

"I may need extra help, especially if this trip turns stressful."

"Must be getting old. You used to love the excitement. You play with bombs, for crying out loud."

"Yeah, yeah. I just feel weird about this one." Elroy surveyed the flat horizon.

"You're scaring me." Becky gave Detach a raised eyebrow.

"When you found me that was my first binge in five months."

"Really?"

"Yup. Getting bored with it and it's not doing my body any good. I'm getting older and it's going to catch up with me, hard."

"You? Bored with drinking?" Becky wagged her head.

"I don't have an inclination for it anymore, except on rare

89

occasions. I'm afraid the stress of this trip and that good Irish ale may encourage me to get too wild."

"Okay, we'll keep an eye out." Becky gave Detach a meaningful stare.

"If I screw up and bite it, I couldn't do it with a better bunch of people," Elroy said with a twinkle in his eye.

"Well," Detach gave a nervous smile. "I suppose that's a compliment."

The humming of the ship's propulsion system vibrated through the floor, punctuated by the rhythmic tapping of Barry's pen on the surface of his desk. Detach marveled at the constant improvements Jams added each time the ship came to port, this luxurious office a prime example. The only differences from any other office were the metal walls, porthole, and the furniture bolted to the floor. Barry even fastened the *Lusitania* model to the table next to his desk with clamps. Breakaway sections of the model's interior were clipped in place.

"What's wrong with you?" Barry said aloud to the ship model.

Detach did not have a clue, either. The model provided a guide for the ship, but it was not supposed to be a rivet-by-rivet image of perfection.

"Hey." Ruby stuck her head in the door. "You're going to turn into a vampire if you don't come up on deck once in a while. Let's go, *now*."

"I suppose so," Barry said.

Ruby led Detach and Barry outside into the brisk air. They moved forward along one side of the bridge and around the fake generator to where Becky and Elroy stood at the tip of the bow.

"Let's go harass them, what ya' say?" Ruby said.

Her cigarette and whiskey voice elicited a snicker from Barry. Detach kept his mouth shut as they approached the others.

"Is that problem still bugging you, Barry?"

"Mmmm." He grimaced at Becky. "Don't ask."

"Think you got problems?" Ruby chortled. "You probably wouldn't want to be in that suit if the sensor malfunctions. It's still an issue."

Detach and Elroy exchanged an apprehensive look.

"Sorry. Didn't mean to upset you all. We only have to be careful and add that hazard into the emergency planning."

"We already did, Rube. That's not to say we love the situation." Detach tugged on his goatee .

"Why don't we forget that for awhile?" Ruby waved him off. "We all need a break."

"Sounds like a great idea." The entire team had been working day and night in preparation for the dive. It wore on all of them. "What do you suggest?" Detach said.

"Why, poker...five card stud, of course!"

Elroy's eyes perked.

Uh oh, another sucker. Detach snuck a glance at Elroy. There was no competing against Ruby. She was virtually unbeatable. It would be fun to see how long it took her to kick Elroy's tail.

SEVENTEEN

The homey wood-paneled conference room reminded Detach of the one back in Galveston, except here, the portholes let in light from a real ocean. Barry, Becky, Elroy, and Ruby sat around the table waiting for him to start the discussion. A day out of Kinsale, they gathered for the first full-scale meeting since leaving home. "Okay, what we got?"

"This is as good a time as any to go over what else we have now. The home team piped us more data, though it isn't anything earthshaking." Barry tapped at his computer keyboard.

"I hope this goes better than that poker game," Elroy said, a crease deepening between his brows.

Detach stifled a smirk. Elroy had lost fifty dollars the night before. He eyed Ruby and she returned his look with a smug grin. "Go on, Mr. Kruger."

"I'm glad I'm not the one going down there," he said, ruefully.

Detach exchanged glances with Becky and Elroy.

"Come on, Hon', no need to boost their confidence any more than you have to." Ruby's raspy voice dripped with sarcasm. She popped an unlit cigarette in her mouth.

"Okay, this is it." Barry sniffed and rubbed his nose as if about to sneeze. He hit a button on his keyboard and the projection monitor glowed to life, displaying the painting of the wreck from the Ballard book. In the top right of the picture an insert of a black-and-white photo of the starboard side of the ship showed with a label underneath: *1914*.

"As I said before, we have a real mess to sift through. First off, they didn't design the ship to carry heavy cargo. In fact,

93

they carried the bulk of any real cargo by hand through the passageways to stow it below." He indicated an area on the black-and-white photo with the mouse pointer. "They used the front of the ship, between the first funnel and the bow for cargo. It also housed most of the coal, which is why Ballard's theory about coal dust may have some value."

"Another theory proposed that the forward boiler exploded from the cold water hitting it," Detach said.

"Add that to the list." Barry moved the mouse again. "They primarily used the upper and lower Orlop decks, the two lowest decks on the ship that are just above the bilge. Now according to the painting, and what Ballard discovered, the ship landed on its side. It has collapsed in on itself over the years. The theoretical smaller opening would have given access to at least the upper Orlop and much closer to the target area. Since the hole isn't there, that point's moot. The large crack further back gives access to the keel, which leaves us the only practical place to enter the hull without cutting in. That's bad for several reasons. A big one is that the crack is a good distance from the bow."

"From what I see," Detach peered at the painting, "we'll need cutting tools just to get in there, even with the opening."

"Maybe, maybe not. There's a possibility the leeward side is relatively free of debris. Your trouble will start once you get over the keel. Since the hull is pretty much collapsed on itself, you'll have some tight squeezes, *if* you can get in there."

"Great," Elroy said, rubbing his forehead. "Why can't we just cut in at the target area?"

"First off," Detach began counting off on his fingers, "we're not allowed to disturb the wreck in that way. Second, with all the ordnance lying around, cutting might not be such a great idea."

"Just wait, Kiddo." Becky patted Elroy on the shoulder. "You'll have to go down there and see if the Navy left any souvenirs inside, and not just around the ship on the seabed. Most likely, those that struck the hull exploded on impact. If they did a lot of multiple runs, it's possible they could've dropped a few that didn't go off." She gave him a sweet smile.

"With all that silt in the water, I hope I'll be able to see 'em in

94

there."

"Got news for you. Though there are times the silt can be really bad, I've found the water is usually clear with a thirty meter visibility range. Just in case, I've attached the filters tuned to the type of silt that's down there. So, you should have visibility even if things muck up a bit." Ruby sucked on the unlit cigarette. "Relatively speaking."

"We'll go in as far as we can and if we run across an explosive blocking the way, you get to go down. If we *do* find one, I propose a vacuum," Detach said.

"You could set it off with the vacuum. Just as bad as cutting through the hull." Elroy tapped the side of his head.

"I guess so." Detach exhaled a long, exasperated breath.

"How much are we going to let that intern do?" Becky nodded toward the door.

"Broce?" Detach grinned at this. "He gets to do the dirty work by setting up the light towers."

"Good." Elroy snorted. "Just keep him away from anything metal until I get a look at it, okay?"

"Look, Matey, we gotta' git' our treasure, aargh," Detach said in his best pirate voice, eliciting a laugh from his team.

Soaked in sweat, Jeremiah still felt the aftereffects of the adrenaline rush as he, Charles, and Pierre fed another traitor to the gators. The man had tried to skim some drug money off the top and threatened to turn them in if they did not let him.

He turned his eyes to his two partners. They had grown up together in the swamps and avoided any significant schooling. If it were not for the TV down at the general store, owned by Charles's uncle, he and his pals would never have learned much about the outside. His world consisted of fishing, hunting, the drug business, and guarding the old lady's property. The TV and small store provided his main link to civilization save for the occasional foray into New Orleans or Morgan City.

Watching reruns of *Miami Vice* gave him the idea for this drug smuggling operation. It was easy money and a lot better than selling fish and crawdads. Gators were also a lucrative trade, especially because of the prohibitions, but a lot harder than moving drugs. Either way, he had absolute control over his environment and his two friends. Barely out of their teens, they had ventured to New Orleans and made contacts in the drug trade, then set up operations outside nearby Morgan City. Over the years, government agents had tried to pin him and his friends down, but when they got too close, he simply took them out, and the bodies disappeared in their special place.

"Aaaah." Jeremiah let out a sigh. "We had us a good day, eh?"

"Yeah." Charles and Pierre gave him matching leers.

Jeremiah thought of them as the evil twins, though they did not look anything alike. Between the three of them, they had created a unique way to kill their victims and continually refined it for the best sexual release. Neither of his friends had enough brains to fill a thimble, but that did not bother him. He liked to lead and they never objected to his orders. Once in a while, they would surprise him with a bit of inspiration to enhance their killing ritual.

"You with us?"

Charles' voice snapped Jeremiah back to the present. He surveyed their new hideout at the edge of Shamblewood Mound. They had spent the past week setting up the cave, bringing in their equipment and supplies, and preparing for a major shipment of cocaine and heroin. He tried to explore the small hill, but could not reach it. The vegetation was so thick and tangled that he could not find a way in. He made several circles around the site looking for an opening, but the navigable water veered him further and further away. Where he could get close, he faced an impenetrable wall of brambles. The barrier was too thick even to hack through with a machete. Water moccasins thrived in the surrounding marsh, which added to the hazard. For some reason, the snakes avoided the cave.

Jeremiah planned for no one but the three of them to see this place. Distributors would hand off and receive goods at a distance from their new hideout. It would be no problem to lose someone in the bayou and he had worked out several diversions to make sure. Additionally, they would never come straight in. The old lady paid him to keep people away from the area anyway.

"I hope someone else tries to turn us in." Pierre grinned through several gaps in his teeth.

Jeremiah chuckled in reply and took the bottle of moonshine from Charles.

"Can you beat this? That old lady is actually paying us to guard this place," Charles said.

"So what if we take advantage of it a little, eh?" Jeremiah raised the bottle and took a giant swig.

EIGHTEEN

The morning broke cool, the sea choppy with a strong breeze pushing against the port side of the ship. With a cup of coffee warming his hands, Detach stood at the railing and watched the dark land mass of Ireland rise up from the horizon. Before his coffee was finished, fog moved in and spoiled the magnificent view. *Time for a meeting with Barry.*

Detach entered the conference room to a blast of welcome heat. "I hope the weather isn't too bad while we're here." Detach shivered despite the warm room and stared into his empty coffee cup.

"Don't forget Murphy, our 'buddy' and longtime friend," Barry said.

"Don't talk about that around Elroy, okay?"

"He's spooked?"

"I guess anyone would be, dealing with bombs all the time. He loves his work but still gets nervous about it."

"Sounds like performing."

"The problem is, he's not allowed to suck, like you do," Detach chided.

"Screw you," Barry said.

"Playing steel guitar in that country band is like scraping fingernails on a chalkboard. Yee-haw."

"Pffft!" Barry gave Detach a raspberry. "Better than that heavy metal vomit crap you and the boss listen to."

Detach approached the model and pulled out a section just forward of the first funnel, exposing a cutaway showing several decks including the two Orlops at the bottom, just above the bilge. On the wreck, the first boiler and engine room lay exposed by the large rip in the hull. The low-height decks, small doorways, and narrow passages were probably clogged with debris if not already collapsed. They would be entering on the wrong side and going down to get to the other side of the hull buried deep in the seabed. "This looks like a friggin' maze."

"Consider it a deadly maze, full of junk, maybe a critter or two, very nasty currents, and explosives."

"Oh, encourage me." Detach made a gun gesture to his temple and pulled the trigger.

"It's too bad we couldn't have got hold of good sonar scans. In a way we're going blind because we have to depend on models, a painting, and pretty pictures. However, with our gear, we won't need all that prelim stuff anyway. It still would've been nice, though."

"We take what we can get."

Barry powered up the laptop and a moment later, the plasma screen lit up. The unedited version of the wreck painting displayed. He picked up a laser pen and pointed to the image as he approached the model.

"See here?" The laser pointed to the smaller hole originally thought to be in the port side. "That's right here." He pointed to the same spot on the model. "That *could* be a good spot to cut in if you have to, seeing as how the hole isn't really there. It's in a good spot that might be relatively clear of debris and explosives."

"I think we'll try and go in the easy way first. I don't like the idea of using welding torches with all that ordnance down there." Detach oriented himself from the starboard side of the model, the insides still exposed to the middle of the keel. He bent down, peered inside, and judged the spot where Barry's laser pointed on the screen. "Besides, the owner and guv'mint won't take too kindly to us cutting on their wreck." He peered closer. "It looks like I'll have several bulkheads to circumnavigate, a few doors, and who knows what kind of garbage piled up."

"Keep in mind it'll be severely distorted." Barry sighed. "Who knows what you'll face once you get inside."

"At least the suit should take care of the current problem."

"Oh yeah, got a new little item for you that Ruby forgot to mention."

Detach arched an eyebrow. It amazed him what the lady could come up with at the last moment.

"We were going to have you use conventional underwater welding equipment."

"Why?" Detach had already checked the welding rig out to be sure it was ready to go. "Why am I not going to need it?"

"She's been tinkering with a new toy that should make welding much easier. It is some kind of laser rig." Barry aimed his laser pointer at the wall. "It has a small working head on a handle that attaches to your belt. Not much bigger than your utility knife. It hooks up through your fusion generator in the suit. That power pack has enough balls to run this entire ship, let alone your suit."

The cold fusion pack gave him a thrill every time he thought about it. No more than a thickening on the back of the suit, that little unit packed a powerful wallop and produced enough current to power ten of their diving suits.

"That's all you'll need now. No heavy rig to haul down there. From what she says, that thing's hot enough to cut through steel like it was butter."

"That's good news," Detach said. "I can crawl around in tight spaces without a lot of crap to worry about. I have a feeling I'm going to need it in there too." He peered into the honeycomb of decks, bulkheads and doors he would have to navigate.

"If you don't mind." Barry grabbed the cutout Detach held and pointed to an area near the outer edge of the hull. "From what we gathered from historical accounts, the bullet crates should be somewhere toward the outside area of the hold on the lower Orlop where the ship's magazine is. You'll probably find copper ingots all over the place. I understand they hand carried all this stuff down there and just scattered it wherever it would lie. They didn't secure it, best we could tell from the reports. According to the manifest, there'll probably be food supplies mixed in. Most of that was supposed to be on the upper Orlop, but they did some creative bookkeeping and arranged it for the customs inspectors."

"Just peachy." Detach stared at the section, now in Barry's hand. He looked up at the plasma display and saw from the

101

painting that the cutaway section on the wreck disappeared under the twisted forward hull, still the most recognizable part of the ship. "At least that part of the ship isn't as collapsed as the rest."

Becky popped her head in the door. "Kinsale ahead. Just spotted the *Cooper* on the horizon."

Detach perched on the bow of *Lothar* with his friends at his side and looked across the waves to the gleaming white silhouette of the *Cooper*. The fog lifted, and despite the choppy water and uncomfortable breeze, he enjoyed the scene.

"There's the lighthouse, way over there." Detach pointed to the west. The dark silhouette of the structure peeked out of the lifting fog.

"Wow!" Elroy shook his head. "They were close, weren't they?"

"Might as well have been a hundred miles away, especially with the frigid water," Becky said.

"Another reason to be thankful for the diving suits." Ruby puffed on her cigarette. The smoke drifted away in the breeze.

"The water even *looks* cold." Elroy clamped both hands around his arms. "Makes me want to take a hot shower."

Detach noted his friend's sour face as he considered the water. "Probably in the forties if that, even at this time of the year."

James Broce, one of the diving interns, threw in his unsolicited opinion. "Looks extreme to me."

Detach gave the kid a sidelong glance. Though an excellent diver, Broce was a major smart ass and thought anyone over twenty-five was ready for a wheelchair. At twenty, he was on top of the world. The product of the extreme sports crowd and a reality TV-bred short attention span, the kid always had a major attitude.

"Wait until you see extreme," Detach said under his breath. He winked at Ruby and caught a glare from Becky. She must have sensed that he and the old engineer had cooked up something to put the young buck in his place. He could not hide an evil grin.

Becky shook her head in disgust.

It's time to let her in on it, but only if she remembers to ask. Detach kept his lips sealed.

Her expression changed to puzzlement. "Who's that?" Becky pointed toward the *Cooper*.

Detach followed her gesture and saw another ship creep into view around the *Cooper* as the *Lothar* approached.

"They have observers here awful early, don't they?" Ruby said in a raspy growl.

"You never know with a foreign government. I wonder what they think of this ragged looking derelict?" Detach patted the railing.

"What kind of flag is that?" Elroy poked a finger at the fantail of the strange ship.

"Let's see." Ruby raised a pair of binoculars from around her neck and sighted them at the unknown vessel. "You're not going to believe this, but that ship's Russian."

"Crap." Detach winced. "I forgot Jams invited a Russian university team to observe and assist. In fact, he asked them right after our first meeting back home. It has to do with limited technological exchange and all that PR stuff. He told me about it a few days ago."

"Great. The lousy Commies are with us." Broce spat over the side of the railing.

Ruby glared at the kid. "Christ, do you ever watch the news or read any history? They haven't been communist since you were in elementary school. Haven't you learned anything from those movies you watch in the break room?"

"Hmmph." Broce shrugged it off.

"I wonder how they're supposed to assist," Becky said.

"For all we know, Jams has already made some kind of technological deal with them." Barry checked his cell phone.

"As a matter of fact, he has, but not the cold fusion thing. We have to keep that under wraps as well as the gold." Detach gave everyone an exaggerated wink.

His gesture elicited snickers.

Detach studied the Russian ship. A line of men gathered at its railing and stared back.

NINTEEN

While everyone boarded the port side of the *Cooper*, Björn Lundgren, the first mate, waved down from the bridge. Detach waved back.

"Jams is in the conference room on video waiting your arrival," Björn called down.

"Let's see who these Russians are," Barry muttered under his breath.

Detach wondered that himself. He tugged his goatee. *Do I know any Russians?* His mind drew a blank.

The *Cooper's* conference room lay buried in the superstructure and lacked windows. Comfortable chairs, bolted to the deck, sat around a large table with workstations and video projection equipment. Jams smiling face filled the plasma display.

"Son." Jams touched a finger to his forehead in a mock salute.

While Detach looked for a seat, the door on the opposite wall opened, and two men entered. The first one wore a surly expression, dark hair, a unibrow and a scowl. Detach's jaw dropped when he recognized the other's blonde hair, blue eyes, and familiar grin. *What's that name again? Vladimir something?*

The Russian smiled at him. "Hey Detach. Long time no see." He spoke in accented but perfect English.

"Vladimir, the Commie spy?" Detach said, his voice dripping with flagrant sarcasm. His mind flashed back to Broce's ignorance a little while ago.

"Not for a long time, since the Gulf. I went back to killing people with rifles, knives, and poison."

Detach half believed him. "What happened to the KGB?"

Vladimir shot him a warning look and his eyes nudged slightly to the side where the other man stood like he had a board up his butt.

Detach caught the cue and backed off. He noticed the other man cock an ear.

"You two have a history?" Elroy said.

"Could say we used to be enemies." Detach turned to Elroy, surprised he did not remember. "Don't you recall that...uh... incident with the alcohol in that little village in Saudi?"

"Hmmm..." Elroy frowned, peered at Vladimir, and shook his head. "I don't know..."

"Remember, how you say it, the shopping block?" Vladimir said, grinning.

"Whoa." Elroy busted out laughing. "That's chopping block. Oh my God, it's you."

I can't believe Elroy forgot that little town! They stumbled from bar to bar, belting Journey ballads in a dissonant chorus. Elroy, drunker than him from a secret stash they had to dispose of before they got caught, made a "boorish pass" at a woman on the street, despite her here being decked out in a full burqa. Nothing but a wink, it was enough to be considered a major crime under Saudi law. If it was not for Vladimir intervening, Elroy might have lost his head at a Friday execution party in the village square.

"I still don't know why you did that. You could just as easily have let them arrest me."

"Uh, hum." Giving Elroy the same warning look, Vladimir said, "Later we will talk."

Without the other Russian even opening his mouth, Detach hated him. The arrogant and suspicious face, the haughty manner made his skin crawl.

"Okay gang, now that we're all gathered in one place, I want to take this opportunity to go over a few things." Jams held up a finger. "First I want to welcome our Russian friends." He nodded as if the two men were in front of him instead of thousands of miles away. "I've been dreaming of a time when we could make our own dive on the *Lusitania*. With our special equipment and technological advantage, we may finally put to rest the mystery

106

of how and why she sank. As most of you know, a single torpedo of the type the Germans used shouldn't have sunk the ship. At best, that thing would've allowed plenty of time for everyone to get off. As it turned out, there was a second explosion. We're going to try to find out what caused that secondary explosion. Dr. Robert Ballard's team at the Woods Hole Institute theorized that the second explosion was an empty coalbunker. The torpedo hit, stirred up dust in the bunker and ignited with a spark. Boom! That second explosion probably ripped a major hole in the hull. However, there are other theories and I want to know the truth, once and for all."

Detach studied the two Russians. *They hate each other.* He itched to get a minute with Vladimir alone. He did not have a clear idea why Jams invited them in the first place. He had to have something else going on with them.

"What we have here is the most advanced diving apparatus ever developed. Thanks to our head engineer, Ruby, Detach, and the research team, we've come up with a way to make the exploration safer than previously possible." Jams frowned. "Despite our technology, you're about to significantly risk your lives because of a few factors we can't control. First, there's unexploded ordnance laying around down there. That's where Elroy comes in."

Elroy nodded in response, his expression neutral.

"The other difficulty is attempting to make sense out of an extremely deteriorated scrap heap." Jams' face disappeared, replaced with the painting of the wreck. "As you can see, it's barely recognizable. The hull's twisted and collapsed to less than half its original width. The only intact section is the very front part of the bow, and I might add, not much of that.

"I apologize for not having more up-to-date images, but we had a bit of a scuffle just to be able to do this. Don't worry, we have our own methods." Jams scanned around the room, which was a bit disorienting coming through the TV screen. "Detach and his diving partner will have to enter the hull at the big tear that was clearly seen for the first time during Ballard's expedition. No cutting, no shortcuts, unless there's absolutely no other way."

107

An arrow popped onto the image, pointing to the spot. "From there, you'll have a very long path sifting through junk to find the answer. It doesn't take a brilliant mind to see that this isn't going to be an easy job, even with our equipment. There's the possibility you won't find the answer. I'll not accept that any more than you will, until you've tried everything within reason. We dove deeper and in more hostile waters, but sifting through scrap metal three hundred feet down is going to make most of our previous dives feel like routine."

Detach risked a glance out of the corner of his eye at the two Russians. They did not look convinced.

"Good luck to you all." Jams smiled and the screen went blank.

"Oh...kay, folks. We have our work cut out for us." *So much for cutting our own hole.* Detach slapped his hand on the table, his eye on the two Russians, who in turn, watched everyone else. People stood and filtered out of the room.

Detach accompanied Becky up on deck to take in the afternoon sun. It did not surprise him to bump into Vladimir, who had wandered near the railing, waiting for Detach to appear.

"Where did you get all that hair," Vladimir said with a grin, his teeth perfect. "You know, you sort of look like Lenin, but with hair and the tattoos..."

"What, no 'comrade' stuff?" Detach shot back.

"I gave that up when the wall came down, long before I ever met you two." Vladimir frowned, glancing toward his ship.

"I get the impression you're not too crazy about your partner," Becky said.

"And you are...?"

"Sorry, this is Becky Mason." Detach motioned to her.

"A pleasure." Becky shook Vladimir's offered hand. "He forgot to mention that I'm his main diving partner."

"I am impressed. If you are *his* diving partner, you must be quite good."

"She's no slouch," Detach said.

"What's with that guy you came here with," Becky arched a brow, "the guy with the attitude?"

"I hesitate to call him a partner, though that is apparently what someone thought. They eliminated my job with SVR, which used to be part of the KGB. To be truthful, I have not been enthusiastic about my work for quite some time. They buried me in bureaucracy. I received an offer to do legitimate research at our local university. My first assignment is to observe and assist your expedition. To be honest, I was...how you say it...laid off from my government job. Cost cutting forced them to release all but the most enthusiastic operatives. As far as I am concerned, it is an opportunity to start fresh. I settled into my new position and thought life would be good until I found out about my team." Vladimir spat over the side. "I think someone forced my university director to send these goons along. Not one of them knows a thing about diving."

"Are they KGB...I mean, SVR?" Detach said.

"Worse."

"Oh?" Detach stared at the Russian. "Mob."

"Mmmmm." Vladimir winced and spat again over the rail into the sea.

"Crew too?" Becky asked, indicating the ship's crew.

"They are merchant marine, and not fond of the government or the mob, as you call them. There has been a lot of tension on board between my so-called team and the ship's crew. I associate mostly with the captain."

"Sounds like a plan," Detach raised an eyebrow.

"I must warn you not to reveal any more than you must with those men."

Detach let out a conciliatory grunt.

"Does he not look like Lenin, but with hair?" Vladimir smiled at Becky then poked an elbow into Detach's ribs.

"Just don't say anything about a pirate." Detach let a note of warning settle into his otherwise casual tone.

TWENTY

Detach gave James Broce a sidelong glance. The cocky little bastard could be a thorn in everyone's side, but he saw something good in the young man. The kid chomped at the bit to get in the water, to get his ultimate thrill, his charge, his shot of adrenaline. Detach turned his head the other way to meet Ruby's gaze. She winked at him.

"You ready, Sonny?"

Ruby's voice rattled like a defective foghorn this morning. Detach pictured her chain-smoking a carton of cigarettes in one sitting. He stifled a laugh.

"Hmmph." Broce gave Ruby an annoyed glare.

The intern's attention span lasted thirty seconds on a good day, and most of the time he seemed to be only half-listening and in a hurry when talking to anyone. Sometimes, Detach wondered if he had made the right choice hiring him. He lifted the helmet onto Broce's head and attached it to the awkward and heavy suit. Out of the water, the suit maneuvered slow and clumsy. He attached the fasteners and clamped the seals, then hit the power button to run a diagnostic check. A display mounted on the chest of the suit provided the same images that projected in front of Broce's face inside the helmet. Ruby kept a limited remote control station in the briefcase at her side, and a full remote in the conference room. Seeing that everything checked out properly, Detach slapped the top of the helmet and gave thumbs up. He winked back at Ruby.

Broce gave thumbs up and a stepped off the side of the ship, plunging feet first into the water.

Vladimir leaned against the rail a few feet away and said, "The young man seems to be, how you say, feeling his oats?"

"Kid's a jerk, but a great diver," Becky piped in, joining them.

"He just needs an attitude adjustment, right?" Detach avoided looking at Ruby.

"What is going on with you two?" Becky crossed her arms, regarding the pair.

"Oh, nothing unsafe, at least not *in* the suit." Ruby then spoke into a small microphone on her headset. "Okay Sonny, how's it going?"

"Stop calling me Sonny!"

"Yeah, pretty cool, huh?" Detach noted the startled look on Vladimir's face. "It's a voice link. Once we go back to the control room, we'll also have real time video, both ways if called for."

"Both ways?"

"Sure, my commie friend." Detach gave him a jovial pat on the shoulder. "The suit has video projection in the helmet. The diver can ask for reference material and view it on site, monitor his environment and all that stuff. Even do a face-to-face talk with us up here, if need be."

"We project all that onto a special coating on the inside of the helmet visor. It fools the eye into focusing properly." Ruby spread her fingers in front of her eyes. "This way, the diver can keep the outside in focus as well. That is, unless your eyesight is real bad."

"How long have you been developing this suit?"

"About twenty years." Ruby said, casually shrugging her shoulders.

"Twenty…" The Russian glanced between Ruby and Detach. "We met—"

"Yup, before I was part of this." Detach held up a hand.

"So you can see what he is doing from the control room." Vladimir's eyes lit up.

"Sure, but we'll get to that in a minute." Detach nodded to Ruby. Out of the corner of his eye, Becky gave him *the look*.

"Sonny boy, what's the depth?" Ruby asked.

"Two hundred thirty feet, ya' old bat!"

"Two hundred thirty feet? I guess he cannot stay down long." Vladimir said.

"He isn't staying down very long, at all." Detach snickered, and avoided another glare from Becky.

Ruby gave him a frantic wave and pointed to the microphone. She switched the feed off on her headset.

"You guys are awful." Becky slapped Detach on the shoulder.

"Time to teach the youn gun' a lesson?" Detach said.

"The teacher is *in*." Ruby gestured to her control console. "Let's see what happens when I trigger the depth sensor." She checked another monitor. "He's well away from the *Lothar's* hull."

Detach eyed the controls at Ruby's fingertips. An amazing piece of technology, the suit still had the depth sensor defect that caused the suit to lose stability and shoot to the surface at high speed. To get around the problem, Ruby designed a manual override to reset or disable the device in case it went haywire. Deliberately disabling it would cause the same effect.

With a wicked grin on her face, she flipped a switch on the panel next to the speaker.

"I'm losing it!" Muffled gasping and cursing echoed all over the deck. Ruby had piped his audio into the ship's PA system.

Detach had to cover his mouth to prevent an outright laugh. *If Broce wants extreme, he'll get it!*

Wide-eyed, Vladimir asked, "What did you just do?"

"Just watch over the side, right about..." Detach pointed into the water, "there." The surface exploded as the suit shot ten feet in the air. With arms waving wildly, Broce and the suit came back down with a big splash.

Ruby flipped the switch again.

"Anyone care to explain?" Vladimir looked around at the crew members for answers.

"Technical thingies. Tell you later," Detach no longer held back deep breaths of laughter.

"I should've known when I didn't see anyone else up on deck." Broce's snarling voice echoed across the ship.

Ruby flipped on her microphone. "Hit the level control Hon', and come back in. You don't actually start work for a few hours." She switched the microphone off, and cackled.

Mumbling erupted from the speaker while Broce manipulated the level control. A loud "oomph" rang out when the suit righted itself in the water. Broce's head and shoulders bobbed in the gray sea. He cussed and said things about Detach and his origins, oblivious to the fact that everyone on board listened in. Detach laughed until tears leaked out of the corners of his eyes. He watched Broce flail the clumsy fat arms of the suit to swim toward the ship, too shaken to remember he could have used the stabilizer jets instead.

"To explain your question," Detach wiped his eyes and turned to face Vladimir, "the suit is loaded with thrusters. Working with the on-board computer, they keep the diver stabilized in more than a ten knot current."

"Amazing."

"Besides the pressure aspects, the suit is somewhat bulky because of the battery and thrust motors." Detach did not, however, explain the *battery* which was really a miniature cold fusion generator.

"What about decompression?" Vladimir eyed the depths of the water below. "He went down over two hundred feet."

"There's no decompression because the diver's isolated from the outside pressure. Plus, the breathing mixture is computer controlled and the gasses are a secret formula that work with the re-breather. So, there are no telltale bubbles." Detach could not hide a grin as he continued. "There's another reason the suit's so bulky. The flex joints are specially designed so that the suit acts like a…what would you say?" Detach looked at Ruby.

"Like the folding plates on an armadillo," Ruby said.

"I have heard of this armadillo animal. It is a delicacy, no?"

"Depends on who you ask. Anyway, computer control enhances manual movement. We made the movement as intuitive as possible. And, to tell you the truth, if it's awkward above water, down below it almost feels like diving naked. Except, you don't get wet."

"What is the theory behind that switch?"

114

"Well, Darlin', we still have an annoying problem with one of the depth sensors. Because of the design we used, we have several erratic loop problems in the control circuitry. When it works, it works great, but when it goes wrong, well..." Ruby nodded over the side toward Broce where he floated next to a platform at the waterline.

"Care to get personally involved?" Detach asked. He pointed to a boom with a hook and cable, similar to a lifeboat davit. "There's an eyelet above the shoulders on the back of the suit. You need to swing the boom over the side and lower the hook and cable with that button." Detach pointed to the button.

Vladimir lowered the hook to Broce. A crewman, standing by on the platform, hooked it to the eyelet. The Russian lifted Broce up and swung the boom around to deposit him on deck, where Detach unfastened the helmet and stepped back.

With his head fully exposed, Broce received a round of laughter and applause.

Crewmen stood everywhere, watching the spectacle. Detach gazed across the open space to the Lothar where her crew watched as well.

"Consider yourself initiated and put in your place." Ruby winked at Broce.

"Come on," Detach stated. "It's time to get to work for real."

Detach pulled Vladimir aside in the hallway before they entered the conference room. "Who are those guys you're with... really?"

Vladimir shrugged. "I do not know. But I will tell you they are after something you have, besides the guided tour."

"Hmm."

"I am guessing you have technology they would love to get their hands on. By the way, if I were you, I would check for KGB surveillance apparatus."

"You mean the cameras and unidirectional microphones aimed at us?" Detach smirked.

"You have a good eye. I only realized they were there this morning. They are a sneaky bunch."

"Just like someone we know?" Detach patted him on the shoulder.

"Guilty as you are, my friend."

"Except this time, you're here in a conventional capacity?" Detach peered into Vladimir's face. They had some encounters in the Gulf, but the Russian had never crossed the line to hostile action. He had actually helped get Elroy out of that jam in Saudi and he wondered ever since how Vladimir had ended up in that little village at the same time they were there.

Detach thought the Russians were interested in what he and Elroy were involved in, but their mission was not exactly above board and had nothing to do with the military. There must have been something else going on in that village and he and Elroy just stumbled into the area.

"It would be a good idea to go over every inch of the path that man walked with me. You never know what you might find."

"Like the microphone he placed under the conference table where you were sitting?"

"There?" Vladimir's eyes widened. "I am not surprised."

"Don't worry about it. We've always had to use a good deal of caution in our line of work."

"Where is it? I would like to shove it up that bastard's behind when I go back tonight."

"Funny you should mention 'behind' my friend."

Detach led Vladimir into the conference room. Jim "Marlboro Man" Caprisi, the current skipper of the *Cooper*, played the tapes from several hidden cameras. The one beneath the conference table revealed the other Russian's hand as he slipped the microphone under the table where Vladimir sat. "That microphone found a new home on the bottom side of one of the public toilet seats in the head. So far, it's recorded several bouts of diarrhea."

Vladimir arched his brow.

Once everyone sat, Barry Kruger punched a few keys on his terminal. The painting sprung to life on one monitor screen while another image covered the second screen. "This is a sonar image of the sea floor around the area we'll be working with today."

Detach scanned the shadowy black and white image. The hull of the wreck stood out amid miscellaneous odd lumps on the sea floor. The resolution still startled him. Though they called it sonar, the technology was different. To keep it simple and secret, Mason engineers kept the *sonar* name and let everyone assume it was just advanced.

"We can't tell for sure, but the area where we want to set the lights looks relatively clear." Barry used the pointer to draw an arc around the large break in the hull, from near the tip of the bow back to about twenty feet past the gash in the side. "The lights will be set in a fairly large spread. We want a clear approach to the goal. The other side might get a similar array depending on how well the initial setup works, except they'll be more or less in a straight line. That'll be the most difficult set to place since the ship's collapsed in that direction. As a matter of fact, you can still see the outlines of a funnel or two if you look closely at the patterns on the sea bed. However, we may not need to go that far. We're going to start with the keel side and go from there."

"What about the bombs?" Broce said.

"That's where you earn your money, Son." Barry aimed the laser at the kid's chest.

Elroy harrumphed.

"You're going down with just your headlamp. The suit will allow you to position yourself at the specific sites for each light tower. We'll guide you from topside. You'll go down to exactly ten feet above the floor. Position the suit so you're facing straight down, aim the light, and see what's there first. If the spot's clear, we'll drop a light tower. You simply scoot out of the way and guide it the rest of the way by hand. Once on the seabed, you'll anchor it in place with the special spikes. We'll do this for each one. I estimate it'll take a day and a half to complete the job."

"And if I find a bomb or something?" Broce asked.

"Then I get to earn my keep." Elroy tapped the table.

"Yes, you will." Detach caught an eager grin on his friend's face.

The occasional passing fish could not satiate the ravenous appetite of the creature. It ventured further and further away from its new home to find food. Before long, it discovered a strange plant moving through the water that trapped fish. The thing dragged

117

the fish as if the whole mass was an individual animal. Though tough, the plant fiber tore easily with a few good bites and kept the food in one place. The only danger was the larger noisy fish with the spinning teeth that the plants followed. It remembered what happened to one of its mates when he attacked the spinning teeth. The creature learned that the large fish would not bite back unless attacked first, so keeping the large animals on the far side of the plant kept it from attacking.

More fish, with spinning teeth, took up residence above his new home, larger than the ones that the strange plants followed. They did not directly threaten, but still, the creature kept a wary eye when it ventured out.

TWENTY-ONE

The ship hummed with activity. Broce continued lowering the lights while Elroy prepared his tools in case they found any ordnance. Ruby gave Vladimir a classroom course on operation of the suit. With nothing to do for the moment, Detach took advantage of the time to go into Kinsale with Becky. He wanted to take in the local sites and do a little research into Mad Jake. The heavy gray clouds had dissolved into a clear, beautiful day and he looked forward to the legwork.

Detach and Becky wandered around the small, friendly town, appreciating the old world architecture and its landscape particular to the English and Irish islands. At first, they meandered down cobbled streets, playing the tourist until they arrived at the hotel where they had rooms reserved for the team. Detach approached the desk and asked about the old warehouse West Winds used.

"Aye, I remember hearing about that." The clerk, Tony McMillan smiled behind Coke-bottle lenses framed in a halo of snowy white hair. "My father worked for them a short while, but they let him go because he was too young and they were afraid he'd get hurt. He didn't believe that, but never found out the real reason. They did the same thing with the rest of our locals."

"Your *dad* worked there?" Detach could not believe his luck.

"Aye. Should be no surprise, Fella, nearly half the town did at one time or another. Of course, there are none left to talk about it except us kids." He grinned through stained, but still-intact teeth.

"From what I've heard, it was an odd deal, wasn't it?" Detach said.

119

"Everyone in town thought that. How'd you hear about it?"

"Oh, we were just doing background on the sinking...how it affected the people...what was going on around here at the time, that sort of thing." Detach did not have to tell the man *which* sinking.

"God, that was horrible business. My ole' man told me how he went down to Cobh and saw all those coffins. They didn't do too much of the rescue from out of here back then. Kinsale was much too small to handle it. In fact, most of the dead were buried over there."

"What do you know about West Winds?" Detach sensed a side story coming and headed it off.

"A weird bunch. They came after the sinking and stayed a few months. Why they didn't settle in Cobh, I don't know. The people back then were not about to turn away an opportunity for work."

"Guess not," Becky said.

"A cute young bird." The old man grinned at her.

"Thank you." Becky smiled back.

"Anyway, they took the old Cork Produce warehouse, used to be over there." Tony moved from behind the desk and to the window of the lobby, pointing to a row of buildings down by the water. "As a matter of fact, see those three buildings over there? The ones with the red tiled roofs?"

Detach noted an odd-looking row of dilapidated, but clean buildings.

"Those three are what's left. In the thirties, they split the warehouse into separate businesses. Over the years, they've seen many different companies, all except the middle one, which has stayed empty. Now they're little more than storage rooms for odds and ends. The town has managed to keep them from becoming an eyesore, but they're still in bad shape on the inside."

"How much of the original building is left?" Becky moved toward the window to get a better look.

"Almost all of it. In fact, the middle section is original on the inside. No one seemed to care for the interior and there was a legal dispute that lasted decades."

"You're telling me that after a hundred-odd years, the middle section has remained virtually untouched?" A tingling in the pit of his stomach rode up through his chest.

"When they cut the building in sections, they erected two walls in the middle of the warehouse and reworked the roof. You can't really see it from here, but what looks like gaps in the roof are actually gutters where the walls exist on the inside. From here, they appear to be separate buildings. I'm afraid I can't tell you why they did it that way. The middle section is the largest. They moved all the leftover furniture and junk to the middle and concentrated on the two ends. Better flooring and other reasons I can't remember. My uncle was one of the contractors that did the work. When it came time to rent out the individual sections, the two ends were ready for business but the middle just collected junk. No one ever came around to renovating it, even after the property dispute was settled."

"Do you think there may be some stuff left over from West Winds?" Detach did not try to hide his curiosity.

"Why the interest in West Winds? They weren't very successful."

"Oh, we're just looking into what existed at the time the *Lusitania* sank. You know, background info," Becky said with a conspiratorial smile.

"Say," Detach leaned toward Tony, "would it be possible to go into the center building?"

"I suppose so. See that bluish rooftop over there, a few blocks down the hill?" Tony pointed out the window.

"Sure," Detach peered toward the area where a blue roof stood out against the other buildings.

"Ask Máire at that antique shop. Her husband owned the place after the legal disputes ended and she still has the keys."

Tony pronounced the woman's name "Moya," using the Gaelic pronunciation, a bit of trivia Detach picked up from a CD Becky had of Máire Brennan, sister of Enya.

"Good luck." The old man moved toward the desk at the other end of the counter to pick up the ringing phone.

They left the hotel and strode down the slope toward the

antique shop. Detach had an urge to hold her hand but she kept far enough away he could not reach it.

"This place is beautiful without crappy weather."

"I know." Detach nodded and sniffed the air. "In fact, I like everywhere I've been in Ireland and England. For the most part, the people here are absolutely wonderful."

"What're we looking for?" Becky said.

"Tell you the truth, I have no idea. It's just that old smuggler's nose, you know."

"Oh yes, I know." She rolled her eyes.

"We'll probably find nothing, but it should be an interesting afternoon."

"Crawling around junk inside an old warehouse?"

"Not much different than crawling around a junk pile three hundred feet underwater."

"Oh yeah." Becky sniffed. "Should be a little safer."

Máire was a spry little old lady who wore wire-rimmed glasses that magnified deep-green eyes set against a fringe of white hair. Based on her appearance alone, Detach, assumed she would be as ornery as a Tasmanian Devil, yet she let them have the key and did not even ask why.

"Stop back by for tea. And be careful in that horrible old building."

"I promise." Detach gave her his most sincere smile.

A distinct shift in light and temperature hit them on the way to the structure. A fog and thick clouds crept in from the south. "So much for our bright spring afternoon."

Becky shuddered. "See what I mean about the weather?"

When they passed a quaint little general store, Detach went inside and bought two LED flashlights and the requisite batteries. He unwrapped them on his way out, popping in the batteries and dropping the packaging in a trash bin.

"Glad you thought of that," Becky said, taking the proffered flashlight.

They approached the warehouse from the ground. He noticed the three sections were not separate as the illusion from up the hill made them appear. The two ends were in much better repair.

Though paint peeled on the wood, metal, and brick sides of the end units, they had an occupied look to them versus the middle section. At a personnel door next to a sealed-up loading dock, Detach spotted a rusty padlock. The key opened it, though it took effort to rotate the mechanism because of corrosion.

"Looks pretty decrepit, doesn't it?" Becky said.

"Oh, geez!" Stale, damp air from inside assaulted his face and he gagged. "Smells like it too."

Paddy held the phone to his ear as the call went through.

Without preamble, the creepy female voice asked, "Did you do what I asked you?"

"We did it, Ma'am," Paddy said, "but we're still starvin' 'ere."

"Your pay is on the way," the voice said. "What's going on there now?"

"They're 'ere right now. They been setting up the spot above the boot'. Gettin' ready for something big tomorrow, I figure."

"Are they going to find anything?"

"How…" The voice held an icy edge that made Paddy shudder, but a rising fury overtook the fear. "How should I know? I just blew the dickens out of yer' bloody boot', but I couldn't exactly go down to check."

"Do you have some left?"

"Have what?"

"The explosives!"

Paddy pulled the phone away from his ear.

"You still there?"

He put the phone back to his ear. "Still 'ere. The explosives, all gone."

"I need a little extra insurance. Here's what I need you to do…"

TWENTY TWO

The air reeked of damp and unpleasant, ill-defined smells. Detach suppressed a shudder stepping into the dark interior of the old warehouse. He inched his way inside with Becky close behind. His eyes adjusted to the dim light leaking in through a half-covered skylight and dirty windows. Piles of junk, rotted furniture, and rusted machinery lay everywhere. He flicked on his flashlight.

"Watch your step." Becky added her light to the gloom.

"You had a tetanus shot lately?" Detach said, only half-joking.

"Shut up, Mister Cheerful."

With due caution, Detach navigated across the rotted floor. The flashlights guided him over the treacherous path. He aimed for the offices he had spotted in the rear that might hold old papers or books.

He worked deeper into the building, avoiding dark holes in the rotted wood, testing each step. Detach had no idea what lay below the boards, and did not want to find out. Tiny indistinct noises erupted around them. He heard a creak here, a skittering there, a tiny squeak somewhere in the back of the room. They did not sound friendly. The hair stood on the back of his neck.

Something caught his eye. He held up his hand. "Stop."

"What'd you see?"

"Look over there." Detach pointed to a rotted pile next to a severely rusted machine. "That looks odd."

"Let's just be careful," Becky said.

With cautious steps, he crossed to the pile on the floor and kneeled down, his left foot next to a gaping hole in the floor. "If we assume this is left over from the original West Winds, they were a fishing outfit…"

"And…?" Becky put a hand on her hip.

He scanned through the rubble, and spotted a rusted piece of angle iron three feet long. Detach picked it up, tested for firmness, then probed the pile, peeling up a layer of disintegrating fabric. After turning over a few layers from the top of the pile, he recognized rubberized canvas. A taint of diesel crept through the smell of mold.

"If they were a fishing outfit, what would they need inflatable bags for?"

"Inflated with what?"

"Exactly."

"Is that a pump of some kind?" Becky pointed to a rusted machine nearby.

"I didn't know girls could recognize technical thingies."

"The pump?" Becky shot him an impatient look, gesturing toward the rusty machine.

"As you guessed, it's a pump, and not for air." Detach moved over to examine it. Belt-driven, it had a large six-foot flywheel mated by a thick shaft to the body of a large volume horizontal piston pump. He could tell from the design that it dated from the eighteen nineties. "It's a liquid pump."

"Inflatable bags, liquid pump. Maybe for diesel? I thought they still used coal back then. What's the deal?"

"Huh." Detach tossed the piece of angle iron onto the pile of canvas and threw up both his hands. "No idea, maybe nothing. This junk may be from long after West Winds left the area. Let's see what's in those rooms now."

He picked his way across the floor to the nearest of three doors in the back of the room. One of the portals was recessed and probably led out the back of the building. The other two were of more interest despite lack of markings or signs indicating what the offices represented. Opting for the left one, Detach doubted it would open without crumbling to dust. He grabbed the handle, gave a slight twist and it turned. "Hmm." With a push, the door opened with a squeal of rusty hinges. Debris from the rotted frame crumbled down in a brown, dusty rain. Despite the deterioration, the wooden slab remained intact.

The room had no window, but in the glow of his flashlight, he spotted a rotted desk. Next to the desk sat a wooden file cabinet, tilted from a bad spot on the floor. In the middle of the ceiling, he found a light fixture with an intact bulb and pull chain.

"Give it a try." Becky's whisper nearly sent him through the roof.

Already on edge, Becky's tone of voice did not help. Detach could not blame her, though. Something about the age and rot of the place reminded him of a haunted house.

He navigated with the flashlight, watching every step for rotted flooring. When he pulled on the chain, nothing happened.

"No surprise. Edison probably installed that one himself. No wait, he wasn't in Ireland, was he?"

"Ha ha." Becky waved her light around the room.

The floor looked solid except for the area by the file cabinet. Not trusting appearances, he tested each step and Becky followed close at his heels. The theme from *The Exorcist* popped into his head and he forced it out, replacing it with the theme from *The Addams Family*. Still a creepy song, but at least it could be a funny creepy song. He made it to the desk at the back of the room without falling through the floor. The smell of mold forced him to take short breaths to minimize exposure and he came close to hyperventilating. When screens formed at the edge of his vision, an indication he was about to pass out, he forced himself to relax.

"Looks like this place is freaking you out, too."

"Oh?" Detach turned to her. "Is it that obvious?"

"Only to someone who has it just as bad as you."

"Then let's make this quick."

Becky searched the desk while Detach held his flashlight aloft, giving her all possible light.

The wooden piece of office furniture had a thick layer of dust on the surface dotted with animal tracks and rat droppings. This model had a center drawer, two deep drawers on one side and three shallow ones on the other. Becky pulled open the center drawer and Detach spotted writing implements attached to each

127

other with thick cobwebs and rotted paper shreds.

"Batting zero so far," she said.

She reached for the two-drawer side and opened each one, revealing shredded paper, obviously rodent nests. "I'm not about to stick my hand in there to search through that."

"I wouldn't either, not without very thick gloves."

"I'll try the other side, I guess."

Detach peered over her shoulder into each drawer and, like the other side, saw the same shredded paper until she got to the bottom drawer. Peeking out of the mess, he spotted an old logbook or ledger. Becky wiggled the drawer fully open then picked up the book, setting it on top of the desk.

Detach reached down and tapped the cover to see if anything crawled out, but the book remained inert. "Want the honors?"

"Let's see." Becky bent over the desk, lifting the cover of the old volume exposing lines with entries on the yellowed old pages. "June 1915 is on the front page."

She reached to peel back another page, but Detach worried the whole thing would crumble on her. "Hold it. Let's take it back to the *Lothar* and see if anyone has an idea how to look at it without destroying the pages."

"I think you're right."

While Becky gingerly closed the logbook, Detach approached the file cabinet. Made of a sturdy wood, perhaps oak, it remained in good shape though the brass handles had a greenish tint. It held five drawers and none looked warped despite the sunken angle of the cabinet. He pulled the top drawer and it slid open with ease. The inside contained shredded paper, though the pieces were bigger and he could still see lettering on some of them. The musty odor mixed with the smell of rat urine. Wood slats separated the drawer into sections and the second one back looked to have intact documents. He leafed through them and they were stiff and brittle. When he spotted a letter, he had to concentrate to keep his fingers from shaking. He feared the letter would turn to dust before he could read it. With great care, he pulled it from the drawer and laid it on the top of the cabinet to look it over.

June 20, 1915
West Winds Trading Ltd.
Glasgow

Kyle,
The bags and pumps should have arrived by the time you
receive this. The diesel will arrive by ship next week. We have
little time to pull this off before someone discovers what we are
doing. I urge you to use the best discretion. We are not doing
this for profit, but for the sake of our country and all the people
who died so needlessly.

I am placing a huge amount of trust in your judgment,
despite your young age. All our years of experimenting and
research are finally going to pay off with my plan. I know you
are the right man for the job. Please bear with me if what we are
doing seems the work of a lunatic. I would give anything to see
the looks on their faces if this works.

Keep the faith, and if not, you know what will happen.

Jake

The hair on the back of Detach's neck prickled, and a shiver
of apprehension racked his body. He had a sudden and strong
premonition of something amiss in Kinsale, but had no idea what.

"Talk to me."

"I have a bad feeling about this." Detach shuddered again.

Becky had to get on her tiptoes to read the paper on top of
the file cabinet. "My God, Mad Jake was really here. This is the
proof."

"Sure is, but the proof of what?"

"What do you think?"

"No idea. It just seems awful coincidental that he pops up
here right after the sinking. But there's no way they had the
technology to dive on the *Lusitania* to salvage anything, not in
three hundred feet of water."

"That does seem pretty far-fetched. But what are the bags,
pumps, and diesel for?"

"I have no clue."

"It's getting late. We'd better get back to the ship and see how our youn gun' is doing with the lights."

"Yeah." Detach chuckled, "We still haven't heard any loud thumps from that direction. If they accidentally triggered one of the loose explosives on the seabed, there's a good chance we'd feel it here."

Detach checked the rest of the drawers but did not find anything of interest. He collected the book and letter, slipping the single piece of paper into the logbook. After shutting off the flashlights, they went outside into the darkening day and he re-locked the door. The prickly feeling returned. Something did not feel right, but he could not pin it down. Did it involve the ship, or was there some other venture Mad Jake pursued that coincided with the ship sinking? He could not shake the possibility of Mad Jake's hand in the pie.

TWENTY-THREE

Dusk fell over the hulking silhouette of the *Cooper*. Detach and Becky returned just in time to hear the crackling voice of first mate Andy Fitzgerald droning over the PA. "Detach to the bridge."

"See you in a bit." He gave the logbook and letter to Becky. "You know where to take these."

Becky squeezed his arm and headed below.

He climbed the staircase, noting the glow of the Kinsale lighthouse in the distance. Its glaring light fading to a haze as the fog moved in.

He found Andy and Marlboro Man sitting on the bridge, watching a set of four video monitors.

"Check this out," Andy said and pointed to the left-center screen.

The image was in infrared, or IR, but Detach had no trouble watching the diver slip over the side of the Russian ship, the *Novosibirsk*, and glide through the cold night water toward the *Cooper*.

"He's in regular scuba gear. He'll freeze his tail off." Marlboro Man fingered an unlit cigarette. "We watched him suiting up where he thought we couldn't see him. Unbelievable. Was wondering what he was up to."

"He's not even attempting to hide the bubble trail. I guess he thinks it's dark enough that we won't notice." Detach plopped into an empty chair between the two crewmen.

"Here we go." Marlboro Man pointed at the screen with the cigarette. "He's trying to avoid our deck lights."

Detach followed the image as the glowing shape veered away

131

from a bright area at the bottom of the screen.

Marlboro Man reached over and flipped a switch. "Going to hull cameras. Staying in IR."

The diver was clearly visible on the IR down to fuzzy, but distinguishable, details. He touched the hull and seemed to be measuring from the rudder along the keel.

"Anyone want to bet he's headed for the bulkhead nearest the conference room?" The captain held out his open palm.

"That's exactly where he's headed," Detach said.

"Over here." Andy pointed to a fifth monitor on the desk next to them.

Messages on the computer screen displayed "POSSIBLE MICROPHONE OR TRACKER," below that, "MISCELLANEOUS DEVICE," and finally "NO EXPLOSIVES DETECTED."

The diver pulled away and headed back to the *Novosibirsk*.

"Should we do anything?"

"Well…" Detach considered for a moment. "Why don't they just ask?"

"Beats me." Andy sighed again. "Such a suspicious lot."

"I wonder why they didn't try that on the *Lothar*?" Marlboro Man snickered and took a drag from the unlit cigarette.

"It looks like it's about to sink half the time," Andy said with a chuckle. "A wolf in sheep's clothing."

"Should we send someone out and do the toilet thing again?"

Detach glanced at the captain and said, "Naaah. We know it's there."

"Not even worth bothering with tonight…oh by the way, do you trust that Vladimir guy?"

"Actually, I do. I have a gut feeling he's being straight with me."

"He sure doesn't seem to like the guy that came with him to the meeting." Marlboro Man sucked on the unlit cigarette.

"I think they're Russian Mafia," Detach said. "My guess is they're after our technology."

"S'pose so."

"Only seen a couple of them on deck. According to what I've seen, there's some that don't show themselves topside. I'm guessing they're seasick and don't have their sea legs." Andy stretched in a chair by the window.

Detach gazed out at the Russian ship. "We could only hope for rough seas tomorrow, but that would affect us too, so I guess not."

"You're so mean." Andy reached up and patted Detach on the shoulder.

"Part of my overwhelming charm." Detach gave him a mock salute and left the bridge.

TWENTY-FOUR

Fog ruled the night and left visibility to a few feet. Detach stood with Becky on the dock and waited for the second launch to come in. The heavy air smelled of salt, fish, and tar. Waves lapped against the pilings under the dock. A faint hum grew louder as the other launch from the *Cooper* appeared out of the gloom, loaded with those from both ships that decided to stay in town. Skeleton crews remained on the ships for security. With a bump, the boat landed and a crewman jumped out and secured ropes to the dock.

"Welcome to Kinsale," Detach bowed and made a flourish with his hand.

"Follow us," Becky said.

He grabbed at her hand as they led the team up the slope into town, but she quickly pulled it away. The procession attracted attention from the locals. Most waved and smiled. Detach assumed they were glad for the business.

At the hotel, Detach let everyone settle into their rooms and told them to meet in the lobby in thirty minutes. He and Becky planned the evening after their trip to the old warehouse. They arranged dinner at a small restaurant and pub nearby, recommended by Tony, the hotel clerk. Kinsale had a reputation as the cuisine capital of Ireland and local restaurants offered a wide variety of tasty meals. Tonight would be a seafood platter containing Sea bass, Monk fish, Salmon and Mussels with garlic and chili butter sauce. The next night would be Ruby's choice, and then Barry's, and so forth.

An hour later, he sat at a table with Becky, Ruby, and Broce.

135

Barry held court at another table with Marlboro Man and the other three interns. The remaining tables held various members of the ships' crews. He spotted Elroy at the bar, chatting with the bartender and enjoying his meal with a pint of Guinness.

"What's with the Russians?" Ruby asked.

"Apparently they're all staying on board. I should invite Vladimir to stay here with us at least one night. You've probably guessed that he's not happy with his situation. I believe he's sincerely interested in the project and has no hidden agenda. One reason I think so is that he was so upfront about the gang that's with him."

"Including the ship's crew?" Broce said.

"He says they're not part of it, and I believe him."

"You have an awful lot of trust for a guy that used to be your enemy in the Gulf." Ruby took a drag from a long cigarette and blew the smoke away from the table.

"We were enemies by circumstance, but that man, despite being one of the bad guys, has more honor than many Americans I know."

"You trust him that much?" Broce rocked back in his chair.

"Yes I do."

"I have to agree," Becky said. "I can sense if someone's good or bad at the first meeting, right Ruby?"

Ruby took another puff of her cigarette and talked as she exhaled. "You've got that radar all right. You're right ninety-five percent of the time."

"Women's intuition?" Broce sat forward. "Okay. I can't argue with that. I've known a few women...

"Exactly. I seem to have it better than most. The man's okay, even for a 'Commie,' as you and Detach say, for entirely different reasons, I might add."

The evening wore on, filled with pleasant chatter and delicious food. Marlboro Man headed back to the launch while Detach led the rest of the procession out of the restaurant and back to the hotel. The heavy blanket of fog settled deeper into the town, with mist so dense he had to follow the line of buildings. He could not see more than a foot or two over the curb and into the street.

"Gather round." Detach made a quick announcement to his crew mates in the hotel lobby. "Six-thirty, we do breakfast on the *Cooper*, so be at the dock by five forty-five." He did not need to worry about anyone being late, even Elroy.

Climbing upstairs to the room, Detach turned right down a long hallway stretching both directions. His room was two doors down and Becky's was the next one past his. Typical of many hotels in that part of the world, the bathrooms and showers were at each end of the hallway. For someone with a weak bladder or the runs, he imagined it would be a serious inconvenience. He felt Becky next to him as he slipped the key in the hole and unlocked the door. *Should I ask her in?* The door swung open, drawing his attention to a piece of paper on the floor. He bent down to pick it up. The world exploded.

Warm pressure on his upper back made it hard to breathe with his face hard against the thin carpet. Detach squirmed and Becky's unconscious form slid to his side. His ears rang and he smelled an acrid burning stench along with an explosive smell that reminded him of chemical fertilizer. He crawled to get out from under the rest of her. Her limp body rolled over face up, eyes closed.

In a moment of panic, he reached to her neck for a pulse, but shoved the paper he still held against her skin. "Aaagh!" On the way to stuffing it in his pocket, he noticed her chest moving up and down. "God I hope you don't have any internal bleeding." His voice sounded far away, like he had water in his ears.

Through the ringing in his head, he made out moaning and strange crackling noises in the distance. A surreal atmosphere permeated the hall. Shock distorted his senses. Faint thumping on the floorboards indicated others nearby moving around. Whatever exploded must have come from down the hallway or he would not still be alive.

He tried to stand, swaying back and forth to keep his balance. Background noises gradually became louder and clearer, overriding the cacophony in his head. The last time his ears rang that hard was after a *Cannibal Corpse* concert he had attended

137

with Jams the year before. He glanced down the hall in each direction. Lights were still on, but he could only detect vague movements through the smoke-filled hallway. The piercing wail of a fire alarm penetrated the muffled noises. *How much time do I have before the place burns down?* He turned back to Becky so he could drag her out of the building. She sat up and held her ears.

"Let's get out of here!" Detach reached down, grabbed one of her hands and pulled her up. He held her shoulder as she fought for balance.

She staggered a bit, then nodded. "Let's go."

Detach led her out. Halfway down the stairs, his mind snapped back to the source of the explosion. For all he knew, they could be walking toward a gaping hole in the floor, but he pressed on, taking the chance of falling rather than burning to death.

They staggered through the lobby and into the street. Detach turned and saw half the roof missing on one end of the building. He counted two rooms exposed through the foggy gloom. Water shot into the air from several broken pipes. Relieved, he saw no signs of fire. One by one, people stumbled out of the hotel, and he took a tally of his crew. Barry appeared with one of his ears bleeding. Elroy came next, sniffing the air, probably already knowing what caused the explosion.

Two interns, Broce and John, came out and ran up to Detach. Broce yelled, "George and Randy are still in there, I thought they were behind us but there's no sign of them."

"Crap!" Detach fought an overwhelming sense of dread. "Where at?"

"Right up there," Broce pointed to the room next to the gaping hole in the roof.

"Was anyone supposed to be in those two end rooms?" Becky said.

"Hold on, there." Tony, the desk clerk, walked up behind them. "I called the fire department and the police. The last room is the lavatory and the first room should've had someone in it." Peering at Broce he added, "Your room, I believe."

"That would've been me all right, but I was talking to George and Randy in there." Broce still yelled. He held his nose and blew, trying to equalize the pressure. "George sent me down to his room to get a paperback while they argued about it. I left them there for just a second. I met John in the hall."

"We have to get the others out." Without a second thought, Detach handed the visibly shaken and groggy Becky off to Broce. "Stay with her," he said, and ran into the building and up the stairs.

Elroy followed close behind, huffing and puffing as he climbed.

Over his shoulder, Detach said, "thanks." He imagined Elroy's moderate ale buzz cleared by the shock. Not a pleasant way to sober up.

"Let's make this quick," Elroy said.

He reached the top of the stairs, meeting the thick Irish fog that filtered through the damaged end of the building. The edge of a ragged wall outlined the gray night, and spraying water glowed in the nearby streetlights. Detach approached the opening where the door to Broce's room used to be. The wall from the door jamb to the bathroom was gone, along with half the floor. He spotted a bathtub sitting on a bed in the room below. A cascade of water tumbled down from jagged shards of metal from the plumbing.

"Here," Elroy said over Detach's shoulder.

Detach followed Elroys' finger and squinted at a pile of debris with what may have been an arm sticking out. "That floor doesn't look good."

The nearest working light from the hallway was too far away to illuminate the room. A streetlight in the distance provided only a meager glow. Every shadow looked like a bottomless pit. He hesitated, waiting for his eyes to adjust. The rush of water, crackling of the building shifting, and other muffled noises saturated the air, the vague light creating a surreal dream-like quality to the scene. He stepped through the shattered portal, testing each step as he moved toward the pile of rubble, Elroy at his heels. He inched closer, his breath catching in his throat. Not just one, but two right hands with arms attached stuck out from under the rubble.

They pulled off the debris and uncovered the two stunned

and bleeding young men.

"Hold on, guys, we'll get you out of here."

Neither acknowledged him.

"Let's be careful so we don't do more damage." Elroy threw a piece of bed frame into the gaping hole in the floor.

"We have to move fast. I smell gas." Detach felt a twinge of fear in the pit of his stomach. Gas had a bad habit of finding a spark at the most inconvenient moment.

They each grabbed a man and dragged him out into the hallway. In an almost synchronized dance, they hoisted them into a fireman's carry. Out of the corner of his eye, he saw flashes at the hole in the floor.

"Move!" Elroy shouted.

Detach made a running leap after Elroy down the stairs taking them two at a time, despite the added weight of a grown man. He ran out the front door.

"It's gonna' blow!" Elroy shouted from somewhere to his right.

A burst of heat threw Detach into the air, blasting him into an altered state. Everything moved in slow motion. He held tight to the intern and it felt as if they floated on the clouds. The dream came to a crashing halt when he slammed face-first into a brick wall. For a moment, he felt nothing. Then reality jolted him back to the present. His world became a tangled pile of arms and legs, ears ringing louder than before, nothing but muffled noises in the distance. He managed to move his head enough to see a blazing inferno across the street. The heat made him squint.

Firefighters and rescue medics worked frantically while Detach watched in a disconnected daze, as if observing it all in a dream. A constable approached the crowd and a multitude of fingers pointed to him. The law officer hurried over, along with a medic who pulled the intern off him and started first aid.

Detach sat up with his back against the bricks. He felt terrible, and felt sure he looked worse. His hair dangled everywhere, the tie for his ponytail lost, and the torn, burned, and dirty clothes made him look like a homeless man. A bright red smear covered the back of his hand, evidence of his repeated attempts to staunch the trickles of blood running down his cheeks. "IRA?" he said to the constable. His voice sounded miles away.

The man gave Detach the once over and shook his head in the negative. "I don't think so. This isn't their usual way."

Despite the ringing in his hears, the constable's voice penetrated.

His crew members gathered in pockets surrounding the blazing hotel. Becky emerged from a huddled group near an ambulance with Tony, the hotel clerk, and made their way to his side.

Elroy moved around the constable and peered down at him. Becky knelt down and touched his forearm. Her hands shook. "Are you okay?"

Detach had a thought to milk his injuries, but decided not to. She would not fall for it anyway. "I'll be okay in a minute."

"Fertilizer bomb." Elroy tapped his nose. "I caught a whiff of ammonium nitrate right after the first explosion."

"That's strange." The policeman rubbed his chin. "The IRA tends to use other materials. Besides, this is not their usual territory and things have calmed down the past few years." He eyed Elroy. "How is it you know so much?"

"I do it for a living…when I'm not helping a friend." Elroy gave Detach a quick glance. "I'm with the *Lusitania* expedition."

"Yeah, everyone in town knows. Luckily, your people were the only ones checked into the hotel. How do you know what it was…the explosive?"

"Smelled it right after the initial explosion."

The policeman turned to Tony. "Do you know of anyone who was mad at you?"

Tony scoffed. "Gaylin, you know me better than that."

"I guess so. But why in the world?" Gaylin gazed at the inferno across the street.

Detach remembered the paper he found slipped under the door when they first went up to their room. Reaching in his pocket, he pulled it out and read it. "Uh, mmm…hey everyone." He held up the paper.

"Well?" Becky said.

141

Detach read the note aloud.

LEAVE NOW. DON'T PUT YOU_SELF IN UNNECESSA_Y DANGE_.

He studied the cryptic warning. Whoever wrote it used a typewriter with a bad or missing letter "R" and left it unsigned. It looked like a piece of trash picked up on the side of the road, maybe the outer layer of what was once a piece of cardboard.

"Me thinks someone doesn't want us here."

TWENTY FIVE

Detach breathed a sigh of relief when the constable finished his questions and moved on. He could not concentrate on anything but his two badly hurt crewmembers. The best the medics could tell, both interns had internal bleeding, ruptured eardrums, and concussions. He spotted the on–scene doctor and approached. "How are they? Please don't candy-coat it for me."

"They'll probably pull through. However, I need to run a battery of tests when they get to the hospital in Cobh before I can tell for sure."

The news was not ideal. Detach stared at the bits of rubble on the ground. *It's my job to keep these people safe.* His jaw tightened, his fists clenched, his knuckles turned white.

"Everyone over here, now." Detach formed a football team huddle. He figured that most of his friends probably could not hear any better than he could. "I guess we'll have to stay on board the ships tonight."

"I'm sure some other inn will be glad to take us right now," Elroy said with a touch of sarcasm in his voice.

"Especially after hearing about the note," Ruby said, cackling through a haze of cigarette smoke.

"What's your take, Detach?" Becky said.

"The Russians? The I.R.A.? I have no idea right now." *I hate being bullied or threatened. Nothing and nobody's going to mess this dive up for us.* Someone was hiding something, and he needed to find out what it was. Derailing more speculation, Detach said, "Where can we find a ship-to-shore around here? My cell phone was in the room."

Ruby, Elroy and Barry held up their cell phones.

"Don't think we'll need it," Becky said. "I'm sure Marlboro Man'll be curious to find out what happened. He couldn't have missed the explosion, even from out there."

No sooner had Becky finished speaking than the ship's captain rushed out of the gloom, a cigarette in his hand, the smoke lazily trailing off into the night.

"Before you ask, someone doesn't want us here," Detach said.

An hour later, the entire crew gathered in the *Cooper's* conference room. Detach invited Vladimir over before the meeting and told the Russian what happened.

"You look like the Devil. Are you sure you are okay?"

Despite having bruises all over his body, cuts on his face and a bit of burned hair, Detach brushed it off, a skill he had mastered in the good old days of the Gulf. Elroy had fared better. Since he came out first, the munitions expert ducked to the side just before the blast and a pillar shielded him and his intern. Outside of getting knocked down with bruised knees and ringing ears, all he needed was a shower. "We'll all live. Now what about your friends?"

"This is bad, but I am not surprised. The *Lusitania* seems to hold many secrets." He glanced toward the *Novosibirsk*. "I am sure it is not them. They have not left the ship since we arrived."

Detach entered the conference room, greeted by Jams' magnified and worried face on the plasma screen. He told the boss about the explosion. Beforehand, he and Becky agreed to leave out what they found at the warehouse until they could talk to Jams privately from the *Lothar*.

Shortly after, Marlboro Man took a ship-to-shore call from the Cobh hospital. "They'll be okay," he said, hanging up the phone. "However, they'll need a few weeks to recuperate."

The room breathed a collective sigh of relief.

"We have plenty of experienced divers on board to take up the slack, so our timetable shouldn't be off." Barry said. He had scratches on his forehead and a cut on his right ear.

"The question is," Detach tugged on his goatee, "who could it be?"

"Save the whales?" Elroy said.

"You mean, Greenpeace?" Vladimir rolled his eyes.

"Don't think so." Barry shook his head. "It's not their style, and neither is violence, at least not at first. If they were involved, they'd have been a nuisance long before it resulted in this. Besides, what are they saving? It's just a shipwreck."

"I have to agree." Detach gave up that train of thought for a moment and asked, "Where are those TV guys? They make it here yet?"

"Believe it or not, they've been on board already, dropped off their gear, and went to Cobh for a night on the town. Missed the whole thing," Marlboro Man said with a snicker. "They spent the afternoon prowling around the ship, shooting footage and asking questions."

Detach frowned. "I never saw them."

"They didn't stay long. Seemed more interested in hitting the pubs," Marlboro Man added. "Said they had to do background on the sinking."

"Wait till they get a load of what they missed," Ruby said.

"That still leaves us with a big question." Becky threw her hands in the air. "Who wants us out of here?"

"All we can do is increase security and watch our backs. Sooner or later, whoever's trying to scare us off is going to tip their hand." Detach looked at Vladimir and silently mouthed, "Are you sure about your friends?"

Vladimir nodded and shook his head, then scribbled something on a piece of paper and slid it in front of Detach.

I think they want something they cannot get themselves. They are hoping you will do the work for them, or, they are here to steal your technology.

Detach passed the note around the room. He had briefed everyone on the bug that clung to the hull, which they decided to leave alone for the time being. "Okay then, let's get some sleep. We have a long hard day ahead of us tomorrow."

After the group dispersed, Detach led Vladimir to the stern,

145

out of range of the listening device.

"What do you want out of all this?"

"What do *I* want?" Vladimir looked off in the distance for a moment then turned to Detach. "Many things. I want the chance to use technology *not* stolen from someone. I want to explore that ship. And for once in my life, *I* want to collaborate with someone who is not full of ulterior motives."

"Okay." Detach kept his face neutral. He debated how much to reveal to the Russian. He wanted to trust him more, but still had to be careful. "See you in the morning." Detach turned and headed for the launch to ferry him to the *Lothar*.

Amused by their accomplishment, Paddy left the pub with pints for him and Sean. He did not want either one of them to slip up and let someone overhear their guilty bragging. He could hardly suppress laughter as he talked to Sean about the explosion. Paddy had enough common sense to know they needed privacy to revel in their dirty deed. They meant to kill maybe one or two people, but not the whole town. He was disappointed to hear that everyone survived until he saw the damage to the inn. The building was almost leveled. He felt redeemed.

Paddy had lied when he told the old lady they did not have any more explosives. Since hearing about the Oklahoma City bombing back in the 90's in school, he had nurtured a fascination with fertilizer bombs. In a shed behind his house, he experimented around, usually setting off those small blasts out in the ocean by floating them on little rafts or inner tubes. The one he used on the inn was the most powerful he had made so far.

Since the old lady had not paid them yet, he had no more money to go to that old man with the IRA connections. He could charge the old lady for the bribes and whatever he wanted to say it cost to buy some explosives. She would never know the difference.

"Boom!" He grinned at Sean.

Sean broke out into hysterical laughter.

Paddy slapped his friend on the shoulder.

TWENTY SIX

The three ships rocked gently on mild swells. The morning broke foggy and cold despite the predicted warm temperatures for the day. He could not see the shore or the Old Head lighthouse, but he heard the eerie foghorn wailing like a banshee. Detach woke up sore, took a couple of aspirin and a second hot shower and felt much better. Despite his best efforts, he still ached in every joint from the two blasts last night. After an early breakfast, he walked along the *Lothar's* deck, surprised to see the TV crew's launch sputter toward the *Cooper*. On the bridge, he grabbed a pair of binoculars and studied the team. Their expressions made it obvious that they were not happy campers.

"Things are getting exciting now, and they missed the first big event," Marlboro Man said in his usual drawl.

The *Cooper's* captain arrived early to discuss strategy, once Detach got his stuff together. He did not feel guilty for taking his time getting up there. "I have a funny feeling that we've not seen the last of our troubles."

"Some things never change, do they?"

Detach shook his head. "Never."

They went over details of the dive. Detach pointed out that the Russians ignored the *Lothar*. "I figure their arrogance or incompetence has a lot to do with it.

"So, are both the suits on my ship?" Marlboro Man asked.

"Right now they are. We'll bring them over here after work, if we have any luck today. We'll look for the evidence of why she sank, and if we happen to run across something early, we'll spot its location and pick it up later. I have a feeling we'll have to dig though."

"Hopefully, the gold is still there…if it ever was."

"Oh, it's there all right. No one else has the technological means to get to it."

"We'll see."

A note of uncertainty tinged Marlboro Man's voice and Detach could not blame him.

After breakfast, work began in earnest. By the time Detach climbed aboard the *Cooper*, Broce was already hard at work laying the rest of the U-shaped pattern of lights on the seabed. At the pace he worked, they would be ready to dive after lunch.

Vladimir arrived, accompanied by a different team member. Detach noted the sour expressions evident on both of their faces. The Russian's companion had an unpronounceable name and Detach dubbed him "Ivan." He deliberately chose Ivan to piss the man off. When the expression on *Ivan's* face turned harder, Detach hid a smile. Ivan acted as if he could not speak English, forcing Vladimir to translate everything for him.

Fifteen minutes later, Vladimir approached alone and pulled Detach to the side, out of earshot of Ivan and the listening device on the hull.

"What's with the sour face?" Detach said.

"Grrr." Vladimir spoke between clenched teeth. "I do not like him."

"He doesn't speak English?"

"So he has led me to believe." Vladimir looked disgusted. "I already know he speaks perfect English, though I have not told him I am aware. That ruse is a way to stay close to me to see what is going on. They cannot be SVR. They are not very good at being discreet."

"The main consensus among the crew is that they're Russian Mafia."

"As I told you before, I think so also. If not, they are the most ill-prepared and ill-organized group of operatives I have ever seen, even considering the downsizing of our government." He smiled and added, "They are all sick and when not throwing up, they spend their time arguing or trying to monitor what you are doing over here."

"To let you in on a little secret," Detach said, winking, "we have nothing to hide from them here." He moved his eyes to the *Lothar*.

Vladimir nodded and grinned.

Detach returned to the action, taking a spot next to Ruby. She ignored his arrival, eyes fixed instead on Broce's image on her laptop. A camera on the front of the suit transmitted his work on the seabed, the same direct feed the videographers watched and filmed in the conference room. Broce's grunts and occasional curses fed through the speakers to the ship-wide audio system. The videographers would have their work cut out for them, bleeping out the unacceptable language.

When the TV crew approached him a few minutes later, Detach briefly considered lacing his explanation of the inner workings of the ship with some colorful language of his own. He resisted the urge and stuck to the basics he had scripted out ahead of time. Behind the cameraman and boom operator, Vladimir translated to Ivan. He spotted Elroy out of the corner of his eye, perched on a side rail off-camera as he waited for word of explosives. So far, there were no surprises.

Wrapping up his segment, Detach turned his attention from the videographers to the laptop where Broce worked to lay another light on the keel side of the ship. This particular light assembly would be closest to the large tear amidships. He watched the seabed approach through an eerie underwater glow. The legs of the light tower bobbed back and forth in the video while Broce guided it down. The view swung up level. A greenish-white and gray object grew large and slammed into Broce, who let off a garbled "oof!"

"Crap and a Crayola!" Broce gasped from the loudspeakers. "Something just hit me!"

Detach crouched head to head with Ruby eyes riveted to the monitor. The object hurtled toward Broce again. His utility lamp illuminated a large shark or whale snout. A glint of razor sharp teeth flashed on the screen, enough of a glimpse to know their man was in trouble.

"Holy mother!" Ruby hit the intercom button and yelled,

"Hold on, you're coming up." She slapped the sensor defeat switch.

The monitor blurred as the suit went crazy, shooting Broce to the surface in a violent rush. This time it was no prank. The stabilizing jets performed the same trick as the day before, but he figured this time Broce would not object.

"Best I can figure, it's some kind of shark, but unlike one I've ever seen before."

Becky's voice over his shoulder startled him and he turned. "A shark that large, here?"

"I guess it's not unheard of."

Detach tapped Ruby on the shoulder. "Can you roll back the tape?"

"Sure, as soon as we get Junior out of the water," Ruby nodded over the side of the ship.

Detach watched a boiling white spot where Broce would surface.

Within seconds, the suit shot out of the water through a geyser of foam and spray. Broce panted and cursed over the P.A. Detach wanted to laugh, but when he thought of the creature, he checked his humor. Besides, they might have lost a light fixture when the crane operator dropped it to help Broce. A crewman snapped the hook onto the suit and the crane operator lifted him out of the water. He half expected to see a gaping mouth jump up and try to swallow the intern, suit and all.

The creature did not materialize. By the time Broce swung over the railing onto the deck, Detach ordered everyone to the conference room to look at the tapes.

The room filled with bodies. Within moments, not a single seat remained empty and latecomers had to crowd in, standing around the edges of the room. Ruby typed furiously on the laptop and pulled up a digitized recording. "I'll start it just before the attack and use stop motion to get a better view of that thing."

"My God, what is it?" One of the camera operators said.

"Looks like a nightmare." Becky gaped at the screen.

"Christ, that thing's not only ugly, but big and hungry looking," someone else said.

"Geez," another videographer piped up, "I bet that's why the fishing sucks around here."

"It sort of looks like a shark, but it's all distorted and sort of scaly." Detach shivered.

"Looks like some kind of dinosaur." Barry played his laser around the image.

"Hey Marlboro Man, did we have sonar going?" Detach looked to the captain, standing near the door.

"Absolutely. My man is playing it back now, and he'll pipe it to the monitor if Ruby would be so kind..."

Ruby grunted and tapped at the computer keyboard.

"Okay everyone, here it is." A disembodied voice from the bridge came through a speaker.

The monitor changed from the underwater camera image to a greenish sonar screen. Detach recognized the distorted hull of the *Lusitania* on the seabed. Tiny random specks, representing the few fish left in the area, flitted about. The semicircle of light towers stood out against the flat bottom and the larger shape of Broce's suit moved as he descended.

"That's sonar?" A videographer asked.

"Yeah." Marlboro Man gave a cagy smile. "It's kinda' special."

"I've seen plenty of sonar before and it looked nothing like that. This looks more like a negative photo than a blip screen. Shouldn't there be a pinging sound?"

"Fool." The man next to him slapped him on the shoulder. "You have to be under the water to hear it, Dummy."

The captain gave a slight shrug and remained silent.

"Let's discuss the creature." Detach did not want to reveal another one of their technological breakthroughs. He noticed Ivan's eyes light up with interest, and the Russian did a lousy job of pretending he did not know exactly what was going on.

"Notice the large tear in the hull?" The sonar operator directed their attention back to the screen, a pointer appearing on the display. "Watch what happens when Broce is just about to the bottom, right about here..."

At that point, a large shape shot over the hull straight for Broce. The two collided once and then the thing came around for

151

another pass before Broce shot to the surface. The larger shape disappeared into the deck side of the ship, somewhere near the third funnel. At that angle, Detach could not see the exact entry point. "That's just great. Some monster fish has taken up residence in the hull."

"First the inn, and now this?" Elroy said.

"At least you guys get a front row seat this time." Becky waved a hand to the videographers, eliciting a few winces between them.

"This thing just gets better and better. I guess it's back to the drawing board." Detach had a feeling they were not through with major hurdles. "Break time."

When he reached the deck, Detach observed the videographers in a flurry of activity, talking on cell phones, typing on laptops, and narrating into recorders. They had finally witnessed something they could report first hand.

The creature's stomach growled. Hunger forced it to search farther and farther away to find enough food. For some reason, there were more of those large fish with the spinning teeth in the thin water above. However, they did not move like the smaller ones that dragged the plants.

It sensed movement in the water from something larger than the fish that lived nearby.

Curious, the creature left the cave to investigate. When it detected the source of the movement and approached, it saw a white fish with odd fins, one eye, and no teeth. White, just like the thing its mate bit into. White was bad. Annoyed, it had bumped the white fish a couple of times to scare it away. After a second pass, the odd white fish swam up to the thin water.

The creature swam back to the cave, hoping that white fish would stay away.

TWENTY SEVEN

Paddy staggered down the street, still drunk from the binge the night before. Smoke and the smell of fertilizer still hung in the air.

"No bloody decent women in this town." Sean whined his usual complaint.

They take one look at you, no wonder. Paddy knew better than to say that aloud.

They entered the Boar and Whistle and sat down at their table, signaling the barman for a couple pints of stout. At the bar, a radio played instead of canned music.

A tinny American voice over the radio caught their attention. *"Just over an hour ago, the Mason expedition on the Lusitania made a startling discovery. A large shark-like creature attacked one of their divers. So far they have not been able to identify it. It's this reporters' guess that they may have discovered a new species. Officials acknowledged that its' presence could explain the extremely poor fishing over the last few months..."*

"Hey, man!" Sean grabbed Paddy by the forearm, sloshing a bit of the dark beer onto the table. "How do we catch a big shark?"

"Hmmph." Paddy's eyes widened. They had caught small ones in their nets, but a big one? The only way they might have a chance was either dumb luck or some kind of lure. "Yer' use bloody chum, Mate."

"Chum?" Sean's eyes lit up. "Yeah, that's it." He frowned into his glass. "What we gonna use to grab it? Think our nets'll do?"

"I don't know." Paddy shook his head. "Maybe. What's the thickest gauge net you have?" He was sure he did not have one

153

on his own boat. His ragged nets would, at best, slow a big fish down. Maybe the reporter was exaggerating.

"How about you start digging up some chum and I'll see if I have a net strong enough."

Paddy eyed the spilled beer on the table, considered licking it off the table, but thought better of it. "Just meet me at me' boat in fifteen minutes."

He had never dealt with a large shark or whale, despite fishing his entire life. Something at the back of his mind told him he should let it go, but an urge for vengeance, mixed with a significant alcohol buzz pushed any misgivings away. "No beast will kill my livelihood and get away with it."

The old lady had been slow on payments. He did not think her weird and inconsistent jobs would supply them with a living forever. The only thing he and Sean knew how to do was fish. If that beast ate all of their catch, they would lose their boats and the only thing they had ever known how to do.

With fishing so bad lately, it would be next to impossible to find much of anything he could use as chum. The processing plant was his best bet. He staggered over there and found what he needed half-spoiled in a barrel near the back door. An hour later, he steered his boat toward the open ocean with the reek of stale chum creeping up to the wheelhouse, despite the breeze. He glanced back at Sean who busied himself fastening his thickest net to the spar, fumbling a bit from the day's intoxication.

Paddy aimed the boat toward the three vessels anchored over the *Lusitania*. He glanced at the net hanging from the spar on the back of his boat and a rush of doubt gave him pause. *How big is that beast? For real?* A glance at the water revealed nothing.

With the engine at idle, Sean dangled the spar and net over the water.

"Drink time." Paddy grabbed a Guinness out of a cooler next to the wheel and handed one to Sean. He chugged his down in one gulp. The fading buzz returned to his head. "Let's throw that crap over and see what happens."

"As yer' say, Mate." Sean slid the huge barrel to the stern gunwale.

154

Paddy joined him and said, "Okay, now!" They poured the contents over the side. The water received the chum with a sickening "glop."

The radio crackled. "Hold on." Sean rushed into the pilot house. He returned a moment later with two more ales. "We have to hurry. There's a 'buncha boots' coming to look for the beast. They may try to protect it."

Paddy glanced at the dark water. "We can't have that. Bloody environmental idiots."

"Aye." Sean gestured toward the widening slick of fish guts and blood. "'Ere it is."

A huge shape travelled under the surface, looking more like a mini-submarine than a living creature. Paddy leaned over the stern rail to get a better view of the large animal as it approached the chum. "Holy Mother of God!"

Their net was inadequate for the task. The beast appeared as large as their boat. He backed away from the rail, chugged the ale still in his hand, and threw the bottle over the side while the creature circled the boat.

"Iss' checking us out," Sean said with a slur.

Nerves numbed by the ale, Paddy ignored the warning alarm going off in the back of his head and checked to make sure the weights were fastened around the perimeter of the net.

"If we can get the beast to the middle of the chum slick, we just drop the net over it and let it tangle itself. Then, drag it to shore and cut its heart out!"

Sean burped in reply.

The ale buzz gave Paddy more bravery than he knew was good for him, but he continued to ignore the warning bells. His friend seemed oblivious to the danger as well.

Sean stumbled past him and swung the spar over the slick, dragging the net further out. It jammed. He pushed harder.

"Watch it. Get back." Paddy's friend was too close to the back rail.

"Huh?" Sean glanced up and slipped in a puddle of blood at the edge of the deck.

Before Paddy could react, Sean toppled over the side and hit

155

the red water with a loud splash.

The water erupted in a geyser. A huge scaly creature rose out of the water. Sean was in its mouth, feet first up to his solar plexus, his eyes bulged out. In that split second, it squeezed down and Sean let out a scream as they both disappeared under the surface.

"Sean!" Paddy made a feeble attempt to reach for Sean but lost his balance after slipping in the same spot of blood as his friend. He grabbed for a rope above his head and got his hand tangled in the edge of the net. Twisting around made it worse and he slipped off the deck with his hand caught above his head. His body slid down the boom and over the water. In full panic mode, he twisted and thrashed about, his wrist straining with his full weight. With his free hand, he reached up to untangle his wrist, realizing it would be better to lift his feet away from the water and wrap his legs around the spar. The movement released his tangled wrist and he found himself hanging head down over the water.

"Oh, bloody God! The water erupted underneath him. Everything went black. He felt sharp pain in his midsection. Then nothing.

TWENTY-EIGHT

"This sucks!" Detach clenched his jaw and studied each face at the table. "How do we get out of this mess?"

"Apparently it's a nuisance to the local fishing industry," Barry said.

"It looks meaner than a Beluga Pike." Vladimir glanced at Ivan and then to Detach.

"A Beluga is that fish the best caviar comes from, isn't it?" Barry played with the cravat hanging from his neck.

"The best." The Russian gave him a thumb's up.

Though he knew Murphy's Law always loomed over any operation, this time everything seemed to pile up on them. The thought of the wounded interns sent a pang of regret, which turned into a surge of acid up Detach's throat. Now, the possibility of some new animal harassing them on top of the thread of explosives down there grated on his already frayed nerves. He threw up his hands. "We have to do something."

"And I thought disarming sixty year old depth charges was going to be difficult." Elroy rubbed his temples.

Becky slammed her hand on the table. A few people jumped, a few finally woke up all the way. Ivan spilled his coffee in his lap. Detach suppressed a chuckle. The reaction took his mind off his troubles for a split second. Before he could respond, Becky did.

"All right, all right. I think Detach is right. We have to do something, but let's not kill it."

Becky's degree in marine sciences from the University of Maine gave her not only academic experience in the field, but a

157

soft spot for ocean wildlife. Detach, however, had little time for lectures on monster conservation. "If we don't get rid of it, how do we *live* with it?"

"It may have been my imagination, but I'd swear it was only harassing me." Broce formed his hands into a steeple and twiddled his thumbs. "I saw an awful lot of teeth, yet it never took a bite."

"That's odd," Barry said. "I thought sharks would bite at anything, no matter what."

"Not necessarily true. They like to make passes before they go in for the kill. But let's go back a bit." Becky waved a hand at the wall toward the wreck. "Who says it's a shark? Maybe it looks vaguely like one, but have you ever seen one with scales the size of half dollars?"

"Sharks don't have scales, right? Okay…" Detach spoke up after nobody could come up with a suggestion. "Say it isn't a shark. It is a *thing fish*, okay? Like that Frank Zappa song. So, it has teeth and like most things with teeth, it bites and therefore it at least eats other fish, if the local commerce is any indication."

"I think we need some chum." Ruby's raspy voice reverberating off the walls.

"Chum? Someone's buddy? What is that?" Vladimir glanced between Ruby and Detach.

"What made you think of that?" Becky arched a brow at Ruby.

"Haven't any of you seen *Jaws*? And that old *Beast* movie that was on some horror channel a while back. Don't you all know anything?"

"Will someone explain this chum to me?" Vladimir said.

"Fish guts, blood, dead leftovers." Detach held his nose. "Since most sharks are attracted to the smell and taste of blood and wounded fish, one trying to attract sharks dumps a load of that stuff in the water and waits. If there's a shark anywhere nearby, it won't take them long to find the bait."

"Ah yes! Primanka. I am sorry I did not know your name for it. I have used it myself."

"Just like bleeding in the water can get you in trouble," Elroy said.

"Exactly." Becky frowned and gazed at the screen. "But this area isn't known to be shark infested, at least with anything that large."

"Hah!" Barry nodded to the intern. "Tell that to Broce."

"As far as we can tell, there's only one. If my guess is right, I doubt we'll find a whole school of them," Becky said. "And like I said before, I don't think it's a shark."

"Ah… so you need to find a load of this chum, try to lure the creature away from the wreck, and then what?" Vladimir spread his hands apart.

"I suppose capture it. Then we'll drag it far away and let it go." Detach hoped that was all.

"Great." Elroy sniffed and poked his thumb at the wall. "Give the problem to someone else."

"Attempting to capture the beast didn't work out too well for the crew of the *Orca*." Ruby obviously could not resist dropping another *Jaws* reference.

"We can't just kill it. It may be one of a kind for all we know," Becky said.

Detach could see this argument leading into uncharted waters. "We'll have to do something pretty soon so we can get back to work. In the meantime, let's have lunch and come back in an hour with some ideas, okay?"

An hour later, Detach and Becky emerged on deck with Vladimir, discussing Beluga caviar and its imitators. "Hey, check it out." Detach happened to look out on the water and spotted a dilapidated fishing trawler dumping something over the sides.

Vladimir and Becky followed his pointing finger out over the water.

The trawler sat on the opposite side of the wreck and well away from the Russian ship. It looked like they were dumping chum over the side. The mast on the back suspended a large net above the water. "Apparently, those guys are going to try to capture the beast. Our problem may be solved."

"How did they find out so quick?" Becky asked.

Detach nodded toward shore. "Those video guys are cooperating with the locals. They must've put the word out."

Elroy joined them. "I heard them talking about it on the radio station in Kinsale."

"They're not going to get it with that flimsy net, are they?" Becky gripped Detach by the forearm.

Detach had his doubts. "I don't think so."

"Do they have any idea how large that thing is?"

Vladimir tapped Becky on the shoulder. "I think they are about to find out." The Russian pointed to a boiling white streak of water heading toward the small trawler.

Detach spotted the streak. It reminded him of the torpedo that sunk the great liner three hundred feet below. A man at the back of the trawler fell in. The water boiled. The creature pounced. The other man tried to grab him and got tangled in the net.

"Oh my God!" Becky grabbed his arm in a death grip.

The creature returned and grabbed the second man off the spar. Blood spread across the water. It churned as scavengers swarmed for a quick meal.

The entire incident took less than a minute.

"Holy crap!" A wave of nausea hit Detach. He gazed in horror at the churning blood spreading out from the trawler. The boat drifted aimlessly with shredded pieces of net dangling above the water. He forced his eyes from the gory scene.

"And you're worried about a few old depth charges?" Elroy slapped Detach on the shoulder. His dark brown face was a few shades lighter.

"Jesus Christ!" Detach could think of nothing else to say.

Becky eased her grip. "Should we do anything?"

"Not much point in that, now," Barry said.

"I'll say." Detach turned to face the newly arrived Barry. His already light skin looked pale as a china doll. "I guess we'd better call the local equivalent of the Coast Guard."

"I'm pretty sure Marlboro Man already has," Ruby said, glancing up at the bridge as she joined them.

Detach spotted the captain through the window with a microphone in his hand. A siren blared far away in Kinsale harbor.

"Just great." Broce groaned. "Next, we'll find a nuclear

warhead down there at the rate this trip's going."

"That's odd."

"Huh?" Detach looked at Vladimir.

"There," the Russian pointed toward the *Novosibirsk*.

The sound of a motor echoed across the water as a launch veered off from the side of the large ship. "It is the entire compliment of my team, and they do not look happy." Vladimir gestured from Detach to the bridge. "May I use your radio?"

Elroy slapped Detach on the shoulder and gave him an annoyed glare. "We're still not going to kill it, right?"

"Oh, boy." Detach nodded. His attention wandered back to the empty fishing boat.

TWENTY-NINE

Detach forced a light mood to keep from getting sick, considering what he had just witnessed. He and Elroy had seen some bad stuff in the Gulf, and he assumed the same for Vladimir. Barry, Becky and Ruby held calm expressions and only Broce looked like he was going to pass out. The kid wanted extreme, and he got it today.

"Okay, people." Detach tugged on his goatee. "We may have to delay things a day or so while we engineer a way to capture it or chase it away. Obviously chum's a bad idea."

"Oh, really?" Barry rolled his eyes. "It is when you use a net designed for minnows."

"Well, who we gonna' call now?" Ruby said.

"*Ghostbusters*?" Elroy quipped as he hummed the *Ghostbusters* theme song.

"Shut up, smartass. How about Zork and Dork?"

"A who?" Elroy stopped humming and stared at Barry.

"It's a name we gave these two geekazoids we take on for technical advice." Becky smiled and winked at Detach. "These two have to be seen to be believed. They have tape on the bridge of their glasses, wear pocket protectors, are uncoordinated, and both have a loud, snorting laugh. They're just like the geeks from high school, except they took that image into their thirties."

"Picture this," Detach took over, "two guys that'll argue for hours about the pros and cons of four or five-lug automobile wheels."

"Or why monkey's sneeze," Barry added.

"That bad?" Elroy gave them a wry grin.

"No kidding. They look sickly most of the time, no hair on either one. I've heard they both have mild cases of Progeria, but don't know if that's possible. Reminds me of my grandpa when he was being treated for lung cancer." Detach gave Ruby a furtive glance.

"Seriously, they do look awful but rumor has it they're both very healthy. Despite their appearances, they're quite friendly, smart, and possibly just the two we need to figure this out." Becky added.

"Their weird way of thinking, you know, outside the box, has come in to help us on more than one occasion. Their whole frame of reference is different. They see things we never will."

"Should I ring them up?" Ruby put her hand to her ear in a universal phone gesture.

"We'd better wait and see what the locals come up with. Remember, it's their territory." Detach said. "We have one saving grace. Somehow, George George has, at least up to this point, kept the owner and government off our case. We haven't heard a word from them. I guess that's all being handled behind the scenes. Then again, with this happening..."

"That's what I'm afraid of." A lack of confidence was plain in Becky's voice.

"I guess I'm on my own."

Detach turned to the sound of Vladimir's voice as the Russian walked back from the bridge. "What's up?"

"My team has deserted me. The good captain said they put their heads together after they finished throwing up. He heard stuff like 'not worth it', and 'get me off this water.'"

"What's going on?" Detach frowned and gazed at the *Novosibirsk* gently rocking in the water.

"My second in command, Ivan, as you call him, pulled a gun on the captain and commandeered the launch. The whole gang piled on board, luggage and everything. Left me a note."

"What did it say?" Detach asked.

"Nothing nice." Vladimir smiled. "I can imagine they will never be able to go back to Russia."

"What are you thinking?" Becky said.

164

"I have no idea what they were after except it was probably going to make them loads of money. As I said before, I suspect it is the technology you possess. The SVR would not give up so easily. 'Ivan' and his gang will not be able to go back to face their boss empty-handed. It is my opinion that they decided to take their chances on the run rather than deal with that beast in the water." Vladimir pointed to the fishing boat.

"Good, you're on your own now." Detach felt luck on their side for a change.

"How is it they haven't dragged you into their scheme?" Elroy gave the Russian an appraising up and down glance.

"I do not blame you for being suspicious, my friend." The Russian spread his hands wide. "I think they put all their pressure on my boss at the university and left me alone to take the fall if they failed. Besides, they know I am ex SVR and must have looked up my profile. They would know I do not take threats or intimidation. However, my boss apparently does."

"What are you going to do?"

"I am going to continue as if they were never here. To be on the safe side, I will delay telling my new boss at the university what happened." Vladimir smiled. "As a researcher, I am still interested in completing this. I do not care how your new suit works, only that it does and I have a chance to use it. I am sure that with the state of our economy back home, no one could afford to make one even if you gave us the plans."

"Sure." Ruby snorted and said, "Fat chance of that ever happening, but we don't mind you participating."

"Thank you." Vladimir did a little bow from where he sat. "It is not just the suit. I am interested in shipwrecks, especially historical ones like this. In Russia we do not have many to choose from, but as for the rest of the world..."

The videographer's boss, Marvin Jacobs, approached. Behind him, another camera operator and two assistants followed like shadows.

"Thought you'd like to know the Irish are sending specialists from Dublin and elsewhere. From what I've been able to sniff out, the verdict is about fifty-fifty for killing it."

165

"Aaagh!" Becky slammed her hand on the rail. "Figures."

"One more thing." Marvin looked puzzled. "It seems that boat over there…" He pointed to the empty trawler. It drifted closer, a bloodstain becoming visible just above the waterline. "Jesus."

"Should've seen it," Elroy spoke up. "Would've fed the fish with your lunch."

"My God! We could never have used the film, even if we managed to tape it."

"What about that boat?" Detach prodded.

"The two locals on board were the town troublemakers. Hated by everyone and suspected of murder a few times. Never pinned anything on them, according to the constable."

Detach shook his head and looked out past the bloody boat. The Kinsale lighthouse peeked through the fog like a gray shadow. He noticed dark shapes popping up in the distance. "It looks like the cavalry's arriving."

"When are you going to give us a peek at that other boat?" Marvin said. "You know, for background?"

"Uh, sure. I need a break from this after what we just saw." Detach gave Ruby a wary look. She rolled her eyes at him.

"We call the geeks or not?" Becky said.

Forgetting Marvin and his crew for a moment, Detach turned to Becky. "Let's wait and see what the locals do, first." After a pause, Detach added, "The wreck will just have to wait a while."

THIRTY

Detach was grateful for the distraction of taking Marvin and his crew around the *Lothar*. After witnessing the scene on that local trawler, he needed something to take his mind off the horror. The ship performed its part magnificently, giving the appearance of a rundown utility vessel. The artfully painted and acid etched surfaces would have held up under *close* scrutiny. He made sure to keep the TV crew away from the more secretive areas of the ship, and they did not act interested enough in the details to dig further.

When he could stand it no longer, he pulled away from the group and called Marlboro Man. "What's going on with the big fish?"

"I hate to tell you this, but we lost it. Sonar rig's acting up. I got a tech working on it, but in the meantime, we're blind." He hesitated. "Doesn't matter anyway. We just got news over the horn that all diving has been suspended until further notice."

"Great!" Detach groaned. "I wonder how long they'll have a hold on things."

"Since they just lost two of their locals, the authorities aren't happy, even though we had nothing to do with it."

Detach watched an IRCG boat tow the empty trawler back to Kinsale. Two uniforms prowled the deck, probably looking for clues. He was glad to see it go.

The *Lothar* had the same sonar system as the *Cooper*, but he did not want to fire it up and attract undue attention. When the TV crew had enough, Detach returned with them to the other ship and called everyone to the conference room. He flipped the

167

switch on the intercom and hailed Marlboro Man. "Any news?"

"Just got a call from our Irish friends in the IRCG. They spotted something large moving southwest, out to sea. Some locals are going to chase it down, but I don't think they have a real plan. Just a bunch of cowboys." Marlboro man's voice boomed in the confined space.

"Think it's our beast?" Detach had split feelings about the creature. He wanted it gone, but he could not accept the idea someone killing it, at least not until they knew more about it.

"Don't know. Could be a small whale. I didn't see it leave the wreck. The sonar is still giving me fits."

"Thanks, Captain." Detach shut off the speaker. "The locals haven't come up with a viable plan to deal with the beast. This news changes the whole slant of things. We need to get the government to release us to dive again."

"I called George George to see if he could grease some wheels." Barry held up a ship to shore phone.

Detach spent the rest of the day pacing about, antsy to get to work. Waiting for word stretched out before him like a slow torture.

The next afternoon, Detach stood at the fantail of the *Lothar* and once again considered going down the sneaky way, through the moon pool in the bottom of the hull. A honk from an air horn drew his attention to the bridge of the *Cooper*. Marlboro Man waved and gave him a thumbs up. "Finally!" Detach exhaled a day's worth of pent up agitation.

Twenty minutes later on the *Cooper*, he scanned the expectant faces of his team sitting around the conference table.

"We going down, or what?" Broce rubbed his hands together.

"What if it comes back?" Becky gave Detach a worried look.

"There's been no sign of it since yesterday. We'll just have to keep an eye out. It's better than just sitting here. Besides, the suit is tough enough to handle a bite or two."

"Bah." Ruby nodded. "No sweat."

"Okay, gang. Let's get to it." Detach slapped the table in uncontained impatience.

After an hour of preparations, Broce continued to set the lights. Detach watched the display through Broce's camera as he sank into the deep. A powerful light shone straight below. He approached the seabed and the light tower he had dropped during the encounter with the beast. Through the gloom, it came into view along with the seabed.

Detach took note of the debris from the wreck scattered about. Coal lumps dotted the sand along with unidentifiable pieces of metal. He spotted the skeleton of a wooden crate, the metal banding still intact. When Broce ran the light along the prone tower, Detach spotted something underneath the collapsed bulk of the tower. "Uh oh."

"We have a problem," Broce said, seeing it at the same time.

"What's wrong, Sonny?" Ruby tapped some keys.

"The tower fell... no, let me show you. Get Elroy."

"Already here. Stay at least ten feet away and aim your camera at it. Close in with your magnifier." Elroy concentrated on the plasma screen.

"Okay."

The image shifted as Broce sank and hovered a few inches above the bottom. He zoomed in on the object, and the image over the field swelled.

"Not good." Elroy mumbled curses under his breath.

"Yup, we have a problem." Detach said.

"For those of you that don't know what that thing is," Elroy looked around the room, "it appears to be a depth charge. Each one has a depth trigger that sets it off. You see that lump there?" He pointed a laser at the view screen. "The tower fell down on the trigger, and from what I can see, that trigger's holding it up." Elroy circled the spot with the laser. "The thin crust that's built up over the years is cracked. It's like a shell over the thing, and now that pole is right on top of it. Moving the pole could set it off."

"Just what we needed." Detach rubbed his temples.

While Elroy suited up, Detach's cell phone rang. He recognized the number as Jams' private phone.

169

"I couldn't sleep. I'm not getting real good vibes from this *Lusitania* thing and I'm worried about you guys."

Detach gave him a quick brief of the daily events so far.

Jams did not interrupt, but when Detach finished he grunted and said, "Mildred briefed me on what you two found from your research here, before you left."

"Mad Jake's been here." He told him what he and Becky had found in the warehouse. "We got a look at the log book and it lists supplies that confirmed what I saw in there. Large rubberized canvas bags, pumps, hoses, and not a lot to do with actual fishing."

"What in the world was that old dirt bag doing over there? It's renewed my interest in him, that's for sure."

"You just bought some more of his property. I'd say your interest has never waned."

"True," Jams admitted. "I've been poring over crap I've gathered over the years, trying to get a handle on him. I'm looking at a photo of him that gives me the creeps."

"Describe it." Most likely, Detach had already seen it.

"He's staring at the camera, wearing a bowler hat and pinstriped suit, and one of those under the chin beards like a Quaker. It's ragged, reminds me of an old lion. The back says it was taken in...uh...1910."

"Just a minute, Boss." Elroy gave him a grin as a crewman dropped the helmet in place. This was the happiest Detach had seen him in a long time.

Jams said something he missed. "What was that?"

"I said what's going on now?"

"Nothing." Detach stared at the diving suit, ready to drop off the side. "Elroy just suited up to go down and see what he can do about that depth charge."

"I'll make this quick then. Maggie, Jake's great-great-granddaughter, hired an investigator and found out that her great-grandmother, Jake's daughter also named Maggie, hated him with a passion. He had a reputation for being ruthless and cold, but nobody outside the family knew he systematically abused his kids. He beat them regularly and even tortured them until they became old enough to fight back. The old man didn't respect anyone until that person stood up to him. Maggie resolved to kill the old bastard, slowly and with a lot of pain. To do this, she poisoned him. A mild dosage wouldn't kill him at once, but was enough to make him sicker and sicker over years, instead of months or even days. She wanted him to slowly become helpless, and know it was coming. Her final triumph came the day she forced him to become dependent on her to live, her ultimate revenge. After Jake died, she went on to live a fairly productive and straight life, bearing seven children. One of them was young Maggie's grandmother."

Elroy disappeared over the side with a resounding splash.

"What was that?"

"Elroy just hit the water. Guess I'd better go."

"Tell him to be careful."

"Said that enough times to piss him off," Detach said with a chuckle.

"One more thing. Maggie ordered an autopsy and the report was inconclusive. The grave was in a swampy area and too deteriorated to find anything useful. The pathologist couldn't even say for certain that it was Jake. Too deteriorated for DNA at that time.

"As far as the public knows, Jake's people murdered him in 1915 and held his body in state in Louisiana, where most of his holdings were located. However, with no definitive proof that the body in the grave is his, I'm not so sure he died like they say. He was a tricky old bastard."

"Sounds like it. What I really wonder is, what was he doing here?" Detach gazed out over the water and tugged at his goatee.

THIRTY-ONE

Detach came close to slapping Broce. The young man fidgeted and paced as if he were a caged lion.

"Why don't we just hook a cable to the thing and lift it from up here?" Broce pointed down to the sea. "Or, how about just leaving that one and using another one. We have plenty."

"Three reasons." Detach held up a finger. "One. If Elroy's right, it'll probably set the thing off and destroy the tower." He did not need to add that it could rupture the cold fusion power pack mounted to it. A second finger. "Two, we don't want any explosions to damage the wreck any more than it already is. It'll make our job that much harder." He held up the third finger. "We can't leave it behind. Period, and you know why." He did not need to go into the cold fusion power pack.

"Four," Becky said. "In case that creature is still in there, we don't want to hurt it, or… piss it off."

"Elroy, how you doing?" Detach spoke into the microphone on Ruby's control box.

"It's what I've been brought here for. While I'm on the way down, power up the other towers. I'll need all the light I can get."

"We'll have to run the cables down from the generator." Barry gave Detach a knowing look.

Detach wished they could just forget the ruse and turn them on by remote, instead of messing with the phony cables. However, they had to protect their secret technology. "Broce, head back out. You'll need to run the cables. For now, forget about the deck side light array. I have a feeling we won't need them anyway, as bright as these lights are."

173

"When I reach the bottom, I'll just hang tight. Get the kid down here, pronto. I don't want to stay here all day."

Detach had been honest with Elroy and told him about the cold fusion power packs. Broce knew the secret also. As a budding electrical engineer, the kid would have smelled a rat when he had to hook up the cables to obviously dead terminals, especially ones open to the water.

With time to kill, Detach found Vladimir back on the fantail, watching the other boats trolling for the creature. He waved to grab the Russian's attention.

"After this is over, I want you to get a good workout with the suit." Detach gazed down at the water

"I am anxious to start," the Russian said with a grin.

"If you pick it up as well as I think you will, you can go down with me tomorrow afternoon, if…" Detach hesitated, "if we can get over a few 'bumps' in the road."

An hour later, and with much grumbling from an increasingly annoyed Elroy, the fake cables hung in place and the lights ready for Ruby to energize from her computer. Detach had gone over the gist of how the light system worked with her and he knew each light would receive a signal that turned on their fusion generators. At the same time, the fake generator on the *Lothar* would kick in and make enough noise to look like it was straining under the load.

"How bright are these lights?" Vladimir said.

"Bright." Detach could not suppress a wicked grin. "Real bright."

Ruby aped Detach's expression and pulled a pair of sunglasses out of her pocket.

Vladimir gave her a dubious look.

"We tested them out in the bay back home in clearer water. Laid them ten miles offshore, about the same distance to the lighthouse over there." Ruby pointed toward the Kinsale lighthouse through the haze.

"At dusk, we could see the glow from shore in the Mason Industries building." Becky spread her fingers apart in front of her eyes.

"Bright," Detach said again.

"Here goes." Ruby tapped a few keys on her laptop.

The dark sea visibly brightened while the generator on the *Lothar* whined into fake labor. Detach smiled at the Russian's startled expression.

"Here, you go." Ruby pointed to the laptop. "I'm going into the conference room to monitor Elroy on the big screens."

Detach, Becky, and Vladimir crowded around the LCD display.

"Please don't slip, dear," Becky said into the microphone. "We wouldn't want the token black guy to meet an untimely end."

"Screw you!" Elroy laughed.

In the right bottom corner of the monitor, the water temperature read 44 degrees. Next to it, the temperature in the suit hovered at 78. Elroy moved closer to the fallen light fixture. Detach made out each light source in the distance, though silt and garbage floated by the camera lens. He estimated the current travelled at three knots. In conventional gear, he would probably miss the target area entirely unless he swam hard or held onto an anchor line.

A chill passed through him while he watched Elroy hover along the bottom and drift over to the tower. Once in a while, a swirl of silt came up from his friend's boots when they got close to the seabed. The view blurred, then refocused. Ruby was right about the light filters. They cut through the silt and minimized the cloudy effect.

"I'm at 295 feet, with an outside temp settling at a balmy 46 degrees. If I'd been in conventional gear, I'd already be heading back up again for decompression, if not for freezing my nuts off."

"Yup." Detach chuckled under his breath. "The wonders of modern technology."

"I see it. I'm going to get down current and take a closer look."

"Looks like you'll have to get on your knees."

Elroy grunted, squatting down to examine the mine. The hum of the stabilizers crackled through the speaker.

"I can't say the exact vintage, but this thing could be a Mark 6, which makes it American origin. World War II. I thought it would

175

be a Hedgehog mine. That's what they reportedly dropped all around the ship. This one is about twenty-eight inches long by eighteen inches wide. The trigger's called a pistol. There's a crank handle on the end that's buried in the mud and a depth indicator on this side."

A gloved hand pointed to the indented center of the barrel. "This one landed with the trigger facing up and a bolt from the tower is resting on the edge of the dial. The impact cracked off a piece of thick scale that looks like fifty or sixty year's buildup. I can still see the numbers stamped on the dial indicator."

The image grew larger as Elroy moved his head closer. A ring around the center showed the depth was set for 300 feet. Detach rubbed his temples. "It's a dud."

"Maybe, or maybe it's just because we're at 294 feet." Elroy responded.

"That means—"

"Ruby, how much pressure can this suit take?"

"Not enough for that thing, I'm sure," Ruby's voice cut into the conversation. "Maybe in a few months when I add the latest technology, but not now."

"I'm going at it." Elroy hesitated, then added, "Oh yeah. If this thing goes off, you'll definitely know up there."

"Don't talk that way, Darlin'," Ruby said, her light tone barely concealing a motherly concern.

"I just hope the critter doesn't show up," Becky said under her breath.

"I heard that!"

Detach winced and gave Becky a dirty look. He glanced up at the bridge where Marlboro Man would be monitoring the now repaired sonar.

Silt swirled around Elroy's camera. He stood and did a sweep of the area. "No sign of that thing, yet."

The camera returned to a close-up of the depth charge.

Sweat rolled down Detach's face. Despite the cool air, he had to wipe it from his eyes just to see. He had been through tense situations, but never got used to them. His knuckles, white with agitation, gripped the rail while his eyes stayed riveted on the monitor. The man had his faults, but Elroy also had a huge set of balls to work on explosives. He admired that.

On his knees again, Elroy dug sand and debris away, exposing more of the depth charge. His movement created a cloud of silt in the water. "Waiting to let this stuff clear a bit."

The current moved the cloud away in a few seconds. Detach checked the readouts and the stabilizer jets drew a heavy current.

Elroy scooped a bit more and waited.

The process was enough to drive Detach crazy, but he kept silent so Elroy could concentrate.

With the steady hands of a surgeon, Elroy continued to brush decades of muck from the surface of the barrel. As more of the barrel became exposed, he noticed severe corrosion and several holes in the sides. Detach gasped when a gloved hand appeared on the screen with a long screwdriver.

Elroy gently poked at the largest hole in the corroded metal and chipped away a larger section about the size of a paperback book. The exposed insides held a grayish-brown pasty substance, speckled with grainy white flakes, though it was hard to tell the color because of the odd tint from the lights.

"The ravages of time and water have ruined it on the surface, but this stuff looks intact. It's designed for a concussion effect and if it's close enough, it'd do a number on a submarine hull."

Ruby's voice cut in. "Or, a diving suit."

"You don't have to remind me, Ruby. If this device had been on land and sat for a long time unattended, the explosives inside would've crystallized. The crystals, or 'nitrogen whiskers,' are extremely sensitive to any disturbance. A gust of wind breaking a single crystal could start a chain reaction that would set it off, the same as a radio wave causing one to vibrate and break. Even under water in the core of this stuff, a hollow pocket could be teeming with those crystals."

"At that depth and in the water?" Detach asked.

"I'm only guessing on the side of caution, here."

"Looks like they stuffed an old oil drum," Becky said.

"It's smaller than an oil drum. The more I look at this one—it doesn't look like a stock Mark 6. Maybe it was experimental."

177

"What is that stuff?" Becky asked.

"Maybe it's high-pressure gelatin," Elroy replied. "The thing is, I think they used a molded charge in the Mark 6, and this doesn't look quite right."

"I remember high-pressure gelatin." Detach chuckled and closed his eyes, recalling his childhood. "Some friends and I found a few sticks in an old construction vehicle when I was twelve. Almost blew up Lompoc, California." He looked into the monitor. "How many sticks worth do you think is in that thing?"

"The equivalent of thirty or forty, by the looks of it."

Detach was not the only one that gasped.

"Okay gang, enough. Let the man concentrate." Ruby held a note of warning in her gravelly voice.

The camera moved to the trigger again, and the device jumped closer when Elroy activated the magnifier. The dial end loomed in the center of the screen.

"Cool." The image swam as Elroy stood. "I forgot to turn off the magnification. That was a rush."

The screen zoomed out again and Detach spotted the row of their lights in the distance. "What's up down there?"

"Just wait a minute." The image moved to the head of the light tower.

Detach did not know what Elroy was going to do until he saw a gloved hand grab the tower and lift if off the depth charge.

"Hey, watch out!" Multiple voices clamored their warnings over the voice link.

"Too late. Already done. Send down a claw and cable. We're going to move this puppy outta' here. The internal mechanism of the timer has rotted away, I think, but this thing's unstable, we need to get it out of here before someone bumps it."

"But what about the claw? Won't it do the same thing? You know, set it off?" Becky said.

"I'll be careful."

Grabbing the edge of the console in a death grip, Detach watched Elroy attach a plastic explosive charge and remote detonator.

A tap on his shoulder broke his trance and drew his attention to Vladimir. The Russian pointed to a crewman who was lowering a lifting hook into the water from the ship's crane.

"The claw should be coming into view shortly," Detach said.

Ten tense moments later, Elroy announced, "Okay, take up the slack just a little bit."

The cable straightened, eliciting a collective wince from everyone watching the monitor. Detach crossed his fingers, almost afraid to watch.

"I'm moving back a few hundred feet." The view zoomed back.

The scene changed, the greenish light dimming until the water turned almost opaque. Elroy had backed away, stopping with the light tower invisible in the gloom. Detach squinted at the dark screen and relaxed his eyes when he realized he would not be able to see it anyway.

"Okay, give her a gentle tug."

The crewman at the crane punched the UP button and the cable tensed, taking up the slack. There was no explosion.

Elroy moved back to look at the charge. It appeared through the gloom until it filled his camera field of view. "Gently now."

The barrel came free and swung toward a large piece of metal detached from the wreck.

"Oh crap."

Detach braced himself for the worst, but just before it collided with the object, it swung back the other direction. The arc subsided in shorter and shorter swings. A few feet off the seabed, it bobbed up and down in time with the swells above.

"I'm outta' here."

The screen filled with a jet of bubbles, trailing toward the surface with the force of Elroy's escape.

A glow leaked through cracks in the dead fish's shell, startling the creature. A sick feeling overwhelmed the urge to go outside and investigate. After eating those strange babies that came from the small fish with spinning teeth, it felt unsettled and lethargic. The two babies tasted different, and it was not sure it liked the flavor. The meal satisfied at first, but as time passed, the creature felt worse.

Rustling, thumping noises outside frustrated its attempt at rest. The commotion piqued its curiosity, but it could not work up the energy to move.

It sensed a larger fish swim by after it settled in, but the growing ache in its belly deterred any thought of a more substantial meal. Whatever the fish was, it would likely come back, prowling for food.

The beast took in a long draw of water through its ancient, unshark-like gills, and blew it out. A cloud of silt obscured everything. The opaque thickness of the water calmed the aching behind its eyes. The outside would just have to wait for another time.

THIRTY-TWO

"All's clear," Marlboro Man yelled down from the bridge.

"Thanks, captain." Elroy waved up to him.

"I was just thinking about Zork and Dork," Detach said, to nobody in particular.

"About the shark thing?"

"No, no..." He turned to Becky. "Not that."

"What is it?"

"Those bags and that pump we saw in town."

"Stumped, huh?"

"Yeah, I can't quite remember what I should know about them. That old bell in the back of my mind is ringing, but the thought won't come to the surface." Detach scratched at his goatee, his brow set in a deep furrow of frustration.

BOOM!

Detach could not suppress an involuntary gasp. A geyser of water shot up from the surface of the ocean four miles from the three ships.

Elroy winked at him and put the detonating transmitter back in his pocket.

"You had to be crazy to move that thing. I know a little about explosives and if that stuff was anything like the high pressure gelatin I've been around, it's unstable once it gets old."

"Well..." Elroy drawled, "A couple of things."

"I'm listening." Detach faced him and waited.

"First off, you're right. It's quite unstable, *if* the temperature's right."

"Oh?" Detach jerked his eyes to the white circle on the horizon,

181

already dissipating.

"According to the readout in the helmet, the temperature was 46 degrees. Add the pressure at that depth, and that would keep the stuff relatively stable. On the other hand, if it was in an old shack in the desert with an ambient temperature of 80 degrees or more, we'd be in trouble."

"Okay." Detach nodded, satisfied with the first answer. "So, a *couple* of things?"

"Second, once I got it up so I could see the other side, it looked like the firing mechanism went off, but didn't work." Elroy paused. "I didn't think that thing could go off even if it wanted to. Apparently I was right."

"Time to make that call?" Becky put a hand on Detach's forearm.

"Hey," he gave her a sidelong glance, "why not?"

"Worst four years of my life."

"That again?" Becky nudged him. "You whining about high school again? That's the only four year period you every gripe about."

The question hung in the quiet hum of the control room. Detach had not realized he spoke aloud. "Just thinking about Zork and Dork."

Eldridge Carter and Mallory Elliott, otherwise known as Zork and Dork, could have been friends with him if he had met them in high school. Detach was always drawn away from the jocks and "soshes" and toward the outcasts, the oddballs. For a substantial chunk of his freshman year, everyone thought he was retarded because he hung out with a mentally disabled kid.

"I guess if you were fully on your game, we wouldn't be calling these guys." With that good-natured barb, Becky handed him the phone.

Within moments, the call connected. "Carter and Elliott Enterprises, your dime."

"It's tha' Zork man. You know who this is." Detach put the phone on speaker and set it on the conference table.

"You're up early, guys." Becky glanced at her watch.

"Early? It's already five o'clock in the morning. We've been up for hours."

"You two 'up' for a puzzle?" She added with a slight hint of sexual innuendo.

"Talk to us," Dork cut in.

"Okay, here goes." Before Detach could continue, both men spoke at once.

"Oh, mighty pirate. How doth thou be-ist?"

"Aaargh, matey, aaargh." Detach resigned to play the part. He had heard the dig before, ever since they made him do the pirate routine for a children's hospital they sponsored. They never let him live it down. "A coastal town, an old warehouse, rubberized canvas bags, very large bags, I might add. A large scale liquid pump."

"That's it?" Zork asked.

"That's it," Detach replied. "Oh yeah...the smell of diesel."

"You actually want to *pay* us for the answer?"

"Usual fee. The check will arrive within a week."

The two argued in the background, but Detach could not make out what they were saying. "When will you be able to figure it out?"

"Oh... ah... give us a day or so."

"Later, guys." Detach hung up.

"What you think?" Becky said.

"I think I don't want to think about it for a while. Let them do all the mental gymnastics." He still had the feeling he already knew the answer, and was pretty sure they already did as well. "Other things to worry about."

THIRTY-THREE

Dusk settled over the water. Detach stood on deck, savoring the gold shimmer cast by the last sliver of sun sinking below the horizon of an unusually clear sky. Ocean swells pushed the ship up and down in a gentle motion beneath his feet. Too soon, the light faded into a heavy purple. The darker the sky, the brighter the water glowed beneath him. The fake generator on the *Lothar* whined away for appearance's sake, but he worried the glow would attract undue attention from shore. He did not want prying eyes hovering when — or if — they located the gold.

To make up for lost time, they would dive at dusk. The plan included looking for a practical way in, and spotting more ordnance. Detach wanted to take Vladimir down on this first dive and felt the former SVR man would be handy. Becky had deferred to Jam's wishes to let the Russian participate. Though he felt more comfortable with her at his side, he also wanted to see how the man conducted himself under stress. This would be his trial by fire.

After fixing the errant sonar rig, Marlboro Man scanned the area for several hours with no large blips moving on the screen. Detach assumed the creature, satisfied with its recent meal, had retreated into the wide expanse of the Atlantic. There was no sense in delaying further.

He walked to the conference room where everyone waited, ready for the briefing, and took his seat.

"Nothing's really changed from before." Barry used the model and painting of the wreck, pointing out the large tear in the hull. "This is pretty much the only opening large enough for

185

easy access. It's probably full of debris, so you'll have your work *cut* out for you, especially since the big boss said no overt cutting on the outside of the hull."

Detach rolled his eyes at the bad pun.

"Didn't Alvin go in a ways?" Becky asked. She referred to the submersible Dr. Ballard's team used to explore the ship.

Barry shrugged. "Sure did, but we weren't able to get much data on that. They wouldn't respond to our emails. So, we're on our own."

"What about the nets?" Vladimir pointed to the screen.

"You should be okay if you approach from the sea bed, around where the lights are placed. Marlboro Man says they're all drifting toward the upper hull, away from where you'll be entering." Barry aimed his laser at the objects on the painting. "The tide's pulling them away from the target area at the moment."

"Be careful of any strange objects. We don't know what's been dropped there besides that thing I blew up this afternoon," Elroy clicked the remote switch, which he still had.

"Okay people, let's get going." Ruby slapped her hand on the table and poked a thumb at the door. An unlit cigarette hung from her lip.

A half hour later, Becky grabbed Detach by the arm, depositing a quick kiss on the cheek before she and Ruby lifted his helmet on. He blushed and his mind raced with all kinds of motives for the gesture, but her expression didn't convey anything other than concern.

He heard Vladimir breathing over the voice link as the Russian's helmet settled into place, amplified by the excellent sound system. Detach's readouts sprang to life and he used his wrist pad to move them to the left side of his visor so he could have a clear view in front. He liked the readouts because they resembled an aircraft HUD, or Head-Up Display. Though he hated to fly, he appreciated the technology that went into aircraft.

"Last one in the water's a Commie, Pinko, Faggot, Junkie, Doper," Detach cracked, reciting an old George Carlin routine.

Vladimir's husky laugh crackled over the comm, and the two dropped simultaneously over the side, hitting the water together with an impressive splash. Following the pre-planned drill, Detach maneuvered to face the Russian while they sank to the bottom. Seeing it from the monitors was nothing but a pale imitation of experiencing it from the suit. He marveled at how well the lights revealed everything. The filter lenses Ruby designed for the mineral content cut through the cloudy water. Tilting the suit down, he spotted the bottom. Soon, he stood in a clear spot on a soft seabed, facing the lights. "Those things are bright!"

"Yes, they are," Vladimir said.

Turning away from the glare, Detach had his first look at the twisted and deteriorated hull of the swiftest and most luxurious ocean liner of her day. A sad testament to the ravages of time, the once magnificent ship looked like a shadowy scrap metal heap.

"Keep a watch out for ordnance ole' buddy." Detach pointed to a suspicious looking canister.

"It is a junkyard down here, no?"

"I've seen auto salvage yards cleaner than this."

"In Moscow, most of the cars on the street would be in the same condition as the ones in your junkyards. Communists."

"Good thing for Glasnost, huh?"

"Heh, heh. I am not so sure that was much of an improvement."

Scraps of metal and unidentifiable junk lay everywhere, among them he saw a pair of suspiciously new looking oil barrels. They reminded Detach of improvised depth charges, but sat far enough out of the way to avoid. Detach felt a prickling at the back of his neck. He expected the crowds of fish and sea life common at this depth, but saw nothing, not even small ones. They approached the huge flattened hull that lay still as a tomb. He scanned the area for signs of the creature, but only tiny specks of debris hovered in the light. *Now would not be a good time for the sonar to act up again.*

With Ruby's special filters on the light towers, Detach could see at least seventy-five feet. Silt coursed along the current toward the wreck, giving him the sensation of moving on an escalator. If not for the stabilizers, he would have fallen flat on his face. The few scraggly plants sprouting out of the seabed swayed in lazy waves in the same direction, making the feeling worse. Small drifts of sand and silt peppered the area, making weird swirling patterns amid the junk. The lamp filters altered natural color, giving everything a flat appearance. It reminded him of an "artsy fartsy" foreign film.

Detach led the way to the tear in the hull, circumventing a lifeboat davit with a chunk of sheet metal lying over the curved end. His jaw dropped at the sheer size of the hull. He pulled within a few feet of the large hole, stopped and scanned the length of the wreck. The black gray mass went both directions into the distance, disappearing in the haze that even the lights could not penetrate.

"At seven hundred and eighty-five feet long, the hull once had an eighty-eight foot beam at the widest spot. However, now it's about half that width."

"Then our job will not be any easier, no?"

Eyeing the dark abyss in front of him, Detach shook his head. "Headlamp time."

They turned their lights on and the unfiltered glow fogged up the view, like turning on the car brights on a foggy night. Detach peered into the gaping hole and it was as Barry described, a scrap yard. The Orlop decks lay exposed, twisted and tilted at a crazy angle. Folded, spindled, mutilated. Casting his gaze upward, he noticed several large dark openings within the gash, inviting nervous thoughts of the unknown. "Follow right behind and watch my tail, all right?"

"To your left, friend," Vladimir warned.

Detach turned left and in the reddish mass of rust, he spotted an olive drab cylinder. It did not look nice.

"Haven't even started and there's another explosive already."

"Need me?" Elroy's voice boomed.

"Hold on, we still have a clear path."

"You watch it, Buster," Becky said.

Detach grinned at Becky's comment and he studied the moving silt. It drifted up and disappeared into the dark opening thirty feet above their position. Despite the comfortable temperature in the suit, his body reacted with a strong shudder, a chill that had nothing to do with the temperature. The dark opening emitted a sense of danger and evil. The twisted mountain of metal loomed like the nasty looking factories and decrepit buildings he saw along the Thames River in London. He always imagined if ghosts existed anywhere in the world, they must be in London. This wreck could be the second place.

"Is kind of creepy, no?" Vladimir mumbled.

"Mmm."

"Reminds me of Chernobyl."

"You were there?" That startled Detach out of his morbid thoughts.

"I did not have much choice. After the accident, I was sent in to look for 'other' causes."

"You mean it wasn't an accident?"

"It was an accident. In reality 'a monumental screw up.'"

"I heard it was pretty bad."

"The deadest piece of land I have ever encountered. My testicles are probably fried, even though I was wearing the best suit available."

"I can imagine." Detach remembered seeing the reports on TV. Many people died because of it, and most of them died slow. "Well, at least this heap isn't radioactive."

"We hope not. Although, the way things have been going…" Becky said.

"Oh, cheer me up."

"I am ready if you are." Vladimir motioned toward the wreck with his gloved hand.

No, but here goes anyway. He began his ascent, using extreme caution. His stabilizers moved him up, but at the sacrifice of stirring up silt. Lucky for them, it drifted up and over the hulk of the wreck. The nearest dark area, probably the lower Orlop deck, sat just above the bilge but it was too narrow to enter at this spot. They would have to rise higher.

"You know, when the ship sank and hit the bottom, a design flaw common to that class of ocean liner forced it to split. The *Titanic* and the *Britannic* split the same way. The *Titanic* actually separated into two pieces because of the great depth in which it sank, when the stern lifted so high above the water." Detach

189

gestured to the gaping hole. "This tear in the hull never had a chance to break all the way because of the shallower depth."

"I remember reading something about that when I prepared for this trip."

Silt covered rusted metal chunks of hull and deck plates. Pieces of wire and porthole frames stuck out of the mess. They continued upward and the silt thinned, drifting back down to the sea floor.

"I don't trust the depth sensor enough to simply float into that dark hole, so let's climb the rest of the way. Ruby figures the sensor acts up most when we free float. The stabilizers still work when we walk, but at reduced power and that seems to limit the effect on the sensor."

"Da. Fine with me."

His boots settled on a piece of protruding inner deck, the metal sloping up to a peak. With a few tentative steps, he reached the top. The remaining deck tilted sharply down and disappeared into the gloom. At this angle, the light tower illumination cut off at the lip of the precipice. With his headlamp, he spotted a large gap that looked like a promising entrance. "We'll have to drift down from here," Detach said.

"Maybe not."

Detach turned to face the Russian. He spotted a rope in the Russian's right hand. He forgot that Vladimir had insisted on a few extras, just in case.

Vladimir picked a thick metal projection and clamped the rope in place. "How you say, honors?"

"Close enough." Detach took the rope Vladimir offered and backed down onto the steep slope of the rotted steel deck. Despite the current hitting him head-on, the suit equalized the force so that he could relax without drifting. Clouds of silt billowed up and drifted toward Vladimir as the stabilizers pumped out a complicated rush of multi-directional jets that kept him upright, the thrumming increasing and decreasing in volume. He hoped that would not be a problem once they got inside. Holding onto the rope, he let himself down into the murky depths. The thrill of being one of the few humans to penetrate the inside of the ship since it sank, sent a tingling wave across his skin.

THIRTY-FOUR

Despite the protection of the suit, Detach could not suppress a shudder. Even with the lights, the dark opening gaped like a bottomless pit. If he had been in conventional diving gear, he never would have attempted going inside. The twisted metal, wires, and junk that hung everywhere would cut him to ribbons. Silt swirled about and colors could not be trusted because of Ruby's light filters, which were also on their suit lights. A surreal alien aura pervaded the already treacherous dive. Whatever she had come up with worked, because the difference between regular and her filtered light startled him with penetrating clarity of what it revealed.

"Current's mild here so turn your jet stabilizers to low and your buoyancy compensator to walk. Also set boot magnets to weak so we have some traction, but without too much work. The silt will make the footing slippery. The jets'll make it so cloudy we'll never see a thing if they're going full blast, despite the light filters." Detach hit bottom on a bulkhead, now positioned sideways relative to the lean of the ship.

"Come on down, Vlad."

He scanned the area. An open door yawned at the other end of the room and the joint between the floor and wall lay filled with sand. A metal rod lay against the deck. He picked it up and poked at the path leading to the portal. The suit performed flawlessly so far. He could move, bend and twist enough to feel like he was in street clothes, at least to a point. With the fusion generator and air recycling system in a bulge on the back of the suit, there were no obstructions to catch on the jagged metal.

191

"Think it will hold our weight?" Vladimir asked.

"Seems pretty solid so far. Our buoyancy compensators will give us enough weight to walk comfortably, but we could also fall through any weak spots."

Detach gave another poke at the floor with the rod. Satisfied it would hold his weight, he took a few steps toward the open doorway. The metal seemed solid under his feet and held sturdy. The mild magnetic field from the boots made it feel like he walked on a sticky kitchen floor. He reached the doorway, and looked into pitch-black. Fine debris drifted from behind, disappearing into the gloom. There had to be an opening somewhere below leading to the outside.

"Here's where it is gonna' get kinda' tight." Detach was not referring to the size of the door which would easily accommodate their suits. "I hope you don't have claustrophobia."

Vladimir acknowledged with a grunt.

"How about an update?" Barry voice cut though over the voice link.

"You're seeing what we're seeing, so hold on. We gotta' concentrate here. It's a little touchy."

"Sorry. We can't get the whole perspective from up here. Still, I'm getting the creeps just watching it on the monitor."

"Thanks, I needed that."

Keeping an eye out for jagged metal, Detach slid into the doorway and the dark unknown. Once through, he held onto the lip of the opening and scanned the inside of the room. Empty and out of shape, the space reminded him of a funhouse. One door gaped at the other end, as did another one down to the right. He let go, and sank to the bottom.

His boots settled into the silt, stirred up a cloud that drifted to the other end of the space. Neither of the openings had a door mounted on them, no hinges, and no sign there ever were any. He looked into the one on the right while Vladimir plodded over to the other. Just as distorted as the room they were in, it was empty. "Nothing here."

"The same."

"Barry, you're on. Where are we?" Detach said.

"Though you went in the hull from the wrong side, you should already be somewhere on the lower Orlop. There should be junk all over the place. About where you are, there's supposed to be rotted wooden cases and the remains of foodstuffs. I thought you might be hitting a coalbunker, but that room's obviously not one of them. From where you stand, to your right should be a door leading to the first boiler room."

"As you saw from my camera, that room's empty. I spotted a boiler above us on the other side of the gash."

"That's a problem all right."

Barry still sounded troubled and that magnified Detach's puzzlement.

"Did you notice the doors missing?" Vladimir asked. His helmet camera highlighted the empty hinge mounts.

"That's extremely odd. As a matter of fact, they should've been on rollers, some of the watertight doors." Barry was clearly puzzled.

"There's no sign of rollers on any doors we've seen so far."

"I know," Barry grumbled.

"Why is it we are able to communicate in here without a lifeline to the outside? In all of this metal?"

"That's a question for Ruby, Vlad."

"Just be glad you're not in a cave," Ruby said.

"I do not understand."

"So which way, navigator?" Detach did not want to discuss technology that the military would kill for. He could hardly believe Ruby let slip that little tidbit about caves.

"Uhhhh…" Barry hesitated a moment before answering. "Go straight down. The door to the right should lead to the front boiler room. We know the explosion wasn't there… well, we don't THINK it was there."

"All right. Vladimir, care to take the lead?" It was time the Russian got a little ownership in this dive.

"Spacebo."

Detach moved out of the way and cut to Vladimir's camera. The Russian's view revealed a clear path through a narrow and distorted room.

"Scan around so Barry can get a good look."

"Da."

Detach spotted a school of tiny shrimp floating by Vladimir's head.

"Here I go." Vladimir maneuvered into the portal and dropped another level to a junction between the wall and floor. More flattened than the previous room, the ceiling showed severe compression and held nothing of interest except a door at the bottom.

Detach switched back to his own video and dropped down next to the Russian, a small cloud rising up from his boots.

"Now wait a minute, this can't be right." Barry had an edge to his voice.

"I have the feeling something's truly amiss." Detach tried for a bad imitation of W.C. Fields.

"Oh, geez." Becky groaned in the background. "Stick to the pirate."

"Take a look in that door," Barry said.

"Which one of us?" Vladimir turned and peered at Detach through his visor.

"Either."

Detach had already moved toward it around Vladimir. His curiosity overcame his desire to let Vladimir take the lead. He peered into the gloom and saw a distorted room beyond. The twisted metal reminded him of looking inside a half-crushed car at a salvage yard.

"Empty again," Barry said.

"I see a door, to the left this time, heading toward the bow, and another one to the right. Want me to go further forward?" The nerves tingled in Detach's stomach.

"No, not yet. Before we go any further that way, I want to find that boiler room."

"Okay." Detach scanned the room. "Why?"

"Just a suspicion, no...actually a hunch."

Detach nodded to Vladimir and got a wave in return. They headed up the steep slope, and he was amazed they had enough traction to make it to the other door, despite the magnetized boots. He followed the seam to the right door, and peered inside.

"Between the two of your videos, I still see nothing."

"Can't argue with that, Barry. We're going in." Detach stepped over the rim of the portal and into another silt-filled seam. When Vladimir reached his side, he moved forward, expecting the boilers to jump up at them in the gloom.

"Wait, Detach, turn your head to the right and up the slope." Barry said.

Detach did as requested and saw huge metal blocks mounted to the deck, empty boltholes clearly visible.

"Can't be," Barry whistled. "No way!"

"I get the idea something's missing." Detach said, his sarcasm tinted with that uneasy feeling he could not suppress.

"The first boiler, that's what!"

"Wait a minute. Isn't there a boiler visible in the big crack from the outside?"

"Exactly." Barry groaned. "If this is supposed to be the boiler room, then that one up there's in the wrong room."

"Holy crap!" Detach raised up more and got a better look at the huge bay. The distorted cavernous space took his breath away. Instead of large boilers rotting in place, he saw rows of empty wells fading into the distance. He poked at the scant debris poking out of the silt and found pieces of pipe and wire, the first real sign of debris deep inside the ship. The current flowed toward the stern and he assumed there were still more openings deeper in the hull. After going twenty feet, he saw no sign of any boilers or steam piping. No sign of the smokestack piping going up to the funnels, though the ceiling, at least what was visible had nothing but a mess of beams and tangled junk. The seam spread out and flattened to over ten feet wide. Small objects littered the area and he spotted a shape.

"I see a wrench, and I might add a real big one." He leaned down and pulled the object from the silt. It appeared to be brass, and had a greenish tinge to it.

"Can you see any writing on it, like a brand name or size or something?" Barry said.

"Why would that…" Detach hefted the wrench to his helmet

and almost dropped it in his surprise. "What the…?"

"Holy…" Barry sounded like he was choking. "Son of a gun!"

"What you think, Vlad?" Detach handed the wrench to the Russian.

"Since when did the British use Russian tools?"

Detach looked at the wrench again. "I don't think the Brits ever wrote in Cyrillic."

THIRTY-FIVE

An uneasy silence filled his sound system as Detach and Vladimir moved deeper into the hull. The large boiler room became more distorted and narrower as they moved astern. From this point on, the ship flattened out more and more and the superstructure slid to the starboard side.

It amazed Detach how fast a huge steel ship could deteriorate into such a mess while some wooden ships, buried in the sand for thousands of years, remained recognizable. "This ship's empty and I'll bet that has a lot to do with why the superstructure is collapsing so fast. Ballard spotted that one boiler, but it's in the wrong place."

"If the hair could stand up on the back of my neck in this suit, it would be doing so, friend." Vladimir sounded nervous.

"The hair *is* standing up on the back of my neck," Detach admitted, though the snugness of the suit's inner lining prevented it.

"Barry, are those pits the mounting wells where the boilers are supposed to go?"

"Yes." He did not elaborate.

Vladimir gestured toward the nearest pit. "I suggest we take a look inside one and see what is there. Maybe there will be some more debris we can look through."

"Sounds good to me, my commie friend," Detach agreed. "Lead the way."

"There's no lack of debris on the outside of the wreck, but inside's a different story. The more I'm seeing, the more obvious the inside of this ship's empty. It's giving me the willies, to be honest."

"Thanks, Barry. I needed that."

Vladimir grunted.

"Sorry, guys. Didn't mean to…" Barry's voice trailed off.

"With that little bit of cheer to spur us forward…" Detach drawled.

The magnetic boots made the trek up the slope easy. Detach followed Vladimir to the nearest opening in the twisted deck. He looked into the pit, knowing exactly what he would find. Nothing. No boiler mount blocks, plumbing, struts, shafts, or other hardware. The rectangular boiler well measured fifteen feet wide and thirty feet long and was relatively level in the distorted hull. He saw the remains of a metal stair at one side. Their lights revealed sand and silt on the bottom, along with a collection of objects he could not recognize.

"Da or Nyet?" Detach said.

"We cannot look close from here. I suggest we climb down."

They maneuvered over the edge of the boiler well and dropped inside, landing softly in the built up silt of what should have been boiler number two service well. The pit reminded Detach of service holes below huge diesel engines in the power plant at Torrejon Air Base. He had seen them while on a visit with an Air Force friend stationed in Spain. Because of a mild slant of the deck, silt filled one side of the area.

"You are not going to like this," Vladimir said, picking up an object.

"This is all wrong!" Barry cut in. "You guys need to come back up for a reconnoiter."

"A what?" Vladimir asked.

"All that spying on us and you didn't pick that up?" Detach added full sarcasm.

"Reconnoiter…" Vladimir gave a puzzled look then his eyes lit up. "Aah!"

"Aah! The light comes on." Detach tapped the side of his helmet and winked at the Russian. Then he looked down at the wrench Vladimir held, saw the Cyrillic writing on it, and shook his head. "Let's hit the road." He poked his thumb upward.

Taking the lead, Detach climbed back out of the pit toward

deck level from the other side. "Jesus friggin' Christ!" He found himself face to face with the largest and meanest looking creature he had ever seen. It was the size of a locomotive and he briefly wondered how it got in the room. There had to be a large hole somewhere, a very large hole.

Vladimir pulled up beside him but did not say a word.

Their helmet lamps revealed only part of the creature, but Detach saw that its body extended well beyond the length of the pit. Its hide was covered in coarse, greenish scales on top and a pink tinted underbelly. The fins were thick, the dorsal ribbed but the others smooth and almost dolphin-like. It also had funny looking gill slits. The thing breathed in and out through large nose holes. Each breath sent a swirl of silt shooting off. The mouth hung open slightly, revealing rows of razor sharp teeth. When he fixated on the creature's eye, he heard Becky gasp.

"Vlad, can you dim your light a bit?" Becky whispered.

The Russian mumbled something unintelligible in Russian. "I must move my arm."

"Slowly," Becky said. "Trust me."

Detach caught a glimpse of Vladimir with peripheral vision as the Russian delicately curled his arm up to the light intensity control on the chest of his suit.

"It doesn't seem to be bothered by the bright light, but we don't want to anger it, now do we?" Becky kept her voice calm and gentle.

"Mmph," Detach exhaled. He still had not budged an inch. "What about my light?"

"Don't worry about it, yet."

Detach exhaled again, afraid he would start hyperventilating.

"Okay, guys, calm down." Becky said. "See that eye?"

"Big as a basketball, can't miss it." Detach sputtered, his voice up a few pitches.

"That's the eye of a mammal, not a fish."

"With scales?" The Russian had a slight tremor in his words.

"I'm no zoologist, but that eye reminds me of the whales I saw back home at the marine park." Barry whispered as well, as if the creature could hear him.

199

"I'm about to drop a load in my pants down here. I'd like to avoid the embarrassment. Oh, and the added annoyance of being eaten," Detach stammered.

"Oh shut up, Darlin,'" Becky kept her voice calm. "Has it attacked you yet?"

"Well, ah…"

"It's looking at you, studying you."

"Wait a minute." Detach had a thought. "If that's a mammal, how can it breathe down here? I see gills."

"Well, ah…" For a moment there was silence, then Becky continued. "From what I can see, this thing breaks several biological rules, so the fact it can breathe water, and maybe air for all we know, is going to take more study. I've been at this for a while and I can guarantee there's no known creature in the oceans like this one."

"Time to get out of Dodge." Detach glanced at Vladimir.

"What is Dodge?" The Russian flipped up a hand and winced, then lowered it slow after glancing at the creature. He gazed wide-eyed at Detach.

"One of his bad clichés, that's all." Becky groaned, not seeing what just happened down below.

Ever so slowly, the two divers lowered their heads and moved the lights out of the eye of the huge creature. Detach prayed for no reaction and breathed a sigh of relief when it did not move. "Me thinks we best look for an avenue of egress."

"That thing had to have come through a very large hole. But it probably isn't a good idea to try and find it," Becky said.

"Good idea. We need to find a way out that's too small for it to follow," Detach said.

"Just move slow, Friend."

Vladimir's voice also sounded a few pitches too high and that made Detach feel better knowing he was not the only one about to stink up his suit. He turned slow and scanned their temporary prison, desperate for a way out. The pit measured an easy ten feet deep, even with the silt buildup on the floor. Up to the port side of the ship, he spotted a black opening in the side of the space large enough to squeeze through. Vladimir's light turned to the same spot and their combined lights showed metal beams deep inside the hole.

"By the way, how much oxygen do we have?" Vladimir said.

"Uh, well..." Detach started to say.

"That'll not be a problem for several hours," Ruby's voice echoed in their helmets. "Just hope you don't have to pee for a while... or worse."

"But, how...?"

"Trust me, just worry about getting out of there in one piece, dear."

"Should we go for it?" Detach looked at Vladimir. *As if we have a choice.*

"After you."

Detach caught the sweet smile on the Russian's face. He blinked and sniffed one time to focus, then slowly moved up the slope to the dark opening. Out of the corner of his eye, he saw part of the huge body of the beast, still unmoving on the deck above them. Taking that as a sign of encouragement, he continued until he reached the lip of the portal and discovered not a door, but a missing piece of the pit wall. He did not see a metal plate in the bottom of the engine well, making him think it was never installed. He scraped the sides while squeezing through the opening.

The creature watched the white fish enter its cave. The things were roughly the shape of those babies it ate the day before, but they were white. White was bad. White was what killed one of its companions. It did not want to bite into one of them and find out.

The two fish moved around, emitting a strange humming and whooshing sound that changed pitch. They glowed too. It had never seen a fish glow like that. The fish also had an odd smell. After a few moments, they disappeared somewhere in a side cave. Good thing. It was not hungry enough to tempt the same fate as its companion.

THIRTY-SIX

A thousand shark attack videos played through his head. What would it feel like? Would the suit stop the bite, crush his lower torso, or have no effect at all? Detach half expected a tug as the creature bit off his lower body, but he made it through the hole followed by Vladimir, who insisted he go first.

"That was close," Detach let out in a long breath.

"What's it doing?" Becky said.

Detach turned back to the small opening and peered out at the creature. It lay on the deck, still watching them. The eye stared and blinked, but the creature remained motionless. *Is it sick?*

"If that thing's a mammal, then how come it has gills?" Detach thought of a duck-billed platypus.

"I can't explain that, except a minute ago I saw a blow hole too," Becky answered.

Detach could not see it now, the way his light was aimed.

"Reminds me of a duck billed platypus," Elroy broke in, echoing Detach's thought. "Not by look, but by the mix."

"Are those video people getting all of this?" Vladimir asked.

"No. They're on the *Novosibirsk* interviewing the crew. We promised them a copy of the video, but didn't want them in the way in case something went wrong. Guess something did," Barry added with a smirk.

"We may need to edit a few of the boring bits out." The sarcasm in Ruby's voice was thick.

"Barry, help us. Where are we?" Detach changed the subject.

"I hate to tell you this, guys, but... I have no idea." The frustration in Barry's voice did not boost anyone's confidence.

"Not good," Detach muttered.

Vladimir said something nasty sounding in Russian.

"All I can tell you is head away, toward the port side. The decks might be impassable, but maybe you can find a way back to the outer hull." Barry took a deep breath. "You seem to be in a crawl space above the upper Orlop. If my guess is right, you should see some kind of service hatches that will open into a larger room."

"Makes sense, I guess." Detach scanned the confined area, realization dawning on him. This space should contain conduits, piping or something. Along the ceiling were holes and a random bracket, but it appeared that someone either removed the plumbing and wiring or never installed it. Reaching the Orlop decks, the two lowest decks on the ship, should be easy from the bottom of the boiler pit.

"Make sure your buoyancy is set to neutral and turn off your magnetic boots. We'll be swimming for a while."

"That way," his partner pointed up the slope. "I see another opening."

Detach followed Vladimir's lead. The four-foot high space contained I-beams supporting the deck above. He saw no debris except for another Russian-made wrench that he passed over fifteen feet from where they entered. The close quarters gave him the first feelings of claustrophobia. Towering above him, stretched tons of rotted steel, ready to fall down and crush them both. He had been inside many shipwrecks before, but this one was by far the most deteriorated.

Ahead, the Russian reached the opening and stuck his head through. Detach watched fine silt drift by, clouding his view. It reminded him of underwater caves.

"Hey, my friend. There is a causeway and ladder in here," Vladimir said.

"Good. We need to head up."

Because of the tilt of the wreck, the causeway led them back toward the boiler room. At the top of the ladder, Detach spotted an opening, door missing of course, that led to a larger room beyond. When they entered the new room, he noticed significant wreckage for the first time.

"Well, well," Detach stood for a moment, taking in the scene. "Finally something to look at."

Distorted into a non-definable shape, the room continued in the funhouse tradition. The wall toward the stern partially collapsed into a pile of corroded debris, silt, and rust fingers. Detach detected a slight current from the movement of the silt as he neared the right side of the room to examine the debris. "This place looks like it'll collapse at any moment."

"Careful what you touch," Vladimir warned.

"The current's heading this way, so there must be another opening." Detach navigated over the debris, avoiding the rust fingers dangling from the twisted ceiling.

Toward the bow end and to the right, the room narrowed, half from the collapse of the hull, and the rest from the piled up debris. It would be a tight squeeze, but Detach estimated they should be able to weave their way through the junk and into the next room if they were careful. If there turned out to be another collapsed room ahead, they would have a difficult time backing up without causing a cave in. "What do you think?" He glanced at Vladimir and noted a nervous look that matched his own.

"That is where the current seems to go. What choice do we have?" The Russians' face broke out in a grin. "Besides, I have no desire to be a quick meal."

Detach turned to the narrow passage. With slow, delicate movements, he swam upward. He pictured chunks of rust raining down on his back, though the suit prevented him from feeling them. Even with the sediment filter altering the color, he noticed a reddish-gray cloud moving around his helmet and into a dark opening ahead. Foot by foot, he closed in on the dark portal until his head penetrated into the next room.

The room contained only rusted walls and bulkheads. He twisted and tilted his head so the light faced up where he saw another opening. The reddish water drifted toward it. "Come on, but be careful."

Vladimir followed his lead.

Detach floated into the open space and turned when Vladimir

tried to come through the door. Just as his head reached through, the suit jerked up, slamming the Russian into the wall above him, half in and half out the opening.

Vladimir yelled out curses in Russian, a mixture of panic and anger in his voice.

"Ruby the sensor!" Detach grabbed at Vladimir's hand.

He did not have time to wonder whether or not Ruby would react, he just knew he had to pull Vladimir through before the whole wall came down on him. A dark cloud of reddish-black muck billowed out and blinded him. He grabbed through the murk with a grand sweep until his thick-gloved hand made contact with his partner's glove.

Detach got a firm grip and pulled with all his strength. With a desperate jerk, Vladimir slipped through the opening, shooting past just as a rumble signaled the collapse of the room. The Russian shot back and forth, up and down like a deflating balloon. Instinct took over. He grabbed out when his partner shot past. Though it was hard to hold on, he kept his grip until the suit went still. Rust and chunks of metal rained down on him, clouding the view.

Vladimir's suit hummed back into action and Detach quickly shut off the stabilizers using the external chest control. He peered into the relieved face of his partner, a foot from the Russian's helmet to see him clear in the murky water. The current made quick work of the muck, and visibility returned to a tolerable level.

"What happened?"

"I do not know." Vladimir shook his head inside his helmet. "The stabilizers were turned off. That was not supposed to happen, right?"

"Vlad." Ruby's voice cracked in their sound system. "Did you disable the stabilizers or just put them in standby?"

"Well…" The Russian frowned at Detach. "I thought I turned them off."

"From up here I can't tell, which in itself, is an anomaly. I should be able to see all of your settings no matter what. I'll have to run a diagnostic when you get back up here."

Detach did not like the idea of things coming on at random. However, he knew Ruby could figure it out, though it would not do them much good in their present situation. He glanced back through the opening and saw a solid wall of metal debris. Just visible through the edge of the door, stood a green barrel with a depth trigger wedged in the pile. The barrel had no corrosion and the trigger dial read four hundred feet. They were lucky it did not go off during the collapse. "Hey, Elroy, my man. You see that?"

"Sure do. That's another new one. Never seen the like before. It's not standard issue. Looks improvised."

Detach could almost hear Elroy frown. "What's going on here? Who'd try to blow this ship up now, especially after all this time?"

"Someone trying to stop us from finding something?" Vladimir said.

"I think I know what they were trying to cover up." Barry cleared his throat. "But let's worry about getting you out of there first."

"Looks like there's no turning back now." Detach had no desire to face that creature again.

"A bad time to be...how you say...claustrophobic?"

"I am, now." Detach glared at Vladimir who returned a grim smile.

"You have to keep moving," Becky said with a loud sigh.

"Yeah, you're right." Detach studied their surroundings. The water had already cleared. He grabbed a glove full of silt and released it to check current flow. It moved into the next black opening. "That-a-way."

"Spacebo."

"Mmph." Blood rushed to Detach's face for a second before he suppressed a shudder, peering through the dark portal. The surrounding reddish-black and gray metal seemed to close in, as if crushing him in a vice. The passage reminded him of swimming above a drop ceiling. The superstructure compressed what was left of the bulkheads, narrowing the passage into a tight squeeze. Rods and turnbuckles stuck up from the bottom as if holding the floor in place. *This is going to be very tight.*

"Don't mention claustrophobia again, Vlad. We got a really

tough squeeze ahead of us."

"My honor." Vladimir promised. He swam up next to Detach and looked into the space, then cursed in Russian again.

"My sentiments, exactly, whatever you said." Knowing they had no choice, Detach plunged ahead, hoping that the sensors did not go haywire again. They could not power down completely or they would lose breathing, buoyancy and communications. Both suits seemed to be running properly. For how long, he did not know.

"Should I ask how much breathing time we have left?" Vladimir asked again.

"At least that's not a problem." Vladimir would have been shocked if he knew how long they could stay down without tanks. Breathing worked so well that the readouts did not even show a gas quantity indicator unless a problem occurred. The biggest drawbacks were dehydration and elimination. Detach had never been down more than three hours, and that had been a strain. They were now pushing just over two.

Weaving through the narrow maze, Detach maneuvered around cross members and rusted-through I-beams, following the drift of the silt. Every few feet, he reached down and threw up another glove full, watching the drift. The further they went, the more nervous he became. That explosive back there had to come from the outside, but it was buried in a solid wall of debris. They couldn't dig through that, let alone work around the explosive, so it was this way or back to the creature. Their direction now took them toward the bow and sideways instead of up. He had no way of knowing how deep inside the hull they were. Outside of the structure itself, he found little debris. For the first time, he saw a small fish, darting between metal rust fingers, watching them. All of a sudden, his forward movement halted and he felt a sickening crush of being wedged between the top and bottom of the space.

"I'm stuck," Detach said, fighting a tremble in his voice. He felt a push against his boots and he popped through the narrow space into a wider area. "Thanks, now grab my boot if you can still reach it and I'll pull you since I can't turn around."

"Thanks."

Detach grabbed a solid chunk of metal before him and pulled. He heard a grunt from the Russian.

"I am through."

"I don't know if you noticed it or not, but did that not look like a dent?" Barry said.

A buckled shape crumpled against a nearby wall. If it turned out to be a dent, they could be near the outer hull, pockmarked with dents from depth charges. "I think you're right. If that's the case, we might be inside the double hull." He turned to the right and looked up for an indication of portholes or openings. Seeing nothing, he probed on, praying that they would find an opening. Ahead, he saw a precipice with vast blackness below it. When he reached the edge, he looked down into a room, most likely the upper Orlop again.

Detach floated over the opening and stood while Vladimir followed suit. They floated above the blackness below, hanging onto the lip of the chasm. He was glad for the small victory.

"Hey, Detach, aim your head just over Vladimir's right shoulder," Barry said.

Faint Cyrillic writing was etched on the bulkhead behind the Russian. "Care to translate?" Detach said.

Vladimir read the black letters still visible on the rusted metal. "Vladivostok Metal Works."

A chorus of curses echoed from above. "Later, okay?" he shouted back to them. "We need to get out of here."

"Look, under there." Vladimir pointed below Detach's waist.

Detach turned and sank down into the room under his feet and saw a black opening with silt drifting rapidly through it. He aimed for the opening and reached it with Vladimir at his heels. Up and into the narrow space again, he spotted the glow of lamps ahead. "About time."

He headed for the light and had no trouble navigating through the narrow space.

They broke into the light, a large hole exposing the way back outside. A large round object partially blocked the jagged hole. Detach let out a breath. "Doesn't that just top the day?"

THIRTY-SEVEN

A current swept stirred-up silt through the opening next to the explosive. Detach eased back as far as he could get from it. He glanced at Vladimir's external control panel to ensure his stabilizer jets were not on standby.

"Switching video to you guys." He used his wrist control to change the view inside his visor to a camera in the conference room above. He moved it to the left side so he could still see the explosive on the right. Sweat trickled down Ruby's face. Barry's was redder than usual. Becky paced back and forth behind the chairs. Elroy's eyes stared off screen where the monitor from his helmet camera showed the others what he was seeing.

A knock at the door made everyone jump, including Detach. Becky cocked an ear to the door. "It's the video guys."

Ruby rubbed at the deep lines between her brows. "This would be great copy for them."

"They've missed most of the major events on this trip." Barry glanced around the room and his gaze ended at Detach. "If we let them in, let's keep our feelings about the ship layout out of it, okay?"

"What do you mean?" Elroy said.

"Until we solve the mystery of what's wrong with the wreck, let's keep it to ourselves. I have a feeling the result might create a lot more publicity than we need." Barry eyed the door off screen.

"As if we'll be around to worry about it." Detach meant it to be a joke, but it fell flat.

"Give me a chance to think." Elroy paced out of camera view.

Before anyone else could object, Barry opened the door and
211

let the videographers in.

"Hey, there." Ruby stood and addressed the newcomers. "You guys missed all the fun, so far."

"What's going on?"

"See that thing on the monitor?" Barry pointed to Detach's right with his laser pointer.

"Looks like a big oh…" The lead cameraman fell silent.

"That, my friends, is some kind of depth charge. Our two divers are presently trapped inside the wreck. That gap around the explosive is their only way out."

"How did—"

"Hey guys, quiet. We'll fill you in later. I need to concentrate." Back in view again, Elroy waved his hand at them.

"What we have here is a predicament," Barry said with a much better W.C. Fields voice than Detach could manage.

"Aarr matey, aarr!" Detach added, eliciting chuckles despite the obvious danger.

"I need to get down there with my tools," Elroy said. "You have another suit?"

"Unfortunately, they're wearing both of them," Ruby said.

"How about conventional gear?"

"No way, especially if you haven't had intensive training and conditioning. That's three hundred feet, well below the safety envelope for conventional diving gear. Besides, the temperature and currents would knock the crap out of you, even if you made it down there," Barry said, matter-of-fact. "Besides, the complications of decompression, we have no conventional gasses to help you out. The breathing gear for the suits uses entirely different technology."

The videographers perked up at that statement. Ruby glared at Barry and he winced, mouthing "Oops."

"Hey pirate," Elroy peered at the screen, "get in for a closer look."

Detach moved to the object and a swirl of silt flowed past the camera lens.

The device had wedged itself into a large dent in the hull. It partially blocked the hole to the outside, creating a quarter-moon shape, jagged and uninviting. Detach moved around, spotting a round lump projecting from it, closing the moon shape even further.

"Hold it there," Elroy said.

Detach froze with the camera centered on the round lump.

"That's the depth trigger. We don't want to touch that, okay?"

"That trigger housing's going to make it difficult for us to squeeze around the device without rubbing against it, but I noticed that the area around it is severely corroded and there's layers of metal peeling away. This isn't like the clean one we saw a while back, set for four-hundred feet."

"How about this, we carefully peel away the metal around the hole to make the opening larger?" Vladimir asked.

"Give it a try, but be extremely careful not to disturb the charge," Elroy said, his voice shaky.

Using the full potential of the high-tech gloves, Detach and Vladimir broke away chunks of the corroded hull plating, careful not to let any pieces fall toward the explosive. They had to stop at an I-beam running the length of the opening, too thick to break loose. They backed off and he groaned. "We can't get by without rubbing against the trigger."

"Go under the thing and let me see what's holding it up," Elroy said.

Detach moved under the device and it looked like it would come down any minute.

"This isn't good!" Detach could not keep the frustration out of his voice.

"You might not want to yell, Dearie." Ruby coughed and continued. "The slightest thing could set it off or make it fall. I need a cigarette, bad."

"It doesn't look like it would take very much to drop that thing right in your laps." Elroy sniffed and his face filled Detach's monitor. "About how far down is it to the floor beneath."

"Actually the floor used to be a bulkhead... no, the inner hull, apparently. Who knows? Anyway, I'd say about seven or eight feet."

"Move up to the trigger again, as close as you can get without touching it."

The device hung above him, taunting. Detach approached it, inching up as slow as his thrusters would allow.

"There." Elroy said. "Don't move."

Detach froze.

"See that corrosion at the base, sort of like a flower?"

"Yup."

"Very gently, with your finger, try and break it away, see if we can expose any fresh metal."

Detach lifted his gloved finger to the layered corrosion and broke off a chunk.

"Whaaa?" Cloudy water swirled outside with the current. Elroy groaned faintly as the explosive moved. "Uh oh."

Detach did a silent prayer as the explosive settled.

A new voice said, "What was that sound?"

"We have mikes on the outside of the suit so we can hear whale song, things like that." Ruby nodded to the screen. "However, in this case, they're off. What you just heard was what they heard from inside their suits."

"If it was that loud, that whole thing could be coming down on them."

"Can you guys stop talking like that?" Detach said, a note of pleading in his voice.

"How heavy are these things?" Vladimir said.

"That one's several hundred pounds, by the looks of it." Elroy answered. "But it's not standard, so who knows?"

Vladimir cursed again in Russian.

"Hey." Detach faced Vladimir. "I know what you were thinking, friend, but no way."

"Yes. If one of us held it up while the other squeezed through..." Vladimir started to say.

"Too risky. That thing's way too corroded." Elroy disappeared from the screen, paced again.

"Do you think the explosive may have lost its integrity?" Barry said.

"Depends on what they used in it. All I can tell you is that I don't know for sure, and we don't have time to find out."

"Hey guys, maybe..." Ruby held up the suitcase.

"The sensor switches!" Detach pointed at Vladimir's chest controls.

Detach noted the camera operator's confused expression on his video link with one eye, keeping the other eye on the explosive. "They're designed to reset a malfunctioning sensor in each suit. A design bug. They can also shoot us straight to the surface." Detach grinned and added, "Our intern, James Broce, can appreciate that."

"I heard that." Broce's face appeared on the camera and he glared at Detach.

"That's risky." Elroy voice came through calm and professional.

"Not much choice." Detach pointed to the explosive. "I mean, what else are we going to do?"

Vladimir eased back and floated a few feet from Detach. "I agree."

"How about going to a safe distance and cutting through?" Barry's eyes lit up.

"No good." Elroy said.

"Why?"

"What if he cuts through the hull into another explosive?"

"Oh, crap." Barry's face sagged. "You have a point there."

"It shouldn't be a problem if you pick a wall that is straight up and down," the video guy said.

Detach recognized the gaping flaw in their plan immediately. "If we try to go back and find a place that is up and down, we still can't be sure if it is hull or bulkhead. We might waste a lot of time cutting into the next room."

"At least here we can see what you're dealing with," Barry said. "And, I might add, you sure don't want to light the torch too close to that bomb. All that electronic noise could set it off."

Detach wondered about their radio and video signals, which were not normal signals and technologically beyond what the rest of the world was aware of, but still, but he did not want to broach the subject. It was bad enough what they faced already. Then there was the obvious problem in the layout of the ship, which gave them no reference points. This had to be their best way to get out, with light on the other side of the hole. He would rather take a chance on being blown up than to crawl through more tight spaces. "What's the plan?"

"See the open space on each side of the trigger?" Ruby asked. The depth charge cut the quarter moon shape in half with the lump of the trigger in the middle. "Considering the bomb, do you think you can squeeze through with the room you have to work with?"

Since the device had shifted, the gap had opened up enough for him to squeeze through on either side of the trigger. However, in doing so, he would scrape against the device and probably dislodge it.

Detach turned to the Russian. "What you think, Vlad?"

"Da. One of us on each side? At the same time?"

"That's the idea."

"When I let my boss in Moscow talk me into this, I had no idea what I was in for."

Detach grinned. "Neither did I."

Ruby drew his attention on the left side of his visor.

"This has to be coordinated. If you two squeeze through at the same time, and the bomb starts to slip, I simply hit the switch and as soon as you're free, zoom, up to the surface." She turned to Elroy. "How many seconds for it to hit the bottom?"

"About two," Elroy said. "Hey Pirate, how deep did you say that suit'll go?"

"Started to notice a slight strain at a —"

"Deep enough." Ruby steadied herself against the bulkhead.

Elroy, fully back in the camera frame, did some quick calculations with his fingers. "It all depends on how much explosive is still intact. The thickness of the casing will also affect the concussion." He stared straight into the camera, his eyes on Detach as if he were in front of him. "I really don't know what to think. Then there's what's left of the hull that *might* help shield you a bit, if it doesn't make it worse."

"I don't see as we have any other choice." Detach almost threw up his hands, then realized where he was.

"I agree." Vladimir said. "The way I see it, if we can get a small start, we might be able to survive the explosion."

"Well pilgrims, let's get the show on the road." Detach did a very bad John Wayne, even worse than his W.C. Fields.

"Get right up there, as close as you can." Ruby hacked out a loud cough.

If Detach could have crossed his fingers, he would have, but he needed to grab onto the metal and prepare to slide past the deadly canister. Next to him, Vladimir grabbed for the edge.

"We are ready," the Russian stated.

"Now, turn your stabilizers to standby."

Detach pressed a button on his wrist controller.

"On my count...one..."

Detach squeezed the sharp edge of the hull plating.

"Two..."

He took a deep breath.

"Three!"

Detach pulled with all his might. When he slid past the explosive, it broke free and started its deadly tumble. Just as his boots slid past the outer hull, the stabilizer jets whined and he lost all control of the suit. Gravity pushed him down into his boots, his stomach did a lurch and the suit shot toward the surface.

A loud thump hit him like a hammer and propelled the suit up in a crazy spiral. Everything went black.

THIRTY-EIGHT

Blackness turned to gray. A frantic ringing penetrated murky, slow-moving thoughts. Sensation returned, a feeling of something crushing his chest. Detach forced his right eye open, and saw a face, mouth moving. *Do I know that face?* He closed the eye again and felt a sudden gush of air. Faint sounds beyond the loud ringing in his ears slowly became clearer. With open mouth, he took in the fresh air that gave him another burst of energy, enough to open both eyes at the same time. The same face looked at him, the mouth moving, and more of that muffled sound. A few words broke through.

"Christ, I think he's gone deaf." The voice sounded familiar. *Is that an angel looking down on me?*

Awareness returned in a rush. Through the ringing, the talking became more distinct.

"It's a wonder he's not deaf after that hotel thing the other night." Ruby stood a few steps back and puffed on a cigarette as she leaned over her suitcase controller. "He's okay. All of his vitals are fine."

He closed his eyes and grinned. *Thanks for the concern, Ruby.*

"They didn't get the full force of the charge. That thing didn't go off as hard as I thought it would." Elroy said.

"Are you kidding?" Barry looked over the side.

"It wasn't exactly a dud, but the geyser should've been bigger." Elroy spread his hands. "Maybe that old hulk had more structural integrity than I thought. Or, whatever they loaded it with wasn't as powerful as I assumed."

Detach caught a whiff of cigarette breath and opened his eyes

219

to see Ruby hovering over him. She doubled as the expedition nurse only because she took a semester of nursing at a vocational school before he was born.

"The vitals are fine, but let's get these suits off them to make sure." Ruby pulled away and took another puff on her cigarette.

"They're stunned, but seem to be intact," Becky said.

A few hours later, the TV crew had left for the night and Detach sat at the conference table, glancing at Jams' worried face on the plasma screen. Everyone was there, including Vladimir. He had invited the Russian to stay, and he sat across the table, tapping his fingers on the polished surface.

"You'll have to explain what you mean by 'something ain't right.'" Jams glanced from Detach to Barry.

"We have major discrepancies in the hull structure, there's Cyrillic writing on the tools and bulkhead, and the boiler room's empty." Barry hesitated, tapped his laser pointer on the table, and continued. "The dimensions and some of the features seem to be right, at least on the outside. After all, it had unique propellers that were salvaged years ago."

"Unique?" Jams asked.

"Yeah. The Lusitania originally had three blade bolted-on propellers. They didn't perform very well, so the owners replaced them with a four-blade cast design. They were salvaged in the thirties, I think, and have been positively identified." Barry took a breath. "There's plenty of debris visible on the outside of the wreck, including one of the boilers, but it's apparently in the wrong place since they found the real boiler room empty. The name's still visible on the bow and stern. The ventilator arrangement's close, though there are some differences, and a host of other features seem to ring true at first glance. The dimensions are about right, despite the twist in the hull."

"What's this all mean?" Jams waved a hand, prodding him along.

Barry's blue eyes gazed in the distance, his mind preparing for the bombshell Detach knew he would drop. He already guessed what Barry would say.

"Okay, here goes." He looked around the room. "Because of

the depth, no one until now has been able to look closely at the wreck. Dr. Ballard's robots did a fantastic job but they had to deal with the currents, the nets, and their lifelines. Their maneuvering was severely limited and they couldn't probe far inside the hull. They also went under the assumption that it was the original ship. Many divers over the years have also been down for short dives here and there and found stuff. Now," he nodded at Detach and Vladimir, "we blew that out of the water...excuse the pun. For the first time, we were able to get past the outside of the wreck, probe deep inside, right to its true nature."

"Okay," Jams said patiently. "What's the verdict?"

"That wreck down there," Barry looked around the room and then at Jams, "is *not* the *Lusitania*."

THIRTY-NINE

Stunned silence filled the room like a thick fog. The creaks and groans from the ship's superstructure reminded Detach that he still had his hearing. When he could stand the silence no longer he said, "We're on a secure link again, right?"

"Absolutely," Jams said over the plasma monitor.

"I had a bad feeling about this before we left Galveston, but didn't really expect to confirm my suspicions. I figured I was just being paranoid."

The way Barry held his head gave Detach the impression of vindication. He could not blame him, especially now.

"If word gets out, this will change the history books." Jam's drummed his fingers on his shiny desk.

"I'd say," Becky looked at her dad, "it definitely upsets our plans."

"Are you sure it is not the real ship?" Vladimir gripped the table, steadying himself.

"Good question." Barry nodded to him and stood. "Since the beginning, I've thought things didn't look right. As I mentioned before, all the discrepancies with the ventilator holes, the portholes. Though they're roughly in the right places, the deterioration and twisting of the ship cannot account for them being where they shouldn't. Also, there has never been a salvage operation to remove the boilers. They would've had to cut massive holes in the hull to get them out. Then there's the Russian writing on everything inside. The ship was built in Liverpool and never got within a hundred of miles of Russia. Finally, you two saw it firsthand navigating through the insides, everything was not where it was supposed to be, according to the original deck plans."

"Well..." Tapping his laser pointer on the table, Detach thought a moment then looked up. "I think we need to pack up and do some discreet investigating. I've smelled something funny about this deal from the start, especially after finding out Mad Jake was here. It has a lot more significance than it did before."

"It's your call. Have a story for the media?" The boss in Houston peered through the electronic ether.

"Simple." Ruby said. "We tried, had too many technical problems and ran out of time and money, or some such bull."

"Heh heh heh." Jams rocked from side to side in his chair. "It'd be entirely believable to give up."

"After today, I do not mind telling you, I have had my fill of diving for a while," Vladimir said. "I will miss every one of you back in Moscow."

Detach felt a pang of regret at the thought of the Russian going home.

"Oh, by the way," Jams said. "Thought you'd want to know I discovered something about your friends."

The larger than life eyes on the monitor aimed at Vladimir.

"Not the SVR, true?" Vladimir asked.

"Igor Romanov, an old adversary. They call him Karandash."

"Romanov...Romanov..." Vladimir's eyes darted back and forth. "I know of this man, Igor "Karandash" Romanov. One of the most powerful and vicious Russian Mafia figures to emerge from the breakup of the Soviets. He has his hands in every illegal activity from spying, smuggling, to mass murder. He fancies himself as a descendent of the Czar, though I doubt Romanov is his real last name. His killing style is legendary in the criminal world."

"What would that be," Elroy asked.

"He got the crazy idea to steal our suit technology. Someone must've tipped him off. When his cronies deserted you, they headed to Morocco. Never made it. They were found yesterday in a tidal marsh near Rota, Spain. His people jabbed pencils in their eyes and mutilated their bodies while still alive." A pencil appeared in Jam's hand and he twirled it between his fingers.

"Aha, so you know." Vladimir held up a hand. "Karandash is the Russian word for pencil."

Jams leaned back from the camera and stretched. "Lucky for me, he has a short attention span...oh, and a few diversions to keep him busy." His gave a wicked grin but did not elaborate.

"I am willing to bet my new boss at the university was strong armed into making them part of my team. He...my boss, that is, seems to be a true academic."

"Okay." Detach nodded at the Russian then to the group asked, "What time is it?"

"Five thirty A.M.," Ruby looked at her watch.

"We can go ahead and announce the end to the public, but I'd like to stay around one more day to do some investigating in town. We may be able to dig up more clues." Detach turned to Jams. "Hook us up with Mildred. She may be able to help."

"Done," Jams gave a devious grin. "So anyone want to hear some Cannibal Corpse?"

Detach joined the room in an emphatic "No!"

Jams laughed and the screen went blank.

After sleeping several hours, they made their way ashore. By seven that night, Detach, Becky, Elroy, Vladimir, Ruby, and Broce sat together at a large table in an eatery in Kinsale.

"You heading back tomorrow?" Detach put his hand on Vladimir's forearm.

"I have to, my friend. There is no more justification for staying. I am also sure the *Novosibirsk* would love to continue to more profitable ventures."

"We need to stay in touch, I have a feeling we may need you again," Detach added, and Becky gave him a thumbs up. "This Russian connection may lead to some real strange places."

"Glad to." Vladimir eyed the room with suspicion. Lowering his voice, he took out a pen and wrote something on a paper napkin. "Here is a way to get hold of me discreetly. This address is a secret email account I set up while I was still with the SVR. But first, you have to log on to this web site." He pointed to a web address added to the paper. "It is a popular sex fetish site from Moscow."

"Is it in English or just Russian," Detach said.

"English, of course. Most of the users are Americans or British."

Detach exchanged a surprised glance with Becky.

"Use the AVS secure system to get in. I will set up a username of...Vlad. Your password will be VpLusitania, case sensitive. It will log you into the site but will mask you from the operators."

"Huh?" Detach arched an eyebrow.

"No worries." Vladimir smiled. "We have our, how you say... hackers too, as your recent election indicated."

"Fetish site?" Ruby, leered across the table at Broce, ignoring the crack about the election.

Detach noticed the young man squirm in his chair and suppressed a grin.

"Yes. The site specifically caters to Americans and was supposed to be used to gain leverage."

"I bet they get lots," Ruby said.

After dinner, they took the launches back to the ship and Detach sat across from Becky in the luxury reading room aboard the *Lothar*.

The rich, deep-brown mahogany shelves held hundreds of volumes from historical to fiction. Each book was sized to fit snug on the shelves so that bars could clasp across the middle to hold them in place. To remove a book, one grabbed the latch and swung it out. In the middle of the room, a large table took up most of the floor with adjustable padded chairs bolted to the floor around it. Multimedia stations popped up from recesses in the table at the touch of a button. Detach settled into one chair with Becky in the one next to him. Their knees touched.

"You know..." Becky played her finger around one of the multimedia unit release buttons and sighed. "I wouldn't have admitted it before, but I had a feeling something was up since we arrived. It got worse when we found that canvas and pump in the old warehouse."

"I had my doubts back in Galveston after Mildred and I found out Jake had an interest in this area."

"What's going on?"

"Maybe the biggest scam of all time."

"But the *Lusitania* really *did* sink here...didn't it?"

"It's hard to believe they could pull that off with so many witnesses. The real *Lusitania* sailed from New York. The real *Lusitania* took a torpedo and sank here. Those big engines couldn't have been removed just before it sank, or even long afterward. Not to mention the fact that what's down there is structurally wrong. Besides, since when did the shipbuilders use Russian tools and metal?"

"I'm lost, dear."

"I think we need to check up on some of those ghost stories we heard about. There's bound to be someone around town who remembers them, or maybe even someone still alive who witnessed something. I've seen some pretty old people around town. At least they look old."

"Enough already, it's giving me a headache."

Detach already had one. He rubbed his temples.

The next morning, as a final insult, the weather turned crappy. As Detach, Becky, Ruby, and Broce headed ashore in the launch, the fog thickened into a heavy blanket of gray. They could not see five feet in front of the boat. The pilot, Marlboro Man, knew what he was doing and Detach had every confidence in his ability. It took a little longer than normal, but they made it to the dock in one piece.

A slight drizzle fell on his shoulders and the cold, damp air held not a breath of wind. Blurry bright spots indicated lights in buildings or street lamps. Vague shadows moving through the mist indicated people out and about.

"Today, I'm the tourist, okay?" Marlboro Man said. "Unless you need me real bad."

"Naw, go ahead. We have enough people to stir up trouble." Detach waved him off.

"Stir up some ridicule is more like it," Ruby said.

Detach noticed her voice sounded clearer than normal on this cold morning.

The four friends each took a direction, heading out on a

mission to dig up ghost stories that related to the *Lusitania*. Detach decided they would concentrate on the stories of seeing the ship itself and not the ghosts of the passengers, unless the ghosts were on the ship. If a story started because of what someone thought they saw, maybe they really *did* see it. Maybe they saw it out of context. He did not know what to expect, but if someone saw something, it might give a clue to what happened to the real *Lusitania*.

The hours passed, and the sky grew lighter, but the already heavy fog thickened, shrouding the village in blindness. The temperature dropped ten degrees, making the day more miserable. Detach arrived at the predetermined pub at noon, and one by one, everyone came in, ordered tea, and sat with him at a table near the back. The bartender eyed them with curiosity, and Detach figured the news of their search had spread around town.

"Well?" Becky said.

"There's people older than dirt here." Broce's eyes shifted around, his attention already drifting.

"Anyone over thirty is ancient to you," Detach said.

"Yeah yeah."

"I'm surprised I wasn't ridiculed." Ruby took a sip of her tea. "I did find out that nobody's left alive that could've witnessed anything except maybe one person. Most of the elderly I ran into were the kids of those people."

"I got a line on an old lady on that hill outside of town, one Enya McMurty, but it'll take a good walk to get there." Detach nodded in a westerly direction inland. "Get this, she's a hundred and nine, and supposedly chased a burglar away with a shotgun three months ago."

Broce's eyes widened. Ruby and Becky cheered in unison. "Go girl!"

"My day didn't go well. Everyone was polite but scoffed me off as some kind of whacko. I heard *Ghostbusters* a few times. Two people told me the same thing. That old lady you mentioned." Broce nodded at Detach.

"Yup," Becky said.

"Me too," Ruby waved her cigarette. "That's the one."

"We have a start. I hope she's not senile." Detach said.

"Handling a burglar with a shotgun at her age?" Becky made a gun sign with her thumb and index finger and aimed at him. "I doubt it."

"Heh heh. Reminds me of Gladys Henson." Detach recalled his trip to New York. "She was quite feisty for her age."

FORTY

The trek up the hill to the old woman's house would have been pleasant if not for the cold and the fact that Detach could see little past the end of his nose. Given excellent directions from the pub's bartender, he led his friends through the shadows without incident. Up the hill, the fog thinned and he spotted a white cottage that would make a postcard-quality photo in bright daylight. A flower garden, shrubs and trees loomed in the gloom. He knocked once on the door and it swung open. The tiniest, most frail person he had ever seen stared out at him.

A petite Enya McMurty stood a hair under five feet tall. A mass of thick gray hair on her head extended her height a few inches. She peered at Detach and his friends through thick glasses. Her hands had a slight palsy, but the eyes, amplified by the thick lenses were bright, green and full of life and intelligence.

"About time." She waved for them to enter. "I'm not going to live forever. After all, I'm the oldest person in Ireland. Did you know that? Probably not. Come, come!"

Detach glanced from Becky to Ruby and sensed their surprise as much as his at how fast word spread in the small town. His amazement extended to the tea set, carefully laid for five on the living room table, one for each of them. In the center sat a metal tray piled high with cookies.

"Sit," she commanded then went through a door to the kitchen.

Everyone found a seat and Detach surveyed the pile of cookies.

Broce grabbed one and bit into it, chewed a moment, made a strange face, and discreetly placed the cookie back in the pile, after blending his bite mark into the edge of the cookie.

231

Detach almost laughed but thought better of it as Enya returned with the steaming kettle.

"So you want to know about the *Lusitania*," Enya stated.

"As a matter of fact, we gave up on diving, but would love to get some background lore to go with our report," Detach said.

"You gave up awful quick. Letting a little old shark get you down?"

"Well Ma'am, it isn't a shark, and then there are other problems, expensive ones." Detach wanted her to talk first, not him.

"That shark creature was the best thing that ever happened around here. Got rid of those two bad men." She paused and stared at him. "Never mind. You didn't come here to hear an old lady rant about the town ruffians."

"Did you see the ship sink?" *Might as well get right to the point.*

The old woman sat back in her chair and took a sip of tea. Her eyes looked off in the distance.

Detach was about to prompt her again when she spoke.

"I remember it as if it was yesterday, even though I was only four years old at the time. And no, I don't have a photographic, or as they call it, an eidetic memory. It was just the most awful thing that could happen and gave me nightmares for years." She tapped the side of her head. "It imprinted, right here. So many people, gone." She frowned. "No, I didn't see the ship sink. Well, yes I did, but not what you think."

"Wow," was all Detach could think to say.

"Oh, yeah." She took a deep breath. "The day of the sinking, I was playing in the garden when I heard the bells. My mother came out of the house and ran to the lane as a man came by. They talked for a moment and she started crying. I had no idea why my mother was so sad."

She sat her shaking tea cup down.

"According to my mother, it wasn't until four days later that we went to town. All I remember was seeing bodies lined everywhere. Years later, I learned they buried some of the victims here at St. Multose Church, and the rest went on to Queenstown. For the next few days, I vaguely remember my father talking about the bodies floating up on shore at the beach. Awful, just awful."

"That's amazing. I can barely remember a thing from when I was four," Detach muttered under his breath.

"Huh." Enya glared at him and continued. "It was three months later, fall was coming and it was starting to get colder. I'd just turned five. I was up early in the morning, sneaking a sweet from the pantry. I went outside to eat it and stood at the edge of the garden. I would sometimes wake early to go out and watch the fishermen take their boats out. Back then, because of the war, they weren't going out that much because of the submarines, but sometimes. Anyway, I looked out across the sea, and there it was."

Detach tensed.

"It looked like a bunch of boats out on the water, and they floated around a sinking ship, a very big one." She blinked and took another sip of her tea.

"Did it look like an ocean liner?" Ruby pulled her hand to her mouth, as if to take a drag from a cigarette, then dropped it.

"Don't keep interrupting me, child," Enya snapped. "Where was I...?" She thought a moment and continued. "I remember seeing a hook-shaped rudder, shiny propellers, the ship silhouetted against the rising sun. But the ships didn't seem to be doing anything, just watching the other one sink. At that distance, and as a five year old, my imagination may have been playing tricks on me. The image is still so vivid. Funny because I can't remember what my bedroom looked like back then, yet I remembered that unsettling sight out on the ocean."

Detach exchanged glances with each of his friends. Even Broce was arching an eyebrow.

"I remember later seeing pictures of the *Lusitania* in the paper and it had big smokestacks on it. This one didn't. The top of it was flat. I couldn't say anything to my mother or I'd get in trouble, but I was just old enough and lucky enough to attend school. I blurted it out in class. Being a kid, nobody listened to me. I became the laughing stock of the school, but I couldn't stop thinking of it.

"For years I thought about that morning. It was burned into my memory. The town would've still been in the dark and the point blocks the harbor from that line of site. I figured the lighthouse must've seen it but the old coot running it at the time told me later that he'd seen nothing." She shook her head.

"What happened then?" Detach kept his voice gentle.

"I was just a kid with an active imagination. Some said I hallucinated, while others were convinced I saw a ghost. I guess that's how the original ghost story got started."

"You were labeled crazy?" Becky looked sympathetic.

"For the most part, yes. I would've been fine if I'd just shut up and kept it to myself, but as I got older, the subject came up once in a while and I stuck to my story. It wasn't until the thirties that everyone seemed to forget." Enya looked into the distance again. "So, I didn't see the *Lusitania* sink a second time, three months later. Or, did I?" She looked intently across the table at Detach.

Not willing to tell her what they found on the seabed yet, he said, "For what it's worth, we don't think you're crazy."

"Well, young man, thank you. Just one thing please." She stared at him for a long moment. "When you discover the truth, would you let me know?"

The old woman *knew* he was holding back. He made up his mind that she was a sharp cookie and he would not be able to lie to her. Somehow, he would let her know the truth, if he ever found out. Besides his own curiosity, he had a sense of urgency to discover the truth before this woman passed. Though she looked better than some eighty year olds, she was still over one hundred years old and very frail. It was still hard to believe she chased off that burglar.

They walked back down the hill into town. Broce spoke up first. "What a character. I'm glad we didn't piss her off."

"This thing's getting crazier by the minute," Detach said.

"How can a ship sink twice?" Becky threw her hands in the air. "Or for that matter, why sink one ship right on top of another one?" She hesitated a moment then added, "And if so, where's the second ship?"

"This whole thing is giving me one headache right after the other," Detach groaned. "And what makes it smell like a rat, is old Mad Jake."

FORTY-ONE

A hum of activity buzzed around Detach. He stood on the fantail of the *Cooper*, the crews of the *Cooper* and *Lothar* preparing for the trip home to Galveston. The weather had relented again and set them free from the oppressive fog, he took in the green vista of the Irish coast. The Old Head of Kinsale rose from the flat sea in the distance, and the lighthouse stood sentinel. A few Irish boats milled around, looking for the creature. The *Novosibirsk* had left a few hours before, leaving an empty gap in their circle of ships. It always saddened Detach when things wrapped up, especially when they could not complete a goal. They had experienced failures in the past, but in this case, he was thankful there were no permanent casualties.

Detach gathered the team in the conference room while Marlboro Man attended to the ship. The TV crew hitched a ride back to shore, disappointed the expedition had ended. Ruby gave them a highly edited version of the tapes from their dive after Detach and Vladimir re-recorded some of the earlier audio where they found the Russian writing.

"You get that bug off the hull?" He turned to Broce.

"Long time ago. Piece of cake." The intern nodded.

"Geez." Detach slapped the table. "Never did get back with Mildred yet. We missed our satellite appointment."

"She's visiting her sister in Phoenix today and tomorrow." Becky twirled in her chair.

"What do we do now?" Barry said.

"Pffft." Detach grimaced. "I guess we have to do some detective work."

"Are we *really* finished here?" Broce sighed and flipped his hair back off his forehead.

"Pretty much. Somehow, I think the Mad Jake angle is our only bet right now. Though I've seen little direct evidence, I smell him all over this." Detach looked at Broce. "He and his history are back home."

"We never did get back with Zork and Dork." Becky said.

"Yeah!" A twinge rippled through Detach's body. He reached for the keyboard set into the conference table and typed out the codes to connect to their telephone back home. In a matter of seconds, he had both men on the line. "What you have for us?"

"Teheheheh." Sniggering penetrated the background noise. "Oh...ah...it took a little work," Zork answered, followed by more sniggering. "But here it is."

There was a pause and Detach knew it was for dramatic effect. If he had been face to face with him, he would have to fight hard not slap him up the side of the head.

"Rubberized canvas bags, a large pump, and the smell of diesel?" Zork asked as if Detach should already know.

"Well, maybe diesel, so what?"

More sniggering in the background. "Didn't you watch that *Titanic* special a while back where they brought up that chunk of hull?"

"A long time ago, yeah."

"Add those three together, and you're going to raise something *very* heavy off the seabed," Dork cut in.

Detach heard the sound of a struggle and the two arguing on who should have dropped the bombshell. Then, what Dork said hit him like a nun slapping him with a ruler, though he was not Catholic. "We've been had! Jake pulled a fast one."

"Whatever dude," Zork broke in. "The usual payment?"

"I don't believe it!" Detach hung up. "This can't be!" When nobody responded, he said it again.

"All right already!" Becky broke the silence. "Now tell us. What is going on?"

"Mad Jake *stole* the *Lusitania*?" Barry slid his chair back and stood. "You've got to be kidding."

236

"I don't know how it could be possible, but it's starting to look more and more like he did." Detach's head swam, his thoughts coming in a blur.

"I'm no expert on such things, but come on now," Elroy said. "If he was going to go through all the trouble to steal a sunken ship, then why sink another one in its place?"

"I don't know. This just can't be right...I don't know," Detach threw up his hands.

"Time to eat. We can get ulcers afterward." Ruby gestured out the door, cutting the conversation to a close.

The stunned silence continued, nobody had a comeback.

On the way to the mess, Detach made a detour to the open deck for one last look at Ireland. He expected to see the flotilla of boats still searching for the creature, but the two American ships were now alone.

FORTY-TWO

The long trip across the Atlantic grew uncomfortable before Kinsale lighthouse was even out of sight. They immediately encountered heavy seas. Both ships took a beating from the high waves. An hour off Fastnet Rock on the Southern tip of Ireland, Detach went outside for some cold, but fresh air. He gazed astern from the starboard side and noticed a fin and shadow bobbing up, then disappearing in the water behind the ship. *What's this?*

He turned and hit the ship's intercom. "Meeting in ten minutes. Conference room." When everyone had arrived, he quelled their questioning expressions. "You're not going to believe this, but we're being followed."

"Yeah, I know," Marlboro Man said. "Been tracking the thing since about ten miles off Fastnet."

"What're we going to do with it?" Ruby rubbed her eyes. "The last thing we needs is extra baggage."

Detach did not have a clue and shrugged. "Everyone give it some thought."

A crackling sound drew his attention to the old engineer. Ruby had pulled out the card deck, and was shuffling and fanning them out like a Vegas dealer. Elroy arched an eyebrow and grabbed his wallet in a protective gesture.

The creature was restless. It was time to move on. The fish carcass cave lost its appeal. Good food was scarce, the memory of the babies that made him feel ill and the inedible white fish turned its stomach. Its ancient home was long gone and it did not know which direction to go to find a similar place, if one

239

still existed. An odd noise drew its attention.

Something about that sound reminded it of the past and instinct kicked in. The beast swam toward the source and saw the two large fish with spinning teeth that had been hovering above the cave. One made a loud noise like similar fish while the other sounded different. This fish had a different shell. There were pronounced ridges on its belly. The hypnotizing thrum reminded it of a long forgotten mating call. Would it lead to more of its kind? Would it lead to a more familiar home? The water here was too cold anyway.

The creature tagged along, keeping a safe distance.

The long awaited call from Mildred came through while Detach sipped coffee in the lounge. He had burned his lip by missing the timing of the ship's swaying and was licking on it when he answered.

"Yeth?"

"You develop a lisp?"

"Sorry, sore lip. What have you found out?"

"I feel really bad because I screwed up emailing you a summary. I sent it to myself but didn't realize because I rushed out the door to get to Phoenix."

"Uh huh." Detach grinned. Somehow, he would find a way to use that later to rib her. "That's all right. You caught me at a good time. We're somewhere in the middle of the Atlantic and the seas are kicking us around pretty good. We have a few days with nothing to do. Takes the edge off the boredom." That was a lie, in a way. The mystery of the bogus ship had made for sleepless nights.

"I have some great news. I found the Kyle mentioned in that letter. His name was Kyle McLaughlin and he worked for Mad Jake. He's dead, but his son is in a nursing home in Pennsylvania."

"If he was an adult at the time Jake wrote him, Kyle would've had to be about 120 years old or more, if he were still around."

Mildred sniffed. "His son is 90."

Detach was still amazed to have found a living person that was around back then, even though she was a little kid at the time. Enya McMurty was quite a pistol.

"Didn't think I'd find much more than a grave, and sure enough, that's what I found."

"How did you track him down?"

"First, I got his name through Jam's archives. After that, I only had one clue. Kyle used to be a pro wrestler, and I know a website dealing with wrestling history. I'm a big fan."

"Mmmphf." After another more careful sip, Detach said, "I liked a lot of the old timers, especially Black Jack Mulligan, Ronald 'Freight Train' Jones, and Andre The Giant."

"Where'd you see them wrestle? You were a baby in their heydays."

"Old videos. My older brother taped them off TV with an 8mm camera. Look terrible, but you can still watch them."

Mildred sniffed again.

"You have a cold or something?"

"Sinuses. Anyway, this website I found tells the history of each wrestler, what they did before they became wrestlers, their real names, and other facts. I'd heard he was called the Beast, so I typed in his name as Beast, and got a hit."

"That's pretty lucky."

"There was a photo of him. He had some guy in a headlock and there was blood running down his face. Looked authentic."

"They would cut themselves in the forehead to get some 'juice' to make the match look more real."

"Pretty gross. Anyway, he was from a little town in Oklahoma called Tipton. I got hold of his family and found out he'd died in the 70's. His grandson, Earl, said Kyle was real close with his son, Kyle Jr., and told me where to find him. He's in a rest home near Uniontown, Pennsylvania."

"Mildred, you're the greatest. His son may not know anything, but you can never tell. I think it's worth visiting this guy."

The moment he hung up, Detach called another meeting.

"Send *Lothar* to Galveston. We have to make a detour to Pennsylvania and the *Cooper* would be better suited for the trip." Detach nodded to Marlboro Man.

"Wait a minute!" Becky poked a thumb toward the stern.

"The creature."

"Oh, that's right. It's still following us, isn't it?" Detach arched a brow at Marlboro Man.

The captain nodded. "Yes, it favors this ship. Why, I don't know, but it seems to avoid the *Lothar*. Maybe it's the hull color, shape, or whatever."

"Nnnnh. Just great," Detach rolled his eyes to the ceiling.

"We have another option," Ruby said. "Once we get within range of say...south Florida, we can bring out a helicopter and pick you up. If we keep far enough away from the coast, hopefully the creature won't detour for lunch."

"How far would that be?" Elroy eyed Detach with amusement.

"Well..." Ruby frowned. "No idea."

"Let's give it a hundred miles, okay?" Becky said.

Detach winced. His friends all knew his aversion to helicopters.

"Oh, boy." Elroy wrung his hands, flashing him a wide grin. "How you ever survived the Navy with your phobias, I'll never know."

As much as he hated helicopters, they were a picnic compared to his phobia of lakes. It was called *Limnophobia* and he had struggled to keep it hidden from the Navy. Lucky for him, all of their training was in salt water and he never had to worry about diving in fresh water. It turned out that he was not particularly afraid of fresh water, just certain lakes. That still would have been enough cause for the Navy to discharge or retrain him to another field. He was proud of the fact that he spent a good part of his stint on helicopters. He had faced his fear. However, once he got out of the Navy, he did his best to avoid them. One day he would have to face his biggest fear and dive in a freshwater lake.

What made this pickup worse, was the thought of floating up to the craft in a harness. If the seas were too rough when the chopper arrived, it would be inevitable. "What makes you think that creature's going to stay with us that long? Maybe it'll lose interest and veer off somewhere."

"Look Sweetie Pie," Becky put a hand on his shoulder. "You know all about women's intuition?"

Detach learned a long time ago that Becky had more perception than most. She knew certain things about people, and even more about animals.

"It'll stick with the ship for a while, trust me. We'll still have a few days before we head across the Gulf to figure out what to do with it. I have contacts."

"Then helicopter it is," Marlboro Man said in a saccharine tone.

Detach bit his lip.

FORTY-THREE

With the Florida coast well over the horizon, the ship veered south for the trip around the keys. Detach waited on the deck, a twinge pulsing in his stomach, the thrumming of the helicopter growing louder overhead. He half-expected Marlboro Man to say the seas were too rough just to see the look on his face as he lifted up in the safety harness. To his relief, the aircraft came in and settled on the landing pad.

He hugged each of his friends as they came out on deck to see him off. He tried to give Becky a kiss, but she pulled away before his lips could reach her cheek. As compensation, or maybe out of sympathy, she gave his hand a reassuring squeeze before he turned to face the chopper.

With a few muttered words of non-religious prayer, he scrambled aboard the aircraft, hoping he would not need a barf bag along the way. The engines revved and the Mason Industries helicopter took off. Detach watched the two ships shrink below them. The chopper pulled away and made altitude.

After an agonizing two hours, where he did everything he could to take his mind off the flight, they reached Miami airport where a limousine waited just off the landing pad. He got out, went down on his knees, and kissed the tarmac while the pilot chuckled behind him. The limo drove to another Mason aircraft, this time a charter jet brought in just for him. The pilot greeted him as he entered the passenger cabin.

"Jock Charles." The man gave a two-fingered salute. "And no, I'm not a sports fanatic. My dad's idea."

"Mmmhm." Detach relaxed a little and nodded. "Pleasure."

"I'm your official pilot as long as you need me."

"I wasn't expecting this."

"Obviously. But the boss told me to tell you..." he hesitated, "and I quote, 'Whatever it takes to put this bugger to bed. You're after the *Lusitania*, and I'm after old Jake.'" Jock frowned. "I have no idea what he's talking about but..."

"Don't worry about it." Detach shook his head. He would hate if things did not work out, and would take it as a personal failure. Yet, he could not linger on it or let guilt eat away at him. There were too many other things to do.

"I have to ask. The *Lusitania* trip didn't go so well, did it?"

"That's an understatement. There are a few loose ends," Detach said.

When Detach did not elaborate, the pilot shrugged. "I'll bet that's why you're here." He grinned and turned to the cockpit.

Detach settled in to try and get to get some sleep on the flight, already missing his friends.

A thump, thud, bounce, and rumble woke him. The plane landed in what felt like a cow pasture. When they came to a halt, the engines died and Jock came back from the cockpit.

"Sorry about the rough landing. We're in the middle of Hee-Haw-ville."

"*Where* are we?"

"A crop duster strip about thirty miles south of Uniontown, Pennsylvania. We're about ten miles from the rest home."

"How are we going to get that last ten miles?"

"Oh, *you* are going to get there in that truck parked next to the plane." Jock pointed out the already open door. "I'm going to lock up and get some sleep." He went to the back of the cabin and folded down a couple of seats that turned into a bed.

"You have a real setup."

"Part of the job. At least I don't have to worry about being shot at in here...this time."

Detach deplaned and approached a relatively new Chevy Silverado, the keys in the ignition. Smiling, he did not even wonder how it got there. He started the truck and turned on the headlights. The coordinates were already programmed into the display on the dashboard.

The airport road meandered through low tree-covered hills and ended at a two-lane highway. The map said to turn left and as he did, he spied a greasy spoon restaurant across the road, a hundred yards down. Coffee sounded good. The light was on so he stopped and picked up a cup. He gagged at the taste of hard water and chlorine that overwhelmed the weak coffee. However, it warmed him and gave him that all-important dose of caffeine. He choked it down as fast as he could manage, wishing afterward he had mints to mask the aftertaste.

The rest home sat on a hill, surrounded by well-kept grounds, a lush carpet of green grass, dogwood trees, elm, ash, and maple mixed throughout. An arborvitae hedge lined the main drive, neatly trimmed square to six feet high. The building had an elegant look that reminded him of a European palace, but smaller.

His thoughts wandered to what he might say to the old man. His great-granddad had lived that long but declined into senility by the end of his life. He was only three years old the last time he saw him, and the only thing Detach remembered was the beret the old man wore. It still amazed him how much Enya remembered of what she saw.

A sour-faced middle-aged female nurse commanded the L-shaped receiving desk. When he asked for Mr. McLaughlin, the sour look turned suspicious.

"Are you a relative?"

"No, just here to see if he can answer a few questions. I have the permission of the family." He showed her his ID.

The nurse tapped on her computer keyboard, looked up at him and nodded, her expression now sympathetic. "Did you know you look just like that Russian guy, Lenin, but with hair?"

"I get that a lot. You know, he really is dead, just like Generalissimo Francisco Franco."

"Hah! You don't look old enough to remember those early SNL shows."

At least I'm getting on her good side. "Reruns. My older brother and I used to watch them."

"Heh heh heh." The nurse's face turned pink. "You probably

still get grief from right wingers, huh?"

"Not that bad. I think they're scared of me because of the tattoos."

She looked him up and down. "If I shake the image of Lenin with hair, you *do* look more like a biker, or maybe a pirate." She let out a laugh. "I hope I'm not insulting you."

"Not at all." Detach had an urge to fall into his pirate routine and give her a salty "aaar," but thought better of it. *No, no. I don't want to start something here!*

The nurse led him down a long oak-lined hallway. Despite the early hour, the place bustled with preparations for breakfast. Orderlies moved about, and lights glowed in every room. She approached a door and whispered, "He's an odd duck, so good luck." She opened the door and announced, "Mr. McLaughlin, you have a visitor."

Detach entered the room and the door closed behind him. The only furnishings were a TV, a painting of a terra cotta pot full of flowers on the wall, and a nightstand. A full-function hospital bed stood against one wall and on it lay the gray and shriveled form of a man with a vacant look in his eyes.

Detach almost turned around, but decided to attempt a conversation. He heard the nurse's footsteps receding down the hallway along with the hiss of flowing oxygen in the room.

The old man's eyes lit up and he growled. "Took you long enough."

Detach's jaw dropped. He saw intelligence and life in those old eyes.

"It's all right, the nurse is gone." Kyle McLaughlin Jr. said as he glanced toward the door.

"It's an act." Taking a guess, Detach said, "You aren't as *odd* as the nurse says, are you?"

"We have a live one now, don't we?"

"I have to ask. Why?"

"Oh, God, do I have to spell it out?"

Detach threw up his hands.

"You see, my son in Oklahoma struggled on the farm and it was getting much harder for me to get around. It was too much of a burden on him financially and emotionally. So, I put on the act, did the 'heel' bit."

"I see." Detach smiled at the reference to professional wrestling. "Were you a wrestler too?"

"Pfft. I was an attorney. Because of my dad, I got interested in the old male soap opera we call 'professional wrestling.' It's sure changed from back in the day."

"I can just imagine."

"A family friend knew a lot of places, good places that would take care of me." He gazed out the window. "Better than staying at home."

"So you faked your mental abilities so they'd have to send you away."

"I had to convince my son of that. It was the only reason I got away from him. I swung a deal with my friend to get me out of Oklahoma so the kid wouldn't be tempted to take me back. This place was the best spot and we happened to roll the dice the right way."

"So, why keep up the act now?"

He winked. "I can't screw em' but I can sure screw with em'."

"Oh, geez, heh heh heh." Detach relaxed.

"Besides I'm hooked to this oxygen and can't go anywhere. I have to do something besides watch TV. Can't read much anymore. Truth is, I can barely see the TV."

I'd go bananas here. Detach admired the old man's endurance. Remembering Kyle's first comment, he asked, "How did you know I was coming?"

The old man eased back on the bed with a look of smug gratification, took a few strong whiffs of oxygen then removed the mask. "Been hearing about another expedition to the Lusitania. I figured eventually that someone would get down there for a real good look."

"It's not the *Lusitania*, is it?"

The old man tapped the side of his head. "We have a smart one, don't we?"

He half expected that answer, but was still surprised Kyle admitted it up front.

FORTY-FOUR

Detach took in the stunning landscape from the window. The lush grounds stretched out for acres, manicured like a park, probably better. He had an urge to wander around after he talked to the old man. The hiss of the oxygen snapped his attention back to Kyle Jr.

"What's down there, and where's the real *Lusitania*?"

"Hold on." Smiling and shaking his head, the old man pulled the mask to his face and took a few deep whiffs. "You're tied in with a character named Mason."

"Ah... yes."

"It figures the kid would eventually hit the treasure-trove." Kyle chuckled. "He's been nosing around that business for years and never had a clue."

"You mean Mad Jake?" Detach said.

"Hmmph.... 'Mad' was hardly an apt word for the fool." Kyle took another puff of oxygen. "More like psychotic."

"What do you know about all this?"

"Me and the old man had the best possible relationship. He was and still is my hero. I'm probably the only man on earth that knows his real story. Even my mom never knew half of it."

"But..." Detach thought a moment. "How come he never told anyone else?"

"He just couldn't get himself to destroy history back then. Besides, there were still too many people left alive that it would've affected."

"What about now?"

"Don't matter anymore. They're all long gone. The last

survivor of the sinking died a few years ago."

"Are you ready to tell me what's really going on here?"

"Heh heh heh heh. I've been waiting my whole life to have a reason to tell this story." He tapped the side of his head. "The plot thickens, so to speak. The old man has a story to tell." Kyle took a few more pulls from the oxygen and put the mask down at his side.

"Old Jake was into every criminal enterprise imaginable. There was the slave trading, the illegal immigration of known criminals, drugs, smuggling, just to name a few. Something set him off when it came to the Germans. Dad didn't know for sure what did it, but Jake developed an irrational hatred for anything to do with them. It was real funny you know, back then at the turn of the century. He had black and oriental, or as you'd say now, Asian employees and treated them equally as bad as all of his white employees. In other words, in that respect he *wasn't* a bigot. But, he had a passion for hating Germans that went beyond mere bigotry. It was pathological. Madness.

"When the war broke out in Europe, he went nuts. The Germans were messing with his friends in England. During this time, he got hooked up with the Czar of Russia and had several secret meetings with him."

Detach gasped at the reference to Russia.

"Wanted to bribe him to do more in the war, but the Czar had his own problems. Sometime during those continuing meetings, the Germans sunk the *Lusitania* and Jake went off the deep end. As Dad found out later, Jake's daughter was poisoning him with maybe lead and a few other *nasties* and it affected his mental stability. That, of course, inflamed his hatred of the Germans even more. He was so pissed about the sinking he wanted to rub the German's faces in it."

"Did you say the Czar?"

"I'll get to that in a minute. Patience, young pup." Kyle took another toke from his oxygen then continued.

"Though he was an ugly customer and difficult to deal with, Jake was also a technological genius and knew how to pick talent. He was sort of an evil counterpart to your boss. The day he heard

252

about the sinking, he went to work and devised a plan to raise the ship." Kyle shook his head. "Crazy guy wanted to bring it back to the states, fix it up, fit it with guns, then 'haunt' the Germans with it. Rub their faces in what they did, sink a few of their boats— maybe blow up a few seaports, too. Dad said it was a half-baked plan, but Jake had the power to do anything he wanted."

"You mean he actually raised it?"

"Sure did. I assume since you already made the connection with Jake, you found at least some evidence he dabbled in the Kinsale area." Kyle shifted in the bed.

"Large rubberized canvas bags and a pump." Deatch spread his hands. "Found them in a warehouse."

The room fell silent except a faint hiss from the oxygen mask. A bird flew by the window. A pan clanked somewhere down the hall. *I hope I never end up in a place like this!* His eyes drifted to the old man.

"I think that was Dad's screw up." Kyle took another puff from the mask after breaking the silence. "He was supposed to clean out every bit of evidence when they were done, but in the rush to get out, I'll bet he forgot to do one last check of the warehouse and missed them. Jake wanted him to burn down the warehouse, but Dad couldn't get himself to risk the lives of innocent locals."

"I'm duly impressed. Even today, they'd consider it impossible to raise a ship that size."

"Hah!" The old man snorted. "You know how many times I wondered about that? It was impossible back then, but they did it anyway. The modern industrialized world has a lot of paradigms they didn't have back then. Jake took the impossible and did it anyway, technology be damned."

"So, which wreck is down there, and why bother sinking another ship in its place?" Detach finally sat in the empty chair, the gravity of the implications on his shoulders.

"Jake became increasingly more paranoid. In his twisted logic, *he* figured that if he could raise the ship, someone else could too. He wanted to make sure there was a similar wreck down there while we prepared the *Lusitania*, just in case. That would really mess with the German's minds." Kyle shook his head. "I had trouble believing Dad when he told me all this. Dad could hardly believe it either, and he was there. Jake's insanity cost a lot of lives and money."

"So he got a duplicate from Russia." Detach tugged on his goatee, his head spinning, still not believing what he just heard even though he had seen the evidence.

"I heard it bore an uncanny resemblance to the Lusitania, if one didn't look too close, but I don't know. Dad and his men raised the real ship and left before the replacement was laid to rest by a different crew. He never saw the replacement.

"They lifted the *Lusitania* over several nights, using a lot of diesel bags and something like twenty pumps, towed her away and another crew brought in the replacement ship. Just imagine trying to do this while keeping the locals in the dark, not to mention the ship traffic and other German submarines. A lot of bribes and threats went out to the local fishermen, local politicians, and the British and Irish Navies to keep them away. The most difficult part was that they were in sight of land and they couldn't control witnesses along the shore. I can still hardly believe they pulled it off, but Dad said Jake knew how to cover things up.

"Someone suggested Jake dress up the Russian ship instead of going through the trouble of raising the real one. That person ended up dead." Kyle ran a finger across his throat. "They say his head engineer was meticulous about ensuring the other crew sank the replacement in the exact spot, same position and all. Once they got the real ship to the surface, they had to strip fittings and miscellaneous junk off her and onto a barge. The other crew planted that stuff on the replacement just in case anyone got down for a quick look."

"The technology didn't exist then, or so I thought." Detach eased back in the chair and rubbed at his goatee.

"It *didn't* exist, except Jake invented his own, barely. Lost three good men on the original dive and lost four more crossing the Atlantic." Kyle held up seven fingers. "That in itself was a miracle that there were so few."

"What happened?"

"When they got her to the surface, she still had one funnel attached. The other three fell off during the original sinking. The key to getting the ship home was to make sure she had a low profile on the water. The bags raised her up to the funnel deck, but to keep the profile flat, they didn't want any funnels sticking up. Besides, the replacement didn't have funnels, so they needed them to stay in case someone got a closer look. Dad knocked the other funnel off himself before they moved her. I saw the book Robert Ballard made from his expedition and that thing fell almost right in line with the others." Kyle Jr. shook his head with an amazed expression. "That was pure accident or dumb luck.

"The worst part of the ordeal was the propellers. They needed them off to decrease drag, and since it was a highly recognizable feature of the original, Jake insisted they be mounted on the replacement. Dad's crew pulled them off the *Lusitania* and left them on the barge for the team with the Russian ship. Later, he heard the other crew had all kinds of problems attaching them because the couplings didn't match. Plus, since the Russian ship was basically an empty hulk, they had to drag it from Russia half submerged to keep it from capsizing from being top-heavy. Attaching those propellers that deep under water was even worse, especially when the winds whipped up.

"Until his dying day, Dad wondered how they got that Russian ship to the site without someone spotting them, despite the low profile being half sunk already. Jake had some powerful friends in England, but, those other countries…" He took another whiff of oxygen. "Not only that, but when I did my research, they went right through the danger zone where the German subs came into the patrol zone above Scotland in the North Sea and slipped right past Liverpool." He wheezed and took another pull from the mask. "Now you tell me, how in the hell did they drag that mother all the way down from the north and through all that without getting caught?"

"I…" Detach came here to find out what happened and the truth was far more bizarre than he ever imagined. "Go on."

"The trip across the Atlantic was no picnic either. On the horizon, they looked like a flotilla of cargo ships moving in an oval shaped formation. The *Lusitania* floated barely below the surface, her funnel deck at sea level. Besides the funnels, they had to get rid of her mast. The bridge, the next highest point, had already slid down on the foredeck, but was still attached by pipes and wires."

"Where did they go?" Despite all, this was the key question now. Did the old man know or would this crazy story just lead to another puzzle? Detach wiped sweat from his brow.

"Aah, the big question..." Kyle took another tug of oxygen. "That trip was a nightmare. They almost got caught three times. One time they sent one of the auxiliary vessels off to lure a sub away and it was sunk. They flew African flags, so the Germans *should've* left them alone, but by then the Germans were actually targeting just about anyone. They managed to save all but four of the crew. Beside those hazards, they had to figure out how to get her up to the original waterline when they reached their destination. Divers worked the whole trip to patch those holes in her side."

"While they were under way?" Detach had a similar experience once with a damaged freighter. He shuddered at the thought.

"Are you okay in here?"

Detach twisted to see the nurse eyeing them. "Just having a nice talk."

"I'm okay, Darlin'. Having a great time." Kyle waved her off.

When she closed the door, the old man gazed at the ceiling. "The outside divers were being trolled like bait. It was an unspoken fear that a shark was going to show up and take a bite out of one of them. The divers inside didn't have it any easier with all that junk and the bodies in the way."

"It's a miracle they didn't lose more divers."

"Did you hear Ballard's theory that the coal bunkers exploded?"

"Sure did."

"Not so. The torpedo hole wasn't that big. It was right next to the larger hole that came from the explosives they had stored in the coal bunker behind a false wall. Yeah, the Lusitania carried munitions, not that many but enough to blow a big hole in the side. They barely had enough sheet metal plates to patch it. Luckily all that stuff didn't break the keel.

"It was all the more dangerous because some of the diesel bags started leaking. Left a trail of diesel and they had to replenish it every so often. He said they could tell when the funnel deck started to get too low. Good thing they had a large store of fuel on one of the utility ships, which all ran on coal, by the way.

"They entered the Gulf of Mexico south of Cuba and headed for Louisiana. Got her someplace just west of the Mississippi delta and hit ground in a remote area Jake had ready for them. Once there, they sealed up all the open doors, portholes and began raising her. Somehow, it worked, and they got her high enough. It took thirty high-volume pumps, and a lot of coal. It's funny that they had access to all of that diesel but still used coal-powered engines, just like the ships that dragged her across the Atlantic." Kyle stopped and took a few pulls from the mask. Then he shifted in the bed.

"What happened after that?" One side of his brain wanted Kyle to hurry, but the other wanted to hear every detail. Detach kept his emotions in check.

"Took three days, but they floated her. The patch job held pretty well, considering. From there, they moved her inland, somewhere deep into the bayou to a dry dock. Dad heard they utilized an old Indian legend to explain the mountain they built around her for cover. Jake wanted it hidden so the ship could be refit in privacy. Rumor had it the false mountain was already there so Jake could conduct his smuggling operations. It was supposed to be a base for a small fleet of boats he used up and down the coast. When she finally set sail, she'd be a deadly 'ghost' weapon. Then it all came crashing down." Kyle held his hand up and dipped it with a whistling sound, barely audible from his cracked lips.

"Jake's murder?"

"Yup. He finally pushed everyone too far. Some of the higher echelon ganged up on him and killed him, from what Dad heard. Jake's daughter never got a chance to see him suffer, or so the rumor goes. Nobody knows for sure the true story. Dad admired him, but was afraid at the same time. He was too low on the totem pole and too young to get that close to him once they returned. I always thought that was a good thing. He might've been caught up in the murder, if it went down per rumor."

Detach stood and went to the window. With his back to Kyle, he said, "Why'd he pick your dad?"

"He was a disenchanted engineering student at a college in New York, a young punk. Jake heard of him from one of his instructors."

"First, the Lucy is somewhere in the bayous in Louisiana. I'm pretty sure it's still there or we wouldn't be having this conversation. My dad couldn't remember where it was. He delivered it, was hustled away, and couldn't keep track of the route. That bayou was a nightmare to navigate and he never got close enough to any local towns. He was pretty sure they were near Morgan City. My suggestion is to look for any hills or high spots near there. One of them isn't natural." He winked and took another pull of the oxygen.

"Second, I haven't a clue where that other ship came from. My best guess is it really came from Russia, but that's just what Dad thought. Might be a good assumption because of Jake's connection with the Czar. I didn't even know the Russians were building ships like that back then."

"I didn't either," Detach said, a deep furrow creasing his brow.

Kyle Jr. took another longer toke of the oxygen, blinked, then his eyes lit up. "I just remembered something. One time, Dad mentioned the name Anastasia. Don't know if it was the name of the ship, or someone he knew."

"With all the witnesses, how come nobody has tried to claim her?"

Kyle nodded. "Good question. However, the answer is simpler than you might imagine. Dad said a hundred and twenty men were involved in the raising, transport and re-docking of the ship. There were at least thirty involved in sinking the replacement."

"That's a lot of people."

"My dad spent years afterward trying to track down what

happened to the ship. He never found it, but discovered that most of those hundred and fifty people died in the war. Those that didn't were so afraid of Jake, they didn't believe he was really dead and they took the secret to the grave. There was one guy that tried to relocate it in the thirties. He disappeared in the swamp and was never seen again."

Detach nodded, filing that info for later. "Are you ready to rewrite history?"

"After all these years, I have no moral obligation to give a rat's patoot."

"Can you believe those two Irish guys are dead?" Grace said, her aged voice thin with the petulant whine of a child.

"Stop whimpering," the old woman snarled. "You don't know how to pick the right help."

Grace suppressed an urge to retaliate. She did not want to start her mother on another one of her spells.

"Is Daddy okay?"

"Of course." Grace did not mention that she had not visited her granddad for several days and had no plans to for a few more. Had her mother known, she would have gone into one of her spells for sure.

She backed out of the room and walked down the hall to the study where Maggie sat at a large oak desk, cell phone in hand.

Maggie smiled, hanging up the phone. "That was Jams."

"What did he want?" Grace Johnson, her mother, asked, trying to hide her anxiety.

"They have a new lead on the *Lusitania*. Remember, he promised to keep me up to date on things."

A wave of panic swept through her gut. She had to stay cool, find out what they knew. "Like what?"

"They found an old man in a rest home that's the son of someone named Kyle McLaughlin. Detach is checking him out this morning."

Kyle McLaughlin? Where had she heard that name before? *Couldn't be! How did they find him?*

Despite her people screwing up in Ireland, Mason's troubles

on the ship should have led them to quit. This thing should have been over and Daddy, her great grandfather, would be safe. This was a turn for the worse. They must have made it down to the ship and seen something.

"Mom, are you all right?"

"What?" Grace glared at her. "Why wouldn't I be?"

"Whoa." Maggie held up her hands and backed away, her eyes wide. "Gotta go."

She would have to get nasty. If those two Irish idiots or the Russian crooks could not do things right, she would have to take matters into her own hands. She still had one ace up her sleeve, but she had her doubts about it. *They must never get to Daddy, for my sake, and for that crazy old bitch of a mother.*

FORTY-FIVE

The welcome thump of the jet's wheels as they touched down on the tarmac woke Detach from a slight doze. Despite Jock's excellent flying skills, he wanted to kiss the ground when he deplaned at Scholes International Airport in Galveston. He said his good-byes to the pilot and walked to a limousine waiting a short distance from the jet.

He nodded to the driver, only mildly irritated that they had sent someone to transport him to the main building at Mason Industries, instead of leaving a car. He had been looking forward to the quiet contemplation driving often provided. The devastation that was still evident from a recent major storm flashed by his window. He noted the many empty lots and piles of debris still not cleaned up, even years later. The sense of guilt that his home, further inland, received such little damage gnawed at him. He knew it was illogical to feel guilty about something he had no control over, but he could not shake it. He wondered if Jams felt the same way. The boss's house was the only one in his neighborhood during the last major storm with no damage except a downed tree.

He arrived at the manicured landscaping and well-maintained buildings of the Mason Industries complex and after the driver let him off, walked inside and up to his domain.

Detach had an office with a nice view of Galveston ship channel. Surrounding his solid teak desk, a collection of ship models sat in display cases. Photos of family and friends covered the walls. Piles of papers, boxes, machinery components and electronic circuit boards crammed every other open space.

261

Though clean, the room looked like a tornado hit it. He turned on his stereo amp, put on a CD of his favorite band, *Clear Light*, and hit play. He set the volume low enough that he could hear the phone ring and went to his mini refrigerator to pull out a beer.

The chair leaned back from his weight when he stretched. He took a sip of the beer. *Clear Light* took him to a different place, a different era, one that he had never experienced, but somehow could relate to. The first time he had heard them was when he was ten and his dad had put the record on their old stereo in the den. It sat buried amongst a wall of vinyl albums Dad dusted meticulously. When the old man was in a mood, he would light up one of the various incense burners and turn on the three-foot long black light mounted on the opposite wall. Oriental tapestries covered the walls and two bean bag chairs lay on the thick carpet. He would invite Detach and his brother to sit with him and listen to one of his albums, volume loud enough that Mom had to go shopping. The music drew Detach in and it was the first time in his life he had ever stopped and really listened to a piece of music. Some he did not like but a few old classics like *Clear Light* resonated with him. He missed the old man, who slipped away, sitting in a chair by the stove with a cup of coffee in his hand, a cigarette in his mouth early one morning. Mom found him. Massive stroke.

With Bob Seal singing the lyrics to *Black Roses* in the background, he powered up his computer and waited for it to cycle through all the annoying checks and boot sequences. He opened his browser and pulled out the web page address Vladimir gave him.

A screen popped up for a Russian fetish web site. An option allowed viewing it in English or Russian. He chose English and waited while it loaded the home page. The menu choices surprised him. They included leather, rubber, spanking, enemas, and a long list of other fetishes with enough graphic images to entice one to join for their nominal fee. At the bottom of the page, he found the email button and almost clicked on it until he remembered that he had to log into the site first. He studied the login Vladimir gave him and moved the mouse pointer back up the page to a "MEMBERS ONLY" button. He clicked on it, typed in the AVS login and password, and waited.

The images that appeared on the screen would have shocked a more conservative person. An old Navy buddy named Jerry, a pornography nut, always had plenty to show him whether he wanted to see it or not. He had built up immunity to the shock.

Ignoring the graphic photos, he scrolled to the bottom of the page and found the "Contact Us" button. After typing in "Give me a call," along with his office phone number, he hit the send button and logged off the site.

The chair creaked as it went back, but settled into a comfortable position. He sipped some more of the beer and listened to the Doug Lubahn composition, *Sand*. His eyes, heavy from a lack of quality sleep, he snapped awake when the phone rang. The CD had started over again.

"Detach," he said, groggy enough not to bother checking the incoming number on the phone's LCD.

"What do you think of the site?" Vladimir asked.

"Hey, you old commie! Not my cup of tea."

"Me neither. I am just too ah…oh yes, uptight."

"I didn't expect a call so soon."

"The *Novosibirsk* crew dropped me off in Liverpool and I caught a flight back to Moscow. I was home before you lost sight of the Irish coast. The chair of the history department was not happy with my lack of results. However, I believe he was more worried about his mob problem."

"That doesn't sound good."

"He is still alive. Maybe that counts for something."

"Can we talk?"

"Sort of."

Though his end was secure, Vladimir's was not. Maybe it was the phone line, or maybe the Russian was in a room where he might be monitored. He would have to choose his words carefully. Before he could answer, Vladimir spoke again.

"What are you doing right now?"

"I'm sitting in my office chair, sipping what a connoisseur might call homogenized and pasteurized piss."

"Oh you mean American beer?"

"Quite perceptive." Detach laughed. "What about you? What's that Russian brew like?"

"Mmm, do not ask." Vladimir chuckled. "I am drinking bad tea. It is still a better choice."

"Ooh, sounds nasty."

"Uh huh. How can I help?"

"Remember our discovery below?"

"Yes."

"Anastasia."

"Hmmm. I will check into it. The next time I call, we will talk more. I have to go now and work on a lesson plan."

"Oh yeah?"

"Remember, I work for a university."

A click turned into an increase of hiss on the line, the first indication that he just talked halfway around the world. Detach wondered how bad the connection would have been just a few years earlier. "Modern technology."

An hour later, on his second beer, he sat before Jams and gave him the rundown on their trip. "Should've suspected something fishy once Mildred and I learned Jake was nosing around there."

"That's absolutely impossible and insane!"

"Tell me about it." Detach shook his head. He was still shocked by Kyle's story.

"I know he had some smart people in his group, but how did they raise a ship that large when we still can't do it today?"

"I guess he didn't have the mindset that it was impossible. He stretched the technology of the time past its limits. Seems to have been a fluke. They might've succeeded more out of plain dumb luck than anything else."

"They make every other ship raising attempt look amateur."

"What's even more amazing is that they did it right under the noses of the Irish and the British, not to mention any German subs patrolling the area. Plus, they managed to drag the thing across the Atlantic and all the way to Louisiana without detection. It's also been hidden somewhere since 1915."

"Fffff…" Jams gazed out the window. "What's really nuts is that they sank another ship in its place."

"According to Kyle Jr., Jake was afraid the Germans had the technology to explore the wreck just like he did, which doesn't make sense since it was in enemy territory. How were they going to pull that off, even if they did?" He raised his beer up and shrugged. "But, oh well. He wanted to be sure that they had something to find. It had to look close enough to the original to pull it off."

"I guess he figured the Germans might occupy Ireland?"

"The guy was nuts." Detach pulled up from the chair, went to the window, gazed on the harbor, then came back and plopped down. "But why not use the look-alike instead of doing what they did? It would've been cheaper and simpler to turn that replacement into the new *Lusitania*."

"But Kyle Jr. said Jake was going mad, especially with whoever was poisoning him. I've heard it was his daughter. He was losing his rationality, yet he had the power to carry out his twisted dreams."

"Yeah, until his people finally turned on him, or so rumor has it." Detach took a long pull of beer, burped and gazed past Jam's hat on the spoked ship's wheel.

"Crazy, crazy, crazy…" Jams shook his head back and forth slowly. "He expected the Germans, or anyone for that matter, to be able to dive on the ship? At that depth?"

"Well after all, *he* did it." *We had to use a specially designed suit that took decades to develop.*

"He bought an ocean liner from somewhere."

"Russia we think."

"Went to the trouble of sinking it along with a bunch of debris from the original ship."

"It sounds crazy to me too, but we can't argue with the fact that they actually pulled it off. After all, you saw the playback from our dive." Detach aimed his bottle at the computer on Jam's desk.

"I did."

"Now we have a mystery ship lying on the ocean floor. The

Lusitania, or what's left of her, is somewhere in the bayous of Louisiana." Detach sipped his beer then added, "What if it's been scrapped already and there's nothing left?"

"Can't be, because there are too many recognizable pieces. Parts of it would've turned up somewhere." Jams waved his hand out the window at the bay. "But now, what about all the artifacts they've salvaged off the wreck?"

"According to Kyle Jr., that was the purpose of the barge. They stripped the upper decks, dropped the last funnel, and even mounted the screws on the replacement."

"Why the screws?" Jams said.

"Too unique. If someone dove on the wreck, they would've discovered the truth from that alone. While they placed the bags in the hull, another crew removed the screws for placement on the other ship. The drag would've made the trip across the sea that much more difficult. It was obvious they weren't going to power up the ship. After all, they couldn't have raised her completely without attracting an awful lot of attention and without putting her in a dry dock, which they didn't have over there."

"Just removing and raising the propellers was an engineering feat. It wasn't until the twenties or thirties that anyone successfully salvaged them."

"Now our problem is finding the story of the replacement ship, and most of all, the location of the original."

"The bayou is a large area. I even own some of it, bought it from Jake's estate. At least twenty thousand acres." Jams sniggered and slapped the desk. "Got it for a song too."

"Jesus, twenty thousand acres of swamp and bayou...kind of the same thing."

"Like I said, cheap. It's throughout Louisiana, Alabama, and Florida, most near the coast."

"I guess everyone has to have a hobby."

"Just my obsession with the man. Besides if I own it, no one can develop it and ruin the environment. I plan to donate it all to the state and federal park services, eventually."

I love how he thinks. "Say," his eyes lit up. "Does any of that bayou have a hill or two?"

"I don't rightly know." Jams frowned and stared off into space. "Tell you what, I'll dig up the topographical maps of the acreage and let you take a look."

Jams turned to his boom box and hit the play button. A din of heavy metal band blared out of the speakers.

Detach gave him the obligatory "who are these guys" look.

"*Cradle of Filth*, album called…I don't remember. Picked it up yesterday." He smiled wickedly then snapped his fingers. "An older classic called *Midian*, that's it. It rocks!" He bobbed his head up and down like Wayne and Garth listening to *Bohemian Rhapsody* in their car.

Detach went back to his office and turned on *Clear Light* for a second round. *I wonder what Vladimir's going to find?*

The water gradually changed as the creature followed the odd fish. The sound was soothing and familiar. The strange fish's mate made a different sound. Similar, but not quite the same. It wondered which one was the female. Wherever they were headed, the water warmed and there was plenty of food. However, in a few spots there was an odd smell and it had to rise to the surface to breathe. The creature had never experienced dead water like that.

After several light and dark cycles, it tasted something familiar in the distance. The soothing sound of the big fish could not compete with the urge to seek it out. With one last circle of the two fish with the spinning teeth, the creature veered away toward the source of the familiar flavor. The dank tang reminded it of home. Now, a different hunger growled in its stomach.

FORTY-SIX

The rich smell of roasted Ethiopian coffee beans distracted Detach from his goal. He reached over and poured a cup from Mildred's *precious*.

"What kind of tidbits have you found?" He gestured to her computer with his cup.

"I've been busy since the updates you gave me from the plane." She sniffed, took a sip of her coffee, and peered at Detach.

"Oh?"

"You know, the British and maybe even the Irish Navy have been using the wreck for target practice for years. Then that American guy bought the salvage rights to it. You're lucky he didn't come after you."

"It is weird. Never heard from him but I bet Jams had something to do with that." He grinned. "I went over the videos and with Elroy's help, spotted several military-type Hedgehog mines around the wreck. That was most likely what the Navies were dropping down there. But, then there's the amateur depth charges. I wonder if someone tried to booby trap the wreck."

"Makes you wonder what they were trying to cover up, and why." Mildred took a sip of her coffee and continued. "I think the owner will get the shock of his life if he finds out he owns the rights to an empty Russian ship."

"It may be years before the owner or anyone else has the technology to go into it as deep as we did."

"Kyle Jr. thought it was called the *Anastasia*, or something, didn't he?"

"He knocked around that name but I don't know if that's the

269

name of the ship, or just a clue leading to the real name. I have Vladimir checking on that one."

"There were Russian tools inside and some of the metal plates still had the foundry name on them." Her eyes lit up. "Tell me more. Fill me in on the rest of the details of your trip to Pennsylvania."

Detach took a big swig of coffee, noted the excellent flavor, then repeated everything Kyle Jr. had told him.

"Figures," Mildred said when he was through. "With the info you called in to me from the plane, I pulled up the property maps of all the swampland Jake owned in Southern Louisiana. Keep in mind, the records may have flaws and the topography has surely changed since the turn of the century."

"Here's what we need to look for." Detach gathered his thoughts. "Kyle Jr. told me they grounded the hull and raised her with a combination of platforms and pumps. Just that feat alone was phenomenal for the time. Once they finished patching her and had her afloat, they would've required a channel deep enough to bring her inland. She had a draft of about thirty-six feet, too deep for most of that water. He didn't say, but I suspect a crew dredged a channel to somewhere in that mess. He needed to keep it away from prying eyes, so it couldn't have been on the river or one of the commonly used channels."

"That thing had to tower over the trees and everything."

"The funnels were missing and they took down the masts, so it had a low profile. Yes, it would've stuck up quite a bit, but deep enough in the bayou no one would be close enough to see it unless they were in a plane. Back then, planes were still not that common."

"We need to look in the delta area or nearby. Not a main channel, but something that can be dredged deep enough to float her into the swamp." Mildred rolled her chair around on the casters as she worked the mouse.

"Keep in mind that she was almost eight hundred feet long so it would have to be a fairly straight shot, or with a large turn radius." Detach aimed a finger at a few possibilities on the screen.

"Okay, but how would they hide it so that it still hasn't shown up on a LANDSAT or Google image?"

"Kyle Jr. told me to look for high spots, hills, and such. He believed they had a false hill just big enough to dock the ship. Covered with vines and other vegetation, the ship wouldn't be invisible from the air."

"Oh...kay." Mildred's fingers danced next to the mouse. "So, we need to look for a long and relatively straight channel into the swamp that leads to a hill of some kind, and happens to be on property owned by Jake." Mildred worked her keyboard, pulling different topographical maps out of the computer database.

Detach sat back, sipped his coffee, and dug his heels in for a long night.

"You trust that Cajun scum?" The old woman yelled from her bed.

"Of course not, Momma, but what choice do we have?"

"It's time to get personally involved." The rheumy eyes glared at Grace. "Time you gave them the old husband treatment."

Grace could not suppress the mix of glee and pride that overcame her when she recalled the legacy she was part of. Passed down from generation to generation, the Malone bloodline had all killed their husbands and made it look like accidents or murder, as in the case of Jake. Men were only good as sperm donors and once that was taken care of, they were nothing but liabilities, especially when it came to sharing the vast inheritance, handed down from Mad Jake.

Unfortunately, her own daughter, Maggie broke the chain. The crazy girl displayed scruples from an early age and it became obvious in her teenage years that she would never go along with family tradition. In a case of bad judgment, Grace had let Maggie gain too much power and now there was no way to reverse it. Though she had thought of killing Maggie, like she did her husband, when it came down to it, she could not do it.

That would not stop her from taking care of Maggie's friends. She already had a plan in motion long before the old bag thought of it.

The two women exchanged wicked grins.

FORTY-SEVEN

The morning sun broke through a light haze to illuminate the large conference room. Around the table, Detach, Barry, Ruby, Elroy, and Becky gathered for the first time since leaving the *Lothar*. Jams sat at his usual seat, eyeing his boom box.

"Can I assume our wounded interns made it back okay?" Becky said.

Jams gave a thumbs up. "Yes, and they're recuperating at home."

"What now?" Barry tapped his fingers on the table.

"Yeah, no ship, no treasure, no more bombs for me to defuse."

"We're not through yet." Detach winked at Elroy.

"Oh yeah?" Ruby arched her eyebrows. "It's a pretty safe bet history's going to be turned upside down if this gets out."

Detach repeated the events of the trip to Pennsylvania and making the call to Vladimir.

"You mean to tell me, the *Lusitania* is here in the states?"

"As crazy as it sounds, Becky, we think Jake raised the original, sunk a replica from Russia in its place, and brought the original home." *I still don't believe it myself, even with all the evidence.* Detach noted the disbelieving stares centered on him.

"We could hardly imagine pulling that off today, even with *our* technology." Ruby had doubt all over her face.

"Let's think about that," Barry said. "Remember how they were trying to figure out how someone on Easter Island put those giant stone heads all over the place without modern technology? What about how the Egyptians built the pyramids? How about Stonehenge?"

273

"Okay, those are conspiracy..." Detach arched his eyebrows. "Come to think of it..."

"Exactly. For a long time, everyone thought aliens did it until a few scientists threw away their technological paradigms and figured it out." Barry waved his hand in the air. "Maybe we couldn't do it today because the technology is actually getting in the way."

"Good point." Jams grabbed his hat and twirled it. "The evidence speaks for itself, crazy or not."

"It's still hard to believe anyone would go through all that trouble just to freak out the Germans."

"Exactly." Detach jabbed a finger at Elroy. "But you have to remember, Jake's daughter was slowly poisoning him, and there was his obsessive hatred of all things German. With his power, money, and technological edge, like it or not, he pulled it off."

"Kind of a shame," Becky let out a long breath, "we've lost so much of our technological innocence."

"So, Son, what were you able to dig up?" Jams said.

Detach punched a few keys on the keyboard in front of him and the plasma screen lit up. Multicolored photos taken from LANDSAT images appeared on the screen. Using a laser pointer, Detach launched into his presentation.

"The first image is a large section of southern Louisiana, in particular, a desolate section not too far from Morgan City. I figure someone would've found the ship by now if it docked in a more populous area. Keep in mind that we also had to narrow in on property Jake owned, and this is the most remote of his holdings."

"My God, he owned all of that?" Elroy said, eyes wide.

"No, not all of it, of course. Some of it is government land, some owned by others, but at the turn of the century, a great deal of it was owned solely by him. Today it's mostly government and oil company land broken up into smaller parcels. In fact a good chunk of it is owned by our boss." Detach nodded to Jams.

"What are we looking for, an actual ship?" Barry waved his laser at the image.

Detach shook his head. "No, no, not at all. Kyle Jr. said they floated her, brought her inland then covered her in some kind of building. He figured it would look like a hill if it still existed. I think it's still there because if it had been found, word would've leaked out. Fittings would've shown up, or something. That's why we have a LANDSAT image instead of Google Satellite. We need contours so we can see elevation."

"After ninety-plus years, do you really think it could still be afloat?" Barry said.

"No idea, but sunk again or not, it's still out there somewhere."

"Hmmm." Elroy tapped the table. "Assuming it's out there, what next?"

Detach held a hand above the table to illustrate. "Even fully afloat, she had a draft of at least thirty six feet. As a safe bet, they would've had to dredge a channel at least forty to fifty feet deep, and without any drastic bends."

"Are you kidding? In all that silt? One storm and they'd lose it all."

"True, Elroy, but apparently they managed a temporary channel that allowed them to get the ship inland. The parameters Mildred and I used were a deep channel that went to a hill or high area. The hill had to be at least one hundred feet high."

"The hill may still be there, but the channel has to be gone by now. There've been dozens of floods and hurricanes that would've filled it." Barry studied the images.

"Also true. So, the first thing we did was look for likely high spots within about thirty miles of the coast." Detach pointed the laser at the second image. Among the reds, blues, and greens, a dozen white X's indicated high spots. "And...there are several. To narrow the search, we added Jake's property lines." He pointed to the third image that had jagged lines superimposed over the image with the X's.

"That still leaves...what...five high spots?" Becky counted out the X's.

"Yup." Detach patted the table top. "The plot thickens."

"But wait." Becky squinted at the screen. "I don't see anything that even remotely resembles a channel where the bumps are. The water seems to be a blotchy looking mess with no rhyme or reason to it, yet there are straight channels all over the place. Just not where we want them to be."

Deeper water showed black on the image against the highlighted reds, blues and greens that exaggerated the topography. In this particular representation, most of the water was green-tinted off-white, indicating shallow water or inlets overgrown with swampy foliage. "That's the tricky part." Detach pointed to the fourth image. "After a lot of study, we noticed vague patterns to some of the blotches. Here for instance." He pointed to two black blotches divided by a green-blue arch. "We believe this may be a growth bridge across a potential channel. Remember, some of the vegetation floats, like floating islands. It's possible that the original channel is obscured by floating bridges of vegetation." He rubbed his goatee. "These images can't show true water depth, but here and there, the water is blacker in color, indicating deeper water."

"Do you know how deep the water is?" Elroy said.

"The average?" Detach peered at some notes he had scribbled in front of him. "Not more than twenty feet or so, probably five or six feet in most spots." He looked around the room and everyone shrugged. "Let's just say that whatever it is, it's not deep enough for an ocean liner, not without dredging." He held up a finger. "Also, you have to remember, it's been a little over a hundred hears and how many hurricanes and floods?"

"Okay, okay. Forget that idea." Becky waved her hands in a dismissive gesture. "Now, surely you have a hint of how to narrow down the search, right?"

"As a matter of fact..." Detach smiled and punched a key, replacing the images on the screen with a single one, blown up. "After a little pattern analysis, Mildred and I came up with these three possibilities." He pointed to the image with the laser. "This hill has a vague line in the water coming up to it. So do the other two."

"Which one is your best guess?" Jams asked.

"Ah...the nugget of inspiration, my chickadee." Detach winked at Becky after doing his bad W. C. Fields again.

"Come on..." Becky said with a groan.

"We highlighted the channels, best guess, mind you." Detach aimed his laser. "Notice how each approach their hill, or hump. Each is more or less oval shaped, this one kind of resembling a peanut. But, look at the angles."

"Aah!" Barry held up a finger.

"This channel comes up to the long side of this one. The same with the peanut shaped one. But this one," Detach pointed to the middle hill. "The channel goes up to the end of this hill. So tell me, how would you navigate a large ocean liner into a swamp and turn it sideways?" He pointed to the other two hills.

"You're right. The middle one has to be it. Both of the other two would have the ship turned sideways. An awful lot of effort for nothing." Barry eased back in his chair and crossed his hands behind the nape of his neck.

"Exactly. Here's the channel, here's Jake's property line, and here's the hill. A hill, I might add, that isn't on nineteenth century maps of the area."

A chorus of murmurs filled the air.

The image changed to a satellite photo. "Now this is about a year old, but it shows that spot. As you can see, it's a mess. There's a little lake there and something sticking out in the water that may be a dock. The only way to find out is to go there directly and look under the hood, so to speak. Should be a snap, as Shamblewood Mound," Detach pointed to the hill, "is owned by none other than our own boss. We start there."

277

FORTY-EIGHT

Dishes clanked and Mariachi music played in the background. Detach stared across the table at Becky. Despite the fact they were not in any way a couple, she at least agreed that this was *their* favorite Mexican restaurant. He had brought her here as a strictly professional lunch between co-workers many times, and they usually ended up being alone when the rest of the gang found excuses not to show up.

He took a swig of San Miguel and studied his plate of enchiladas, rice, and beans. Becky had exactly the same dish in front of her. It had been that way since the first time they entered the place. Yet, he could not call this a date. She kept her distance, eyeing him from across the table.

Steam drifted off the plate, rising across her face. The tendrils curled through her dark hair. She took a bite of the beef enchilada, then grabbed a corn chip out of the basket and scooped up a portion of the *Fuego Supreme*, their local brand of super-hot salsa. "Aaah!" She waved a hand in front of her mouth, then went back to her enchilada.

Detach turned his attention back to his plate and savored a bite of his own cheese enchilada. "Mmph...mm."

"You eat noisy," Becky said between bites.

Detach nodded to her and closed his mouth while he chewed. Sometimes she acted like a wife.

Becky gave him a disgusted look then resumed her meal.

He concentrated on eating quietly. When hardly anything remained on his plate but a bit of sauce and a couple forkfuls of rice, he said between bites, "Guess I'll fly up there and you can follow in the *Lothar*."

"Fine with me. I'll have time to try and figure out where that creature went. It left us in the middle of the Gulf."

"I'd say follow the trail of bodies, but so far, I haven't heard of a single attack."

"Maybe there's plenty of food to keep it busy. If it stays in deep water, the only ones that might see it are oil rig workers. I wonder what it's eating since that *Deepwater Horizon* did a number on everything in the area." With a deep tug from her beer, she burped and sat back in her chair.

Detach nodded, finished up his plate, and took another swig of the San Miguel. "I remember there was a huge dead spot off the Mississippi Delta anyway. It was there long before the oil."

"Keep in mind that it can be extremely dangerous territory, out there in the bayou."

"I can hardly believe sport fishermen, let alone Cajuns venture in there. I don't see how they can trust to eat the fish they catch in that smelly place."

"How's that?"

"All the pollution that washes down the Mississippi. All the chemicals and garbage they dump in the river upstream. It ends up in the delta and the bayous, and eventually that dead spot out in open water."

"You have a point." She took another, more delicate sip of her San Miguel. "It's a wonder fish are safe to eat anywhere in the world."

"Skeeter's and crocks' a thrivin' there." Detach spoke with his best country-singer-from-the-north's-fake-southern-drawl. He chided Barry with it all the time.

"You just be careful." Becky reached over and poked him in the chest.

"Huh?" Her eyes widened. She stared over his shoulder toward the door. "That guy looks an awful lot like Vladimir."

He turned and recognized the Russian. *What is he doing here?* Detach waved and Vladimir walked up to them.

"Sit," Becky motioned to a chair.

"They told me at your building that you two would probably

be here. They even flagged down a cab to bring me."

"What in the world are you doing here? I just talked to you on the phone the other day."

"The excuse is to tell you what I found out. Actually, I needed to get away from home for a while." He looked off into space. "I spent many years with the SVR and now that I am out of it, nothing seems right back there. Besides, there is not much call for diving research right now."

"What did you find out?" Becky got right to the point.

"First...I would like to try some of that, what you call it... homo piss?"

Detach sniggered and caught Becky rolling her eyes in his peripheral vision.

"Why? What did I say?" The Russian glanced between them.

"Pasteurized and homogenized piss," Becky said. "Detach has called his beer that for years."

"Yes, that." Vladimir acknowledged.

"Please?" Detach waved to the waiter and asked for another San Miguel. "This stuff is a little better than that."

"San Miguel? Is that not from Spain or the Philippines?"

"True, but American beer just doesn't fit in here."

"Okay, friends." Vladimir huddled down in his seat, lowering his voice. "The Czar was jealous of the British, with all her large ships. He wanted one of his own and ordered the construction of the *Anastasia* based on the *Lusitania* deck plans." His beer arrived, but he let it sit. "However, money was tight and he stopped the construction with little more than a hull and decks. At least on the outside, it was down to the finest details, including the gun placements the Royal Navy insisted upon but never implemented. They were covered up or how you say, disguised on both ships."

"That's what others have found."

"If he decided to finish the ship, there would have been a few people on the chopping block, as you say." The Russian smiled and tapped the side of his head. "The Czar's brilliant engineers failed to install the engines and boilers before building the rest of the hull. Now there was no way to install them below decks because the pieces were too large. Lucky for them, the project stopped and they did not have to answer for that major mistake."

"Hmm." Detach tugged on his goatee. "That explains the empty engine room."

"The Russian empire had millions of rubles invested into an empty hulk. Lucky for them, an American came along and bought it." He took a sip of the beer and looked from Detach to Becky, his eyes full of anticipation.

"Old Mad Jake did a switch and sunk the *Anastasia* in place of the *Lusitania*."

"This Jake fellow was, how you say, crazy?"

Detach and Becky exchanged a wink.

"Since you're here..."

"Say..." Vladimir's eyes lit up. "I would be honored to continue assisting you."

"Done," Detach said. "By the way, are you afraid of alligators?"

"Time ta' ditch da' boat." Jeremiah gazed at the channel behind them, their wake still lapping at the floating muck on either side.

"The usual way?" Charles said.

"Yeah. Sail it back to da' docks in Morgan City and leave it there." There were more boats to choose from along the seedier docks, many with no apparent owner. To quell his paranoia, he had them switch boats once a week to avoid someone seeing the same boat going the same direction.

The only transactions they had carried out in town were to pick up their loot and buy an occasional prostitute, leaving the drug movement to couriers. Since they killed the last courier, Jeremiah had to arrange the odd night delivery until he could recruit a reliable replacement.

"How bout' a cabin cruiser this time?" Pierre spat tobacco juice to the side.

"Too conspicuous," Jeremiah said with a sigh, the same answer he gave every time Pierre asked the same question.

"Yeah, yeah, I know." Pierre motioned to Charles and they climbed back in the boat.

"Bring me back some more rounds for da' gun." Jeremiah

held up a .357 magnum he had found on their most recent victim.

His two friends nodded and headed through the myriad of channels to Morgan City, miles away. Standing at the decrepit dock, Jeremiah watched them disappear into the swamp.

FORTY-NINE

Detach and Vladimir met Jock at the airport, boarded the jet, and headed for Louisiana. Detach struggled not to show how uncomfortable he felt flying. He did not want the Russian to lose confidence in him. Looking out the window would only aggravate his nerves, so he concentrated on the highly sophisticated tracking apparatus Ruby stuffed into a briefcase. With it, they would be able to get real-time satellite views, plus it would let Becky and the rest of the team know exactly where they were. Outside of that, each of them traveled light, with overnight bags.

"You are afraid of flying, no?"

A flush rose to his face. It reminded him of the time he got caught stealing a CD from a record shop when he was a freshman in high school. He could not deny his guilt.

"Do not be embarrassed that I know this." Vladimir put a hand on his forearm. "You do not hide it well, but I understand."

"I'm not sure you do. I travel all over the world, and to this day, I'd rather take the boat, but because of time constraints, I can't usually afford that luxury."

"You were in the Navy."

Detach chuckled. "I can fake almost anything for so long, but I didn't make a career out of it."

"I guess you were a better actor back then to stay in the Navy, or my KGB training on reading people is better than I thought. You had to fly between assignments, no?"

"Pfffft." Detach made a raspberry sound. "The training was very intense, and I learned a lot. Had to do a lot of things I didn't want to. When my time was up, I couldn't run out that door fast

285

enough." He eyed the Russian. "I faced my phobias, but that doesn't mean they all went away."

"Such as?"

Detach swallowed hard. *How much should I reveal?* Before he could think about it more, he blurted out, "As you know, I hate flying, but especially helicopters. I also have limnophobia."

"I do not know that word."

"I have a deathly fear of lakes."

"Ah...oh." The Russian arched his brow. "And we are going into a swamp filled with hundreds of lakes."

"I don't know how to explain this, but the swamp doesn't scare me. I mean, sure, there are many lakes, but..." He was not sure what he meant. When he thought of the bayou, the old fear that usually crept up through his gut did not materialize. Even being on a river did not seem to worry him. "I can't explain why, but what we're about to do doesn't even give me a chill. Yet, when I think of the lakes in California, for instance..."

"Do not worry about it. Let us talk about other things." Vladimir waved a dismissive hand and squirmed in his seat. "You know, we have a long history together and funny how our paths have crossed again. We used to be enemies."

"True." Glad for a change of subject, Detach said, "but despite everything, we weren't deadly enemies, just on opposite sides. I always wondered how you managed to stay in the KGB. I thought that breed was supposed to be nothing but ruthless killers. You didn't seem that way. Then again, maybe that was the point."

"The KGB division I was in turned into the SVR when the new government decided to break us up. However, back to your comment, many of them were killers, but you have to remember we are real people too. Not everyone was a ruthless killer and not everyone was nice. Just like your CIA."

"You kill a lot of people?" Detach doubted the Russian would answer that question, but he could not resist asking.

Vladimir gazed out the window. He frowned, turned to stare Detach right in the eye. "More than you might imagine. However, I will be honest. The vermin I killed deserved it and I did not assassinate them." He hesitated. "None of them were American."

"That's a relief."

"Not for me, not really. Okay, friend, what is the word...? Yes, 'turnaround is fair play?'"

"That's turnabout is fair play." Detach smiled, but it quickly dissolved into a grimace. "I've had to kill a few over the years, all in self-defense, even in the Gulf. What I was into over there never made the news, and to this day, there are only the dead and a few in the Pentagon besides my buds that know what happened."

"One of those things you cannot talk about?"

"Exactly. But I've killed more since I got out, all in self-defense. In the course of working for Mason Industries, we've drawn ourselves into some hairy situations."

"Hairy?"

"Tight...bad...let's see." Detach scrunched his face. "Difficult is a better word."

"Aha!" Vladimir's eyes lit up. "Though I learned English in a rigorous immersion technique, I have never had to use it much, and there are still a few of your phrases that I do not understand."

"To answer your question, I've killed a few, and they all deserved it as well."

"I did not have much choice either." Vladimir looked pained then turned silent, gazing out the window again.

Detach almost felt sorry he asked the question, but it confirmed what he suspected about the Russian. Though he used to be in the most ruthless organization of the Soviet Union, he guessed Vladimir's heart was not in it. He would have smiled but for his own memories and the recurring nightmares he had of the dead faces. Did he really have to kill those men? He knew he did, but that did not make the memory go away.

When they landed at Harry P. Williams Memorial Airport in nearby Patterson, Detach had enough restraint to resist kissing the tarmac, and they took a pre-arranged ride into downtown Morgan City. After checking into the hotel, they walked to a car rental agency and found a cheap four-cylinder model. Detach drove to the docks along the Atchafalaya River and picked a seedy area where they were more likely to find an inconspicuous boat. *The more unobtrusive, the better.*

287

He walked along the dock. The smell of diesel, dead fish, creosote, and a vomit-like odor assaulted his nose. A myriad of potholes dotted the pavement. Though the river flowed right in front of them, the water near the edge had a sickly greenish color, a stagnation that matched the attitudes of the people milling about the ramshackle buildings. A succession of hurricanes had done considerable damage to the docks, years earlier, and it looked like this area was going to be way down on the list for repairs.

"From the scenery, I am guessing even if we *do* find a rental, we will have to dredge it off the riverbed first, and clean it ourselves."

"Speak of the devil," Detach pointed to a poorly painted sign ahead. It read, "BOAT RE T LS" the "N" and "A" peeled off. A boarding ramp led to a variety of dirty and broken-down boats, most with oil-covered engines. Even the ones with electric motors had a tinge of grease on them. He spotted a clean craft with a newer, larger motor. It stood out among the wrecks. Despite contrasting with the other boats, it was still a small and indistinct craft, perfect for what they needed.

"Help ya'?"

A voice at his back startled Detach. He turned to see a grizzled old man with a white sailor's cap, a striped shirt, and black pants. The man had only two teeth to back up his grin, and a cigar stub in his yellow-stained hand.

"Uh, yes. We're looking for a good boat to rent." Detach said.

"Take yer' pick." He motioned to the loading ramp.

"That one." Detach pointed to the fancier boat.

The old man followed Detach's finger to the boat, looked startled for a second, and quickly smiled. "That's my best one. It'll cost you extra."

When the old man grinned, he wanted to recommend a good dentist, but kept his mouth shut. Detach paid for two days in advance, and he and Vladimir hopped into the boat, inspecting it for seaworthiness. Satisfied, he started the motor with one try, and left the dock. "Notice he didn't ask us to sign a contract?" He said, once they were out of earshot.

"I would not know about your American way of those things.

Did you notice his expression when you pointed to this boat?"

"Sort of."

"Maybe nothing..." Vladimir glanced back. "He was surprised to see this boat. The way he reacted, I believe we just rented a boat from the wrong owner."

"You may be right. Let's hope that if the real owner shows up, he'll understand." Detach slapped his knee. "So much for keeping a low profile."

"Maybe I am wrong, but my government training says otherwise."

Just like how you noticed I'm afraid to fly?

"How far do we have to go?" Vladimir asked over the noise of the engine.

"About twelve miles before we start looking for the opening."

"Looks like impenetrable swamp to me."

"There are breaks here and there where we can get through. We'll see better when we get to the spot. Take this." Detach indicated the helm.

Crawling around each other, Vladimir took over the helm while Detach opened the briefcase and turned on the locator. He called up an overhead view of their location.

"Dirmo!" Vladimir gasped. "Is that real time?"

Detach could not suppress a grin. "I don't know what you just said, but pretty cool, huh? It's our own satellite and not many people know it's up there."

"The resolution is very good."

"The on-board optics are state-of-the-art, and much larger than what you'd find in any other satellite. The CCD chip is in the higher end of the megapixel capacity, too. The intent was to be able to read a newspaper from up there."

"Uh huh." The Russian grunted. "Do not tell me you can."

"No, of course not. But it was a goal, and we almost reached it. We use it in combination with LANDSAT images for all kinds of things. You do know what those are?"

"Of course. We have stolen...well...never mind."

The two fell silent while Detach turned his attention to the screen. An hour passed in companionable silence before he said,

289

Fred Rayworth

"Okay, it looks like we have about another mile and there's a small creek-like offshoot heading east. That should take us into the ballpark."

FIFTY

The brackish green water back at the dock thickened into a light brown sludge the farther they ventured along the river. Detach wondered if it was always this color. At least the smell was not as bad, though he detected a taint in the air that reminded him of methane. As they moved farther away from civilization, his apprehension increased.

"Do you really want to be out here after dark?" Vladimir asked over the racket of the put-putting motor.

"Not one bit, actually." Detach cast an anxious glance at the darkening terrain around them.

"How much time do we have?"

Detach shot a glance toward the sunset, which enhanced the long shadows. "Maybe an hour or so."

"We will never make it there."

"Yeah, I know, but at least we can get an idea of what we're up against." Detach turned to face the Russian, taking his eyes off the screen of the locator. "Besides, it's better than sitting on our cans until morning. We wasted half the day already on the trip here."

"Is there not some American saying about wasted days?"

"Hmmm...let me think." Detach screwed up his face a moment in thought, then replied, "All I can think of is that song by Freddie Fender, *Wasted Days and Wasted Nights*."

"I am sure I was thinking about another witty American saying. I am surprised you are not aware of them all."

Detach shrugged and turned his attention back to the locator.

"This is a big river, wide." Vladimir spread his hands apart. "In Russia, we would more than likely be hiking across ice."

291

"Not as big as the Mississippi." He eyed the broad distance to the opposite bank. A huge oil tanker plowed their direction from the south, and he spotted a host of barges, some parked and some moving in different directions. Lights came on, twinkling in the distance. He shuddered. "I'm allergic to the cold."

"That madman took a big risk, bringing such a large ship so close to civilization." Vladimir jerked a thumb behind them.

"Nah." Detach waved to the southwest. "He came in from the other direction, along the coast, and the area was more remote at the turn of the century. I bet we'll have no trouble seeing the sky glow of the city from the site, though."

"We are coming in from behind?"

"More or less. The actual channel we think they used is about twenty or more miles south of us, along the outer coast. Even today, that side is fairly secluded except for some fishing and Cajun communities."

"You know, I am already feeling a shiver down my spine."

"You, a KGB agent, afraid?"

"It is…was SVR. Die, you American swine."

"It'll always be KGB to me."

"Same difference."

"Ha ha ha ha." Detach once again concentrated on the locator screen. His thoughts drifted to the water surrounding them. Though it was fresh water, he did not get the feeling of utter terror he felt around regular lakes. His fear had no logic. Maybe it was the shallow nature of the water surrounding him that quelled the terror. It struck him funny that this area was more murky, mysterious and dangerous than any of the lakes he had avoided all his life. *Maybe I do need to talk to someone one day.*

He scanned the tanker and barges on the screen, and a host of smaller craft out of their immediate line of sight. Their boat was highlighted in light green. He spotted their target opening. "Okay, commie bastard, see that cypress over there?" Detach pointed just ahead and to the left.

"See? Even that tree is sagging with the burdens of your capitalistic society."

"Hmmm." At a loss for a comeback, Detach said, "About ten

292

feet past it should be the creek."

The opening did not look like a creek, but more like a ragged opening in the floating muck. Despite the large and steadily flowing river, the water ahead of them was brackish and full of unidentifiable dead things skimming the surface. Trusting the locator, Detach steered toward it.

"Look at that." Vladimir pointed beyond the mouth of the opening.

Detach followed the Russian's finger to a half-submerged boat, similar to theirs, sticking out of the muck to one side of the opening. An air of menace surrounded it.

Once in the creek, the water stagnated. A thin green mass of vegetation, or more accurately slime, lightly covered the surface, spotted here and there with open areas. Detach guessed the width of the creek at thirty feet, jagged with bushes and cypress tree branches jutting onto and in the water. A myriad of lesser channels veered off in all directions. Spanish moss hung in wispy trails off everything more than a few feet tall.

The tracker showed the creek as a light squiggly line heading south by southwest. Their boat stood out clearly in the channel. A thrill rushed through him as he regarded the device, built with technology not available to the public, or possibly even the government.

Vladimir navigated while Detach instructed. They floated deeper into the bayou.

We're just breezing right along. Detach watched slime and debris float by, yet they moved easily in what should foul their propeller. *On the other hand, all these boats have their propellers in a wire mesh cage. No wonder.* A few more turns down the creek and the water opened to twice the width, the clear areas in the muck becoming more common. The locator indicated they would have no problem navigating for at least several miles. "You know, we could continue even after dark, but the locator would be using infrared and navigation wouldn't be as good."

"Personally, this place gives me the creeps, is that how you say it?"

"I have no argument with that. If I'm guessing right, we best turn around now while we still can." Detach noticed the fading light.

Vladimir maneuvered the boat back the way they came.

"We went in about two miles." Frowning, Detach peered at the locator. "That's odd."

"What, my friend?"

"Why would someone be tailing us?"

"Who else knows about our venture?"

"That's the question. No one else does."

"Are you sure you can trust all of your people?"

"Absolutely. The ones in the know are beyond doubt. I'd put my life in any of their hands. A leak from within isn't even a consideration."

"Hmm." Vladimir scratched his chin. "If you are that sure, then what else could there be?"

"Are we encroaching on someone else's territory?"

"We are not on your boss's land yet, are we?"

"His property line doesn't start for at least several more miles. But still, I thought most of this land was government owned."

"If that is the case, then that makes me think a criminal venture is involved."

"Now we have that to deal with too?" Detach leaned his head back. "Mmmmm!"

"How do you know we are being followed?"

"See this little boat?" Detach turned the screen so Vladimir could get a better view.

"Yes, it appears to be at the mouth of the creek."

"Exactly. I never really paid attention to it before. It was behind us on the main river and when we went around that first bend in the creek, it pulled up about where that sunken boat is parked."

"What about fishermen?"

"Too coincidental. Besides, why's it pulling out 'coincidentally' as we're heading back?"

"Suspicious."

"No kidding."

"What do we do? We do not have a gun with us."

"Yeah, I know. And that was a dumb move for other reasons too." Detach eyed movement at the edge of the creek. A green snout poked up through the mire. The large gator made him think they might need a cannon instead of a pistol.

FIFTY-ONE

Vladimir pulled up to the dock and Detach let out a sigh of relief he did not bother to hide.

"I agree, my bourgeois capitalistic friend."

Detach grabbed the bowline and tied the boat to the dock. They hopped onto the boarding ramp and walked to solid ground.

The old man waited at the front of his shack, a big grin on his toothless face.

"Sir. We're done for the evening."

"Find what yer' lookin' fer'?"

Detach shook his head.

"Well, you take yer' time now. The boat'll be here tomorrow."

"Yes, I do believe we still have two more days to use it." Vladimir said between clenched teeth.

"Where's that accent from?" The old man eyed the Russian.

"Blagoveshchensk." Detach remembered the name from the far-eastern part of the Soviet Union. Back in elementary school when he discovered the town on a map, the long name fascinated him. That lasted until he discovered the names of some towns in Wales.

"Blat....what-ski?" The old man frowned and scratched his head. "Sounds Ruskie to me."

Vladimir followed Detach toward the car as if the old man had not said a word.

Once out of earshot, Detach snickered and noted the Russian's arched brow. "Old fart was being nosy. It also sounded like he wouldn't favor anyone that wasn't French or Cajun."

"When was the last time you heard the term Ruskie?"

"Heh heh." Detach thought a moment. "In a movie from the 70's, I think."

"Why Blagoveshchensk? You managed to pronounce it correctly, by the way."

"Wayell…" He related the story from elementary school. "Sheer coincidence I pronounced it right. Figure I'd mess with the old guy's mind."

"I have been there a few times but was not sorry to leave. Not exactly a…how you say, party town."

Once they settled in the hotel, Detach suggested Cajun food and asked at the desk for a good place to eat. They walked a few blocks and found a noisy, crowded little restaurant on a side street. He and Vladimir ate to a background of high-energy jazz. The crowd whooped it up.

"We'll take a quiet walk to work off our dinner, and talk then," Detach shouted over the din.

An hour later, they ambled down a street lined with bars and small stores on the way toward their hotel. "We'll make it an early morning. Is that all right with you?"

"No problem." Vladimir yawned, drawing a hand to his mouth. "I will be ready to sleep as soon as we get back to the room."

"Me too, but before we do, we need to acquire some protection."

"After seeing those large green noses pointing our direction this afternoon, we will probably need something big enough to be illegal."

"Hah, no, no, not that bad. But we do need something with a kick to it."

"Like one of those Dirty Harry pieces?" Vladimir made a shooting motion with his hand.

"Why not?" Detach smiled and kept his eyes straight ahead. "That sounds good to me."

Vladimir's eyes shifted sideways.

"Yeah, I saw them too. They've been with us since we made it to the restaurant."

"That is when I spotted them, but did not want to give it away."

"Remind you of old times?" Detach asked with a sneer.

"Actually yes." He had no humor in his voice.

"They could be the same guys who were tailing us on the water."

"Possibly."

"They're about to get a thrill when they see us go into that gun shop." Detach motioned to a sign across the street. "Hold on." He pulled out his cell phone and called Jams.

"How's it going?" Jams said over a din of heavy metal noise in the background.

"Morgan City. *John's Guns and Ammo*. Are you still good with them?"

"After you hang up, wait five minutes and go in."

"All set." Detach slipped the cell in his pocket. "See? There's a reason we walked back to the hotel this way. We just have to wait a few minutes."

Out of the corner of his eye he caught a glimpse of two men up the street. They hovered around a newsstand, deep in conversation. What struck him odd was that they looked almost like twins, and were so average and nondescript, had he not spied them earlier, he would have easily missed them in a crowd. Their casual clothes gave them a cloak of mundane invisibility.

Five minutes passed, they entered the gun shop and went straight for the counter. Detach handed the owner a card, then his ID.

"That was quick." The man broke into a wide grin. "How can I help you?"

"Do you have a pair of .357 Magnum Smith & Wesson Model 686PP's with the 6-inch barrel?"

"Just a minute." The shop owner nodded and disappeared behind a curtain at the back of the store. He returned holding one in each hand.

"Oh, my." Vladimir's eyes widened. "They look like they will do the job," he said, his voice tinged with sarcasm.

"And then some." Detach turned his attention back to the shop owner. "We'll take two boxes of 158s. No need to blow our arms off."

"Right here." The man reached behind him and grabbed two boxes off the shelf. "These'll still make your wrist sore. They're for hunting, not target practice."

"Exactly." Detach winked at him.

Without paying, they left. Neither said a word until they were back at their hotel room.

"Goodnight." Vladimir flattened out on the bed and closed his eyes.

Detach nodded and stretched out, his only thought sleep, and whether the Lothar had made port yet.

FIFTY-TWO

A thick layer of pre-dawn haze made visibility outside Detach's hotel non-existent. He could not quite tell if the gloom was smog or just the town's usual morning fog. He detected a distinct chemical odor, reminding him of Los Angeles, which he thought strange for such a small town. Then again, this was an oil industry hub so he would not have been surprised to see a refinery nearby. They decided it was safer to leave the car at the hotel and chose to walk to the docks. Two blocks along the way, the air turned marshy. It reminded him of Galveston, when the wind carried the smell of the tidal bogs close to his house.

They woke early, found a small all-night bistro, and pigged out on bacon and eggs. Before heading out, they requested a couple boxed lunches of sandwiches and soda. Detach remained quiet throughout breakfast. An ominous sense of foreboding ate away at him and he saw the same in the Russian's eyes.

The quiet morning contemplation continued on their walk to the docks, until Vladimir broke the silence. He had volunteered to carry the tracker case and switched it from hand to hand. "This is not much different from the tropical bogs of Vietnam. I hated that environment. My milieu is snow, ice, and hazardous creatures other than crocodiles. I had a nightmare this morning. I was drowning in a green slimy pool with a tree branch just out of reach."

"They're alligators here, by the way, not crocodiles, but just as dangerous. In my nightmare, two giant alligators tore me apart, and I watched from above as they munched away at my arms and legs, helpless to do anything. You went to Vietnam?"

"Several times in the nineties. My uncle was a technical advisor there during the war. He warned me what to expect. Words were not enough."

When the Russian did not elaborate, Detach dropped it.

The farther they walked, the heavier the pistol and ammunition in his pocket felt. They chafed against his skin and he wondered if it was a wise move to leave the rental car behind. Instead of the tracker, he carried an overnight bag with their food and an ample supply of bug repellent. When he spotted the decrepit boat rental sign, he muttered under his breath, "Bout' friggin' time."

"About' frig time," Vladimir repeated.

Detach grinned. Under duress, Vladimir's English slipped and his accent became thicker than normal. The joker in him searched for a way to exploit that. *One day it'll come to me.*

They found the boat where they had left it the night before, and hopped in. Detach checked the fuel and found it nearly full. It surprised him that the boat made such good mileage with the powerful engine. They traveled at least twenty miles, round trip, yet the tank level showed close to the fill cap. "I guess the rental man fueled it up after we left last night"

"I have my doubts about that." Vladimir took his position at the helm.

While the Russian started the engine and let it warm up, Detach turned on the locator and switched to infrared. An eerie glow filled the screen and reddish blobs displayed traffic on the river. The heat sources were less distinct than the daylight visual mode, their edges fuzzy, and the shapes harder to define. "Head that way," he pointed into the river, "we'll have to circumvent something large over there." He aimed to their left.

"We will not drive right into its path?"

"Not yet." Detach managed a slight snicker as he answered. "Instead of letting it ram us, let's try and get tangled in the prop."

"We still have a shadow?" Vladimir dipped his head toward the tracker.

"Yup." Detach frowned at the screen. The tail stayed at least a mile behind them but with an unmistakable pattern that shadowed their movement.

They reached the mouth of the creek and Vladimir turned in next to the half-sunk boat just off their bow. The haze began to lift and he switched to day TV on the tracker. Though a bit muted, the image still showed the area plain enough to work. It would improve as the haze dispersed completely.

The morning remained silent except for the muffled sound of their boat engine. The tail remained on the screen. "Okay, Mr. KGB. When someone is following so far back, they can't possibly see you. So how are they keeping up?"

"A bug, of course." Vladimir smirked. "A transceiver like the one you are going to turn on once we are there."

"Yup, the beacon we'll use to pinpoint our location for the *Lothar* as it approaches the coast from the other direction. Should've thought of that sooner since I'm pretty sure they don't have one of these." He patted the real-time satellite tracker. "Slow down, but keep going that way, remember the route?"

"Da. So far."

Detach set down the case and examined the boat. He started with the bow and worked his way to the stern. He checked the inside and came up empty. On the outer hull above the waterline, he hit pay dirt on the port side, three inches below the upper lip of the hull.

"Sure enough." He pointed down.

Vladimir put a finger to his lips.

"Ooh!" Detach winced. He leaned over the side and took a closer look at the device. He recognized it from an adventure three years before. "We have Feds after us. No mike, just a transmitter."

"Your own government?" Vladimir looked surprised.

"Yeah. I recognize the transmitter." Seeing the question on Vladimir's face, he added, "Don't ask. Anyway, what do we do?"

"What *do* we do?"

"I guess we let them tag along for the moment. After all, we don't know their intentions and we haven't knowingly led them to anything."

"Yet."

"Besides," Detach grinned wickedly, "just suppose they're using our beacon as navigation. Deeper in the bayou, what if the signal suddenly went away? I know it's a stretch, but…"

Vladimir grinned back and tapped a finger to the side of his forehead.

The Russian steered through a myriad of channels while Detach gave an occasional direction. They traveled through an endless path of green slime, no clear water in sight. Detach studied the screen, and it showed a safe path, so he ordered Vladimir to plow right into it. After hitting the third slime-covered area without incident, he decided the electronic device would not let them down.

More than a few times Detach noticed signs that they were not the first to venture through these channels. Damaged branches and disturbed areas showed above the water. It did not look like the work of animals.

The haze disappeared, replaced by muggy heat. Detach had only swatted one or two bugs up until that point, when they rounded a bend into a visible mass of swarming mosquitoes. The atmosphere changed for the worse. The greenish slime floated in thicker blotches, the trees cast an unhealthy pallor, and the moss hanging from them had a brown rather than grayish-green tint. The foul smell intensified, and the light dimmed, even though they passed underneath patches of open sky.

"Did we make a wrong turn, friend?" Vladimir said.

"Not according to the finder. We should keep straight on. We still have a way to go. I hope it doesn't get worse than this."

"I think it already did."

Detach followed Vladimir's finger and spotted a telltale green snout poking out of the mire.

FIFTY-THREE

Buzzing insects, the smell of wet rot, and the sweltering heat amplified the tension weighing on Detach. He kept one eye on the tracker and the other on what lay in front of them. At least the surrounding water did not remind him of a regular fresh water lake, or he would have been petrified. He hated having limnophobia, especially in his line of work. Why this swamp did not send him into a continual state of paralysis, he could not fathom. "We have a junction coming up ahead."

"Which way?"

"According to the view, it'll be much clearer access going left, just past that dead tree over there." Detach pointed to a huge dead cypress ahead.

"We still have our tail?"

"Yep. They're staying a mile back. We're only about two miles from the mound. It's time to sever our connection."

"Why now? They may guess where we are headed."

"Maybe, but why make it easier for them?"

"True."

Detach reached over the side and gently pulled the transmitter from the hull. He knew how the device worked, and rather than smashing it, he had a feeling it would be better to save it. He removed it from the barb holder, flipped the micro-switch to OFF, and stuck it in his pocket.

"Why not toss it in the water, or smash it?"

"Don't know, just a hunch."

"Must be this place." Vladimir's eyes darted from side to side. "Sure wish we could see something above all of this mess."

305

Detach shaded his eyes and looked up at the tree tops.

"Speaking of Satan." Vladimir pointed to a large cypress tree.

"Speak of the Devil." Detach followed his gesture. "Looks good to me."

Vladimir guided the boat toward the tree and the water allowed him to approach the much wider trunk. "Hey, my friend. Look." He pointed to the base of the tree. Shiny bark from repeated boot wear led up one side. "Look for traps."

"Gotcha." Detach stepped onto a soggy mat of green near the tree. It held firm enough to keep his boots from sinking in the muck and he made it to solid footing a few feet beyond that point. He studied the ground and the nearby bushes. The search continued for a couple minutes, but he found no sign of a trap.

It was an easy climb, the path well-marked. He wondered who could have been out in such a remote area often enough to leave this kind of trail. Cajuns fished and hunted out here, but he doubted too many amateur sportsmen would venture this far out. Thirty feet up the tree, he stopped climbing and gazed to the southwest. The dark lump of Shamblewood mound loomed ahead. *No wonder this place has stayed anonymous.* Though obviously higher than the surrounding ground, it blended in, looking like a grove of slightly taller trees. Detach cast a glance back toward where they came. A flash moved in the distance. It could be their tail, but they seemed to be moving too far to the east. *I'll check the finder later.*

"What did you see," Vladimir asked when he returned to the boat.

"Almost there. We have to go around this lump of high ground and we'll be there in no time." He scanned the dense vegetation closing in on them. "I'm getting a real bad feeling here."

"We are being watched."

"Hmmm...I can't see anything on the finder, not with all these trees for cover. But I do know it's not the other guys. They're still floundering about a mile back and to the east."

"I think we are in trouble."

"Let's play dumb and continue on. Just have your piece ready." Detach patted the heavy lump at his side.

With the locator low in the boat, Detach saw they were less than five hundred yards from the edge of the mound. Ahead, a mass of cypress trees stuck out of the water. The only clear path opened to the left. The locator showed solid trees ahead and they covered any clear water under the branches. From this point, he would have to navigate from the ground. The small blip of the craft tailing them had meandered off, and lost them. He turned off the locator and closed the case.

"Vlad, try there." A narrow channel between the trees looked deep enough to navigate.

The Russian turned the boat, all the while scanning the dense growth on each side.

The hairs stood on the back of Detach's neck, and he sensed they had just crossed the point of no return into an ambush.

A loud click drew his attention to the right side of the channel where a rifle muzzle pointed out of the nearby bushes. Following the length of the barrel, he peered into the eyes at the other end and saw death. He grasped for the Russian beside him screaming, "Duck!"

A volley of gunfire rained on the boat, throwing splinters over the water. They dove for the inside bottom of the boat. Detach exchanged a glance with Vladimir. They were sitting ducks

"If we get separated, don't worry about me. Just take care of yourself. Will you do that?"

"Vlad." Detach stared at his partner. "Are you serious?"

"I am used to this kind of situation. I am trained for it. Just run. Trust me. Please?"

After barely getting off a nod to the Russian, they simultaneously dove over opposite sides into the brackish water. He swam for cover, hoping the Russian was doing the same.

Detach held his breath and swam for dear life, trying to stay under as long as he could. The water was too murky and dark, and he did not see the large tree root until it slammed into his head. The pain sent a shock wave down his spine and he floated to the surface, stunned and disoriented. Shouts echoed as the assailants went for Vladimir.

After a few seconds, he recovered his wits. With an eye out

for suspicious movement, he swam to the nearest tree bole and climbed out of the water to get his bearings. Something sliced through the water and it did not look friendly, sending a shudder through his already sore spine. His head throbbed, but the pain dulled with the surge of adrenaline coursing through his body. An outcropping of high ground stuck out a hundred yards to his right. He headed in that direction, hopping from tree root to tree root to avoid the water. With each successive hop, he put distance between himself and his pursuers. He did not have a destination in mind, just *away*.

Four new bruises on his shins later, he came to the edge of a small lake. On the other side stood a rotten boat landing, and in the background, the mound. The lake narrowed to the right, and he had to do a dance across the branches and other debris to circumnavigate it. Adding a few more bruises to his shins, he came to a gap between the roots and the high ground. He would have to swim or wade across.

A wave of panic hit him like a frying pan to the side of the head. No. No, not *fresh water*. They had been floating over it since they left the dock and it had not bothered him. He even dove in it to get away from the crazy men and had not given it a second thought. However, this was a small lake, some would call it a pond, but to him it might as well be the Atlantic. He thought he was cool with the shallow brackish water, but this pond looked clear, reviving his old fear.

"Calm down. You have to do this!" He danced on his feet, realized he spoke aloud and spun around for signs of pursuit.

He hated being scared of fresh water lakes, and this was not the time to let it get in the way. "As long as I can feel the bottom… as long as I can feel the bottom—"

Three shots rang in the distance but he could not tell where they came from. *If they're still firing, Vladimir must be giving them a run for their money.*

A quick scan revealed no creatures lurking nearby. He took a deep breath and waded into the water. It was chest high, and he had trouble lifting his boots off the thick muck on the bottom, but at least he knew it was there and could feel it. Like walking in molasses, he struggled to make the other side of the gap, and almost reached the other side when he heard a splash. Instinct took over. With a burst of superhuman effort, he shot out of the water, away from the alligator's smiling jaws. His struggling made noise, but no gunfire came his way. When he reached high ground, he turned and spotted a long, dark shape moving under the water. It turned and headed away, losing interest.

Detach collapsed onto a boulder to catch his breath and fight back the panic attack. His fingers gripped the rough stone, and he focused on the black and gray grain of the rock to calm his mind. A rush of excitement flooded his senses, squashing the panic. *This is granite. Boulders like this aren't natural to the area.* The few rocks he had seen were a different color and texture, like sandstone.

Solid ground made the going easier on the way to the dock. Though he had to dance with the boulders, he found a rough path. When he reached the ancient structure, he spotted an established path leading toward the mound.

A shot and faint yelling in the distance made him smile. "Go Vlad!" He trusted the Russian still had the skills he promised. Maybe his friend had turned the tables on them. Right now, he had to find out where the path led and maybe he could discover a way to communicate with the outside world.

A few yards up the trail, an opening gaped on the side of the mountain. He ducked to the side. Nothing moved. After a few moments, he decided to take a chance and get closer by keeping to the side of the trail to stay out of sight of anyone inside. For the first time since diving out of the boat, he reached for his gun and felt the reassuring lump still strapped to his waist. With all the struggling, swimming and thrashing through the bush, he still had it. Drawing the weapon, he shook it and sprayed the ground with mucky water. The trigger pulled back easy and he and hoped the thing would still fire.

Detach crept closer, stopped, and listened. Nothing but silence. He pushed the door open with the barrel of the gun and peered inside.

A meager forty-watt bulb gave off a sickly glow. He smelled

sweat and alcohol along with the distinct aroma of marijuana.

By the half-eaten sandwich on the table and the still smoldering joint, he guessed they had left in a hurry.

The wheels in Detach's mind went into overdrive. Did they know ahead of time that he and Vladimir were out there? They could not have heard the boat that far away. He wondered if they had some kind of electronic warning device, which might mean they would also have a radio. Where would they place the generator for powering their gear and the light bulb over his head?

The room held scattered bits of debris, but nothing of value. He suspected these guys were drug runners or survivalists. However, this den had no evidence either way except the smell of the reefer. Stepping back outside, he surveyed the surroundings, and discovered a box with a series of lights on it. Three of them blinked while the rest were out. The only markings on the panel were numbers for each light. One, three and four blinked.

Another shot popped in the distance. "Go Vlad, go."

Under a shoddy metal cover, he found a ham radio setup with a whip antenna hooked to a marine twelve-volt battery. Cables attached to a charger that had a cable trailing off in the distance. A faint puttering indicated a generator. With a grin, he flipped the power switch and was rewarded with a flash of static.

He could not remember the frequency to contact the *Lothar*. Racking his brain, he gave up and randomly punched the frequency buttons. Number after number displayed but they did not look familiar. His eyes darted toward the last sounds of gunfire and he spotted movement in the distance. An epiphany struck him and the correct frequency popped into his head.

"Marlboro Man, come in!" Sweat poured down his face. He had a moment of doubt when he realized the Lothar still might not be within range.

"Where have you been?"

Detach recognized the captain's voice. "Just listen. I'm at the mound. I found it, but some crazies attacked us. I have no idea why, but they want us dead. I don't know where Vladimir is. I'm in a heap of trouble."

"Whoa, slow down!"

"No time. I'm leaving the thing on as a beacon. Have to run."

"But…"

Detach cut him off and unhooked the charger cables. He carried the radio and battery to the dense brush nearby. He hoped the battery had enough juice to last a while. He rigged the transmit button to the ON position and turned down the receiver volume. The signal would provide the *Lothar* with a beacon. Then in a sudden burst of inspiration, he remembered the bug from the boat in his pocket. He pulled it out, turned it on, and sat it next to the transmitter.

At the edge of the water, he skimmed along the boulders until they played out and the brush took over. In front and to his left stood an impenetrable barrier of dense vegetation while to his right, water. He either had to get back in the water, or return to the cave. Neither sounded appealing, especially with the large green snout poking out of the muck a few yards away.

He turned to go back to the cave, and came face to face with the business end of a rifle, held by a nasty looking man with a leer on his face.

FIFTY-FOUR

The face at the other end of the gun sent a shudder through Detach's whole body. A mad light lingered behind the coldness of those eyes and he knew there would be no opportunity to reason with this man. The feeling intensified when a second man came up behind the first.

"Who are you guys?" Detach kept his voice nonchalant, though his blood pressure spiked and made it hard not to squeak out the words.

"Who are you?" The one with the gun poked the barrel at his forehead.

Oh crap oh crap oh crap! Detach did not know where this conversation was headed, but decided to tell the truth, at least for now. "I'm Detach. A friend and I were out here looking for an old boat."

"Riiiiight." The one with the gun sneered. "You're one of them agents from the guv'mint."

The eyes left no room for argument. *I've walked into a drug operation. I'm dead. Where are you, Marlboro Man? I've got to do something, fast!*

"Pierre, pat him down."

"On it." The other one approached and found his gun. "Oooh, look at this!"

"We have a special place for you." The one with the gun smiled.

Detach did not like the gleam in his eyes.

Motioning with the gun, the leader directed Detach to the cave opening.

The one holding his gun went inside and came back out swearing. The gun stabbed into his side.

"D'you steal our stash?" The gun poked harder.

Stash? All he had seen was a single half-burned joint on the edge of the table. If he answered the wrong way, they would become more pissed off and act sooner. He held out his arms. "What stash?" He turned to face the leader and did his best baffled expression.

The man stared back. After an eternity, he dropped his eyes.

"Never mind. Charles must've taken it with him." He studied Detach a moment and broke out in a wide grin. "Let's go have some fun."

They led Detach down the path to the dock and a boat that was not there when he first spotted the lake. *I don't think this is going to be a pleasure cruise.* With no choice but to get in and play along, he did not resist. *What happened to Vladimir?*

"Your friend made a mess out of Charles." The one with the gun grumbled.

Detach tried not to smile as he asked, "Who's Charles?"

"You piece of guv'mint trash!"

The leader punctuated his oath with a blow to the side of Detach's head. It did not knock him out, but he wished it had when the throbbing stabbed through his brain. He stumbled into the vessel.

The boat pulled into the swamp, away from the mound. *I can't believe I let my guard down for these clowns!* Detach scanned the bayou for an opportunity to escape. It would be impossible with the two men hemming him in and the gun sticking in his side. Opportunity after opportunity slipped by, possible escape routes just out of reach. Sweat soaked his shirt and his nerves were strung like high-tension wire. His mind raced, knowing he would meet his end soon if he did not escape.

The plain excitement on their faces disturbed him the most. They reminded him of religious fanatics at the point of rapture.

The boat entered a narrow passage where trees hung over the water in dark curtains. Detach felt the gun over his shoulder relax. With lightning quick reflexes, he reached over and snatched

314

it. The gun went off and the head of the man in front of him exploded in a mass of blood and tissue. The crack of the gunshot produced a sharp pain in his right ear and his hand burned from the blowback. A second shot came from the side, hitting the skull of the dead man before the body could fall. The shock of the second bullet caused only a split second hesitation before he dove into the water.

Staying under as long as he could, Detach swam away from the boat. Soon, his hands hit mud. With feet down, he emerged from the water and ran as fast as he could. Frantic splashing followed but no shots rang out. He could not gain any speed in the muck, and he spent his energy making a tough target by bobbing and weaving, moving from tree to bush and back again. He did not dare look back. *Please don't shoot now!* He crossed his fingers, even as he struggled on. The way cleared and he burst into the open on solid ground at the edge of a pond. A few feet away, a large tree hung over the water and from it dangled a bloody rope.

The gun barrel stabbed in his back. "Not so fast."

"Aw, crap!" Detach had no choice but to comply.

FIFTY-FIVE

Flies buzzed around the bloody rope. A taint of dead meat mixed with the strong swampy aroma. Detach stood on the edge of the pond and stripped off his clothes as slow as he dared.

The man, who the others had called Jeremiah, pointed the gun at him, an overconfident sneer on his face. He stared at Detach's tattooed body and his lip trembled with anticipation.

Please Vlad, burst through the bushes, gun blazing. Detach scanned the remote swamp. Nothing.

"Over there." Jeremiah pointed to a spot under a large bald cypress that stretched its drooping branches across the pond. Holding the gun on Detach, he reached into a nearby bush and grabbed a long pole with a hook on it. He lifted it out over the water and snared the bloody rope.

"Turn around. Arms in the air."

Waves of panic sent his knees into a quivering mess. *He's going to hang me over that lake!* Detach thought of going for the gun, but with his back now to the man, he could not be sure where it was. If he grabbed wrong, he would be dead. He lifted his arms and handcuffs clamped around his wrists. "Who are you, anyway?"

"I told you already, Jeremiah. Your executioner."

"Why are you—"

"Shut up!" Jeremiah slapped him in the back of the head.

The rope wound around his wrists and through the handcuff chain.

The crazy man went to the side, slipped the gun into his belt and untied the other end of the rope from a bush. He pulled and Detach had to swivel to keep from falling over. A pulley overhead squeaked with the effort of dragging him toward the pond. A sudden jerk sent him to the ground and the rope pulled him along the ground until he hit the water, face first. He could not scream, his face full of brackish water just below the surface. The rope shortened, pulling his arms and then his body into the air.

Detach hung over the pond, his hair hanging from his shoulders, his ponytail tie gone. Naked except for his underwear, tired, and scared, he wondered why this nut would want to hang him over the water. A downward glance answered his question. Sun bleached bones lay clearly visible below the surface. A skull grinned up at him. Movement on the edges of the pond drew his attention to a swarm of dark shapes, moving too swift to be fallen logs, cutting through the muck. He should have made his move while undressing.

Jeremiah's laugh prickled at him through the curtains of swinging Spanish moss. "This is going to be fun."

He twisted around to see the whacko trembling in anticipation. Jeremiah grabbed the hooked pole and gouged Detach's thigh, sending a searing pain through his leg. Blood dripped down to his foot. Though he dangled with his feet just inches over a freshwater lake, his limnophobia was replaced with the all-consuming fear of being eaten alive.

Jeremiah threw the hook to the side and danced, muttering words that might have been French. A big leer covered his face.

Detach could not bring himself to watch anymore and twisted to face the other way. His blood dripped into the water and the gators reacted. More slipped under the surface of the lake, joining the others slicing through the water toward him.

Between the awkward position of his arms, panic, and severe pain from the cut in his leg, he could hardly breathe. The blood coursed down his shin, making his foot itch. Though he knew his insane captor had missed his artery, he could not shake the image of being a bullfighter, gored in the thigh, just like Paquirri, a matador that died in Spain. In an ultimately futile gesture, he folded his legs up.

FIFTY-SIX

His shoulders and wrists throbbed. The rope twisted above the water and he rotated around in time to see Jeremiah jump up and down. The Cajun watched him with a mad gleam of delight in his eyes while he toyed with the rope.

"Just a little bit at a time." Jeremiah eased up on the line.

Detach's toes touched the water. He caught movement in his peripheral vision and twisted to the right as two pairs of yellow eyes cut through the water. Warm blood trickled down his leg and dripped into the lake. Despite the agony coming from his wrists and shoulders, he got ready to pull his feet up.

A commotion drew his attention beyond the gators. Whatever it was, the animals sensed it too. Their beeline for his feet veered away at the last minute.

Behind him, Jeremiah cursed and the rope jerked. For a second, Detach thought he was going to drop down, but instead he continued to dangle, his toes grazing the surface of the lake. He tried to pull his legs up, but the throbbing pain in his arms made any movement excruciating, and he gave up.

A white shape flew into the pond with a tremendous splash. The massive creature from Ireland pounced on the unfortunate alligators. Detach barely had time to let his mouth sag open in surprise when he heard the click of a gun hammer being pulled back.

He twisted to face the crazy man and saw the barrel of the pistol aiming at his head. He had seen the business end of a gun before. He heard how people's lives would flash before them as they faced imminent death. In his experience, that was nothing but an overused movie trope. All he could think about this time was that he never found the *Lusitania*.

A muffled roar came from his left. He twisted in time to see an airboat explode through the side of the pond. It went airborne and arced down directly at the madman holding the gun. He caught a quick glance of Becky, Elroy and Vladimir ramming the front end of the machine directly into Jeremiah's chest. The gun flew out of his hand, hit the ground and went off. The bullet flew off somewhere.

The rope jerked as the airboat slammed into the tree that Jeremiah had tied it to. Detach sank toward the water. He curled his legs again, screamed in agony as the weight and movement dug the handcuffs into his wrists. A spurt of blood poured out of the gaping wound in his leg, but when it hit the water, there were no hungry reptiles waiting. Through the tears in his eyes, he spotted white and green shapes thrashing in a pool of blood at the far edge of the pond.

A sudden jerk on his arms drew his attention back to shore. Elroy and Vladimir pulled on the rope while Becky grabbed the hook and reached for him. The next few moments flew by in a hazy blur. His friends dragged him to shore and untied him. In the cool moss, while Elroy worked off the handcuffs, he glanced toward the airboat and saw the red lump of what was left of Jeremiah.

The creature had followed a small, but noisy toothless white fish until it sensed a large meal nearby. Many lizards thrashed somewhere ahead. The urge to feed overwhelmed curiosity and it sped up.

The water was too shallow immediately in front, but it sensed deeper water beyond that. Too hungry to look for another way in, it surged ahead and jumped over the shallow spot. In an instant, it went from the thin water back into a clear pool. The smell of fresh meat urged it forward.

FIFTY-SEVEN

Though his leg was numb, Detach felt every stitch. Ruby patched up the gash in his leg with all the gentleness of a territorial grizzly bear. The comforting thrum of the *Lothar's* machinery beneath him felt like home.

"You're lucky it missed the artery." Ruby finished the last stitch.

"What happened?"

"We saved your butt," Becky said. She inspected Ruby's work.

"Whose idea was the airboat?" Detach winced as Ruby pressed a bandage over the wound.

"Elroy." Becky patted an unwounded part of his leg. "We got here but couldn't get any closer in this big boat. When we got your call, he spotted a fisherman going by and we sort-of commandeered the boat."

"Aaar! Avast me hearties. We pilfered us a boat for yon plunder. Aaaar!" Since Detach did not have his eye patch, he covered his left eye with his hand.

"Ugh!" Becky rolled her eyes. "Good thing we had it instead of a regular motorboat. Wouldn't have made it there in time."

"Turns out that saved my life."

"About a mile from the place, Vladimir jumps out of the muck and aims this huge gun our way. Good thing he recognized us. After we picked him up, we moved on. I was the one that spotted you all through the trees. I barely pointed your way to show the others when Elroy goosed the engine. We hit a bump and went airborne. You saw the result."

"Where is he?"

"In the galley getting a decent meal."

"Once I can get up, I need to thank him."

"Almost done, Pirate. Hold still." Ruby waved a wad of gauze and tape in his face.

"Gotta go." Becky walked out the door.

Detach wanted to thank her, but with only Ruby in the room he asked, "What's going on out there?"

"Right now the area is swarming with federal agents."

"The Feds? What're they doing here?" Then he remembered the tracker and their tail. "So, I guess it really was the Feds following us. This means we have to lay low for a while."

"You don't have any choice, Bub." She glared at him. "You almost died."

"Mmmph." He was in no shape to do much of anything, for the time being. "We're ten miles from the mound, but basically at a standstill."

"Elroy and Vladimir got the rental boat and the tracker case back before the Feds found them."

"Good, wouldn't want to have to explain that technology."

"Me either." Ruby said. "One other thing."

"What?"

"The creature followed us."

"Yeah, I know." He remembered right before passing out, a sideways view of the pond with a white shape thrashing in an alligator buffet feeding frenzy. "Where's it now?"

"It took off. After Becky talked it over with a fellow marine biologist, they concluded this swamp's probably similar to its original environment. It seems right at home in either salt or fresh water. Alligators, or something like them, were probably one of its primary food sources. As far as those two can tell, it's still out there." Ruby waved an arm out in a circular direction.

"Has anyone warned the authorities?" Detach wondered what the two women would do, if they would even say anything yet.

"Tried to but they wouldn't believe us.

"Just great. Wait until the bodies pile up, then react." Detach relaxed and let Ruby finish his leg.

"Yesterday, federal agents cracked a drug ring operating in a remote area near Morgan City. A gun battle between suspected rivals resulted in the deaths of the three ringleaders. The remote location is making it difficult to extract the remains and determining the extent of their operation. Authorities made a grisly discovery at a nearby pond that was allegedly a dumping ground for their victims. This may be the site of the largest serial killing spree in Louisiana history. Authorities suspect there may be as many as thirty bodies buried in the sediment, making it comparable to mass graves in Bosnia. The number of victims may rival the legendary killing of several hundred women along the Mexican border. You won't believe what they're saying now..."

Detach turned off the radio and let out a sigh of relief. They did not mention him, or anyone attached to his group.

"You know," Elroy said, sprawled out in a deck chair next to Detach on the fantail of the *Lothar*, "it's going to take months to excavate all the bodies."

"I heard the count of thirty is grossly underestimated," Becky said from her own chair on his other side.

"What I heard is that those sickos shot their victims up with meth so they wouldn't pass out while they were being killed." Ruby stood away from them so she could blow her cigarette smoke downwind.

"Unbelievable." Detach was not sure where she got that inside information, but guessed it was from Jams who had friends in high places. He tried to stretch his leg but it throbbed. The stitches felt like they were going to rip out. "I hate sitting around, especially with what might be right under their noses."

"Dad worked something behind the scenes and we're now a bunch of scientists on a research expedition."

"Is that right?" Detach gave Becky a knowing grin. "We didn't see or hear a thing, did we?"

After a week of sitting around on the *Lothar*, Detach had exhausted all his go-to tricks to keep from going crazy doing nothing. He needed the rest to heal the gash in his leg, but being idle wore on his nerves. The wait to get back to Shamblewood Mound killed him, but the area had been swarming with federal agents. With a sip from his sixth cup of coffee for the day, he called Jams via videoconference. Ruby and Becky sat on each side of him while Elroy hung back in the corner. Marlboro Man sat across from him and played with an unlit cigarette, while Vladimir leaned over the table and tapped his fingers, his eyes off in space.

"My sources tell me they're concentrating on the druggies original hideout which is several miles from the mound. Keep in mind, you still have to be discreet because the pond excavation team isn't too far away, but they're a minimal crew with a bit of heavy equipment now. If you're quiet, you can snoop around Shamblewood without attracting too much attention," Jams said.

"From what we've been able to determine so far, it's impenetrable. The whole land mass is surrounded by some of the tightest-packed brambles I've ever seen." Detach relayed the results from a couple discreet scouting trips Becky and Elroy had made.

"The cave has to be the way in." Jams peered straight at Elroy.

"We need to blast, no doubt about it. I'm sure it's a false wall." Detach had reached that conclusion a long time ago.

"That'll definitely attract attention." Ruby stared at the door.

"Hmmm." Elroy leaned forward, rubbing his fingers together. "Maybe not too much if we do it once and do it clean."

"How?" Becky turned to him. "How do you make an explosion quiet?"

"A couple of well-placed shape-charges and some insulation," Elroy said off-handed, as if he did that every day.

"I understand that as far as the cave is concerned, but what about the mound?" Detach raised his hands, mimicking the shape of the mound. "If it's hollow like we hope it is, won't that open space inside be like a giant amplifier?"

"Maybe not. All that growth on top may muffle it for us."

"A distraction would certainly help." Becky flipped her hands open.

"Like what?" Jams eyes lit up with a mischievous grin.

"Easy. Jock can fly helicopters can't he?"

"Yeah, they make enough noise to wake the dead." Detach smiled. "But why would he be there, in the first place?"

"Wait a minute guys. Haven't you been paying attention?" Marlboro Man flipped up his cigarette, missed catching it and it fell to the floor.

"Okay, I'll bite." Detach turned to him. "What you mean?"

"They bring in a chopper every day to collect the bones." He stooped down and picked up the cigarette.

"Wait a minute." The thought had not even crossed his mind. "I guess you're right," Detach said.

"I have heard them at least three times." Vladimir held up three fingers.

"That's our answer. Elroy needs to set up his rig while we wait for a chopper. The racket should muffle any noise that we can't." Jams winked at Elroy, his big face on the screen staring right at the man, thanks to the camera mounted next to it. "Do you have the stuff?"

"Please," Elroy said. "That and more."

"Well, uh." Jams frowned and held up a finger. "There's one other thing that may complicate matters."

"Oh?" Detach got a sinking feeling in the pit of his stomach. "What now?"

"Maggie, Mad Jake's great great granddaughter left me with a warning."

"Oh, it's that name again." Becky groaned. "What else can go wrong?"

"Well, maybe nothing. Yesterday she told me her mom went off her nut and is up to something that has to do with Mad Jake."

"Is it necessarily *this* something it has to do with?" Detach jerked a finger vaguely in the direction of Shamblewood Mound.

"Maggie specifically said that her mother is after you guys. And she mentioned you all by name."

"How does her mother know where we are?" Becky's eyes scanned everyone.

"Maybe she doesn't yet, but guess it's my fault. Apparently

she overheard Maggie talking to me. I've been keeping her up on things. She's been a long time trusted friend, and since she sold me that...Never mind." Jams rubbed his forehead. "If her mother was behind all those problems in Ireland, she may have been tracking you the whole time. Are you sure those crazy guys were drug smugglers?"

"For sure." Detach nodded. "However, that doesn't mean they weren't guarding the area for something else, also." That twinge in his gut told him Shamblewood Mound had to be the place. Mad Jake's granddaughter after them could not be a coincidence.

"Oh...kay." Jams' brow furrowed with consideration. "Though this might not help, I have a little more to go on. Maggie's into real estate and has quite the head for business. It runs in the family. However, one thing that makes her different is that she's not nuts. Her family is very rich but another trait the women have, hidden from the public, is that they're borderline psychotics. Maggie is the only one that doesn't seem to have that problem. We've talked about it a lot over the years. I think she's truly worried about what her mother may do. But, she doesn't know what that is, or when, or where. Just keep an eye out, okay?"

"Federal agents, alligators, and now some madwoman. Nothing's ever easy." Detach made a flatulent sound and eased back in his chair.

FIFTY-EIGHT

"This could be it." Detach turned to his friends while Elroy finished wiring the charge on the back wall of the cave. He studied the series of shape-charges and wires leading outside to a detonator.

Upon careful examination, he confirmed his guess that the back wall was concrete made to look like rock. He had no idea what lay beyond the barrier, if anything. The day before, he and Becky made one final circle of the mound and he understood what she and Elroy had meant by an impenetrable barrier. The tightly packed brambles and snakes made a hostile wall.

The original channel flowed to the right of the cave with the dock at the end. He could not understand how or why the place became so impenetrable if they were going to sail the ship out again to haunt the Germans. Jams figured that after they had killed Jake, his gang closed the site in an attempt to forget the fiasco. Even though he accepted most of what Kyle Jr. had told him about why nobody except that one man went after the ship, he still doubted how such a massive feat of engineering could be kept secret with so many people involved. Detach wondered if anything would still be inside.

Another thing that amazed him was how something so huge could remain hidden for so long. He guessed the original mound was almost the size of the Astrodome. Given that the area was remote, how was it nobody took notice of the huge hill? After approaching it several times over the past few days, he almost understood. Overgrown with deliberately planted brush and trees, it did not look all that large until one got up close. It seemed

327

to sink and blend into the bayou, though it had to be at least eighty to a hundred feet tall, even now. He wondered what the view would be like at the top.

A wave of doubt hit him. What if they picked the wrong mound? He would feel pretty stupid if this was not the place. His doubt vanished when he took a last gaze at the concrete wall. Why would someone build a phony rock wall unless there was something behind it? There was only one way to find out.

Detach went outside after Becky and Vladimir had a chance to admire Elroy's work. They walked fifty feet from the cave entrance and waited in silence for the thrumming sound of the helicopter on its way to pick up a load of bones. Usually it showed up before nine o'clock in the morning. It was hard to keep still as they waited, and it was not until nine twenty that he heard the telltale thumping of a helicopter in the distance.

"Get ready." Detach crouched down.

Elroy smiled and put his hand over the trigger. Sweat rolled down his forehead from the humidity.

In a stroke of luck, the chopper swung low and came right for them, zooming directly overhead as it navigated to the pond pickup point. Just as it passed, Elroy hit the trigger.

A muffled thud reverberated through Detach's body. The ground shook under his feet but blended in with the vibration from the aircraft. The helicopter and its accompanying vibrations disappeared into the distance. They diverted their attention to the small column of smoke seeping out near the base of the mound, to their left.

"Look." Detach pointed. "It must be hollow inside, unless there's a vent from a natural cavern."

"Natural? Not a chance," Becky said.

Elroy stood, went to the cave entrance and opened the door he had closed to help muffle the sound. A slight puff of smoke rolled out, but most of it sucked back into the gaping hole at the back of the cave. He waved for everyone to approach.

The shape charges did the job well, almost obliterating the wall at the back of the cave. Rusty I-beams with shiny edges framed the sides of the opening, and beyond it, pitch black. The ground just beyond the wall was coated in slime but the rocky floor seemed to be solid. A wave of dank air hit Detach in the face and he almost choked. "Whew!" He waved a hand in front of his nose.

Becky made a face.

Detach pulled out a smaller version of the fusion lamps they had used on the bottom of the Irish Sea and powered it on. The light exposed a tunnel. The ceiling hung ten feet above them, covered with hair-like tendrils of roots. The passage went in fifty feet then ended in an open area beyond. He spotted a reddish glint, too far away to identify. He looked at his companions and said, "Let's find out if this was all worth it."

"After you," Becky said.

Vladimir turned on another one of the lamps, adding to the intense light.

The weight of the backpack, which held the fusion generator, dragged at his shoulders. He told Vladimir they were batteries, but knew the Russian had to suspect at the huge amperage draw the lamps put out.

Detach moved forward, careful with each step on the slimy floor. Water trickled in the distance. There were no bugs and for that, he was relieved. The nauseating smell of mold and rot turned his stomach. He concentrated on the sides rather than what lay in front of them, watching for traps, bad spots, and critters. Thirty yards in, the walls gave way and he emerged into a huge open area.

Becky gasped. "Oh my God!"

The roof and walls were covered with black, white, and green roots from the myriad of plants covering the outer surface. It was all held up by rusted steel rafters. To Detach, it seemed to go on forever. Here and there, lamp fixtures with the bulbs still in protruded from the walls, moss and rust hanging from them like fairy lanterns. His jaw dropped when his eyes found the orange-black hulk of one of the largest and fastest ocean liners of her time, the real *Lusitania*.

FIFTY-NINE

A combination of thrill, awe, and horror paralyzed Detach. He gaped at the surreal scene laid out before him. Large dry-dock frame sections surrounded the rusting hulk, many of them rotted and leaning. Portholes, dotted the severely corroded hull plates, and stared at him like ghostly eyes. The hull rivets wept rivers of rust down the side of the once great ship. They faced the port side, directly below the rotted remains of the wooden bridge that dangled precariously over the side of the deck high above. Clearly visible, the brass letters *LUSITANIA* bled waterfalls of green, reminding him of the opening titles of a monster movie. Some of the portholes still had the black paint on them, used to subdue light while out to sea. Many had lost their coating and stared like eyes into another world, their secrets dark and sinister. The huge apparition posed for him in all its deteriorated splendor.

Breaking from his paralysis, Detach aimed the light down the length of the hull, to the stern. The large hooked rudder dangled over a finger of greenish black water. Empty propeller shafts bulged out of the streamlined hull.

"We did it." Detach could not keep the tremor out of his voice. The corners of his eyes grew damp. The once great ship exuded grace and beauty, yet with the ugly, sinister aura of decay.

"It is so huge," Becky said.

The curved ceiling of the mound cleared the hull by less than ten feet in places, making it look even larger.

"It's also out of the water." Detach noted the gap under the keel.

"Sounds good to me." Elroy slapped his hands together.

331

"How do we get on board?"

Vladimir aimed his lamp to a precarious scaffold with a ramp that extended up to an open cargo door.

"Oh boy, that looks safe," Becky drawled, her Texas accent thick with tension. Her teeth chattered.

"Do we have a choice?"

"It's what we came here for, my friend." Detach gave Elroy a shrug. "Come on. I'll try first and you can follow if I make it up all the way." He headed for the scaffolding, still carrying a slight limp from his leg wound. *Hope I can make it. No...I'm going to make it or die trying!*

When they reached the scaffolding, it was in worse shape than it looked from the entrance. The corroded iron railings bowed and looked like they were about to fall off. The remaining wood planks were rotten and black. Damp and age had dissolved most of the wood. "The way up's gonna' be scary, but the metal bracing underneath should hold if I keep my feet away from the open spaces." Detach stepped onto the structure, eliciting a loud creak of protest.

"Hey, don't..." Becky started to say.

"Too late." Detach climbed up toward the gaping cargo door. His fingers and palms triggered cascades of rust with each place he grabbed.

He made it to the cargo door and peered inside. The glow of his powerful lamp revealed a reddish interior. He waved down to the others.

"We all have to take a chance sometime," Elroy said. He stepped onto the structure. One by one, the group followed, Vladimir taking the rear to provide light for the rest.

Detach leaned out the door and gazed to the stern. It curved out of sight as it tapered at the rear. He imagined himself as a steerage passenger boarding this way from a dock in Liverpool. His thoughts turned to the Czar's attempts to duplicate this majesty, only to have the project die in the turmoil of his last years as the leader of Russia.

The passageway led to a four-way intersection. He spotted a rotted wooden staircase toward the center of the hull. Detach knew where they were as he had memorized the deck plans from Barry's extensive archives. Easier to navigate than the wreck of the *Anastasia*, this ship remained relatively intact, and happened to be the real thing.

Detach gestured toward the bow. "This way."

He ventured with ever cautious steps down the rusty hallways and even rustier metal stairways. Despite his doubts about the overall stability of the deteriorating structure, the deck plating held his weight. The smell became even more intense the deeper he went into the hull. Skeletons lay halfway through doorways and in the middle of the hall. He had to step over one at the base of a stairwell.

When they reached the lower Orlop, he spotted crates that once held butter and food stores, part of the legitimate cargo listed on the manifest. Even after a hundred-odd years and the ravages of scavenger animals, the room retained an odor of rotten food and animal feces. Detach made for a door at the far end of the large room. More crates lay in rotted piles, thrown all over by the sinking. Animals had torn through it all leaving moldering heaps. The metal door on the other side had a large round handle. "We may need some more explosives."

"Uh uh." Elroy frowned. "Hope not, I'm afraid this whole thing'll collapse from the shock."

"Let's see what happens." Detach reached for the round handle and found it had rusted in place. He gave a firm jerk and the whole door came off, pushing him to the floor.

The weight crushed at his chest but before he had to take a breath, Elroy and Vladimir lifted it off and placed it to the side.

"Thanks," he said, struggling to stand on his still sore leg.

"Hey!" Becky slapped his shoulder. "Be more careful next time, okay?"

The spill did not harm the backpack or the lamp, and he aimed it into the next passageway. A pile of crates were strapped to the floor, and all were intact except for two. He squatted down, examined the exposed contents of one of the broken crates, and discovered bullets covered in white corrosion. Next to the crates a skeleton lay sprawled on the floor. The unfortunate's clothing had long ago turned to dust. Detach pried one of the slugs loose from the box. With a scrape of a fingernail, he exposed a glint of gold underneath the corroded jacket of lead. It was hard not to grin too wide.

Vladimir asked, "We must move on, no?"

"Yup." Detach discreetly pocketed the slug, he had not let the Russian in on the secret yet.

Becky and Elroy stared at Detach. He moved his eyes to the crates and shrugged sheepishly.

Before they left the room, Detach paused to study the skeleton. *Could this be the remains of Emil Straub? Who else would be down here and not try to escape the sinking ship?* He leaned down to the skeleton and picked up an object lying on the victim's chest bone. Becky gave him an odd look and he winked. He took the lead again and navigated the passageways toward the stern.

When they entered the engine room, Detach spotted a huge boiler, cocked at a crazy angle, the mounting jarred loose by the impact with the bottom. The remains of canvas bags like the ones they saw back in Ireland lay everywhere. "Aha!"

"Now those bags make sense." Becky gave Detach a nod. "They must've removed most of them everywhere else because this isn't near enough, is it?"

"Did I miss something, here?" Elroy said.

"See that pile over there?" Detach pointed. "That's the remains of one of the rubberized canvas bags they used to float the ship. We found several of them in that warehouse in Kinsale." Even after more than a hundred years, Detach detected the faint scent of diesel in the tainted air. "They must've removed the rest when they finally floated her."

"Should we not find out what really sank this boat?" Vladimir said.

"My thoughts exactly." Detach headed for another door. "This way."

Detach led his friends to the starboard side. He weaved around a pile of skeletons to a large door toward the bow. The portal stood partially open, allowing him to squeeze through. Beyond it, a passageway led toward the coal bunkers. The walls buckled and twisted. He came to a gaping hole in the floor and a large space to the right. "This must be the place."

"Hey, look at this." Elroy stood toward the back and peered into a side door. "It wasn't coal that blew up."

Detach backed up and stared into the room. It contained piles of coal.

Back at the hole, the superstructure bubbled out, and it reminded him of what a firecracker does to a soda can.

The wall showed the hastily done patch job the divers performed while the ship floated across the Atlantic. It looked watertight but Detach did not know if it reached to the outer hull. The wall toward the stern buckled, a large gaping hole in it leading to another bunker. The mottled texture of coal chunks littered the floor and walls, some of them runny looking, turned into slag by the heat of the explosion. The inner wall had warped and the sheet metal peeled away from the beams. In the hole, he spotted crates of what were probably munitions, maybe gun cotton and artillery shells. He was not about to climb down there and look.

"No wonder it sank," Vladimir said, muttering something in Russian under his breath.

"I guess we can believe the rumors. They were definitely carrying munitions, and from the looks of what's left, quite a few of them." Detach backed away from the hole.

"This place is starting to make me claustrophobic," Elroy shuddered and glanced at the walls.

"Agreed, especially for us after our little escapade in the *Anastasia*." Detach grinned at Vladimir.

"Then I guess it's settled. We go topside," Becky said.

"I'd like to go on deck once before we leave." Detach pointed up.

"As long as it's out of here," Elroy sniffed and eyed the unexploded munitions.

Detach led the group back through the engine room and the stairs leading up to the main decks, far above. The skeletons and weeping walls along the route made everything claustrophobic and creepy. The crew that brought the ship to Louisiana never

335

bothered to clean up the dead, though they did most of the fuel bladders. He guessed they barely had the ship docked in this spot when they supposedly murdered Jake and deserted the project. They left the corpses to rot along with the ship, somehow forgotten over the decades. Rusticles dripped down everywhere, especially along the walls where they had plenty of support to grow. It reminded him of a natural cavern with stalagmites and stalactites.

They entered the grand ballroom and the sight sent a chill down his spine. At the same time, it inspired awe. He gazed upon the remains of what once represented the upper crust of English society. They could not climb the greying wooden staircase as its rotted remains were held in place by a few rusted bolts. The intricately carved wooden fittings along the walls, and a few half-fallen paintings showed little more than unrecognizable ghost shapes. Expensive Victorian furniture lay rotting in heaps on the floor, tossed into piles by the violent collision with the seabed. The skylight revealed a spectral blackness above, dismal through the few panes left intact.

"Christ, we're almost at the stern already." Detach said amazed.

"True enough." Beck said. "We've made it to the grand ballroom near the stern, well behind the rear funnel...where it used to be anyway."

Detach spotted a metal service staircase. When they reached the upper deck, he gazed toward the bow along the rotted teak deck. Gaping holes spotted the wood, some of it looking intact, but probably unsafe to walk on. He stood on the stair landing and gazed at the unique ventilators that distinguished the *Lusitania* from its sister ships, the *Mauritania* and *Aquitania*. He counted a surprising number still in place, all red and black from corrosion. At the stern, a lump of cloth and rope still hung from a flagpole, the tattered remains of a British flag.

"Wow." Becky stood with her hands on her hips.

"I have to agree with that sentiment." Detach blew out a long breath. "We can't do anything more without help and a lot of safety gear, so let's get out of here." He led his friends back down through the bowels of the once great ship.

"Did you hear that?" Becky held up a hand and cocked her head to one side. Everyone froze.

"It sounds like bad music," Vladimir said under his breath.

"Why didn't we hear it before?" A tingle crawled up Detach's spine.

"Where's it coming from?" Elroy roamed around the passageway, cocking his ear.

"Down this way," Detach moved to a doorway leading to the center of the ship.

The sound drifted through the ship. He traced it, pausing to listen. The music resolved into a screeching violin, accompanied by a high-pitched off-key voice which made the hair stand up on the back of his neck.

"I think I'd rather listen to Jam's music," Elroy said.

Detach followed the noise to a large ballroom. The off-key music echoed against the rusted walls. In the center of the room stood a bed surrounded by ancient medical gear. The large bed had an ornate brass frame. Next to it was a nightstand with a cheap cassette recorder, the source of the awful music. The mummified remains of a bearded man stared back at him, the bed sheet up to his shoulders. He wore a black felt top-hat on his skull.

"Oh, no no no." Stunned, Detach said, "you've got to be kidding me."

SIXTY

Detach had seen many weird things in his travels, but nothing crawled under his skin quite like this. The scene was not particularly gory or bloody, but it was just not right. Someone had to have turned on that cassette recorder. The thought chilled him. Whoever it was, they were most likely not a candidate for normal person of the year.

"Oh, boy," Elroy said. "I think we'd better—"

Boom!

The gunshot blast caused rust to rain down from the ceiling. "You're contaminating Daddy!"

"—get out of here," Elroy finished through gritted teeth.

"Day-dee?" Detach picked a piece of rust out of his collar.

A woman materialized through a doorway to his right. She stepped into the room brandishing a gun at them and walked to the bed.

"You found Daddy, and you won't get away with it."

The crazed gleam in her eye reminded Detach of that whacko, Jeremiah. "Day... Daddy?"

"You know who. You and that Jams tried to buy Daddy from me and my momma." She laughed, a note of hysteria creeping into her voice. "Can you imagine that? Trying to buy the greatest man that ever lived?" She glared at Detach, then at the corpse on the bed. "Daddy? Daddy? What do you want me to do with them?" She tilted her head back and forth, eyeing the corpse, then the gun, then the corpse again.

"Who're you?" Detach did not know whether to raise his hands or be still. *Any sudden movement might set her off.*

339

"Don't mess with Grace! Me...Grace." The woman screamed then her voice went down an octave. "Daddy is my great granddad. He's so much better than you." She cocked her ear to the bed. "Do what, Grandpa Jake?" With a gleeful giggle she said, "Did you say kill them?" Her expression made that suggestion a sure bet.

"I thought we were over all this crazy stuff." Detach said.

The last screeching strains of the cassette crackled to a halt, and silence filled the room. Grace seemed lost for a second. Her eyes turned cold, then her voice changed to a growl. "I tried to stop you in Ireland. If I'd hired better help, you never would've made it back here. They couldn't scare you away at that hotel, and they couldn't drop a few simple depth charges. Then the idiots got eaten by that shark thing." She shook her head in disgust. "Even that Russian gangster and his people couldn't stop you. I underestimated Jams." For a moment her eyes turned clear and lucid, cold and hard.

"You sent the Russians?" Detach flipped his eyes to Vladimir, who acknowledged with a shrug.

"Well..." A slow grin spread across her face. "Actually, I just sent along a hint that you had something valuable. I thought they'd take care of you for me in their effort to get it. I heard they ran away like scared little boys."

"I can say they're now dead scared little boys," Detach said under his breath.

"They really were Russian Mafia." Vladimir's eyebrows shot up in surprise.

"Oops." Detach gave him a sidelong glance. "Sorry, forgot to tell you. Has to do with pencils."

"Shut up!" She glared at Vladimir. "I didn't give you permission to talk!"

"Pencils...whaa?" Vladimir cocked his head at Detach.

"Of course they were Russian Mafia!" She waved the gun around. "Easier to influence than those commie bastards that think they run the place."

"They're not com—"

"Shut up!" Grace cut Detach off, her glare settling on Becky.

340

"Here." The woman motioned to a cardboard box in the corner. "I have to do everything myself. You even managed to get through those crazy druggies I hired to guard this place. Just can't find good help these days. I've been paying them for fifteen years to keep people out. They got too lazy, stupid and greedy. Now you've blown a hole in that wall. I'll have to get someone to plug it up again."

"It wasn't just Murphy's Law, then."

"Shut up! Shut up!" She screamed at Detach, spittle flying his way. Grace waved the gun at Becky then aimed it at the cardboard box again. "Now!"

"All right all right." Becky went over to the box and looked inside. "Handcuffs."

Detach involuntarily jerked his wrists. *Not cuffs again!*

"Get to it. Everyone!" Grace's voice became hoarse. She waved the gun toward Becky then motioned to the others.

Becky picked up a handful of cuffs and fastened a set to everyone.

"Now you. I've got to get you out of here. You're contaminating his air." She gazed lovingly at the corpse on the bed.

"Took you long enough." As soon as Becky snapped a pair of cuffs on her own wrists, Grace stuck the gun in her waist and went to the box, removing a long chain with numerous snap hooks attached. She fastened everyone to the chain. "I should've been a Girl Scout. Always come prepared."

"I've never had a thing for women in bondage." Detach eyed his cuffs. *At least they're in front. She doesn't know much about cuffing people.*

"I can understand that after what happened the other day at that pond." Becky's eyes moved from him back to Grace.

"There, there, Daddy." Grace went to the bed, ruffled the blankets on the corpse, took a washcloth from the nightstand and patted the leathery skull. "I'll take these nasty people out of here."

She faced Detach and pointed the gun toward the way they came in. "Go!"

Like a line of convicts, the group made their way back to the

341

cargo door. Detach considered reasoning with the woman, but the look in her eye told him it would be futile. They were in deep trouble and running out of opportunities to escape.

They climbed down the scaffolding as one, and though it creaked and groaned, they made it to the bottom without anyone falling or the structure collapsing under their combined weight. Grace guided them to the hole Elroy blasted, then out through the cave entrance. Detach took a deep breath. The air outside smelled like pure oxygen.

"Well, friends, I guess this is it," Vladimir said.

"Not yet." What Detach really thought was something more vulgar, but did not dare say it aloud.

"You can never leave here alive. You can never reveal this location, or my other entrance."

How did she get in and out of here? Detach had not seen any sign of previous travel up and down that scaffolding at the cargo door. There had to be another way in. "A hundred people already know about it."

"No, you're lying." Grace's eyes darted from left to right. "I'll just kill them too." Her mood shifted and she grinned. "I told those crazy druggies to stay away from here. I should never have let them get away with this."

"They did not," Vladimir slipped out.

"Huh?" Grace shook her head, and continued as if talking to someone else. "This place is off limits and they defied me." With a shudder, her gaze fell on Detach. The mad gleam had returned to her eyes. "Now I'm going to dispose of my little problem before Daddy catches his death." Grace strode to the rotted dock, gave Detach a wicked smile, and pulled a bottle from her pocket. "This is a little something to attract my friends." With the gun aimed toward them, she walked along the beams to the end of dock and turned to face them.

Her grin reminded Detach of someone with their throat cut. *Too bad that can't happen right about now. Right about now? Come on.*

"Ha ha ha ha hahahahahahah!" She poured the bottle's contents into the water. Hitting the surface of the pond, the liquid made a glopping sound.

"What're we gonna' do?" Becky whispered out of the side of her mouth.

Detach spotted movement in the water.

"These gators are messy eaters. They'll rip you apart, piece by piece. You have to suffer, for what you did to Daddy!"

"Look out!" Detach pointed behind her.

"What?" Grace twisted toward the water and almost lost her balance. She turned back to Detach and grinned. "Nice try."

"Crap." Detach's hopes sank. He hoped she would lose her balance. *What now?*

"Where are those gators?" Frowning, she turned again to the water, leaned over for a look, the gun still waving in their direction. "Ah, there they are."

Three snouts cut the surface and made a beeline to the substance Grace had dropped near the dock. At the outlet to the right, a large white shape glided in. The three gators stopped their advance, swirled around to see what it was, then erupted in panic. They scattered, thrashing about in all directions. One of them swung close to the dock and collided into the outer pillar. With a loud crack, the structure tilted down. Grace lost her footing.

"Nooooo!" She tumbled into the water.

The massive shape of the creature from Ireland went after one of the gators that tried to get onto land. The animal only made it half out of the water when it jerked back and into its gaping maw. With the gator's body thrashing away, the creature slid back through the outlet.

An agonizing scream drew Detach's attention to the end of the dock.

Grace frantically grabbed at the half submerged dock only to be jerked back as one of the gators lost their fear and let hunger take over. The pair submerged and came to the surface in the middle of the pond. Detach caught a glimpse of dead eyes staring before they submerged again.

Becky threw up, just missing his shoes. Detach wanted to put a hand on her back but the cuffs would not allow it, especially with the chain linking them together. It was horrible to see someone eaten alive, but he had seen worse. She hunched over, body shaking with dry heaves. He heard the thumping of another helicopter climbing overhead.

"Anyone know how to get out of handcuffs?" Detach held out his wrists.

SIXTY-ONE

"At last!" Detach breathed a sigh of relief when the handcuffs clattered to the ground. He turned to Elroy. "Thanks."

"Ain't nothin' but a tha'ang." Elroy winked at him and moved on to the next in line with the paperclip he pulled from his pocket.

"You're leaving?" Becky turned to Vladimir.

"Unfortunately, I have as you would say a *real* job. I have debts to pay, and most of all, I have a whole era of history to explore that no one knows about." He gazed off in the distance and added. "It was a dangerous way to find the truth, but I can say I enjoyed most of it."

"It was a pleasure having you here." Detach slapped his friend on the shoulder. "We'll have to do it again someday."

"I hope not." Vladimir said.

Detach took a final glance at the bloodstained pond.

Back on the *Lothar*, Detach stretched out on an easy chair in the ship's lounge and watched Becky blow her nose. She suffered from an acute sinus attack caused by the excursion into the old ship.

"Oh, geez." She threw the tissue into a wastebasket bolted to the floor. "You didn't tell him, did you?"

"Uh, no. It just seemed to get lost in the events of the last few days. Really didn't think about it, to tell you the truth."

"After all he went through with us, I would've figured you'd cut him in."

"Don't worry, I'm going to," he said.

"I've seen that look before. You're up to something."

Detach did not respond.

345

"Did our guys get all the crates?"

"Every one of them." He sat up and grinned. "We have at least two tons."

"That's a lot of gold."

"Yeah, and according to Barry, that's taking the lead coatings into the calculation. The actual weight was a bit higher than that."

"Not bad for what we went through."

"Guess so." He gestured to his steaming mug of coffee, then hers. "Try breathing the steam. Maybe that'll help."

"Mmmm." She hovered her face over her cup and took a few deep breaths, drawing in the steam. "All our misfortunes were orchestrated by Mad Jake's great granddaughter. She even hired those crazy druggies. They were a lot worse than the average dealer."

"They were serial killers, if you can believe the reports."

"I really do. I saw a few of those skeletons lying on the bottom."

"So did I." Detach said.

"I don't know how you did it." She sniffed then grinned at him.

"Did what?"

"Your limnophobia. Do you realize over the past few days, you floated on a lot of fresh water? You even swam in it." With that, she drew in another long draw of steam. "Aaaah!"

"Pffffft." Detach let out a long breath. "I was too busy most of the time. It hit me hard as Jeremiah hung me over the lake. I would've been more worried about getting into the water than what he was about to do to me, but never had time to think about it."

"Man, oh man." She shook her head. "What started as a simple salvage operation turned into a monumental fiasco."

"But..." he held up a finger. "We're here, relatively intact, and a lot richer."

"When we get home, let's go somewhere."

"Are you asking *me* out on a date?"

"Well...ah..." Becky blushed. "It's not like that...not exactly."

Detach eased back and closed his eyes. *There's a little hope for us, yet.*

346

SIXTY-TWO

The first thing Detach did when he got back to Galveston was to fill a small shipping crate with the bullets. He nailed it shut to the rhythm of a song by the death metal band *Vomitory*, compliments of Jams who stood by, idly watching.

"You think he'll figure it out?" Jams said.

Detach was about to put the last nail in when he had a thought. He laid the hammer and nail on top of the crate and went over to a nearby workbench. He found a piece of blank cardboard and took out a pen.

> *Hey, my Commie KGB friend,*
> *Don't get lead poisoning if you happen to scrape one of*
> *these things.*
> *Detach*

"I think so, now." He pried the lid up to create a thin crack and slipped the piece of cardboard into it. "You're sure it'll get to him, and him only?"

"No sweat." Jams waved a hand. "I have connections."

"Okay, then." Detach pounded the loose nails back in place, drove in the last new nail and nodded to the warehouse manager. "She's all yours."

"He's the last one. Everyone else has got their share." He put the hammer on the table.

The music came to an abrupt halt. Jams hit the stop button on the CD player. "Are you done?"

"I have a few more places to visit before I'm done."

"I figured as much. I'll be ready to give you your next job."

"Next job?"

"Eeeyup." Jams smirked and spread his hands apart. "I have a list."

Kinsale was pretty much the same as they had left it, except colder. Detach approached Enya McMurty's house. The garden did not seem quite as cheery as the last time he was there. Maybe it was the change of seasons.

He almost got in the first knock when the door burst open. The old woman stared at him and her turned-down mouth changed to a grin.

"Welcome back. Do you have news for me?"

"As promised." Detach hesitated. "I must warn you, please don't tell anyone else. We're working on that end."

She motioned him inside. He was glad she did not offer more of those cookies. The tea, however, was excellent.

"You were right. You did see another ship sink."

"Lord have mercy!" She slammed her fist down on the arm of her chair. "I knew it! I'm not crazy."

"This may be hard to believe, but this crazy man stole the *Lusitania* and replaced it with a substitute."

"Ah...huh?" Enya did a double take. "Why would someone do that?"

"Well, you see..." Detach took a deep breath.

The creature slowed down its eating. The lizards were tasty, but something was wrong. With an increasingly tighter belly, it was time to find a more permanent spot to settle. There was too much activity where it originally settled, so it wandered until a nice large area opened up, far away from everything. Once in a while, a noisy fish flitted by in the thin water, but it rarely saw the fish with the spinning teeth.

Relaxed, the creature settled into a muddy mound for some much-needed rest. After all, she was going to have a baby soon.

SIXTY-THREE

Normal life resumed at Mason Industries. Detach did nothing for a few days after returning from Ireland, and spent most of his time at the Mason's house, playing with Buster and Doodles. "What you think, doggies? Should I go away for another adventure? Should I get busy?"

Doodles yawned and collapsed on the ground for a nap. Buster farted and gave him a dopey look.

"Lost in thought?"

"What's up?" Detach looked up as Becky approached.

"I was hoping you could give me a rundown."

"I've been vegging out the past few days." Detach plopped down on the grass and faced her. His hand automatically went to Doodles' belly for a good rub.

"Barry's camped out at the *Lusitania* site, heading a team exploring the ship. Your dad's decided to keep the discovery secret until we finish our own exploration. The ship's on his property, but being a historical item of great magnitude, we all know what'll happen once word gets out."

"Yeah, that'll freak out historians for decades."

"So far, Barry's managed to glean a few facts."

"Okay." Becky stretched back in a lounge chair, yawned and closed her eyes. "Like what?"

"First, the dome was intended it to be a hidden harbor where Jake's ships could dock in secret, away from prying eyes, but before it was finished, the *Lusitania* sank. Though long enough, it didn't have the height for the ship so that's another reason they left the funnels with the other wreck, besides keeping a low profile. They did the same with the masts. As is, the ship barely fit inside. I've thought of Shamblewood Mound as a smaller version of the Astrodome, hidden in the middle of the swamp. It's not likely anyone could pull something like that off now."

"I must say," she wagged her head back and forth, "Jake was an amazing guy for being crazy."

"Not to change the subject, but Ruby vowed to quit smoking and made it an entire week."

"No kidding?" Becky slapped her hands together. "I've been out of touch too long."

"I can't even picture Ruby without cigarettes."

"I went to Abilene to see my cousin. I got a huge dose of babies."

"I'll bet." She was not the motherly type and had to take kids a little at a time. "Did you hear about Elroy?"

"No?"

"He went home to Vegas with his share of the gold, and called me last night to tell me what he's been up to."

"Partying, I suspect."

"Actually, no. The *Lusitania* thing made him think that he needed a lifestyle change. He realized that he simply lost the desire to risk his life with munitions work on a daily basis. He secured his loot in several banks, sold most of his demolition gear, paid off his gambling debts, and is now writing an adventure novel. Despite having enough money to while away his time in any casino, he's saving most of it."

Becky sat up on the side of the lawn chair and gazed at Detach.

Doodles, tired of the belly rub, got in his face for a few kisses. Buster noticed, and came over for his share. Detach obliged.

EPILOGUE

Detach shivered in the hallway, waiting for Granny Twinkletoes to return. He heard the door open downstairs and backed away into the shadows. It had been too easy to get inside the apartment and he was not surprised she had so many locks on her door.

The old woman huffed and puffed up the stairs and approached her apartment.

"How do you make an old lady curse?"

Gladys Henson stiffened and turned. Who's that?" She reached into her purse.

"Hey, it's okay. I'm a friend." Detach emerged from the shadows.

"Detach?" Her eyes lit up. "You came back!" She dropped her purse and grabbed him in a hug.

"Glad to see you too."

She leaned down just enough to grab the handle of her purse and straightened up. "The answer is, "yell BINGO!" Her laugh turned into a coughing fit.

Inside, after re-locking a myriad of security devices on the door, she put her bag down and motioned him into her sitting room.

"I didn't know if I'd ever see you again, Detach. What brings you back to the city?"

"Well..." He drawled. "You remember that little quest you sent me on?"

"Have any luck, besides what the news has said? Last I heard, you gave up and came home from Ireland with your tail tucked between your legs."

351

"Don't believe everything you hear."

"Thought so." She slapped her knee. "Good. Spend it while you can Sonny." She picked up her cigarette pack and lighter.

"You sure you don't want a share?"

She scoffed. "Goodness no. I don't need it and I don't want my kids to get hold of it either. They're doing well enough. Besides, you know what I got each of them when they turned eighteen?"

Detach shook his head.

"Luggage," she said with a wide grin and a wink.

"Ha ha ha ha! Anyway, there's a twist to the story."

"Oh?"

Detach told her everything.

"My God. That changes history."

"It's a good bet that Churchill and Wilson were playing dirty, or at least Churchill and his cronies were. They may have deliberately let the ship sail when it shouldn't have."

"Reminds me of what Roosevelt did at Pearl Harbor."

"Pffft." Detach gave her a knowing grin. "My grandma swore up and down that FDR let the Japanese attack Pearl Harbor to get us into the war."

"I agree, but I don't make a big deal out of it anymore. Now back to the Lusitania. Captain Turner may have screwed up too, slowing down and all."

"I don't think so. I truly believe he was Churchill's scapegoat," Detach said. "He was called into the Cunard office in New York just before departing, and during the trial afterwards, he was never directly asked what that conversation was about. I think that bothered him till his dying day. He had too much honor to go to the press with it. Even if that rumor isn't true, all the real investigations deemed that he was completely innocent and basically got the royal shaft."

"What's next for you?"

"I've been relaxing for a while but it's time to go back to work. I have to get back to Galveston. My boss has a list."

"I'm glad to see you again, but you could've called."

Detach stood and headed to the door. "Not to deliver this." He smiled and dug into a pocket.

"Oh my God..." Gladys said. With a trembling hand, she reached for the locket on a chain he held out to her.

"I found this on remains next to the gold."

"Oh." Gladys grinned and said, "Hate to tell you, but this isn't my mother's locket."

He bit back a curse. Then whose skeleton was that, lying by the crates? "There goes my Titanic moment."

Gladys opened it and laughed.

The original photo had disintegrated long ago. Instead he had inserted a photo of himself in full pirate gear, patch over one eye.

"This is so precious." She fondled the locket.

"Aaaargh, Matey, aaarrrgh!" Detach raised a finger to his forehead in a salute, and left.

Fred Rayworth found his passion for writing in 1995. He's so far completed eleven full-length novels and is currently working on number twelve, in genres including science fiction, icky bug (horror), adventure/thriller and fantasy. Multiple short horror stories made it to publication including *The House*, which appeared in the anthology Between the Pages, 2003, *The Walk Home*, in Writer's Bloc 2006, and *The Basement*, in Writer's Bloc II, 2008. His short science fiction story Fun In *The Outland* appeared in the anthology First Voyage in 2008 while his short fantasy story *Don't Mess With A Snorg* saw publication in the anthology A World of Their Own in 2009. His autobiographical short story, *Galf*, appeared in the anthology Writer's Bloc IV, 2012 and his short autobiographical story *Dye-No-Myte*, appeared in Writer's Bloc V in 2014. His latest supernatural short story, *The Mine Pit*, was selected for the upcoming Writer's Bloc VI in 2015.

To follow Fred's writing tips
and news of his other adventures go to
www.fredrayworth.com

Made in the USA
Monee, IL
28 September 2023

43577995R00208